A WALL OF F...
ENCIRCLED...

The surface of ... ...aves
were ablaze, t... ...elly of
the stone horse... ...have easily stood upright
under the horse, except for the fire and the water
and the energy with which this bespelled creature
of stone was stomping around. The horse's stone
rider leaned low across its neck, scything around
with his sword, preparing to chop down at a knot
of people trapped beneath a stall he'd already cut
down.

I've always known I'm not the world's greatest
swordsman, but I didn't need to be when I had
Monoch, the sword with a life of its own. I
subvocalized the call to Monoch and stepped
forward.

Immediately I was stumbling, almost falling to
one knee as a vise grabbed my hand and twisted
me around toward the ground. Somehow I kept my
balance and came out of the almost-fall hurtling
forward in a dead run. Cold flames sheathed my
own hand, tearing back from the outline of my
humming, vibrating walking stick; then the outline
firmed into the rune-etched metal of a very nasty
sword indeed. Monoch had arrived. . . .

Mayer Alan Brenner's
delightful DAW fantasy series—

THE DANCE OF GODS:

CATASTROPHE'S SPELL (#1)

SPELL OF INTRIGUE (#2)

SPELL OF FATE (#3)

MAYER ALAN BRENNER

SPELL OF FATE

THE DANCE OF GODS #3

DAW BOOKS, INC.

DONALD A. WOLLHEIM, FOUNDER

375 Hudson Street, New York, NY 10014

ELIZABETH R. WOLLHEIM
SHEILA E. GILBERT
PUBLISHERS

DAW Book Collectors No. 876.

First Printing, March 1992

1 2 3 4 5 6 7 8 9

DAW TRADEMARK REGISTERED
U.S. PAT. OFF. AND FOREIGN COUNTRIES
—MARCA REGISTRADA.
HECHO EN U.S.A.

PRINTED IN THE U.S.A.

For my parents

PROLOGUE

"Aunt Leen! Aunt Leen! Look what I found!"

Aunt Leen, also known as the Keeper of the Imperial Archives, raised her eyes above the lenses of her reading glasses as the three-year-old figure of her nephew skidded to an uncertain halt next to her desk. In the midst of a frenetic bustle of waving arms she could see that both hands were empty, and the pockets exhibited no more than their typical bulge. "Very well," said Leen. "I'm looking. What are you hiding, and where are you hiding it?"

He was tugging insistently at her hand. "Here! Come here!"

Robin had been rummaging somewhere off in the back, playing hide-and-seek with himself among the uneven aisles and coating himself with his usual cloud of grime. With her free hand, Leen slid an acid-free marker into the ancient book and closed the crumbly cover, leaving it perched on the reading stand, and picked up her lantern. Although her work area was liberally furnished with candles, thus slowing the deterioration in her eyesight, the deeper reaches of the Archives had only the illumination one brought to them. How had Robin been able to see whatever he'd discovered?

As Robin trotted ahead of her off into the darkness, a blue glow spread out ahead of him, lighting his way through the crates and leaning piles of scrolls and books. Leen scowled to herself. She must be getting prematurely dotty, on top of blind, or perhaps it was mere engrossment in the book, although that was an excuse with more charity than Leen was usually willing to allow herself. Nevertheless, absentmindedness was the least dangerous explanation she could claim. Puttering about in the dust while mumbling non sequiturs was professionally expected of an Archivist, but when you stopped backing it up with a lucid mind it meant trouble. One day you're forgetting the trick tunic you yourself had given the boy with the very goal of making it safer for him to prowl through your domain, as she had done at his age when it was her grandfather at the great desk, and soon you've advanced to fuddling the sequence for disarming the door wards, with the immediate sequelae of an expanding cloud of Archivist-shaped vapor and, of course, the election of a new Archivist.

Robin pulled up next to a long spill of books and more than a few freely floating pages and stood hopping impatiently from foot to foot. The glow from the runes on his shirt diffused out through a hanging cloud of fresh dust. Come to think of it, Leen did vaguely remember a crash and thud some ten pages earlier in her own reading, but it hadn't seemed nearly serious enough to rouse her. Leen took a look around. They appeared to have arrived at a wall, or at least a room-sized pillar. There were many similar spots around the catacombs. "Show me what you've found, Robin," Leen said patiently.

Robin flopped down on his knees and felt around under the next-to-lowest shelf. The bottommost shelf was a single thick slab of wood extending to the floor, and the next shelf above it was only a book's span higher, so Robin was about the largest person who would have been able to discover something that far down. Three, or four books from the lowest shelf had been removed, judging by the gaps in the line of snugly fitting spines; without the added clearance, even Robin's three-year-old-sized arm wouldn't have had space for maneuver. "Watch!" Robin commanded.

Leen barely heard a soft click. The bookcase made a much louder creak and pivoted slowly away from them into the wall. An opening large enough for a person of Robin's size appeared on the right side, then continued to widen until a Leen-and-a-half could have fit comfortably through. Robin took hold of her hand again and dragged Leen toward it.

How long the shelves and books had been there was anyone's guess. Leen had found a journal kept by the fourth Archivist before her own tenure which set forth his theories. He had been the only member of his particular dynasty, if she recalled correctly, which explained his works not being handed down through the line as her own family had done, although in his case that was not the only plausible explanation. On the basis of flimsy (not to say cryptic) evidence he had speculated that the structure of the Archive catacomb itself dated from the time of the Dislocation, if not before. Leen had her doubts. After all, the same archivist had apparently gone loony himself soon after writing his conjectures, closing his career by triggering the trivial third-bend gate and letting loose a construct that had taken half the palace strike team and three senior-level magicians to dispel. His flattened image was still embedded in the wall just past the bend, the expression on the stretched face oddly untroubled. Her grandfather had hung a tapestry over it.

Behind the sliding bookcase was a narrow alcove and the top of a tightly wound circular stair. Leen followed the unstoppable Robin down it, refusing to give in to a sudden maternal rush and tell him to watch his step. She kept her left hand on the central support pole and glanced up periodically as the stairs wound around it; it was fully two complete turns, or perhaps even a quarter more, before they reached bottom.

Leen had no idea where they were, compared to the overall layout of the Archives and the catacombs and the palace complex as a whole. The palace was the kind of place where outside and inside measurements rarely added up, anyway, with the discrepancy as likely as not to indicate that the inside dimension was significantly the larger. Still, the Archives occupied the lower levels of its corner of the complex, so it appeared reasonable to presume that the staircase had taken them down into the midst of solid rock. Or into what she had previously assumed, for lack of any particular reason to think otherwise, was solid rock.

The floor was cold and certainly felt like unbroken bedrock rather than some construction team's marble or concrete subbasement. Leen was no longer quite as willing to give it the benefit of doubt as she had been even moments before, though. The other two features of the room were suggestive. One was the wall that faced her at the bottom of the stair. It, too, was solid and cold and obviously thick, but unlike the floor it was metal. *Metal.* Not a crude iron alloy or a thin beaten sheet of copper or some lumpish bronze implement, either, but a deadly serious, absolutely flat, medium-gray slab that reflected its dull sheen beneath the centuries'-long accumulation of sifted dust. She had never seen a piece of metal like that in her life. As far as Leen knew, there had never been a piece of metal like that anywhere in the world. Since the Dislocation, of course. Although there was no evidence of hinge, lock, or control, Leen was certain the slab of metal was a door.

It wasn't a certainty born of unfettered intuition. The wall adjoining the metal one on its right had its own feature. From the level of her waist to a spot above her head and for a span of an arm-and-a-half or so in width, the solid rock wall, retaining the same texture and feeling of cold stone, turned inexplicably transparent behind its coating of filth. Leen slid a finger through the grime. As the clear rock became clearer behind her finger, she could see that her initial impression was no mirage. The transparent area glowed a pale green, the green washing over her finger in a faint necrochromatic smear. Where her fingertip pressed against the wall a brighter green spot appeared beneath it. She brought her eye close to the smudge her single wipe had left.

Although it was difficult to tell exactly how thick the crystal actually was, it was incontrovertibly not thin. The depth of her forearm, at least. That it did have a far side, though, was also evident, since Leen could see something beyond it—a circular spot of green, coin-sized. A light. Not a flame, or a sorcerous torch, or a rune like the ones on Robin's tunic, but a light of some different type entirely, a light that glowed its perfect, unceasing, monochromatic glow in the darkness where no eye had seen it for—

The light turned orange, flashed once. Then it winked off.

Leen's head snapped back as though the light had leapt forward through the crystal and slapped her instead. She shook her head once, trying to still through sympathetic magic, she supposed, her whirling thoughts. She looked down at Robin; he was happily pounding away at the metal door, making not the slightest dent or sound, except for the very mild thump of his small hands against the material. Leen discovered she was rather proud of him, even in the midst of her quite un-Archivistlike mental turmoil. Even as the young child he was, he was revealing the appropriate inclinations of a first-class Archivist himself. One of them, unfortunately, was dredging up things better left hidden. Still, he had most likely finished his part; now it was her turn. Leen told herself to remember to get him something special for bringing her such an interesting puzzle. Interesting? Well, this *was* interesting. Indeed, it was more than interesting. Something ancient was still alive in there.

1

It seemed like the first decent sleep he'd had in ages. Of course, his standards had grown significantly more lax since being on the road, but even so you could scarcely deny—

Again, a boot tried to separate his ribs. Again? Jurtan Mont tried to think back into the immediate past. Something must have roused him far enough out of sleep to kick his mind into gear. Could it have been the same foot? And if so, whose foot was it?

"Come on, get up already."

The voice was unfamiliar. Jurtan cracked an eye and craned his neck around. The shaggy figure with its unkempt beard that loomed over him in the predawn murk was not one he recognized either. But his warning sense hadn't given him an alarm, and he hadn't been robbed and strung up in his sleep. "Who are you?" Jurtan said.

"Who do you think I am?" the unfamiliar figure said irritably. "Shoulda slipped a knife through your belly instead of just a friendly boot. That might sharpen one thing about you once and for all, since I've just about given up on your mind."

The figure might be new, but Jurtan was well and fully intimate with the irritation. "Max?"

Maximillian the Vaguely Disreputable, looking more than ever like his sobriquet, grunted down at him. "Five minutes, then we exercise."

Jurtan piled out of his bedroll. It was chilly out in

the air, but at least the dew hadn't frosted over on his face. "How long do we have to keep doing this for? How long until we get somewhere?"

"Never fails, does it," Max muttered. "Awake for ten seconds and the first thing he does is start to complain."

"But we aren't just going to keep traveling forever, are we? When do we get someplace we want to *be?*"

"We *are* someplace."

"No, I mean—"

"So do I." Max raised an eyebrow and directed his gaze meaningfully over Jurtan's shoulder. When they'd stopped after dark the previous evening, they'd gone just beyond the line of trees that marked the margin of the road before settling themselves down. During the night, Jurtan had rolled up against what he'd thought, in the gloom of sleep, was a hard tree. It wasn't a tree. It was a low cairn of stones, with a small signpost on top. He went around to the front and squinted at it. The arrow-end of the sign pointed ahead down the road in the direction they had been traveling. The legend on the sign read "PERIDOL."

Jurtan grunted. "It doesn't say how far." It *did* seem like they'd been traveling forever. "How long has it been since we slept in a bed?"

"Day before yesterday."

"Really?" Well, okay, maybe. Still, it had to be more than two weeks since they'd made it out of the swamp; maybe as much as a month. If Jurtan had had anything to say about it, they'd never have gone into the swamp in the first place, especially since all they had to show for it was a sack of moldy papers neither one of them could read. Of course, if Jurtan had anything to say about *anything,* he'd be anywhere at the moment but out at five-thirty in the morning on some nameless road in some useless countryside on the way to somewhere he had not the slightest interest in arriving at. With a maniacal self-improvement freak. Jurtan was still surprised Max didn't make the horses do calisthenics right along with the two of them.

13

To his credit, if you were in a positive frame of mind, you could note that Max never sat on the sidelines just calling instructions to Jurtan. Jurtan scowled at his own thought as he laced his fingers together behind his back and began his first ten-count of creaking his way over backward. That wasn't a positive at all; all it meant was that Max pushed both of them as hard as he pushed himself. "What do you think you're glaring at?" Max said, finishing his own back-bend, holding it, and then moving his upper body up and over in a slow lithe curl that culminated with his nose touching his thighs and his arms pointing straight ahead of him behind his inverted back.

"Why do we have to do this *every* day?" Jurtan grunted a moment later, coming back upright and pausing before doing the whole thing over again. "We're already in shape. Okay, maybe I wasn't when we left Roosing Oolvaya, but I am now, so—"

"You're in shape now? Good, then we can go on to the next level. There's no standing still in this outfit." Max tilted backward again and Jurtan reluctantly followed.

Max had already told him that standing still meant going back; that was aphorism number ten-thousand thirty-three. Thirty-four? If Max tossed him another Rule to Live By today, Jurtan thought he'd . . . well, it wouldn't be pretty.

It wouldn't be so bad if Jurtan's music sense didn't seem to agree with Max. Well, it might be as bad physically, but at least he wouldn't have to accept the fact that his own body was in league against him, too. He didn't care at this stage if something was good for him or not. So what if he actually did feel better than before he'd met up with Max and Shaa? Great, he was in touch with his body, he had muscles and supple joints, his coordination had improved, and he had a new repertoire of skills. All this had done was give him a new appreciation of the under-recognized appeal of sloth as a lifestyle.

A fluegelhorn honked querulously at him from the

back of his head. That was another thing—what was the good of an extra sense that spent most of its time editorializing? Anybody who had a conscience had to be used to having it tell its owner what it thought of them, but Shaa (who was supposed to know about things like that) had never heard of one that orchestrated its critical commentary with multipart harmony and a comprehensive palette of tonal colors.

Of course, the standard wisdom on consciences was that they concentrated on reactions to issues of right and wrong, weighing in with a compulsion to do right and feelings of guilt if you violated a previously recognized ethical principle. What a conscience wasn't supposed to do was step out proactively, jumping in with helpful hints and suggestions of its own when it hadn't been asked to do anything more than shut up. In fact, shutting up was the one thing Jurtan's sense had thus far refused to do.

On the other hand, Jurtan wasn't complaining, especially now that he'd reached an accommodation with his resident talent. In the old days of all of several months ago, his musical accompaniment had been jealous to a fault. Back then, as soon as Jurtan had heard music from outside his head—music that someone else was actually playing—his eyes would glaze and his mind would grind to a useless stop. Eventually he'd come back to consciousness with a blank gaze and no idea where he was. Sometimes he'd even be jerking and kicking, too, or worse. It had been pretty embarrassing, and sometimes kind of dangerous as well. After all the training and the practicing, though, that didn't happen anymore.

Max finally called a halt. Jurtan felt tingly and fully wrung out, but of course the day was really just starting. Back in the grove of trees and parallel to the road was a stream. The horses eyed Jurtan suspiciously as he eased down to the water; they hadn't quite forgiven either Jurtan or Max for their experience in the swamp. Max had been eyeing the horses back. For Max's own part, the look on his face implied he'd been considering whether he was going to continue viewing the horses as part of the team, rather than as a source of ready cash or, in a so-far unexperienced emergency, as dinner or lunch. The horses and Max had for the moment fish-eyed each other to a standstill.

Nothing snapped at Jurtan out of the water, and a quick splash took some of the edge off his own snappish mood. He was almost back to their small camp when he saw the strange device standing near the shoulder of the road at the edge of the treeline thirty paces or so west, in the direction of Peridol.

"What's *that?*" said Jurtan. It certainly wasn't another signpost, unless it was pointing the way to a place you couldn't get to on a horse, and not a place merely across the ocean either. One of the trees, a small sapling really, had been stripped of its side branches, leaving little more than a wooden rod protruding upward from the ground to the height of Jurtan's head, a rod with a prominent root system still anchoring it to the ground. A carved icon had been strapped to the top of the tree facing the road and doubly secured there with a peg. Jurtan couldn't make out any details of the carving since a wisp of ground fog was still clinging to the icon in a soft glow.

"Better stay away from it in that state of mind," Max called over.

"Stay away from *what?*" muttered Jurtan. "I'm not a kid." Ignoring the sudden blare of discordant brass and the familiar snare-drum roll that usually warned him when something worth paying attention to was about to happen, he aimed a kick at the pole. Without quite knowing how it had happened, Jurtan found himself for a brief instant hanging upside down in the air, where he had been dragged when something that felt like an enraged beehive had latched onto his foot and lashed it up over his head. Then he was sprawled out on the dirt fifteen feet away, at the end of a five-foot furrow, with his face covered with mud and his leg throbbing and tingling as though Max had had him exercising for three days straight without a rest break.

Jurtan got an elbow under him, wiped dirt out of his eyes with an equally filthy hand, and spit loam out of his mouth.

Max was standing nearby, looking the shrine over with a professional eye but from a prudent distance. "What did you think was going to happen?" Max said. "It's an active offering to an active god, looks like the Protector of Nature. Whoever set it up obviously had the concept a little vague, since they mutilated a tree to do it instead of just honoring something green in its natural state, but I guess the Protector wasn't being too picky that day either, or maybe she was just hungry. You're just lucky it didn't call an enforcer."

Jurtan dragged his head free of the dirt and sprawled up to a sitting position. "You wouldn't have let me get near it if it would have set off something real bad."

"Oh, you think so," said Max, "do you?"

"Not if it would have called attention to you, no I don't."

The kid was probably right, but that didn't mean Max had to let him know he knew it. Give him an inch and, well, who knew where you'd end up. Max gave Jurtan a hand instead and pulled him to his feet. "Get yourself put together again while I finish breakfast. We still have some eggs from that last village."

Even in his newly reinstated morose mood, Jurtan had to admit that one of Max's other talents was knowing how to make the most of cuisine on the road. With some decent food inside him and after his second bath of the morning, Jurtan was also more willing to take a longer view of his situation. He was prepared to acknowledge that the pace Max had been setting since Iskendarian's swamp was by no means a killing one even if it wasn't downright leisurely. They'd been in and out of several countries and city-states since then, wasting a fair amount of time talking and hobnobbing in towns and farms. They'd even made a few outright side trips to check out local legends or hot spots, and in one case to visit a ruined castle where Max had climbed a toppled mound of wall-stones festooned with moss and trailing ivy to declaim several stanzas of ancient poetry. Far to many stanzas, if you asked Jurtan, who had never been a big fan of high literature. When you added it up, though, you had to conclude that they'd been staying on back roads and avoiding the larger thoroughfares. On the more traveled routes there would have been more people who might have remembered them, Jurtan figured, but there would also have been more excursionists to lose themselves among. On the other hand, the smaller towns they'd been through wouldn't see ten visitors in a year, so they'd most likely remember the two of them if anyone asked.

How much did Max really want to shake the Hand off their trail?

Something else Jurtan had learned was how to think and work at the same time. While he'd been mulling Max's plans and intentions back and forth, he'd succeeded in getting the area cleaned up and the horses packed; more skills Jurtan couldn't recall wishing he possessed. At least sitting on a horse all day was no longer a more drawn-out form of one of Max's tortures. Jurtan was almost at a stage where he could say he felt comfortable with riding.

"No," said Max.

Jurtan paused, one foot in its stirrup and halfway into the saddle. "What?"

"We've been pushing the horses enough. Let's give them a break today."

Jurtan let himself down to the ground. They hadn't been pushing the horses, they'd been virtually coddling them. What was Max up to? This bit with the horses wasn't the only strange thing this morning, either "Why are you wearing that beard and that grubby disguise?"

"Practice."

If there was anything else Max didn't need, it was practice in deception or dissimulation, which meant his answer this time had meant about as much as any of Max's answers ever did. "If you told me what was going on, I could help," Jurtan volunteered.

"Oh, you could, could you?"

"What do you have against me, anyway?" Jurtan mumbled. "I thought apprentices were entitled to *some* consideration."

"They probably are. Are you coming or not?" Max had led the other horse onto the road. Jurtan grimaced and dragged his horse after him.

Something *was* up, though. Max wasn't usually quite *this* testy, especially in the morning; he *liked* getting up early and seemed to hit his stride right around the time the sun came out. Maybe Max did need practice. Max was always suspicious, but this morning he was out-and-out on edge. Something was putting him especially on his guard.

Max had produced a floppy, wide-brimmed hat of a piece with the rest of his ratty disguise. It was ratty only in appearance, though, not in effectiveness. If Jurtan met this fellow on the street, he wouldn't give him a second look except perhaps to make sure there was enough of a buffer space around to steer clear of him. As the trees thickened around them and the amount of morning light reaching them through the canopy of leaves declined, Jurtan thought he saw a pale pink glow begin to peek from beneath the brim of Max's headpiece.

Max settled his hat more firmly. While his hand was in place next to the brim, he slid his fingers underneath it and adjusted the control matrix above his right ear. *Camouflage,* Max thought, *camouflage and subterfuge, always hiding one thing behind another; what a world. If we didn't have all this magic running loose, struggles of power and battles of will, it would probably be a much nicer place overall.* But on the other hand it probably wouldn't. People were people and power, after all, was power. The enhancement disk in front of his right eye firmed and Max's overlay-view of the scene ahead of them settled down. Off to the left on the trunk of a tree was a squirrel. Between its bark-colored fur and the gloom of the lighting level, it was all but invisible to the unaided eye, even once Max knew where to look. To the disk, though, painting the squirrel's body heat in a glowing orange, it might as well have been under a spotlight.

There were other animals out and about, too—a streak that could have been a fox, an assortment of birds, a few more squirrels. No larger game was in sight, though, and certainly nothing on two feet, unless they were using countermeasures. Screening aural emanations was a standard enough trick in the right circles, but heat signature suppression was still largely unheard of. Infrared sensors were such an obvious idea, too. Still, it was a fact that remote sensing never really seemed to catch on, like so many facets of magical technology that were deliberately subtle and designed to keep you out of trouble rather than blowing up situations with flash and pyrotechnics. Most practitioners weren't nearly as clever as they thought they were, and on top of that they'd didn't much like to do research. *Of course,* Max thought, *there's research and there's research.* Everybody liked to steal good stuff if they could. Their problem was that they went after it the hardest way, trying to lift the secrets of a living competitor, or reverse engineering back to a piece of leftover stagecraft from its residual fallout. It was safer all around and usually more productive to mine where the guardians were dead.

When you wanted certain kinds of answers, though, going through ruins and books was nothing but a waste of time. Max glanced idly around again. There was someone around here laying for them, he could feel it. Beyond the matter of foiling whatever the somebody had in mind, the larger question was whether they were just freebooters out to waylay travelers in general or whether they had a particular target in mind. The options weren't exclusive, of course, if you were going to be logically comprehensive, since the kind of customers who'd ambush someone in particular in a forest probably were the sort who wouldn't mind an extra spot of fun and profit if someone else happened along while they were waiting.

Until proven otherwise, you had to assume every plot was directed at you personally. Even with this carefully cultivated paranoia, however, Max had to acknowledge that the most likely scenario here was the old scout-them-out-in-the-village, rip-them-off-in-the-forest routine, with the innkeeper in league with a few of the local toughs.

After all the waiting, when it happened the whole thing was there and over with almost as soon as it had started, in the typical disorganized flurry and commotion.

Max had unbent enough in his didacticism to warn Jurtan to stay alert and keep his eyes open. They had entered a section of forest where the path was both narrower and twistier than it really needed to be, and also happened to be snaking through a series of chest- and then head-high gullies. Reddening leaves covered the ground. It was, after all, fall, but it was still early in the season, and these were a lot more leaves than they'd seen anywhere else in the forest. It could be that this particular area had had a recent windstorm, Max was thinking, perhaps coupled with too little foot traffic to disturb the leaves since then. He'd seen the obvious trace of a wheel-rut in various places they'd already passed on the path, but Max knew he wasn't a good enough tracker to tell how long ago the cart had gone through. Still, even with these plausible natural explanations, was it possible that someone had deliberately spread leaves out across the path?

Max looked around him at the forest on either side. Unfortunately, this was one of the spots where the banks of the gully were above his head. From the back of the horse, though, his vantage point would be significantly better. He raised his hand to tell Jurtan to stop and stepped up into the stirrup.

Following behind Max, Jurtan had been hearing an undulating, traveling string motif in a succession of major keys that he supposed was symbolic of forest murmurs or some such. For background accompaniment it was fairly pleasant, as his internal music ran; it was nicely tonal and more representational than conceptual. Jurtan was much fonder of melody than the atonal screeching stuff, which tended toward sour harmonics and sharp sudden squeals, but even now, with his greater level of control, he didn't usually have a choice. Over the last few minutes, though, a menacing deep bass theme had gradually appeared behind the forest music, which itself had just modulated to minor. Jurtan was looking around himself, too, trying to figure out which direction the menace might be coming from, and so he didn't immediately see Max raising his hand and pausing his horse. As a result, when the loud harsh voice of a steerhorn opened up with a quivering blast from the edge of the gully just behind Jurtan's head, spooking his horse and Jurtan both, Jurtan had no idea how close he had drawn to Max and *his* horse. In the process of leaping out of its skin, Jurtan's horse only knocked him spinning off to the right and into the earthen bank, from whence he went sprawling toward the leaves, but it hit Max full on just as its stride lengthened and it really started to dig in.

Max separated from the stirrup and hurtled toward the ground just ahead of the charging horse's front hooves. Jurtan, watching with slow-motion clarity and stunned fascination on his own trajectory toward the ground, could see that at the same moment as Max's chest hit the path the horse was going to land on his back with its full galloping momentum and punch Max's spine through his heart. Then, an instant later, Jurtan was equally sure that Max had pulled off some slick piece of sorcery and had teleported or dematerialized himself out of the way, since he had hit the layer of leaves and disappeared. An instant after *that,* as the horse's forelegs began to disappear as well and the horse lurched forward off balance, Jurtan realized that no magic had to be invoked after all. Just ahead of them the leaves had concealed a pit.

Max knew if there were spikes in the pit he was in

trouble. He used the thump the horse had given his back to wind himself forward and headfirst down. Above him, Jurtan's horse, still on solid ground beyond the edge of the pit, pushed off strongly with its hind legs, trying to use its momentum to clear the pit's far rim, which was now visible since the net that had held up the leaves was collapsing under Max's weight. Unfortunately, the front of the horse was already twisting downward after Max. The horse started to do a forward cartwheel and hit the far lip of the pit halfway along its forelegs.

Jurtan rolled over once in the leaves just short of the pit and came to rest facing upward, giving him a perfect view of another net with lead weights woven into its sides descending from the top of the gully straight toward him. Also centered in Jurtan's field of view was the underside of Max's horse, which Jurtan had fetched up next to in his roll. Max's horse was tossing its head and stamping its legs nervously, but it hadn't decided to take off like Jurtan's. Accordingly, instead of draping itself over Jurtan, the thrown net settled over the horse.

Jurtan rolled back out from under the dangling corner of the net and staggered to his feet as the steerhorn sounded again. Something swooshed past his ear—an arrow! Whoever was up there was going to hang back behind the ridge above and try to pick them off. But what if Jurtan just tried to run away? He heard a crunch, a clatter, and a loud grunt from his left, in the direction they'd just come from, and turned to see a heavily built man with a wild black beard and a broadsword getting his balance on the path; a spill of earth showed where he had jumped and slid down into the gully.

Max landed inverted at the bottom of the pit, in a handstand, his arms tangled in leaves and netting. The horse with its broken legs was sliding in after him. Max let himself fall carefully backward. Something narrow, scratchy, and tall pressed up against his back, yielded, and then snapped with a crack. There *were* spikes, but obviously not enough of them to carpet the hole. Max kicked another spike over out of the way and sprang backward onto his feet, then leaned forward to press himself against the side of the pit. Next to him, the horse finished collapsing into the pit, impaling itself on the spikes. An arrow thonked superfluously into its flesh.

There would be at least four of them, Jurtan thought. The hefty guy guarding the path with his sword, the archer, the one with the steerhorn, and probably another swordsman to watch the path on the other side of the pit. Max had been tutoring him in swordwork, but even after Max's usual intensive crash course Jurtan didn't think he could take down all of them with his blade, especially considering the tactical situation the terrain put them into. The blade was scarcely the only weapon at hand, though. The music in his head left Jurtan an opening. Drawing his own sword, he hurled himself forward at the hefty man, yelling out "Heda!" in tune with the music.

A blare of internal trumpets matched him. The edge of Jurtan's vision swam, but with the last month's practice behind him his concentration locked solidly into place and held his consciousness together. Instead, the man ahead of him reacted slowly, as though he'd fallen into a sudden daydream, his eyes vague and sluggish as he began to adjust his stance and bring up his sword.

Max and Jurtan had determined that vocalization wasn't nearly as effective in projecting paralysis as the flute in Jurtan's pack or the harmonica in his pocket. On the other hand, his voice was close to hand and left both arms free. Jurtan slid past the man's guard and whacked him on the side of the head with the flat of his blade. Music stabbed at him; without thinking, Jurtan leapt back. Another arrow flashed in front of him through the space he'd just left and punctured the falling man's chest.

Max vaulted over the thrashing horse before it could crush him against the wall and rolled upward out of the pit. Not pausing, he pushed out of the roll and sprang up the side of the gully. Just above him, sticking over the edge, an arrow was slapping into a bow. Max snatched at an exposed root just below the lip, pulled himself closer, grabbed the bow with his other hand, then let go of his grip on the root. As he fell backward, he pushed off with his feet and yanked. With a crazed howl a man appeared in the air above Max, still holding his bow. The man twisted over Max and followed his bow headfirst into the pit.

Two sets of footsteps crashed above, retreating rapidly into the trees. Max was scrambling back up the embankment to give chase when the charging footsteps stopped and were replaced by first a whinny and then a gallop. The path beyond the pit jogged to the left; presumably it snaked around to the spot where the ambushers had their horses hidden. Max dropped to the floor of the gully next to his own horse. "What?" Max demanded of it.

The horse had its head cocked to one side and was giving him a reproachful look from beneath its weighted net. The horse hadn't moved a foot throughout the entire affair. "Be that way, then," Max told it.

"Are you all right?" said Jurtan, from a location safely beyond Max's reach.

"No thanks to you. Next time take better care of your horse."

Jurtan was relieved to note that Max's tone of voice was relatively mild, for Max. "I don't think anyone's going to be taking too much care of that particular horse in the future."

The kid was right. The horse in the pit had one last thrash in it, and it had expended this by rolling over onto the bowman. Most likely the guy had broken his neck anyway, but that still left no one to interrogate. Max picked up his hat, which Jurtan's horse had demolished by falling on it, then tossed it into the pit. So much for a field test of the infrared detector. It would have found the ambushers if he'd had a line of sight to them, but of course he hadn't. "It could have been worse,'' Max said. After all, they did have the one horse, and the Iskendarian papers. The ambushers might have tossed down a torch.

Jurtan was standing over the man on the ground beyond the pit, the one he'd hit over the head, but who'd then been shot by the archer when Jurtan had moved out of the way. "They're . . . dead," Jurtan said.

"Yes. Yes," said Max, "they're dead, all three of them." Max noted that Jurtan was now looking off into the air, studiously avoiding the sight of the body lying in front of him in its heap of leaves splashed red with blood, and the other man and the horse behind him in the pit, and in fact Max himself. Max made no move to approach Jurtan. If you were going to live with violence, you had to deal with this situation eventually.

"I, ah, never killed anybody before," said Jurtan. "I mean, I didn't even *mean* to kill him."

"Well, you didn't kill him, either. His friend did."

"But if I hadn't hit him the way I did—if I hadn't moved away when I did . . .''

"Yeah?" said Max after a minute.

". . . Then either he would have killed me or the arrow would have," Jurtan said heavily. "Right? But it still—I mean, they were *people*, they had lives, and all of a sudden—''

"They might even have had mothers, too," Max said, "but it's still worth remembering that they were the ones trying to ambush *us*. You didn't see them trying to run away; they took the job, no one was forcing them.''

Well, Jurtan thought, *at least I haven't thrown up.* "I'm just glad my father isn't around," he muttered. "He'd probably want to see me drinking their blood instead of standing around talking.''

"If we ever see your father again," Max said, "I won't tell him about it if you don't want me to. Keep in mind that your father is not exactly typical when it comes to these things.''

Now Jurtan *was* looking down. It wasn't really that bad, except for all the blood. It would probably only give his father an appetite, and the satisfaction of a job done well. His father *was* weird.

But Shaa and Max had been teaching Jurtan to be professional, and there was nothing weird about *that* that he could he think of. What would be a professional thing to focus on? "Was this the Hand again?" asked Jurtan.

"No," said Max.

"So you don't know who it was?"

"I didn't say that, did I?"

"Well, who was it, then?"

"I didn't get much of a look, thanks to you, but the main guy could have been Homar Kalifa."

"Another friend of yours? Is he someone else who's after you?"

Max closed one eye and squinted up at the sky. "Kalifa's a third-rater, strictly small-scale; more of a tough-for-hire than a decent adventurer. A riffraffy sort, but he does like to carry a steerhorn. Not too many steerhorns around these days, either. Now that I think about it, I seem to recall crossing him up once, dropped him out a mid-story window into an ornamental pond, it might have been."

"So this could have been just a not-so-friendly hello for old times' sake."

"Maybe," Max said dubiously. "Even if the pond did have something nasty in it; eels, maybe. Doesn't seem very likely to be Kalifa, but it's not totally implausible. Kalifa's the sort who could easily wash up in a spot like this. It's quiet countryside, he could ease back and terrorize soft locals or dumb travelers."

"Really?" said Jurtan. "You think this was just random violence? I thought you were the most suspicious person on the continent."

"There's no real way to tell, kid. It *could* have been a robbery. Anyway, you've got to remember it's Knitting season. A Knitting always kicks things loose; everybody's out taking care of any business they can think of.'' Max glanced into the pit, then looked away down the path. ''Whether or not someone sicced Kalifa on us, could be there's more of this stuff up ahead.''

2

It was early morning, and these were the high seas. Actually, the sun had cleared the headlands, which meant it couldn't be all *that* early, and since the headlands above the seasonally fog-shrouded coast were in easy sight off the starboard beam the seas couldn't be all that high themselves. Zalzyn Shaa had appropriated his accustomed morning-watch position on the quarterdeck of the *Not Unreasonable Profit*, and, with his sea legs long since thoroughly entrenched, was balancing easily against the coastal swells with a steaming mug of herb-brew tea in his grasp. This fine if slightly foggy morning, Shaa was reflecting back on his early acquaintance with the *Not Unreasonable Profit* and its similarly not unreasonable captain and crew, on the middle reaches of the River Oolvaan. The River Oolvaan, as was typical of intracontinental and landlocked waterways, had a fresh-water source, even though it emptied ultimately into the sea. Its navigational challenges had been those of sandbars and shifting currents, punctuated by the odd flood and the occasional cataract. Didn't that mean, Shaa was wondering, that a vessel which made its habitat on such a river would have been designed specifically for fresh-water navigation in areas of restricted passage, rather than for the vicissitudes of the open ocean?

Despite his brief tenure as captain of this very ship, Shaa did not consider himself enough of an expert on nautical matters to speak authoritatively. Such a sage was, however, present. "Captain Luff," said Shaa, addressing the slicker-garbed individual standing beside him at the rail, where he had been keeping his usual weather-eye peeled for any fresh pandemonium Shaa might feel compelled to unexpectedly unleash, "this ship and this crew and, one might add, yourself, are used to sailing the River Oolvaan, is that not true?"

"Aye, Dr. Shaa," Captain Luff said warily, "that is indeed the situation."

"Indeed," said Shaa. "Have you found, then, that the forces at your command have been equal to the transition to the salt-water environment we are now cruising so pleasantly across?"

Captain Luff removed his pipe from the corner of his mouth, extracted a pointed implement from beneath his slicker, and set to work scraping at the pipe's inner recesses. "Why do you ask, Dr. Shaa? Do you have a criticism to lodge?"

"Not at all," Shaa told him, "not at all. I was only reflecting on the reservoirs of seamanship and marine expertise present on this ship, not to say within its very sinews."

The captain looked at Shaa for a moment, his hands still and the pipe forgotten. "You know, it is true," he continued, after the pause for consideration, resuming work at the same time on his pipe, "that a mariner does not often get the chance to engage in conversation of the sort I have engaged in with you, especially while at sea, don't you know. That being said, and that being no less than the truth, it must also be said that never in all my years of roaming the waterways of the known world, aye and seas and oceans beyond the commonly known, too, never, as I say, I can state with confidence, have I heard before today any person refer to any ship as having sinews."

"It is my honor to be the first, then," said Shaa. "But the matter of sinews remains, nevertheless, with or without the delineation, as does the matter of the difficulty in realigning ship and crew from one environment to another. That would appear to be just the sort of challenge to appeal to an old sea dog such as yourself. Wouldn't you say so, Captain?''

"There be more than enough challenges aboard this ship,'' stated Captain Luff.

Shaa inclined a guileless eyebrow. By this time, however, Captain Luff had been through enough of these encounters to realize that if Shaa had a guileless bone in his body it had not yet revealed itself, even by implication. "More challenges than that, Captain?'' Shaa said. "A hardy sea dog you must be indeed, and no doubt about it. Surely there must be some way I can help lighten the load of your burden.''

"I would doubt that very much, Dr. Shaa,'' said the captain with a sidelong glance in his direction, "seeing as you yourself contribute mightily to it, don't you know. You are a challenge yourself, sir, and no doubt about *that*. You must have been quite a vexation to your mother, if you don't mind my saying so.''

"So she often commented,'' said Shaa, "which was all the more curious considering the overall balance of terror in my family.''

Captain Luff examined his now-clean pipe with relish before propping it securely back in the corner of his mouth. "How was that, now, then?''

Shaa had been lulled by the pleasant swells and the motion of the ship, which was for a change gentle to a degree approaching placidity. "I had an older brother, you see, compared to whom I was the merest pussycat.''

" 'Had,' then, you say.''

"Had, have, it's all the same anyway.''

"Is that how it is? I lack the personal experience, don't you know, being an only child.''

"A prudent philosophy,'' Shaa told him, "Have no doubt about it.'' To the east, the sun broke through the last wisps of the morning mist and cast a clean light across the ship. Below them and forward, the main deck was spotted with clumps of crew members adjusting ratlines, coiling ropes, swabbing the deck, and checking the lashings on the few crates of trade goods that had failed to fit down in the hold with the rest of the cargo. Much more of the deck was open than had been the case on their run down the Oolvaan. Perhaps this was also related to the different demands of sea and river. Shaa decided that, all things considered and curiosity aside, it might be better not to reopen the topic.

Members of the crew were not the only ones abroad on the deck. Ronibet Karlini and the young Tildamire Mont were ensconced at their small writing-desk over by the starboard bulwark. Tildamire was not so young as that, actually, Shaa reminded himself, noting the appreciative glances the deckhands were giving her whenever they had the opportunity. She and Roni were both dressed in shirts and shipboard trousers, with loose jackets as outer wear, and Tildy had similarly followed Roni's lead by cutting her sandy hair short. In Shaa's professional opinion as a physician an adolescent woman could do much worse than adopt the sensible Ronibet as her role model. Shaa hadn't known Roni at Tildamire's age, though, so it was possible that could have been a time when the model had broken down. As Shaa well knew, even sensible adults are not necessarily sensible from birth.

Tildamire had been following Roni in more than just deportment, though. Roni was easygoing, but that was not the same as being easily impressed. In discussing their plans for the near future just the previous evening, in fact, Roni had commented on Tildy's rapidly developing aptitude for symbolic math and theoretical magic. Tildy didn't have practical spell-knowledge or casting skills, but her grasp of their underpinnings was significantly the harder to achieve. It could also ultimately take her further if she chose to continue with wizardry as a career. Still, the thrill of discovering an astute disciple did not totally account for the fervor with which Roni had been alternately encouraging Tildy and egging her on. Observing Ronibet, the situation made Shaa wonder if she was not reenacting one of her own formative experiences. Perhaps Karlini knew, but if so he had thus far been unwilling to spill those particular beans.

Not that the Great Karlini had been all that communicative on any other topic for the last few days, either. This morning Karlini was at his accustomed place, too, up on the foredeck wedged into the bow. Karlini had spoken vaguely about keeping a watch for icebergs, and indeed he had been spending an inordinate amount of time gazing off into the water ahead of the ship. True, Karlini at the best of times was noticeably absentminded. At the moment, though, Shaa had observed that Karlini had been taking preoccupation to new levels of intensity. This did not seriously interfere with his value as a deterrent, and was clearly playing a role keeping the sailors at a healthy distance away from his wife and Tildy. Sailors were a superstitious lot by tradition, and Shaa would not have been surprised to discover that this was codified in their guild rules as well, but it took no superstition for them to treat Karlini with vigilant respect, only powers of observation. They had viewed Karlini's pyrotechnics earlier in the voyage.

Of course, as far as the issue of deterrence went, there was Svin, too.

As Shaa watched him along the length of the ship, Karlini suddenly stood, brushed himself off, shook one leg clear of the coil of rope that had decided to tangle itself up with him on his getting up off the deck, and began to make his way aft. Some ancient philosophies had claimed that observer and object were linked in a complementary relationship, with an act of observation causing some reciprocal change at the other end, and indeed a certain class of spells were based directly on this principle, not to mention its ramifications throughout the treatment of action-reaction coupled pairs. Outside of the direct application of this philosophy through sorcery, Shaa did not believe its effect could be felt at the level of the macroscopic world. Nevertheless, it was certainly true that the world was full of surprises. Shaa had been watching Karlini, and

Karlini had taken that moment to spring into action. Of course, nothing said the world's surprises had to be any more than inconsequential.

Shaa heard a discreet cough at his elbow. "Excuse me, sir," said Wroclaw, Karlini's retainer. "Might I bring you a refill for your tea? And you, sir, captain, a fresh pouch for your pipe?"

Indeed, Captain Luff had just started to fumble beneath his slicker with an increasingly furrowed expression, which Shaa had interpreted to mean that his tobacco had somehow eluded his grasp. As Wroclaw deferentially extended a full pouch of the captain's blend toward him, it became clear that he had, in fact, been even better than his word had implied in anticipating the needs of the moment. "Thank you, Mr. Wroclaw," Captain Luff said, taking the pouch and beginning to prime his pipe. "How do you do that, man?"

For Wroclaw, "man" was a generic honorific, what with his lime-tinted skin and extra-jointed arms, but then you had to allow species terms a certain laxity in modern society in general, unless of course bigotry was your all-too-common philosophy of life. "I've always looked on it as more a calling than a job, sir," said Wroclaw. "And you, Dr. Shaa?"

Shaa had thoroughly inspected Wroclaw as he'd handed over the captain's pouch; both of Wroclaw's hands were now free and there were no noticeable bulges around his coat or trousers. "Yes," said Shaa, "I will thank you for your offer and indeed take a refill, since it is after all for medicinal purposes rather than raw sybaritic pleasure, but only if you can produce it now from about your person."

Wroclaw cleared his throat again with a genteel "ahem." Then, when nothing had happened after a few seconds, he stamped lightly on the top step of the companionway up which he had first appeared. "*Ahem,*" he said more forcefully, aiming it down the steep stairs. An earthenware teapot appeared at the top of the companionway and rose into the air.

"Not beast of burden am I," said a crackly voice. His attention now focused in response to the new speaker, Shaa could perceive that the teapot was not in fact floating on its own in midair. Instead, the teapot was clutched in a set of black-cloaked arms that Shaa had lost at first against the similar gloom of the unlighted below-decks passage. Beside him, Shaa felt Captain Luff find something else to observe on the quarterdeck, and edge carefully away. Captain Luff did have his limits.

Shaa had his own limits too, but he made a point of drawing them much more liberally, and on a time-varying basis of relativity. "Thank you, Wroclaw," he said as Wroclaw poured more brew from the teapot, "and you, of course, Haddo. That was quite neighborly of you, I must say," he added judiciously.

"Hmph," said Haddo. "Low is fate, for teapot the porter I to become. If not on vacation was bird, different would be things. Wroclaw, speak with you would I."

"Please excuse me, gentlemen," Wroclaw said. "Is there anything else I might get you?"

"Thank you, Wroclaw, no," Shaa said. "Off with you now. The path of wisdom is not to keep friend Haddo waiting."

"Indeed, no, sir," agreed Wroclaw, followed by another "hmph" from beneath his feet. Wroclaw disappeared down the stairs.

"Quite a crew you are," commented Captain Luff from his new position behind the helmsman, "and about that there's no mistaking." He fingered his nattily short growth of new beard. "Speaking of which, where's that other young fellow this morning? The one with the cane and his mind in the haze."

"The Creeping Sword?" said Shaa. "I'm sure he's skulking about somewhere." He had not actually told a lie, Shaa reminded himself. He had merely neglected to mention the fact that the "somewhere" to which he had alluded was no longer onboard the boat.

Captain Luff gave a noncommittal grunt and puffed

vigorously on his pipe. A cloud of aromatic smoke engulfed his head before shrédding away in the breeze. "And our other amenities are adequate, I hope? And our navigation? I trust we are approaching Peridol at a quick enough rate to suit you, Dr. Shaa?"

" 'Alacrity' is a word that comes to mind," said Shaa. This was not necessarily an unmixed blessing. The circumstances of his last departure from Peridol had been what they had been, nor were they likely in the interim to have changed. Back then, it had been made clear to Shaa that Peridol was not what he would be able to call a healthy place. Nevertheless, one characteristic of interims was that they did offer an opportunity for situations to evolve. His heart gave a sudden palpitation and broke into a run of rapid beats. Be still, Shaa told it, and took an extra swig of the glycosidic tea for good measure. Surprisingly, his heart *did* quiet, resuming its regular rate and rhythm. Pharmacologically speaking, the double swallow of brew he had just downed would not have yet had an opportunity to affect things one way or another, but Shaa was never one to devalue the role of a timely placebo, even on himself. For all his crustiness, Shaa knew well just how vulnerable he could be to suggestion.

In the classical texts, suggestibility was tied up with susceptibility to a curse. Learning that there was such a thing as a curse-prone personality had not improved Shaa's attitude on the subject of curses as a whole. Unfortunately, one's conscious attitude, whether approving or disapproving, was not a side of the issue that had any impact on the results; one's receptivity remained. So did Shaa's track record. To the extent that Shaa's vulnerability to curses might depend on his suggestibility, Max had tried to browbeat him out of it, and Shaa had also submitted to various arcane therapies from the deepest ranges of science and superstition both, but still the curse remained. Shaa was resigned to it. *I am,* he thought, *really I am.*

Resignation in this case was as much a matter of practicality as anything else. Too many oaths would have to be broken—and for that matter too many people would have to die—for the effects of the curse to end. The thought always left Max undaunted, but then Max was an undauntable kind of guy. Shaa was much less so, at least in this case. In this particular case, the most probable single person whose death would bring the curse to a close was Zalzyn Shaa, himself.

Down on the deck, the Great Karlini had reached Roni and Tildamire. He had been joined partway along his path from the bow by a seagull, which had perched itself on his shoulder. This being the sea, there were many seagulls about, and a small flock of them had taken up regular station just astern of the boat. This particular seagull, however, had not entered their company with these others but had been dogging Karlini's steps since even before he'd come to Roosing Oolvaya, having joined up with them the first time at a spot far inland.

"There's something not quite right about that thought," Karlini muttered. " 'Dogging your steps' is a common enough expression, but doesn't it sound kind of odd when applied to a seagull?"

"Many things you say sound odd, dear," his wife told him.

Karlini's face had furrowed itself in thought. "Isn't there some tradition that looks at the seagull as a harbinger of doom?"

"Not as far as I know," said Roni. "That's not to say you don't hear about seagulls here and there in some of the out-of-the-way texts. Usually they're put in a concrete rather than metaphysical role, though; avatars of pelagic ecology, that kind of thing. The seagull?—maybe a harbinger of ocean carrion and bivalve • mollusks, but doom? Why aren't you talking to Shaa, anyway? He's the student of natural philosophy, not me."

The seagull stretched out its wing and flapped Karlini once over the head. "Urr," Karlini said. "It has to mean something! The thing's been following me for months."

"It probably knows you're an easy touch, dear."

I simply must take up tennis, thought Tildy Mont. Her father had sent her off with Roni to get an education and see the world. The academic stuff she supposed she was getting, all right. What she'd been seeing of the world, though, was less scenic than distressing. Tildy had lost count of the number of conversations she'd witnessed that were just like being a center-line spectator at a tennis match, only without the ball, although sometimes with the rackets.

Tildy was used to it enough by now that she didn't swivel her head back and forth to follow the volleys; she could observe with her eyes alone, and even with her eyes closed. The way the Karlinis played the game was different from the way Shaa did it, though, or for that matter most anyone else she'd run across. The things Karlini said often didn't seem to have much connection at all with what was going on in the rest of the conversation. Karlini did this with everybody, but with his wife he was getting to be the worst. Was that because they'd been married for so long, or was Karlini just heading off on a different plane? Tildy glanced idly at the seagull, which as usual was paying no heed to Karlini's comments except for an occasional nip at the closest ear, and sat up straight with a start.

For a change, the seagull had swiveled its eye around and seemed to be watching *her.*

"No, you don't," Tildy hissed. "You've already *got* a shoulder." The seagull squawked and tossed its beak, then turned and wailed straight into Karlini's eardrum.

"Yow! Stop that, will you?" Karlini growled at it. "When we land in Peridol I'm heading straight to the college library to look up an exorcism for sea-fowl."

"Sit down and have a piece of cheese, dear," Roni suggested. "The grapes are still fresh, too."

"I don't want a grape," said Karlini, sitting down anyway and immediately regretting it. Why was Roni looking at him like that? "What? What is it?"

"What's *wrong* with you, dear? You've been snapping at everyone ever since we left Oolsmouth."

"Nothing's wrong, I'm fine. I'm bored. I don't like boats. It's nothing. I'm fine."

"So you said."

Karlini managed a strained-looking smile. "See? Nothing's wrong. You like to see smiles, right?"

"Okay, fine."

"What did I say? Now you're mad at me."

"You're just fine?" said Roni. "Okay then, I'm not mad."

"Okay then, fine," said Karlini.

"Fine."

"Great."

". . . Uh, guys?" Tildy said, watching the two of them sit there glaring at each other, Karlini with his arms folded belligerently and Roni matching him with a sour enough expression to make you think she'd just taken a swig of milk a week out from under its freshness spell. "You love each other, right? Why are you beating up on each other all of a sudden?" It was sort of like watching your parents argue. Part of Tildy wanted to slide under the table and shrink away. Of course, that was the part her father, the former Lion of the Oolvaan Plain, had tried to totally expunge, along with any other personality features that smacked to the least extent of anything less than no-holds-barred straight-ahead attack-dog ferocity. No weaknesses were tolerated in the Mont family. That was surely why Tildy's brother, Jurtan, had had such a hard time, what with his seizures and all; the Lion had looked at him like he was a strange invertebrate dragged in by the cat and dropped on the rug with a binding set of adoption papers. Tildy wondered how Jurtan was doing. Karlini might have been able to snoop in on him and Max to find out what was up, but Roni was right—Karlini hadn't done much of anything since they'd left Oolsmouth except mope around and be peckish.

"There's more to a relationship than love," Roni said, after a pause long enough that Tildy had just about decided neither one of them had heard a word she'd said. "You decide what's important in the relationship and then you stick to it. Trust. Openness. Sharing. Communication. Old favorites like that."

"I've got nothing to share!" protested Karlini.

"So I see," said Roni. "I guess we've communicated."

"Good, I guess we have."

"Right."

"Fine."

"It seems to me," said Tildy, "that if you, Karlini, were working on some project instead of—"

"I don't need marriage counseling from an adolescent," Karlini sputtered. Maybe he'd also been listening after all. "Give me a break! Okay, I'm on edge, big deal. We're heading into who knows what-all kinds of trouble in Peridol, that's enough to put anybody on edge. There's—oh, why bother. And there's always Haddo."

"Yes," said a reedy voice approaching from astern, "always is Haddo."

Tildy looked over her shoulder behind her. There was no doubt from the voice, of course, that Haddo was heading their way, but you could always hope. Haddo was trailed by a distressed-looking Wroclaw.

"Thanks, Haddo," muttered Karlini. "Perfect." Karlini didn't enjoy knocking heads with his wife, especially with Tildy tossed in the mix to boot, so that should make the idea of being rescued more appealing, he thought, *right?* Unfortunately, rescue by Haddo promised its own set of new aggravations. Haddo's industrious scuttle ground to a halt next to the table. Ready or not, Haddo was upon him. "Time for more contract negotiations, Haddo?" Karlini said.

Haddo aimed the black opening in his dark hood at Karlini, the twin floating red sparks in its depths canting reprovingly and the cloth of the upper rim drooping over them like accusingly furrowed eyebrows. "Master, O Great," said Haddo. "Homage give we small laborers. Master are you, light can you treat serious the matters.''

"I guess that means yes," said Karlini, his scowl (if that was possible) deepening further. He pushed himself to his feet. "I guess I'd better deal with it."

"Guess?" said Haddo. "Guess not. Only do."

"What?" Karlini muttered. "What, you want me to start paying you for those pearls of wisdom now too?"

Roni watched Karlini move reluctantly off with his retainers, and Tildamire watched Roni. She hadn't seen Roni like this before. Roni sighed. Actually, Tildy thought, remembering that all of them kept telling her precision was important, it was more a masculine exclamation of "huh!" than a feminine sigh. To say it was a sigh would put the wrong spin on it. "I don't know, Tildy," Roni was saying, oblivious to Tildy's internal battle with vocabulary. "You spend years with somebody, you start to think you know them, then you blink at them one day and see they've turned into someone else."

"Uh, maybe it's like he said, he's just worried," Tildy suggested. "He thinks he's got to watch out for me, keep the sailors off me. I wish he'd back off a little. I mean, there's my father and everything. My father thinks I can take care of myself or he wouldn't have let me go off with you." She noticed Roni wasn't listening again. Just as well; Tildy thought she might have gone overboard a little with the bit about her father. As far as the Lion was concerned, the only one who could take care of himself was the Lion. "Karlini said he doesn't like boats."

Roni was playing with a grape from the bowl on the table. "He *doesn't* like boats, but he's never reacted like this before. He usually just turns green and sits in a locker moaning. I'm not a shrew. It's him—he's keeping something from me. He was always a terrible liar."

"Okay, maybe he is. Why would he do that? If he is, he sure doesn't seem very happy about it either."

"Well, whatever it is, I'll tell you this. I'm going to find out." Grape juice squirted. Roni wiped the crushed grape skin off her fingers.

Tildy found she was staring at the remains of the grape. Don't go making a metaphor out of this, she told herself. The image of the pulped fruit stayed with her, though. If this kept up, somehow Tildy didn't think grapes were the only things that might get crushed.

The Great Karlini stopped on the far side of the deck, leaned on the rail so he could look over the side, and said in a low voice, "Is this far enough out of anybody's earshot for you?"

Haddo regarded him, his arms beneath his cloak planted solidly on what in any similarly proportioned humanoid would have been his hips. "Bum are turning yourself into, you."

"What Haddo means to say—" Wroclaw began.

"What means Haddo to say," snapped Haddo, "Haddo will say. Not for you is business this, you with for liver the lilies. When tough must get—are doing you what?"

"Would you like to sleep with the fishes?" asked Wroclaw, in the same urbanely unruffled tone he always used. The other incongruity in the scene, aside from his words, was contributed by the way in which Haddo was now dangling over the side of the boat above the rushing water below, suspended by the bunched material of his hood caught up in Wroclaw's clenched hand. "Answer now, if you would, Haddo my colleague."

From the strangled sound of Haddo's voice, Karlini thought, you might think Wroclaw had him by the neck instead of by the hood. "Down put me!" he gargled. "Point have you made!"

Karlini blinked. Haddo was back on the deck. There'd been a slight black-tinged blur in the air, but that was the only sign that Wroclaw had swung him back rather than using some kind of quick-zap teleport number. Haddo shook out his cloak and reached up to adjust the hang of his hood. "Regret will you this," he muttered. Rather than a manifesto of vendetta and doom, though, the remark sounded to Karlini like a statement made *pro forma,* for the sake of appearance and conversational nicety.

But Wroclaw? "Uh, have you been taking some kind of martial arts lessons or something, Wroclaw?" Karlini said tentatively.

"As always, sir, my services are yours to command," said Wroclaw. "As Haddo was commenting, though, with his usual velvety manner, we have been noting a certain . . . *decline* in your condition of mind of late, sir. We beg your pardon for our boldness in raising this, but there it is."

"Condition of mind? What are you talking about?"

"A term that comes to hand, sir, is 'mope'; also 'brood' or 'sulk.' We would all much rather see you engaged in some productive activity than slipping into, excuse me sir, as I mentioned before, *decline.*"

There it was. A sorcerer in "decline" was one who'd lost his or her touch and was an accident waiting to happen; raw meat for the next predator who walked up with half an appetite, a sinking ship to be deserted. The seagull shifted its balance uneasily on Karlini's shoulder. "Is that what this is about?" said Karlini. "Are you telling me you're quitting?"

"No, sir," Wroclaw stated, "certainly not at just this moment. Peridol in this season is likely to be rather a challenge, though, if I might say so."

"I'll be ready! Don't worry about me, I'll be ready."

Wroclaw scrutinized him. "Indeed, sir, of that I had no doubt. Please pardon our impertinence. Haddo, shall we go?"

"I've got something else to discuss with Haddo," said Karlini. "Leave him with me."

"As you say, sir." Wroclaw bowed and withdrew.

Karlini directed a hard stare at Haddo, which the seagull still perched next to his head duplicated. Haddo stared back. "Well?" Karlini said. "Is that what *you* wanted to talk about?"

"Close enough is matter. Better can you do than doing have been you."

Karlini closed his eyes, and kneaded his forehead. "All this plotting and scheming, scheming and plotting. It never ends, Haddo, it only gets worse."

"Word gave you."

"I know I gave my word, Haddo, but this is not going to work. I haven't kept anything from Roni since I met her. Now I'm supposed to work against her behind her back?"

"Not as extreme as statement is situation. Know this you."

Karlini turned back to the ocean and drooped over the rail. The seagull squawked and hopped off his shoulder, flapped once, and came to a neat landing next to him on the gunwales. "I can't do this, Haddo. It's only going to get worse, it's not going to get better."

Karlini felt Haddo's leathery hand on his back. "Do it you can," Haddo told him, "because do it you must. In Peridol perhaps will be all things resolved."

"You don't really believe that."

Haddo shrugged. "Happen it could. Happened have stranger things."

"That's not very reassuring."

"How things go, that is. Help you perhaps can I. On this think I should."

Karlini had fallen silent. Haddo watched him a moment longer, though, before deciding Karlini was in no significant danger of falling or leaping over the rail. As he retreated, Haddo cast another glance back to be on the safe side. Karlini was still drooping, his back to Haddo, but the seagull fixed him with an intent, watchful look.

Checking periodically over his shoulder, Haddo made his way below decks and into the hold. The crates and lashed bales of their cargo had been packed tightly into the available space, with only a few narrow passageways left to twist and dodge their way between them. Haddo, however, was a being of less than average size. He had also assisted in the packing. This was not the first time during the trip he had been down in the hold, either. He was sure no one had been following him, and no one was in sight when he scuttled around a bend in one of the passageways, dropped to the deck, and slid himself to the left. Anyone carrying a lamp through the hold would have seen no hint of an opening, since the sacks that flanked the passage at that point bulged out at the front, casting a maze of shadows on everything below them. To detect the narrow recess at the bottom where a cleverly raised palette kept the sacks off the deck an observer would have had to crawl, hope for a quiet bilge as he put his eye down on the deck, and aim his light just right.

Of course, it was a ship, so there were rats. As Haddo wriggled through the narrow space, pushing the sack he'd picked up on his way past the kitchen in front of him, something chittered at him from up ahead deeper in the blackness. Haddo growled back at it. The squeaking persisted, joined by a blinking set of green eyes. Obviously this was a rodent he had not previously encountered. ''Warned you did I,'' muttered Haddo. A red glow spread from under his hood, then focused down and became twin beams, straight, clear, and narrow with a color like spotlit rubies. The rat's green eyes fluoresced and its chittering turned to a squeal as its sharp-edged shadow spread out behind it. Where the beams converged, a puff of smoke rose out of its fur. Then the rat had had enough. It twisted away with a final wail and was gone. The beams and the red glow died. Haddo edged through the area the rat had abandoned and reached the lower edge of a crate. He rapped on it. ''Who is it?'' said a muffled voice.

''Who think you it is?'' Haddo snapped.

''You can't be too careful,'' grumbled the voice. The wood panel clicked and slid upward, and Haddo edged through the opening. The panel glided shut behind him. "Hold on while I get the lights." A ripple of shining green ran around the wall over Haddo's head and snaked off at right angles, outlining the inside of the crate. Then yellow burst out through the green, the two colors pulsated once or twice as they worked things out between them, and the light level settled down to a constant low but serviceable glow.

The crate measured perhaps eight feet on a side. As you'd expect from a crate in a cargo hold, the space ahead of Haddo was crammed tight with stuff—rolled parcels concealed in oilskins, boxes with latches, a lashed set of short metal rods, a hand-ax. Barely visible atop the mounds of equipment was the curve of a spherical cauldron.

Behind Haddo, a ladder was fastened to the inside surface of the crate. The same lattice-work retaining wall that kept the contents of the crate from collapsing into the entrance-space continued upward along the ladder's path. Haddo grasped the ladder and scurried up. At the top of the ladder a two-foot-high gap separated the cargo and the crate's upper lid. Protruding from the center of the cargo was the upper swell of the round ball, and swung back from the center of the ball was a domed lid. "Outside met I rat," Haddo told the creature perched inside the sphere, its head propped on the lip.

"You want to tell me about inconvenience?" said the creature, its pointed ears splayed at conflicting angles. "Try taking an ocean voyage inside a box." He moved his head around in a slow circle, carefully stretching his neck muscles, then worked one shoulder back and forth to match. "I'm getting to be nothing but a mess of hog-tied ligaments."

Haddo tossed the sack he'd lugged up the ladder onto a cluster of skyrockets protruding out of the baggage next to the ball. He gestured at the metal sphere. "Have you not your vehicle, Favored? Life support facilities has it, said you not?"

"There's a big difference between support and comfort,'' said Favored-of-the-Gods. ''At least *you* get to walk outside on the deck.''

''My idea this was not,'' Haddo pointed out.

''You could have tried to talk me out of it.''

''Frozen permanently in frown is mouth,'' asked Haddo, ''or is just to make of visitor with supplies to welcome feel?''

''If you weren't bigger than me, I'd whomp you one,'' Favored muttered.

''Testy is getting on ship everyone,'' Haddo reflected. ''At throats people are.''

''Is that supposed to make me feel better?''

Haddo shrugged. ''Not alone are you. Good or bad not is, fact is only. Of it make what choose you. To Peridol ride wanted you.''

''Well, yeah, all right,'' said Favored. ''You'd think if my patron wanted me in Peridol for the Knitting she'd at least have supplied transportation, but no.''

''Insensitive ones work you for,'' commiserated Haddo. ''Downtrodden masses are we.''

''You starting with the dialectic again?'' Haddo shrugged. ''Anyway,'' Favored went on, ''as long as you're bringing up insensitivity, how's that Karlini of yours doing? You keeping an eye on him?''

''Faith has kept Karlini. Speak to wife will he not.''

Favored shook his head. ''I don't know about him, Haddo. He could be a weak link. If he lets something slip to her—or, worse, directly to Max—Max'll come after us the first thing he does. I don't mind telling you I'd rather not face him head-on.''

''Danger is Max. Getting around it no way is. To check put on Max, options limited are. Karlini most attractive option is.''

''You're sure he's not going to fall apart?''

''Sure am I not,'' snapped Haddo. ''Said I not under strain is he not. Observing closely am him I. Difficult position have put we in him.''

''So we're just going to watch while his fuse burns down?''

''Credit give me for brains,'' Haddo said. ''When

47

Peridol reach we, mood of Karlini must we lift. Cycle must we break. This for, place Peridol perfect is." Haddo hesitated. "Problem only is Karlini not. Told I not you about ice the attack."

One of Favored's eyes snapped wide open and the other squinted half-shut, his nictitating membranes twitching. "Did you say 'ice'?"

"Ice said I," said Haddo reluctantly. "On trip down river to Oolsmouth attacked by icebergs was boat. Thought Karlini and Shaa against them was aimed strike this."

"Does that mean what I think?"

"Know not I, suspect I only."

Favored slumped back into his sphere. His voice echoed with a hollow metallic tone. "That's the last thing we need right now."

"Last need we, first yet but may we have."

"Ice, you say?" Favored repeated, with a note of disbelief. "That's not good. What the hell business does he have heading out of the frozen wastes to come after you down here, anyway? I thought he was out of the picture for good. You said he couldn't survive out of that climate, either."

"Maybe someone he got refrigerator to build."

"Damn," said Favored, now thoroughly morose. "You got anything else you want to tell me? What about that seagull?"

"Bird speaks not yet."

Favored hung his head back over the lip of the hatch. "I don't like that either. The idea of that bird makes me nervous. As long as that thing's walking around . . . Well, I don't like it."

"Much around is there that like you not," said Haddo. "Agree with you do I, yet strike we preemptively can not. To be on guard, to wait, to watch is of wisdom the strategy."

"Wisdom? You trying to turn yourself into a sage now, too?"

"Particularly wise am I not. Open merely are eyes."

"Yeah, well, you're probably right," Favored said.

"You've had more fieldwork than me anyway. There sure isn't much we could do on a boat even if we wanted to. Once we get to Peridol the story'll be different."

"In Peridol will be many things different," Haddo said. "Enjoy you of refill the fruit." Always a useful ally, was Favored, Haddo mused as he squirmed his way back out of the crate and into the passageway in the cargo hold. Seeing adequately as always in the minimal light, he padded quietly toward the exit, dodging around the jogs and corners. Two to the left, then one to the right, then—whoompf!

"Where from came wall?" muttered Haddo, taking a step back. There hadn't been a surface at this spot on his way in. Then all at once he realized that what he'd run into wasn't a wall at all. It was a man. A large man, in fact a *very* large man. A man whose mass owed nothing to sloth or fat and everything to cord upon band of muscle, that and his hereditary ceiling-scraping stature.

"You," whispered the man.

"Down keep your voice," hissed Haddo, feeling the cargo shift around him in resonant vibration with the subterranean rumble of the speech, "or avalanche cause could you. Around boat seen you have I. Svin are you. Dark corners liking are you now?"

"You," Svin repeated, with a bit less rumble this time, but with the same hollow bang and boom. "I have seen you, too. You have been avoiding me. You are Haddo."

"Avoiding have I been not," protested Haddo. "No reason would have I—"

"I have tracked the snow leopard. For three days have I followed him through the tundra, through the empty plains. When someone tries to hide from me, I know. You are Haddo. I know you."

"Serve we both same masters," Haddo said, his own voice a bit scratchier than usual. "Met did we in service together, recently, on boat."

49

"No," said Svin. "I know you. I am a barbarian from the frozen north, like my parents before me."

Haddo stared him up and down. Even in the gloom of the hold, lit only by the stray beams of sunlight that had wormed their way through gaps between the planks of the deck above, it was apparent that this statement was out of date. "Barbarian *were* you," Haddo stated. "Now wear you trousers and shirt, cut you your hair; abandoned have you loincloth, are gone your furs. Civilization have you entered."

"You may be right," Svin said reflectively. "Perhaps now I am something else. That is not the point. You will not change the subject, you with your games of language and your culture of deceit. Men are not born to—"

"If to something say have you," said Haddo, "stop you can I not, but favor do me this—forget at least of noble savage the spiel. Old has it become."

"Words are a trap," Svin acknowledged. "I leave the snares of rhetoric; the truth is this. At the top of the world my people lived with the land; with the caribou, the ice hawk, the polar bear. We lived the way of the warrior. Man strove against beast, family against nature, tribe against tribe. Who would dare rule us? Chill wastes were our home. Even the hand of the gods was light. Then came Dortonn, Dortonn the sorcerer, Dortonn and his Kingdom of Ice." Svin spat, as though to clear his throat of something vile.

What was vile to Svin was not merely the content of his speech, Haddo knew. Not that long ago Svin had been down with tuberculosis. Since then it had been hack and hack, cough and cough all over the ship. Svin got his throat back under control and continued. "With his power Dortonn forced my people to serve him, to build his castle. We called to our gods, but they were with Dortonn. They told us to submit. We would not submit, even at the word of our gods. But we were not the only ones under Dortonn's hand. There were others in the wastes. Those like you."

"Many relatives have I—"

Svin squatted down in a smooth powerful motion and closed one hand over Haddo's cloak next to the hood, where his shoulder probably was. "One among them served Dortonn as his chamberlain, as Fist of Dortonn. He, too, was a cunning sorcerer. He was called Haddo."

"Among my people common of Haddo is name," Haddo said quickly.

Svin's hand tightened. "Under Haddo, Fist of Dortonn, life was hard, but before this time Dortonn himself was even worse. There was little difference; we hated both Dortonn and his Fist. Then one day there was lightning and fire in the castle. One tower fell. We fought Dortonn's soldiers shoulder to shoulder with Haddo's people, who seemed to come from the very walls. Some said this was Haddo's doing, his plan to overcome Dortonn.

"Many fell. Many fled. Dortonn survived, though his strength was now weak. Haddo was not seen again."

"Interesting perhaps this is," allowed Haddo. "Happened what then? Events these must years ago have been."

"Yes," Svin said, his voice lost in memory, "years ago. I was a child. Yet it was I who saw Dortonn escape into the cliffs."

"Do not understand I why to rule frozen wastes would want someone," said Haddo. "Of better places are there plenty."

"That is what I need to ask you. Why? Why did Dortonn come to us? What was the true story, and the story of Haddo?"

"Release you your hand," Haddo instructed him. To his surprise, Svin realized that his fingers had obeyed almost before his mind had had a chance to process the demand. Still, rather than grab Haddo again he stood up and moved back a step. In Haddo's voice, croaky though it was, Svin had suddenly heard the same tone of nonsense-is-over that he'd been trained to recognize across from him at the other end of a sword. The twin red embers beneath Haddo's cloak looked hotter than usual, almost like the actual pit-of-hell flames Svin remembered from bedtime tales as a youngster, and seemed to circulate like whirlpools of fire as Haddo stared up at him and spoke. "If *that* Haddo were I, if there had I been, think would I that behind this story, really was there a god, that his tool Dortonn was. For gods games these are."

"That is not enough. I must know more."

"Your time bide you," Haddo said after a moment. "If *that* Haddo were I, lightly not would take I this. Much means this to you. . . . Against this Haddo swore you vengeance?"

"Of course I swore vengeance," said Svin, taking another step back. "My people are always swearing vengeance for one thing or another." The elders had told him to watch out for magicians, especially ones who weren't human, but they'd never really explained how to rationalize the craftiness you needed around sorcery with the forthrightness expected from a warrior born. "But now I am older," he went on, more thoughtfully, "and have seen too much for things to be that simple. Perhaps knowledge may be a kind of vengeance, too."

A sudden creaking at the far end of the cargo hold, and a new glow in the air, indicated that someone else was undogging the door across from them and coming in. "Perhaps talk will we again," hissed Haddo. "One question pose will I for you. Name know you of god, master of Dortonn?"

"They said Dortonn's allegiance was only to Death," said Svin. "That's all my people ever thought of him as: Death."

"Many deaths there are. To tell them apart, names they have."

". . . I was only a child," Svin said tentatively, "but perhaps I did hear something else, at night, when the elders were talking. Is it even a name? Pod Dall?"

"Is a name," Haddo reassured him. It was quite an interesting one, especially under the circumstances.

The god whose creatures had terrorized Svin's people had kept an uncharacteristically low profile; this god had apparently not wanted his identity bandied idly about. Still, Svin's information corroborated Haddo's own suspicions.

Quite interesting. Especially under the circumstances. Did Svin know about the ring they had picked up in Roosing Oolvaya? Probably not. It would be just as well not to tell him. In particular, it might be better, at least for the moment, that Svin not know about the god trapped in the ring. The god by the name of Pod Dall.

3

There had to be land around here somewhere. I dug the oars in again, stroked against the swells for at least the ten-thousandth time since I'd left the ship, and felt the dinghy move another fathom farther toward what I hoped was still the east. The water-hugging mist had enough of a pearly glow that I knew the big moon was up there someplace, even if by now it was surely declining toward dawn. The fog bank had gotten thicker as I rowed, though, and it was now useless to think about putting the moon squarely astern and rowing away from it, since I couldn't see the disk of the moon to save my life. Hopefully it wouldn't come to that. After all, I did have a compass. I was confident enough of my ability to row in a straight line that I couldn't have been checking it more than once a minute. But how hard could a continent be to find when you were sitting just offshore?

As creative as I'd been at getting myself into trouble, I might find out.

I looked out at the haze and stroked. Maybe one reason the fog was so thick was that some of the murk that had been clouding my own mind was finally leaking out. Wishful thinking, maybe, but you could argue that was the same philosophy that had already carried me alive and intact over more than a few rapids in the last several weeks. Wishful thinking and luck.

Riding the rapids does take a toll, though. The end of the mess in Oolsmouth had left me in a daze; how much so was only becoming clear to me now that I was coming out of it. In my stupor, flowing along with the current, I'd taken some actions that didn't seem entirely well-chosen in retrospect. Drifting out to the Oolsmouth docks and linking up with Shaa and the Karlinis for the ride to Peridol was one of them.

It had seemed to make sense at the time. I'd felt like I needed reinforcements around, enough to provide me with a breather to rethink and regroup. I also hadn't been looking forward to walking or hanging onto a horse all the way from Oolsmouth to Peridol. On the other hand, for anybody who might be watching me, I'd now reinforced my connection with the others and in effect dragged them even deeper into my own problems. I know, I know, "anybody who might be watching me" sounds paranoid to the extreme. Paranoid I may have been, but there was still the evidence of recent twists and turns to show that in this case paranoia was the most conservative of strategies; I was as sure of that as, well, as my own name. Of course, considering that I didn't have the slightest idea of what my name actually was, that gives a pretty good outline of the state of affairs.

They'd been calling me the Creeping Sword. An alias like that is enough to send anyone with a modicum of taste back to bed with an icebag, I know, but unfortunately it was really my own fault. There'd been that case I'd just finished involving this Sword guy, see, and the name was so cheesy it stuck in the front of my mind. When I fell in with Max and Shaa and they wanted some handle to address me by, it was the first thing I could think of. Like most first thoughts, it left endless possibilities for recrimination after the fact. It beat "hey you over there in the corner," I guess, but both of them had about the same relationship to anything approaching the real me. At least, I hoped they did. None of us really knew, which was yet another way of popping the situation into a nutshell. Of course, a handle like the Creeping Sword was certainly the least of my worries.

Just because I had problems, though, didn't mean they were all equally difficult to address. Even if joining the *Not Unreasonable Profit* had been a bad idea, it still might not have been too late to escape the repercussions, which is why I found myself out alone in a rowboat in the middle of the night in the middle of the ocean. From my vantage point at the moment, this was not the first time one of my solutions looked less appealing than the problem it was supposed to solve. Nevertheless, if I could make it to shore, it shouldn't be more than a three- or four-day walk into Peridol along the coast road. That sounded like a good investment. A stout hike was probably the perfect prescription for draining the last dregs of goo from my mind. That's what Shaa had said, anyway, and prescriptions *were* his business.

There wasn't much question about the hike's destination, either; Peridol was clearly the place to be heading. Whatever your question might be, Peridol was always the leading place to find answers. Of course, Peridol being what it was, there were usually more answers than questions, and if you hadn't thought to bring a question with you, Peridol was more than happy to provide you with more than enough of its own. That was Peridol during normal times. During the Knitting season, that should apply at least double; maybe even triple, who knew? Since Peridol was Peridol, someone probably had the multiplier posted somewhere, with a back room full of probabilists arguing over the odds.

There it was again, math. Things kept coming back to math. For me, math had always been a dark room and me without a match. I didn't think I had any better grasp of mathematics now than I'd had before I'd run afoul of Max and his crew. Well, fine, I'd never wanted to be an accountant, and I'd certainly never wanted anything to do with the other major discipline that required a solid grasp of math, both abstract and applied. It was an axiom that you couldn't do magic unless you could work the math, but that had always been just dandy with me.

Just look at me now, though. Whether I'd had anything deliberate to do with it or not, at the very least you had to admit a lot of magic had been working itself around me lately; not only around me but through me. "Through me" just about describes it, too. I wasn't real happy about it; I didn't like being the next thing to a conduit or a trade road, sitting there minding my own business while magic stampeded over my head like a herd of runaway buffalo, but then I wasn't real fond of magic in any guise. On the other hand, I wasn't entirely complaining either—there had been a couple of situations where I'd have been in a terminally tight spot if I hadn't succeeded in sucking something useful out of Gashanatantra through our metabolic link. At least that's what I'd assumed was happening. Now I wasn't so sure.

There was a lot I wasn't sure about, and even more about which I absolutely *knew* I understood too little. Even something as simple as the cast of players, whether they were there by deliberate intention or had just been swept up by the swelling broom of events, was far from clear. There was Gashanatantra, who had had an important hand in getting this thing started in the first place. He'd hauled me in to be his front man back in Roosing Oolvaya, using the hook and gaff rig that bound his metabolism to mine. One of the worst things to do if you want to live to an advanced age is to surprise a god, but I'd surprised *him,* all right, when it turned out the metabolic link was more than a one-way street. Drawing fragments of his knowledge as well as his power through the link had helped me out in the short term, had helped me enough to save my life more than once. Whether the long-term situation was any more than the same fated death stretched out for the sake of excruciation remained to be seen. What didn't seem open to question was the extent to which the events just past had focused Gash's attention on me. At best I was a tool he'd found unexpectedly useful; at worst I might have actually become a center of his serious interest.

As Shaa and Max had told me and I'd come to see for myself in Oolsmouth, Gash's reputation for plots with more layers than a ripe onion was honestly earned. The mess in Roosing Oolvaya had been downright intimate by comparison. There, Gash had only sent me up against Oskin Yahlei, the necromancer and would-be god who'd taken charge of the ring holding the trapped Death, Pod Dall. The ring had swept Karlini into the situation, too, and with him Max, but if Gash cared about them or even knew they were there I hadn't seen a sign. Of course, it now appeared that, whatever he had said at the time, Gash's main interest then had been with the ring; after all, he'd been the one who'd trapped Pod Dall in it in the first place.

Throughout the Roosing Oolvaya and Oolsmouth side of things, though, Gash hadn't seemed to necessarily want the ring in his own possession. Instead, it was lurking out there serving the same purpose as a fishing lure or a piece of flypaper or a nice ripe tarpit—to work as a catalyst and a decoy, both, pulling folks out of the woodwork and getting them enmeshed in a situation that appeared to be one thing on its face, but that in fact involved Gash behind the scenes pulling strings toward his own inscrutable goals. Every time I thought about it, his hand only looked more subtle. He wasn't one for brute force; instead, the core of his style as I'd seen it rested in giving players the opportunity to do things their inclination naturally disposed them toward anyway. Once the framework was in place, all Gash had to do was point them toward the right target and stand back while they took off after it like a hound after a plumped-up rabbit.

Of course, this kind of stuff was easier to talk about than to pull off. No matter how much you wanted to hide behind the screen, sometimes someone just had to be out on stage helping things along. The problem with that was that once you were out in public, you made yourself a target for people to come after later if and when they thought they'd figured out what had really been going on. In Oolsmouth there had indeed been such a front-line figure; Gashanatantra, right? Of course not.

No, they thought it was me.

Actually, if it had only been that, it would have been simple, or simpler, anyway. The players Gash was working with were ones he knew. They knew him, too, but more than that they were already out for his hide. Rather than dodging indefinitely he'd decided to face them, in a manner of speaking. Because of the metabolic link and the aura it projected, they thought I was him. I was more than a front man, I was a full-fledged surrogate. I was there not only to advance Gash's plot but to take his heat.

Of course, no one actually bothered to tell me this or fill me in on my role; no, I'd had to figure it out as I muddled along. At least Gash hadn't decided to re-arrange my face, or my anatomy in general. Fortunately for me, in his circles no one seemed to raise much of an eyebrow over a new body here or there. Still, the first person who'd showed up believing I was him was his *wife*. At least Jill hated him; that I could deal with. I could sympathize with it also, since I wasn't exactly fond of him myself; given the circumstances, however, sympathy didn't seem like the most productive approach to take.

If Jill had succeeded in killing me straight off, I didn't think Gash would have been too unhappy either. After all, if Gash was supposed to be dead it would have given him even more freedom of action, as well as relief from Jill and anyone else on his trail. That I hadn't obligingly caved in had only opened the door to an extended high-wire act. In the company of Jill and her partner, Zhardann (or Jardin), the Administrator of Curses, I had somehow succeeded in extending the masquerade for days; in fact, they might not realize it was over yet. I was sure that the way we'd parted company, though, had left them more than eager to renew our acquaintance at the next possible opportunity. The least they'd be looking for would be answers

I either didn't have or couldn't give them and expect to remain alive.

Would they be in Peridol? Hah! That was a sucker bet. For a Knitting *everyone* who thought they were someone would be in Peridol. That didn't mean I had to make things any easier for them than they already were. If they'd picked up my trail in Oolsmouth, they could have learned I'd shipped out on a boat. With all the sea traffic converging on Peridol it'd been impossible to tell if the ship was being shadowed, but it wouldn't have been surprising. Even if we weren't under observation, it was only elementary to figure that showing up in Peridol on foot rather than on water might keep them off balance. Of course, knowing my traveling companions, a welcoming party might be waiting for any or all of the *Not Unreasonable Profit*'s passengers. That being said, any reception waiting for me would probably be the nastiest; these were *gods* I'd been fooling around with, after all. Even if someone was merely waiting for the boat to come in to pick up our trail, I didn't want to give them that much of a break.

Unfortunately, that wasn't the only possibility to consider. They could be waiting for me to split off from the others before coming after me. They could—

But there was only so far you could go in trying to anticipate how someone would surprise you next. The more reactive you became, the more initiative you threw out. I was pretty damn tired of being tossed back and forth by the whims of fate, chance, and the plots of others. I wasn't planning to wait for another god to show up on my doorstep and sling me into another maze of their own devising. It was time to assert myself, to become again an active participant in my own story rather than just getting bounced around the landscape by the events unfolding around me.

That didn't mean I wasn't perpetually looking over my shoulder, waiting for the next hand to reach out from the unknown and grab me around the neck. Just because I'd come to an ideological breakpoint didn't mean I'd lost all sense of reason. I was still half-expecting someone to pop out of the water next to the boat and hoist themselves onto the gunwales. You could say a rowboat in the middle of a fog bank had to be one of the safer places to hide out. On the other hand, these *were* gods etcetera etcetera; you go over the same ground often enough and it gets less and less interesting, unless you have a particular appreciation for churned mud.

Mud or no, the situation hadn't changed. Who knew *what* the gods could do? More to the point, *I* sure didn't know what they were capable of, other than lots of nasty surprises. They had to have limitations, but other than the ones I'd observed, which centered primarily on a shortage of good sense and on energy supplies and the recurring need to refuel, I didn't yet know what they were. It didn't go nearly far enough toward evening the scales to remember that my sparring partners apparently thought I was a god, too. Aside from its dubious value as a deterrent that didn't help me a whole lot. More than outweighing the deterrent value on the downside was the fact that it seemed to keep the scheming lot of them interested in me.

The thing that bothered me more than having them think I was a god was the chance they might be right.

Even though I'd been listening for it, it suddenly occurred to me that the sound I'd been waiting for had gradually snuck up unawares. More than the constant swish and gurgle of the swells, there was now the added crash and whoosh that implied the presence of breakers and a shore. It was behind me, too, exactly where I'd been hoping for it. There's that old proverb about watching out what you wish for because you might get it, but in this case I couldn't see how it was going to bite me, unless the shoreline was actually one of jagged rocks and I was about to have the keel ripped off the rowboat. In the larger case the proverb was a different story. Even so, I didn't see how that story would pick up again until I'd made it to Peridol, though, or at least before I'd gotten through the waves onto the beach.

Everything was in place, not that I'd brought much with me off the boat. A pack of supplies sat underneath my seat, and jammed through the top of the pack lengthwise was a stout walking stick just the right heft and length for a two-hand broadsword. I left off rowing for a moment and felt around for it to make sure it hadn't wandered off—yeah, there it was, all right. "You got anything to contribute?" I asked the stick.

It didn't say anything, which was no more than I'd expected, but it did vibrate quickly under my hand, sending a low tingle up my wrist and into my arm. Was that a message with real content, or was Monoch just letting me know it was still alive, or whatever it really was? I couldn't say. I didn't know its language, if it *had* a language, but I had come to know its moods. At the moment it was placid enough, for a change. I didn't know its purpose, either, beyond the fact that it was at best a reluctant ally foisted on me by Gash. That meant that it had to be a spy, and quite possibly a homing beacon, too. Unfortunately, things being what they were I just couldn't toss Monoch in the sea and be done with it, if tossing it in the sea would *let* me be done with it, which was another question entirely.

The sound of breakers behind me was now distinct. After perusing a navigational chart, Shaa had assured me that given the currents and the topography of the coastline I'd be encountering beach rather than rocks. I didn't exactly trust Shaa's seamanship, but he'd assured me he knew this section of the countryside well, and anyway I didn't have much choice. A predawn seagull cawed somewhere overhead. Off to the left I saw white-capped foam, then the rowboat creaked and lifted. I played with the oars, trying to keep the dinghy headed straight-on, and as the wave dropped beneath me the keel grated on sand.

I splashed and sloshed my way up the beach, dragging the rowboat by the painter in the bow, as the breakers rose to my knees and ebbed away. I was going to take this as a clearly good omen. It was anticlimactic, true, but I was hoping to find more anticlimactic episodes in my life in the days ahead.

I left the rowboat overturned on the beach under a bed of tangled kelp and headed inland up the sand. I sort of wished I could take the boat along; I never liked to waste a good piece of equipment, and who knew what I'd need for those same days ahead, but on the other hand clawing my way up a cliff and then hiking for days along a road carrying a rowboat on my back or hauling it behind me could easily attract just the kind of attention it was my intention to avoid. There was also the condition of my back and other assorted joints and muscles to consider. It was the sort of stunt you sometimes hear about in myths, and it certainly had the mythical characteristic of being essentially pointless, but maybe that was just the kind of thing gods appreciated. Probably not the ones I'd met, though; they seemed to like to avoid anything that smacked of direct work.

I could have camped at the edge of the water until the day arrived or the fog lifted, but I didn't want to push my luck; I had images of somebody sending giant lobsters out of the surf to snap pieces off my hands while I dozed. So I moved up the beach in the fog, the sparse light giving me a ten-foot circle of visibility before the mass of the fog won out over the glow of the moon, stumbling over piles of driftwood and popping the flotation bladders of tendrils of slimy kelp, until I discovered the cliff by the simple expedient of walking into it. That was good enough for me. No way was I going to try to climb an unknown cliff in the dark and the fog when there wasn't even any need for it. I flopped down on the sand, rested my head on the pack, and closed my eyes.

If there was any particular subject one or another of the members of Max's crew weren't interested in, I hadn't discovered it yet. One of the topics they all had something to say about was dreams. In my case, afflicted as I was by the effects of the Spell of Namelessness, they thought my dreams should be a fertile area of study; mirror of the unconscious and all that. I hadn't been much help. Max had a technique for monitoring the surface thoughts of someone he could physically lay his hands on, but it hadn't picked up a thing from me. "If he's got a mind in there at all, I can't find it," was Max's only comment on the question. Actually, that was okay with me. I'd been starting to have doubts about how far I could trust Max, especially if my original identity turned out to be someone he didn't like. What if I really *had* been a god? If the Spell of Namelessness was a weapon mainly used by gods against each other, as Zhardann's use of it had seemed to imply, that was a possibility that couldn't be ignored, not that I felt like a god, whatever a god was supposed to feel like. If I was or had been a god, though, regardless of what I felt like, the trick to survival might very well involve keeping out of Max's sight.

Karlini with his hypnosis and Shaa with his bedside manner hadn't had any better luck in prying hidden visions out of me either, though. As Shaa had pointed out, it was true that none of them had ever examined a victim of the Spell of Namelessness before, and such cases were also underreported in the literature, so as far as any of them knew loss of dream content could be a standard effect. I had a slightly different slant on it. As far as I was concerned, dreams were even more of a myth than me and the rowboat, since I didn't think I'd ever had one in my life.

Well, that wasn't entirely true. Not the part about the dreams, that was accurate enough, but the slight exaggeration about my life. The fact was, I knew very little about my life. The Curse of Namelessness had taken more than my name, it had erased all memory of whoever I might have been and whatever I might have done prior to my arrival in Roosing Oolvaya. Physical evidence was lacking, too—I didn't even have an evocative scar.

Which made it all the more unexpected, as I dozed off there on the sand next to the cliff, to discover I was having, in fact, a dream.

Not that it was much to talk about, I suppose. There was a landscape of mist. I knew it wasn't a real landscape, though; it didn't feel real, it felt *too* real, as though it was the mother lode ideal against which all mists in the real world were just cast shadows. It crackled with clarity, it sparkled, it shone, as though I was examining each wisp simultaneously with a microscope. By comparison, the genuine mist I'd just been rowing and slogging through was a cheap castoff imitation let loose by someone who didn't have a clue how a real mist was supposed to be put together. But all it was, for all its hyperrealism, was fog. *Great,* I remember thinking, *all this time waiting for a dream, and what I get is fog?*

The fog and I contemplated each other. Maybe it was my metaphor about the conditions inside my head made concrete. It did hold my attention, in a way actual fog never had, but even so it wasn't exactly an epiphany of meaning. Then I saw the face.

It had actually been condensing for a while without my growing aware of it. When I did realize something else was there, it was already a rough head-and-shoulders bust, still the grayish-white of the mist surrounding it and without any discernible features, as though someone had cast a wizard spotlight on their sculpture garden after a season of extreme erosion. Even in that state it projected the same realer-than-real effect as the mist itself, but as it formed a thin nose and a straight-edged mustache, a close-cropped cap of silver-blond hair, and eyes of glacier-ice blue, I had the feeling that if I ever met this person (since I'd never seen him before in, well, my life) I would recognize him instantly, even if all I could glimpse was the tip of an ear around a door in the dark. The image looked too intense to be a person; if I didn't know better, I'd have said someone that vivid must be something superhuman, like a god. I figured it must be an artifact of this dream business—the gods I'd encountered hadn't seemed any more radiant than anyone else you'd meet on the street.

The face hung there for a bit, and after a while I had the feeling I could put a name to it. No voice pronounced it, and I didn't hear the name, per se, it just sort of seeped into the back of my awareness. For some reason I couldn't actually pronounce it myself, either; instead it had sneakily bypassed the usual paths of speech and memory to plop down, latent, on the tip of my tongue.

How long the experience lasted or exactly when it ended I had no idea, but the next thing I knew I was staring down a length of rock and earth. *Up* a length, really, since I was lying on my back and the cliff was still stretching up over my head, although now into the retreating fog under the brighter glow of dawn. I got to my feet and set about putting myself together.

In reconnoitering the base of the cliff, I came across the one artifact I'd been most hoping for right at the moment—a trail. Shaa's map had indicated villages scattered here and there along this stretch of coast, and a small fishing port slightly to the south, so it wasn't like we were talking about unexplored wilderness; a prepared path up the cliff hadn't seemed unreasonable. The path had its share of switchbacks and crumbly spots, but the patches of wildflowers clinging to cracks in the rock and spills of earth made the short hike surprisingly scenic. The fog had retreated enough so that the top of the cliff began to condense into view when I was barely halfway up. Emerging over the lip at the end of the climb brought me out of the fog entirely and onto a meadow of wild grasses waving gently in the morning light. Behind me, the cliff submerged into the fog as though it was the edge of the coastline and the sea was the gray of clouds, and the beach I'd crossed was off in another world beneath the waters.

I adjusted the pack and pushed off toward the road. It was farther back from the cliff than I'd expected, but I still came upon it soon enough. The road was wide enough for a lane and a half of traffic, but it was paved with stone; this deep in the heartland of the Empire you wouldn't expect anything less. Still, it wasn't being maintained as well as it might be, especially with the Knitting coming up and all. The status of maintenance was driven home even further when I topped the ridge of a low hill and saw a canted-over barouche at the trough at the foot of the hill ahead of me. Two men were standing next to the carriage looking down at the right-front wheel.

As I drew up to them, it was plain to see what had happened. One of the paving stones had shifted and the wheel had wedged itself into the resulting gap. Fortunately for them the wheel hadn't splintered and the axle was intact, but the carriage was plainly stuck tight. Both men were covered with road dust and breathing hard. Scattered around them on the road were several boxes, a large luncheon hamper, and a trunk.

The man in livery, his hands on his hips, called to me, "Give us a hand here, then, will you?" The driver wasn't the one of interest to me, though. The other man, his black and silver traveling clothes now distinctly the worse for wear, had fixed me with his full attention and, I thought, a fleeting touch of surprise. "Well met," he said, "and timely. You're the first person along in the last hour."

"And a pleasant morning it is, too," I said, indicating the roadside wildflowers glistening in the sun. "Wouldn't you say?"

"It now shows signs of improvement," agreed the man. "You're a stout fellow; the three of us should have no trouble accomplishing what the two of us could not."

Even if they'd been straining at the carriage and unloading its contents for the last hour, which looked perfectly plausible given their appearance, the guy still had a sword slung on his hip. He hadn't reached for it to put it on as I'd approached, either; he'd been working with his sword easily at hand. It wasn't only that sign that made me recognize him as a pro. I'd seen that aura of latent menace before, along with its subliminal aroma of congealed gore. He'd be a nasty one to cross. I didn't want to cross him; I didn't even want to get within his range. I've sized up enough swordsmen to know which ones are deadly and which ones only think they are.

But that wasn't the real reason I was reluctant to approach. He—

"You've recently been to sea," he stated.

"Actually, I spent the night down on the beach. Unfortunately I picked a part of the beach that was a little closer to the tide." I wasn't about to volunteer to anyone that I'd gotten drenched while landing a boat, especially not him. I didn't trust the situation; it was a classic setup for all kinds of things. Of course, it could have also been an honest case of a random busted wheel, but there was more to my feeling than just the setup. It wasn't merely the situation, and it wasn't just the look of him with his sword. Was it just my paranoia acting up again? Was I just going to automatically distrust anyone I happened to meet? No, because—"I beg your pardon?"

"Together we will extract this wheel and then you will ride with me; I insist."

"If it's just the same to you, I'd just as soon walk. It's a nice day for a stroll."

"No, no, I won't hear of it," said the man. His hand seemed to drift, of its own accord, toward the pommel of his sword. "I *insist*. What is your name, so I may know in whose debt I find myself?"

"Okay," I said slowly, momentarily taken aback because no one ever insisted on knowing my name, "if that's the way it's going to be, that's the way it's going to be. My name's Spilkas, and before you start in after my life's history I'd just as soon tell you I'm a fellow of no particular account." I'd resolved not to be caught short reaching for a moniker like the Creeping Sword again. I figured I was due a few free throwaway names to toss out at random, anyway, but I didn't mind borrowing some from people I'd known. Spilkas was a jittery cutpurse back in Roosing Oolvaya. He was so fidgety, in fact, that he couldn't do a job unless he was halfway soused. Spilkas existed along a fine line—too drunk and his coordination would go and he'd start to fall down, not pickled enough and he'd twitch himself straight into jail. I wasn't one for getting sloshed myself, but the connection with his fine-line lifestyle still made the name a sure fit for me. "Who might you be?"

"I am Joatal Ballista," he told me.

But he wasn't. He was lying. I'd have known he was lying even if it hadn't been for the dream, but the dream put the capper on it. The dream where I'd seen his face; had it scoured into my memory as though it was etched on the business end of a branding iron. And the name that went with it, the one that had perched itself on the tip of my tongue, was . . . was . . . Redley? Fredley? No, Fradgee. No, not that. Fradi. Fradjikan, that was it.

4

His business down the coast had gone tolerably well. There was always far too much to be done given the time and resources available. Still, things were coming together. With his new insights into the motivations of his patron he was coming to be more prepared for the aftermath, and with his recent recruitments and alliances the short term was looking bright as well. The outcome had always been fairly much ordained, of course; he had been commissioned to deal with Max, and there was no doubt Max would indeed be dealt with quite comprehensively. It was how one managed the loose ends and overall aesthetics, though, that set the brute practitioner apart from the select virtuoso at the top of the form, or at least that was the ideal Fradjikan always preferred to pursue. Rather than the sudden descent of calamity from the skies, Fradi was partial to the gradually tightening web of encroaching doom, the progressive dropping away of escape routes and camouflage both, until the noose was finally drawn tight in an orgastic passage of revelation and inescapable ruin. It made one feel glad to be alive.

Nevertheless, being master of the web didn't mean that one foresaw or planned out every last detail. Planning was only part of the game, anyway. If you were a commander of troops, perhaps the greatest satisfaction might come from watching your plan reel itself out with every particular precise, the forces of each side marching as automata through their prescribed evolutions; an ideal rarely achieved, to be sure. Those who plotted plots, on the other hand, whether as their livelihood or just from innate disposition, were either flexible or found themselves cracked across the fault line of their greatest rigidity. That was the source of the real challenge—proceeding toward a fixed endpoint through an ever-changing flurry of random events and the workings of fate. The real challenge and, to be honest, the real fun. But what was the harm in that? The most effective practitioner was the one at one with his job.

In Fradi's experience, though, fate rarely got its workings into gear this early in the morning. Yet here was this Spilkas fellow, producing himself right into Fradi's lap, as it were, of all things. Spilkas was now sweating as much as Lowell, the driver, or Fradjikan himself, but as Fradi had predicted the sweat had been both timely and effective. Lowell and Spilkas finished manhandling the last unloaded piece of baggage, the big trunk, back into the cab and stood back for a moment to pant. "Have you breakfasted?" Fradi asked Spilkas. "The inn provided a jug of freshly squeezed orange juice."

"Orange juice, you say?" said the man, retrieving his pack from the side of the road. "A swig of that wouldn't be a bad idea."

"After you," said Fradi. He opened the door to the coach. "Don't hesitate now, come come. I won't hear of it."

"Did you make a promise to some god you'd meet a good-deed quota?" Spilkas said, "or is this just some compulsion to hobnob with the lower class?"

Spilkas had been deliberately trying to be irritating, and was succeeding rather well for that matter. "I also have some cheese and a modest assortment of fruit," Fradi told him. "Look as it as payment for services if you like."

Spilkas grunted but at least gave off arguing, and let Fradi follow him into the carriage. Lowell mounted to the box and got them underway. Fradi doled out the refreshments and considered the situation.

Spilkas; a dispensable name, to be sure. Surely the name was as false as the one Fradi had used himself. (Which one *had* he used?—oh, Ballista, of course.) Names were quick camouflage on the cheap but nonetheless effective for all of that. At least the fellow wasn't using one of those horrid tacked-on appellations, wasn't calling himself Someone the Something, for instance. During a stint as facilitator to some court or another early in his career, a higher-level factotum (the principal chamberlain, in fact), had taken to referring to Fradi himself as Fradjikan the Assassin, as opposed to Fradjikan, the assassin, which was how he had been hired. Well, Fradjikan had squared accounts with him, and ultimately with the entire court. Not out of spite, or anyway not spite against the court; it had been a pure question of business. His real employer in that case had been the court's subsequent inhabitant.

In such ways are reputations built. Yet what was the background of this Spilkas, now at work with determination at demolishing a hearty wheel of Brie? Until he had appeared boarding the ship following the denouement in Oolsmouth, Fradjikan had not detected his presence. Perhaps he'd merely taken passage with the others; it was too soon to tell. If Spilkas didn't look any more impressive at close-up than he'd seemed from afar, he did have some potential in his own right. In particular, he was proving very adept at giving no information of any substance. On the other hand, he affected a cane even though he had no obvious impairment, and vanity was something that could be played upon.

"You must be on a lengthy excursion to need such a stout walking stick," Fradi tried.

"Not much to look at, is it? If it wasn't an heirloom, I'd chuck it in a marsh."

Well, so much for vanity. "What *does* bring you out on the road, then, and camping out on beaches?"

"Maybe you've heard there's going to be a Knitting

down the road here a piece? You got any more of those wheat crackers in there?''

Fradi passed over the hamper. It was likely this fellow would be nothing but a waste of time; most people were. Considered as a limbering-up exercise, however, even going through the motions wouldn't be entirely a waste, and anyway all he'd be doing otherwise would be sitting with his own thoughts looking out the window of the carriage. On the other hand, perhaps Spilkas really represented something key, but something that needed a bit of digging to exhume. Fradi wouldn't discard him until the possibilities had been exhausted; Fradi was not one to frown back when luck smiled. ''Had you been long at sea?''

''What sea?'' said Spilkas, his mouth full of cracker. ''I said I was on the beach, not on the water, didn't I?''

''Perhaps you did.'' There was no way Spilkas could know he'd been observed getting on the boat, and as a result no way for him to know that Fradi recognized his position as a lie. Not that Spilkas had actually come right out and stated that he hadn't been on a boat. The difference between misdirection and outright mendacity was primarily a semantic one, or at most question of tactics. That wasn't the issue. If Spilkas was at pains to make a casual acquaintance think he hadn't been at sea, there was obviously something there he deliberately wanted to conceal. His association with the others seemed most likely. Was the plan for Spilkas to act as their deep-cover agent in Peridol, clear of surveillance and free to carry out any secret schemes?

Could there be even more here? Could they be trying to set *him* up? Fradjikan, himself?

Fradi decided that that brief consideration was about all that possibility deserved. Yes, it was a possibility, but no, the chance was too low for reasonability. How could they plan against him; they didn't even know he was there. Surely he had not tipped his hand to reveal, even by implication, his presence on the scene. The sun could flare and the oceans could boil, but the cost/benefit ratio in planning for the eventuality was similarly too stacked to make it worth worrying about. There was only so much looking over one's shoulder one could engage in before one's neck became irretrievably frozen in a retrospective attitude.

Nevertheless, it was useful to remind oneself occasionally that one was not a sorcerer. One might employ them, and one might know how to bend them to his purposes, and one might even have a professional but limited respect for them as lower-order tradesmen and functionaries, but one still had to admit they did have their own annoying tricks and their own peculiar delusions of grandeur. Indeed, delusions notwithstanding, there was no reason to get one's own hands dirty grubbing around in the mystic arts. Why stoop so low when there were magic practitioners for hire begging on the streets, almost, when one's own patron was a god of not inconsiderable power, even among gods, and when one's allies included such as even a high contender for the throne of Gadzura? And when one was who one was oneself?

Why, indeed?

"Why do you keep harping on this sea stuff?" Spilkas said suddenly. "You looking to recruit a sailor?"

"I, ah, I was just on my way back up the coast," Fradi began, his thoughts racing barely ahead of his words, "after a quick trip down to the cape to seek news of a ship overdue for its arrival in Peridol."

"What ship's that?"

"The *Flying Pelican,* out of Oolsmouth."

"Who thinks up these names?" muttered Spilkas. "Any boat with a name redundant as that deserves whatever it gets, if you don't mind my saying so."

"I suppose you're right." Actually, Fradjikan had just made up the name himself out of whole cloth; not one of his finest moments, it was true, especially given his earlier thoughts on the adequacy of acceptable names or the lack thereof. "I don't suppose you saw anything sailing past, while you were camped out there on your beach?"

"No pelicans, that's for sure."

"Perhaps some sailor colleagues of yours?"

"I know coincidence is golden and all that, but don't tell me you were expecting to get the news you're looking for from a guy you picked up at random on the road. Come on, Ballista. Here's one for you that's a lot more reasonable—you know any decent places to stay in Peridol that still have room?"

"No, I'm afraid I don't," said Fradi. He had a few bottles of assorted spirits packed away in the bottom of the hamper, including a fresh one of aged rum; was it time to crack one of them? Maybe if he could get Spilkas drunk, it would make him more helpful, either by making him talk more or making him talk less. If worst came to worst, Fradi could drink enough himself so he wouldn't care. No, that would be unprofessional. It was still too early in the morning, anyway. "I do know that lodging is scarce; you may find yourself back on the road home as soon as you've arrived." Fradjikan leveled a finger at Spilkas. "You should also know my personal staff complement is full, so don't think about taking service with me to stay off the streets. Unless you have some particular talent I should know about?"

"I don't know. What kinds of talent would you *like* to know about?"

"Anything you're proud of. Or we could converse for a while and see if something comes to light."

A sardonic smile crossed quickly along Spilkas' face and was just as quickly gone. "Go ahead and try. Talk's cheap. It's still a waste of time."

Hmm, thought Fradi. *Was there something there?* "I'm certain you undervalue yourself. Everyone has *some* skill. No one is entirely a blank, a complete unknown."

The sardonic grin flickered back. "Oh, yeah?"

"Any person with—" Fradi stopped himself, or more precisely the words faded away on their path from his brain to his mouth as his mind lost interest in them. Something much more interesting than words had just occurred to him. The more unknown Spilkas was the better. Fradi could soon change that anyway. In fact, he could—

The plan seemed to spring together out of its disjointed parts like an exploding clock viewed in reverse, cogs and gears and springs spinning out of the air in a jumbled cloud of glinting streaks, forming into a greater order as the cloud condensed, and then fitting themselves together one against the other in a chorus of clicks and snaps. It was all Fradi could do to keep from rubbing his hands together in a paroxysm of satisfaction and beaming a triumphant smile at the man opposite him munching crackers, his guest, his patsy, the gear around whose hub his plan would turn. Oh, Fradi was in the groove now. And Max—

Just *wait* until he got to Max. He'd make him a— well, just *wait*.

5

The thing had defeated all her efforts. Admittedly, Leen hadn't directed the full force of the Empire against the ancient door and the window with the tantalizing lights; in fact, the only talents to be ranged against it thus far had been her own. Her skills were not meager but neither were they first-rank, or she might very well have been occupying a position other than Archivist. Things being what they were, with the impending Knitting and its inevitable accompanying realignments of the various coalitions and interest groups, palace cabals and pecking orders, she'd thought it best not to become an open-field loose ball in someone's power game by attracting attention to a forgotten mystery. To be honest with herself, Leen had to admit that the thought of a horde of specialists descending on her library had been a strong argument in favor of keeping knowledge of the whole affair secret; restricted, in fact, to herself.

As far as the records showed, the Archives themselves had never fallen under direct military administration or the control of any organization of secret police. Leen had no intention of becoming the Archivist who'd let that happen, either. She took her oaths seriously, and the heritage she'd been handed down. One of the main tenets of that heritage was that Archivists were independent, owing their primary allegiance not to the Emperor (except as required for the needs of protocol and good sense) but to the Archives they served and to the ideals of the past they recalled, whatever those really were. In practice, that meant that Archivists did their best to do what they damn well pleased which, considering that they hung around in basements all day reading old books and pushing dust from this surface to that, didn't generally amount to much one way or another. To be *brutally* frank, the Archives were a largely forgotten backwater, overlooked in the midst of the Empire's sprawling management structure. When all was said and done, though, that was just fine. There are worse places to be than the basement, and many worse things to do than read, especially when you're interrupted only for the odd bit of puttering.

The problem was, the strange room seemed impervious not only to direct force, both physical and sorcerous, but to analysis as well. Its seals and shields were so strong it might as well have been off in another dimension entirely, rather than underneath Leen's own cellar, for all the good her probing had done. The thing just downright ignored her; it was as aloof to Leen's efforts as she generally tried to be the world at large. Actually, Leen admitted, the thing was better at its act than she was at hers. She could learn that much from it, at least. An outside observer with a contrary streak and a captious perspective might pose the thesis that you'd gone a long stroll indeed down the road to dottiness when you sunk to the level of using ancient artifacts as role models. Fortunately this hypothetical observer wasn't around, though, and in any case Leen wouldn't have listened to her if she had been. The commentary of her own hyperactive superego was more difficult to evade, but all that really meant was that she wasn't working as hard at ignoring it as she needed to. A talkative superego was probably another warning sign of encroaching dotage anyway. Senility was not something that ran in Leen's family, but it never hurt to be watchful.

She sat back on the bottom rung of the circular staircase in the hidden room and stared ahead at the polished metal wall. From a purely aesthetic standpoint the place did look nicer with the grime of ages gone, the metal gleaming in the lamplight, the crystal in the adjacent wall sparkling, the air no longer prone to send her into sneezing fits at the slightest swirl of a dust-raising motion. Still, all this cleaniness was clearly a sign of defeat. To have gone unsuccessfully through the interesting options only to arrive at housework was not encouraging, either from the standpoint of solving the mystery or from that of the inherent statement of housework itself. Not encouraging, but there it was.

The thing didn't seem to be anti-magical, per se, it just seemed to stick its nose in the air and disregard it. Leen couldn't *detect* any active shielding, but the fact remained that as far as any probe she'd been able to look up was concerned the space behind the wall was no different than any nondescript hunk of solid rock. Actually, the rock would have been more interesting; a probe into rock would at least give you some mineralogical or metallurgical data back. Transverse defects, grain size, and veins of tin weren't Leen's particular gratification point, but data return—even if the data themselves were boring—was good enough for calibration, and for reassuring you that you were doing more than just pouring energy down a hole. Except in this case she couldn't even detect that there *was* a hole. Action-at-a-distance work had proved similarly useless, and as far as her efforts with a pry-bar, well, she might as well have stayed in bed. It was time to hit the stacks again.

Leen trudged up the stairs and out through the secret door in the bookcase. Even if the sole source of illumination hadn't been her lantern and she could have seen all the way to the ends of the Archives in every direction, Leen was convinced that some of the rows of cabinets and bookshelves would have stretched out to a vanishing point like the margins of a road on an endless plain. That is, if the rows of shelves had actually been straight, and the aisles hadn't been heaped with their own mounds and crates of stuff. One Archivist had done little in her seventeen-year tenure but try to map the floor plan. The Goldhound brothers had done a bit better in their survey, but unfortunately they'd been more interested in artifacts than textual material; artworks and treasures and whatnot.

Of course, the Goldhounds had had the question of their personal survival to take into account. They'd had the unhappy fate of serving during the reign of Abyssinia the Moot, in the earliest days of the Empire. The reign of the Moot had almost ended the days of empire once and for all, too, what with his goal of never appearing in court or public without wearing an assortment of treasure that weighed more than he did, and never the same pieces twice. From the histories and the portraits, he hadn't exactly had an asthenic body build, either. Still, Leen did have the Goldhound directory and Carla's map, and the half-dozen other catalogs and indexes that had come down to the present time. Perhaps one of them would have something useful to contribute.

Then, too, there were the even-more-secret annex volumes to the main indexes. Those could be the real source of paydirt. If the thing genuinely dated to the Dislocation, it made sense to go where the Dislocation was. Even if time travel was nothing but a theoretical proposition, that didn't mean the days of the Dislocation were necessarily out of reach, though in a more vicarious sense.

One of the genuine treasures of the Archives was the truly remarkable amount of pre- and trans-Dislocation material scattered around. Among the many secrets the Archivists kept, the scope of the Dislocation collection was both one of the most closely held and one of the most dangerous. When an Archivist was assuming the mantle from his or her (or its, there having been a few nonhumans in the office over the years) predecessor, the time of greatest anxiety, of nervous glances over the shoulder and words in a hushed voice, was when the Dislocation stuff was discussed. Nothing would transform the Archives from a backwater to a strategic asset faster than an Emperor finding out just what-all was warehoused beneath his feet. Telling the truth—that most of the Dislocation material was worthless for military or political purposes—would have been the most futile kind of damage control, the kind no one believes.

The ancients had certainly wielded great forces and powerful technologies and had clearly been masters of devastating might, but there was little doubt that the mythical stature to which their accomplishments had been elevated over the years was drastically exaggerated. They'd been helpless against the rise of magic and the coming of the gods, hadn't they? But reason would not be something to count on in a politician let loose in a candy store of presumed militaristic delights. So it was a tenet of the Archivists' office not to let the problem arise.

But that wasn't even the real problem. The gods were a jealous lot, and an insecure one to boot. They might natter on about the natural state of man being inconsistent with ever-more-sophisticated works of the hands, but the real reason large-scale or particularly useful technology was proscribed was that they were afraid of it. This was not merely Leen's own theory. The Dislocation texts weren't the only forbidden materials squirreled away in the Archives, and for that matter weren't the most hazardous either. That dubious honor had to be reserved for the small collection of fragmentary holograph material attributable to some of the gods themselves. In one of the most intriguing manuscripts, a certain god, Byron, had written quite directly about the very issue of technology and the gods' interest in it.

Unearthing the Byron letter during one of her girlish rummaging expeditions had been the turning point that had irrevocably set Leen on the path to Archivist-dom. While her grandfather had tended to what he liked to grandly refer to as Business, Leen had begun her first serious research project. Over the years, a stereotype had developed of the Archivist as not exactly human, but rather some hybrid of ferret and mole, living a solitary life in dark basements, with eyes grown large and weak through excessive use under conditions of insufficient lighting. If this characterization was true, and Leen was willing to admit that was more than likely, her own transformation had begun at that time. But what else could she do? The Bryon letter was *interesting*.

The letter wasn't interesting only for its contents, either. Intrigued by Byron's openly subversive remarks, Leen had set out to learn more about him. She'd gone first to the standard suppressed sources, Pink's *Compendium* and the *Divine Roster,* and *Men Into Myth* to boot, but drawn a total blank. Even *Acts and Actors,* for all its demonstrated errors still the most readable general history, and with significant chunks of narrative that the others skipped as unsubstantiated hearsay, didn't have a smidgen.

The only conclusion Leen could reach was that Byron had been purged, his very name blotted out from among the lists of the gods. Nothing like the Spell of Namelessness for him; Byron had been eradicated as though he had never existed, and the memory of the eradication had been eradicated as well.

If that wasn't enough to intimidate, Leen still thought now, thinking back on it, she didn't know what was. It gave a pretty good intimation of how the gods would react if they discovered the extent of the Archives' special holdings. The Empire and its ruling families might hold special stature with the gods, but that was because they played a designated role in the gods' world order and understood their limits. Even *they* couldn't sidle over the edge without being slapped down as an object lesson. Itting III and his deal with the monks of Leebo was a perfect case in point. Over a singularly uncomfortable half hour one afternoon, Itting had rotted from within in his robes of state, while the monastery where the monks had been tinkering under his patronage with an arc lamp was now a scenic pond in the north of Gadzura, a stream having filled in the glassy crater.

So for the Archives there were only two courses of action. The one that was thinkable—secrecy—was handed down as a central tenet of office. Leen supposed that every Archivist spent an odd moment here or there contemplating the unthinkable option, that of actually destroying archival material, and with no comprehensive record of the Archives' full holdings it was possible that some Archivist in the past might have indeed followed that course. One of the prime candidates for destruction, if such had really occurred, would have been any documentation concerning the enigma in the hidden basement. Leen looked out at the stacks and sighed. It might be a hopeless task, and it was unquestionably a dangerous one, but when it came right down to it that what was she here for, after all. Not just to dust spines and sweep up the floor, that was for certain.

Well, Leen had learned a lot since her first days under her grandfather's guiding but not necessarily watchful eye. One of them was the true nature of the Archivist's Business. While a pleasantly large part of it was exactly the rummaging and reading she had fallen in love with in the first place, there remained other duties as well. One of the inflexible laws of Other Duties seemed to be that they always most needed doing just when you'd rather be doing something else. Well, there was no help for it; Tuesdays were Tuesdays. She secured the secret door behind her and set off across the floor.

Leen paused at her desk. The three herb volumes and the illuminated bestiary were already loaded on the two-shelf trolley, along with several books by an obscure novelist of the previous century which she'd rescued from the family of mice who'd been in the process of abridging them. Was there anything else Vellum had requested? Where was his last note? Oh, there, in the clutter atop her to-do box, just where she'd put it. Right, he was still after the missing volume of Hali Shee's conflict precipitation treatise; it had thus far proved elusive, but she'd have to assure him she was still on its trail. She had come up with the old hound-care omnibus, though.

That was everything—darn it, no, not quite. Leen sat down at the desk, opened the right-hand drawer, and retrieved a cigar-box-sized chest from behind a sheaf of uncollated notes. She propped it on the the desk blotter, flipped back the lid, and made a face. Beneath an untidy cap of black hair streaked with premature strokes of gray a face frowned back at her, itself also streaked with the totally characteristic gray of dust. Leen wrinkled her nose at her image in the mirror and set to work with a cloth at making herself presentable.

Leen's sister had finally prevailed on her to at least keep the mirror and a comb at her desk. "You're not the only one in this family, you know," her sister had told her menacingly. Leen had tried for the umpteenth time to explain to her sister the difference between hygiene (unquestionably important and socially relevant) and appearance for the sake of vanity (transitory and a sink of precious time). Her sister had been intransigent. "*You* may not care, but just think what it does to the *rest* of us," had been Susannah's ultimatum. It wasn't until their brother had weighed in supporting Susannah's position (at least Leen thought that's what he'd been doing, when he quoted an allusive couplet whose source was as obscure as most of the things he came up with) that Leen had capitulated. It hadn't been a total surrender—Leen still refused to waste time dyeing her hair, and her makeup was no more than a few strategic token splashes—but it had gotten Susannah off her back and away from her throat. On that issue and for the time being, anyway.

There was only one way to handle chores—if you were going to do them, you might as well do them right. In this case that meant not only good but fast. A couple of minutes, which was all her appearance deserved in any case, and she was ready to move out.

Pushing the book cart ahead of her, Leen headed for the door.

Leen was aware of two entrances to the Archives proper. A place with the size and convoluted geometry of the Archives would always give rise to notions of disguised tunnels in the stygian depths, sealed passages, concealed doors, and whatnot. Indeed, certain Archivists had been fiends on the subject, fishing out rumors and indulging their speculations for pages on end in their logs. Leen remained skeptical. To her knowledge no additional exits or secret passages had ever come to light; none but the one Robin had found, anyhow. That was just as well. The Back and Front Doors might have been there for centuries, but that didn't make them prosaic. They were a handful-and-a-half all by themselves, which had always been plenty for her.

The Front Door actually *had* a door, in contrast to the Back Door which was more of a trick of light and shadow behind its alcove. The Back Door also had its terminal pit and the Inclined Labyrinth, of course, making the Back Door a more scenic traverse overall, if a somewhat longer one. Leen could navigate them both in the dark, and had, and had half a thought she could make the excursion in her sleep, not that that was an eventuality that seemed likely to arise. One thing she did not do, though, was let herself get over-confident and hurry through. Certain things just took as long as they took; either you finished them or they finished you.

That didn't mean one didn't get impatient, Leen thought, waiting for the Front Door to recognize her and creak open. One just had to deal with— The large creak-and-rumble began and the heavy arch-topped door pivoted slowly away from her. It was hinging on the right and outside today, Leen noted, which might mean it was entering a new phase of its cycle. The next few days would likely tell. She pushed the cart through the door into the safety zone in the vestibule and saw the cart tucked away in its dumbwaiter niche, took a few deep breaths from her diaphragm, and set her feet on the first keypoints of the recessional path.

Time always came to resemble taffy on your way in and out, Leen had been taught. This go-around, for some reason, the null zones zipped past without note while the Watermark, of all junctures, was turbulent, its airspace dragging at her with the approximate consistency of flypaper. Have to check my hair again, she found herself thinking irrelevantly, as she gyrated her way through and into the Great Room with its self-importance field.

Finally Leen debarked through the door at the other end, at the top of the flight of invisible steps. Archivist Creeley had known what he was doing when he'd set up the wards guarding the Archives, and the whole tradition of Archivism as well, but he'd clearly possessed a sadistic streak. Leen staggered past the door jamb and collapsed into the chair just beyond. After a moment, when her heartbeat had slowed, she took up the pitcher of tea from the end table next to the chair and drained half of it in one long gurgle; rehydration was important. But so was exercise, and Leen could tell she was getting out of shape.

She'd have to reorganize her schedule to allow more time for a workout. Leen wasn't ready to turn things over to a new Archivist, by any means, and anyway who was there who'd be up for it? Robin was barely more than an infant, although already a promising one, and even though Vellum wasn't an infant he might have already gone as far as he could.

On cue, the man appeared. As librarian in charge of the Reading Room, traditionally the senior member of the Archivist's small staff, Vellum had been a political appointee, but had proved nonetheless qualified even given the patronage involved. Still, the talents required to navigate the Doorways were more than just a sense for books. "Good day, Archivist," Vellum said. "Another early morning, I take it?"

"Uh-huh. The books I could find are there if you want to haul them up."

"Oh, good," said Vellum. "The Potamian herbal?" He grasped the large windlass crank mounted in the wall and began to haul it around.

"Yes," Leen said, "I found the herbals. The bestiary, too."

"Lord What's-his-name will be pleased about that."

Lord What's-his-name? Who had she seen around lately? "Lord Farnsbrother?" asked Leen.

"Lord—? Yes, the very one."

"Farnsbrother doesn't read," Leen muttered. "What's he doing, starting a zoo?"

Vellum was of middling height, a bit stoop-shouldered, his most notable features the matching set of bifocal spectacles and watery eyes; a recruiting-poster image of a bibliothecary, in fact. Like the typical librarian, he also had a dangerous tendency toward aloofness and a disregard of the occasional political implications of the job. He certainly had a spirit for books, though, and had thrown himself into the work—he'd adopted his new name when he'd taken the position.

Vellum gave a final heave on the crank and the cart of books rose into view in the dumbwaiter slot, none the worse for wear. The books, being in the traditional sense lifeless, were able to transit the maze without destruction. And a good thing, too—you'd never get a handcart up those stairs. Leen followed Vellum and the cart into the back stacks of the Reading Room.

Leen sometimes thought of the Reading Room as a decoy for scholars, to keep them away from the real stuff squirreled away in the Archives proper. In truth that was actually an understatement; the Reading Room was impressive in its own right, even by comparison with the Archives. In fact, to the extent the public mind knew that something called the Archives existed, it thought Reading Room and Archives were one and the same. Anyone surveying the Reading Room's holdings, its warren of shelves and reading nooks, of drafty ceilings and precarious overhangs, would naturally wonder how there could be that many books and papers in the whole world; anyone who didn't know better, at any rate. They turned a corner and now Leen could see the large central chamber ahead. To their right at the intersection was a section walled off with iron bars and a locked gate, the tomes inside it lashed to their shelves with stout chains. Leen patted her key ring out of reflex and saw Vellum do the same. State secrets or arcana of the gods weren't the only perilous materials in the stacks. The Thaumaturgical area was off-limits to all but qualified readers, at least as much for the protection of the browser as out of a need to control dissemination of that particular information.

The cool hush of the great room beckoned as they drew closer, and then the hall itself was opening around them—the clerestory windows around the base of the dome, the allegorical frescoes marching up the curves of the dome itself, the mahogany balconies, the long reading tables and stand-up lecterns, the statuary, the portraits of emperors and Archivists both, the marble floors; all in all, quite an edifice. And it was Tuesday, so the Archivist was In.

The be-monocled Lord Farnsbrother was already waiting at her desk, his jowls waggling with impatience. The ends of a marten stole dangled by his waist, crossing on their way down from his neck an assortment of chest jewels and a brocade robe. Farnsbrother's family tree had its roots back before the Bones. For the last few generations they'd done little but live off their foreign rents and an imperial grant at one of the smallest Living Mines; the last time Leen had reviewed the peerage Farnsbrother had been the sole hope of continuing the family line. From the look of him, a judicious wager on behalf of extinction might not be inappropriate. "I say," Lord Farnsbrother addressed Vellum, "do you have it? The Beast-Book?"

"As you requested, Lord, it has been found." Vellum passed it over.

Farnsbrother eagerly flipped pages. Leen winced; several of the signatures had already seemed loose, and the spine itself might not stand up to extreme handling. As he neared the back of the book, though, Farnsbrother's face darkened. He spoke in an ominous tone. "This—this *book* has only *land* animals, and a few birds and things." Farnsbrother struck the current page with the back of his hand. The page he struck was one of text illuminated in black and red pen with gold leaf accents; the facing page illustration showed a nicely executed griffin rampant, clutching, of all things, a salmon in its upraised claw.

"Why, yes," said Leen. "They are what Fernandez was known for."

"But—" Lord Farnsbrother sputtered, "but—there's no *sea* creatures. There's barely enough time as it is! I absolutely must get the shipyard to work today, or my barge just will *not* be ready. Do you understand? It will—not—be—*ready!*"

"Your barge? Not ready?"

"Not in *time,*" said Farnsbrother crossly. "And I'm *certain* this Squid-thing won't wait."

Squid-thing? Oh! Of course, *that* Squid-thing. "You plan to decorate your barge for the occasion, Lord—"

"Not just *decorate*, woman! It's the whole *superstructure;* it has to be *rebuilt*. It must be the right theme! These birds and cattle just will not do, they will not do at *all.*"

Leen raised a hand. "Lord Farnsbrother, you have still come to the right place. Now that I understand your needs, we can show you just the reference you're looking for."

Farnsbrother paused in his gesticulations. "Oh, can you really? That's dashed timely, I don't mind telling you. If I—"

"Say no more," Leen told him. "I will not keep you a moment longer from your destiny. Vellum, please show Lord Farnsbrother to the oceanography section, and stay to assist him in his research, will you?"

"This way, my Lord," said Vellum, leading the suddenly uplifted peer toward the stacks. Leen collapsed into her chair. Tuesdays, bah! Business!

And the "Squid-thing." Unfortunately that was only the barest part of it, although it was indisputably a highlight. Fortunately, these were days of stability and the emperors had lately been a hardy lot; Leen didn't think civilization could stand a Knitting more than once a decade at the outside. Already Peridol was getting to be so crowded with out-of-towners you could barely cross a street at three in the morning, and the revelry hadn't even officially started yet. It would be difficult to fit a decent day's work in edgewise. With such a round of parties and festivities coming up she couldn't possibly arrange to miss *all* of them, could she?

Her well-known absentmindedness would no doubt be good for a few, even if there were far too many far-too-loyal retainers around to keep reminding her of where she needed to be and when, but even she couldn't use that excuse for everything. Being unpleasant wouldn't help much either; in Leen's circles most everyone was unpleasant, but that never stopped them from being invited or expected to attend. *Damn*, Leen thought. It wouldn't be just makeup, either. *I suppose I'll have to break down and have my hair cut.*

Susannah, Robin's mother, would unquestionably be in the thick of it, and their own mother, too, for that matter. Her sister was a bit of a dope, but you certainly couldn't say that of Mother. Or Lemon for that matter. Leen might have inherited her grandfather's archival talents down the line through her father (who, for all one could tell, had missed out on brains entirely himself), but her brother Lemon had gotten the legacy of her mother's side of the family in full force. Lemon would be having a fine time for himself over the next few weeks as well, if not for quite the same reasons as Susannah and Mother. There would be the usual flirting and dalliance, eating to excess and dancing, too, if not quite enough of the latter to compensate for the former, but above all for Lemon there would be Business. Not the same Business as Leen's, of course. He'd be out for himself and his own machinations, that went without saying; Lemon's entanglements were almost impossibly complex. She'd have to ask him again what he was up to. Not that he'd tell her, or at least not that he'd tell her in a straightforward enough fashion that a mere person could understand, but—

"Excuse me, my dear."

Leen looked smoothly up from the ledger where she'd ostensibly been reviewing Vellum's account of the recent repairs to the dome. If you were going to go through life gathering wool, she had decided many years ago, it was only prudent to develop a few devices to keep the habit under wraps. After years of practice, she could now dream off standing up, that was an easy one, and she could go into fugue seated at a desk without her shoulders slipping or her head nodding, so that a casual observer, especially from the back, would presume she was merely engrossed in study. The bigger trick was to return smoothly to full awareness and orientation without a gap in conversation, and without the audience becoming aware you'd ever been away.

"My apologies for disturbing you," the man went on. "You appeared lost in thought, but the sign here on your desk does indicate your official presence."

Well, sometimes it worked and sometimes it didn't. The face looking down on her was tanned, bearing a dark mustache in bold contrast to the flashing white teeth set in an insouciant grin; above were blue eyes and a shock of dark hair. The body, all swelling shoulders, muscular chest, and trim waist, was encased in a discreetly flashy outfit of scarlet and jet, except for the peak of the left shoulder blade curving around to the back, which shone with a swath of silver. Leen could see the shoulder blade since the man was leaning over her with his left elbow on the desk just in front of her ledger, bringing his head within whispering distance of her ear, but even if his rippling back had been hidden from view she would have known the silver of office was there. "Good day, my Lord Scapula," Leen said. "Is there a particular title I might assist you with?"

"A title?" said the Scapula. "Ah yes, a title. Well, then, let us say my title of interest today is Arleen."

Is this research or just casual browsing? Leen thought. She didn't say it, though; she didn't want to get started with him. "Shall I show you to the card catalog, or will directions be sufficient?"

The Scapula made his eyes smolder. The man did have exceptional animal magnetism, not that that was any concern of hers, of course. "Your personal accompaniment is exactly what I was planning on," he told her. "Although the idea of instruction does have interesting potentialities. Please, then, instruct me in your will. Or no, on second thought, please don't." He flashed his teeth at her. "I feel I know your true will much better than you do yourself."

"Tell me how much I've left to my nephew Robin, then," Leen said under her breath.

Did his eyes narrow the merest bit? Well, probably, and she didn't care if he'd heard her, either. But she couldn't just tell him to get lost, not the Scapula; he wasn't exactly some run-of-the-streets masher, no matter how he acted. Was he here alone, or had he brought an entourage? Over by the encyclopedias was a small knot of minor Digitals; that was the sort of gang he might have trailing along behind him. They were arguing in low voices over something spread out between them on the top of the half-height bookcase, though, and now that Leen thought about it she half-remembered them straggling in by themselves a quarter hour or so before. Assume the Scapula was alone, then. That meant she could speak more openly, without the fear of precipating some vendetta necessitated by the presence of witnesses.

On the other hand, absence of witnesses meant that he could act more openly, too. He raised a hand as she began to speak again and applied it gently but firmly across her mouth. "The festivities of this season of our joy are almost upon us," the Scapula murmured. "Shortly the new lord of us all will walk in our midst for the first time in his aspect of state, and the great gala will begin. Surely, even with the demands of your responsibilities you will venture forth into the season? At the Inauguration Ball, say, in particular? It would be my honor to have you accompany me. I warn you, you may speak only to indicate assent.'' He raised an eyebrow at her.

She frowned down at the hand still covering her mouth and wondered about biting it. Better not; that would most likely only encourage him. Had she once heard that he liked to be nibbled? Violent eroticism would be fully in keeping with his public persona, and what she had heard of his private one, too.

But why was he after *her,* of all people? Aloof though she tried to be, Leen knew she wasn't beautiful enough to be anyone's ice lady, and no one had come after her for her mind, either, but that was just as well; she had long ago decided she was well-suited for spinsterhood by natural temperament and inclination anyway. True, she was in the line of succession, somewhere, but no one was about to arrange her marriage for the good of the state. And a good thing no one was dumb enough to try, either.

So what was the Scapula up to?

Well, as long as she could breathe, she could ultimately outlast him. He couldn't be very comfortable bent across the desk like that. And then there was the possibility of a diversion—

Leen heard an awkward cough next to her chair. Yes, Vellum, and about time, too. ''Excuse me, my Lord. Archivist, might I help you?''

The look the Scapula turned on Vellum was no little smolder, it was a full-scale roast. But his grip did relax enough for Leen to slip backward out of his grasp; she kicked her chair away from the desk, too, for good measure. ''Thank you, Vellum,'' she said, ''but no. My Lord Scapula and I were just discussing the catalog holdings.''

''As you say, Archivist,'' Vellum muttered with relief, and quickly vanished back into the stacks.

The Scapula's gaze had toned itself back down when

it returned to her. "Let us discuss the arrangements, then, shall we?"

"This is a place of serious business, my Lord Scapula, not a spot for assignation."

"Are the two ever long separated?" asked the Scapula. "Very well, let us say I make *you* my business. Will this simple entreaty suffice to win me the pleasure of your company, or must I pursue you further? You will see, I will not be denied."

Leen paused. They moved in the same social circles, or would, if Leen bothered to circulate socially more than the required minimum. This was not to say they'd ever been anything more than casual acquaintances. Well, that wasn't entirely true; they'd been partnered at one of the Pectoral Duke's out-of-town weekends a year or two back. Leen had avoided him as much as possible, sitting through meals and doing the required dances but otherwise escaping to her research in the old duke's library. As Leen recalled, she hadn't slept with him either. Her ignoring him could have caused a bit of a stir if he hadn't been so clearly pursuing Crewtenfield's young wife; had gotten her, too, if Leon recalled correctly. Oh, Leen knew who he was, all right, but then so did all of Peridol. The Scapula was clearly one to watch. The buzz had him a clear contender; at the rate he was moving, the next Knitting might very well be his.

There was some shady bit of family business in his past, which only made him fit right in with everyone in the upper crust. There was also more than a whiff of menace. People who opposed him had a tendency to shift their views abruptly, or equally abruptly decide to leave town for an extended stay in some out-of-the-way province or another. That, too, was only the way the game was played; the Scapula wouldn't be a serious prospect for emperor if he couldn't take care of his affairs with the efficiency of any appropriate means.

But Leen didn't want to be a player, even at second hand. "You're not after me for myself, Lord Scapula, and you certainly don't want me for my looks. I'm aloof, I have a nasty temperament, and I've got a bad habit of speaking my mind, so you're not here for my charm either. Why are you bothering me?''

"Spirit is a rare commodity," said the Scapula, "the genuine sort of spirit at any rate. As one moves up in the world, one primarily encounters the sycophant in all his servile guises; the flatterer, the toady, the truckler. Not that there isn't some satisfaction from the cringing masses flinging themselves at your feet, you understand, but the gratification is limited. Mastering those who aren't fully alive; what challenge is there in that?''

So you say I'm fully alive, and you've decided to master me? Hah! thought Leen. *A likely story.* "Is it my brother," Leen said, "you want something out of him? Or if it's Susannah you've got in mind, there's no need to bother with me; just walk up to her and ask her. Toss a sterling silver rose at her feet if you want, she'd like that even more."

The Scapula had adjusted his position, seating himself companionably on the edge of her desk. He passed one hand over his opposite sleeve, and when he turned over his palm a flower nestled there, its thorny stem trailing up his arm; a sterling silver rose. He tossed it down in front of her. "You are a far rarer catch than you give yourself credit for. In addition to your strength of personality, intellect, and figure, you are also unmarried and unattached." He raised his eyebrows guilelessly. "Your sister is none of these."

"That's never stopped anybody before," Leen muttered. She stared at the flower lying across her book. "What am I supposed to do with *that?*"

"A bud vase is the usual implement, filled one-third to halfway with clear water."

Everyone always thought he was a comedian. "You have one of those up your sleeve, too? . . . Oh, *really.* You're not serious." She was sorry she'd asked.

"There you are," pronounced the Scapula, inserting the rose neatly through the neck of the vase. It was foolish, she knew, but she had always had a soft spot for crystal; was this gift accidental, or had he known? Regardless of his motivations, the vase was actually rather nice; the classic fluted shape with splayed petals at the top and a family crest etched delicately into the neck.

"Do you have any more parlor tricks you intend to show me, or were you ready to leave?"

"This is scarcely a parlor," the Scapula said softly, "nor are all my skills appropriate for a general audience."

"Indeed," said Leen. "Your reputation speaks for itself. It speaks quite widely, too, I might add."

He turned up the heat on his gaze again. "Madame Librarian, it is a time to be seen, not to cower away in this tomb of an Archive. Perhaps I've offended you? Well then, let me make amends. Accompany me. Be at my side. After that, who can say?"

"I can say, and I can say it right now. Thank you, but no."

"Very well," said the Scapula, getting to his feet. "Since you prefer to think about what you plan to wear, you give me the pleasure of conferring with you again on the final details." He cocked his head for a moment in thought. "I will have my couturier call," he decided. "A cosmetologist, too, perhaps."

"You're forgetting your vase."

"Not at all. Accept it as my gift, in memory of our little tryst." He moved in a blur; before Leen knew what was happening, he had her hand clasped firmly in his and was pressing it to his mouth. He paused, launched a last few eye-embers at her over her upraised arm, then laid her hand back down on her ledger. Finally he bowed, said "Good day, my dear," and turned and glided toward the exit.

As her grandfather liked to say, land's sake! She didn't have time for this. What a bother. . . .

Of course, he *was* rather attractive, in his way, and she *was* human. . . .

No, Leen told herself. *Totally out of the question.* She was a professional person, at the top of her profession, in fact, and he and his balls and galas and vases and whatever-else were nothing but a distraction. Probably part of some plot, too, for all anyone knew. Completely out of the question. She'd just take the vase and hide it in a back drawer somewhere, or better yet drop it in the trash. . . .

But the vase really was rather striking, at that. It rang at the touch of a fingertip, and the etching was fairly remarkable, with a delicate sense of line and a nicely executed jaguar head in profile. Perhaps she'd let it sit for a day or two before she tossed it out.

6

"Looks like we'll be in port soon," commented Zal-zyn Shaa.

"Aye, that it does," Captain Luff said.

"This vessel is seaworthy and shipshape as ever?"

"It's my job to make sure that it is, don't you know."

"You are ever zealous of your job," Shaa said. "Whatever vicissitudes may befall, that much is indisputable. Therefore it would be the blackest and most unexpected of luck were something to arise that would keep us from the docks, say a sudden typhoon or a seismic sea wave or a submarine boarding party of pirates."

Captain Luff looked deliberately upward. The sky above the *Not Unreasonable Profit* was sunny, sparkling blue, and cloudless, filled with wheeling sea- and land-birds screeching and cawing with frenetic delight. For that matter, the quarterdeck allowed a particularly pleasant vantage point for enjoying the spectacle, too, if one was so inclined, at the cost of an occasional dive-bombing run from above. The captain lowered his gaze to the scene around them. The ship had passed the famous Hutchinson Point lighthouse at dawn to enter the South Channel, and had by now progressed to its middle reaches. The island landmass of Gadzura-the-Home was much the closer, off the port beam, and so close that the small group of hook-and-line men casting from the end of the narrow landspit they were now passing were clearly visible, without the need of deploying his spyglass. The headlands of the Ruponian mainland were nothing more than a smear of gray far off to starboard across the breadth of the channel.

The water itself was running a sou'westerly light chop, but as they were now behind Gadzura's sheltering bulk the influence of wind would be somewhat moderated. The prudent seaman would take heed of the amplified tides, of course, and keep a weather eye peeled for the intense storms the Channel brewed up now and then. As Captain Luff didn't mind admitting to himself, the prudent nature of this crew—and this captain—had behind it the testament of years and leagues of unassailable fact, unblemished save by the questionable decision to give passage to the current load of excursionists. In any case, though, prudent or not, it was as perfect a day for being at sea as you were likely to find in the normal course of events. Theirs was by no means the only vessel to be taking advantage of it, either.

Under normal circumstances, the port of Peridol was already the largest and busiest in the world. On any day of the year, save those of the fiercest weather or the greatest nautical festivals, the navigation channels would be filled with the traffic of global commerce as well as the local fishing fleet. By the look of things around them today was no exception, but the situation today didn't end there. On top of the normal business congestion, the weather had brought out a raft of pleasure boaters in their schooners, ketches, and other fore-and-afters, and even a few hardy rowers in their caiques. Add to all that the Knitting—well, what more did you have to say?

Captain Luff was a practical man; he would never accept the possibility of crossing from Gadzura to Ruponia dry-shod by leaping from deck to adjacent deck. No, it was clearly an optical illusion; it only *looked* as though it could be done. Several pilot ships were out trying to keep a rein on the congestion and herd ships into the proper navigation lanes, but their cause was clearly lost. They were beset on every quarter by clippers, galleons, galleys, barges, hoys, junks, sampans, xebecs, luggers, packets, ferries, dhows, round ships, lorchas, caravels, feluccas, galiots, smacks, trawlers, cascos, a coasting patamar, a baglo, even the occasional dahabeah with its lateen rig, and there a twin-masted pindjajap with the characteristically cantilevered stem and stern. At least the fishing vessels were not actually setting out nets; now *that* would be madness. Even so, Captain Luff observed as a pinnace darted out from behind the barkentine off the starboard quarter and flashed under their bow, you could conclude there was a fair bit of a crowd. Shaa's hopes for extraordinary intervention notwithstanding, the only danger they were running at the moment was that of collision.

It might be wiser not to suggest that to him, though. "If you're bent on contemplating unnatural fates," Captain Luff told him, "you can rule out any leviathans of the deep while you're at it, seeing as the waters are shoaling rapidly, and the lures for the Running will not yet have been placed."

Shaa grunted, his glower ostentatiously underlining his singularly unimpressed attitude toward the waterborne spectacle around them. "Yes, I thought as much."

Captain Luff peered into his pipe. It had gone dry a few minutes or so back, in the middle of a sticky spot involving a wizard-drive sternwheeler that had come tearing out of nowhere and half swamped them; expensive piece of work that vessel had been, though, even without the mahogany railings and the gold-leaf and mother-of-pearl figurehead. Some god's pleasure yacht, more than likely. "Second thoughts are we having, then, Dr. Shaa?"

"Always," Shaa said gloomily.

"Didn't I hear sometime back that Peridol was once your home?" commented the Captain. Might as well just stow the pipe away, there'd be no time to get it started again, especially with that four-master up ahead looking to be shortening sail any moment now.

"In certain cases, 'you can't go home again' is more than just a figure of speech."

Ronibet Karlini topped the stair from the lower deck just in time to hear Shaa's last pronouncement. "I've a good mind to smack you over the head," she told him.

"Free speech is an ideal always in risk. Smack away, then, if you must." Shaa spread his arms wide and tilted his head back to expose his throat.

"That's your whole problem," Roni said. "You can't look at yourself anymore without seeing a victim. Who was it who used to bore everybody's ears off with all that stuff about the limits of fate and the power of will? Couldn't have been you; you've got a martyr complex."

"They say it's a profession with a future."

Roni studied him suspiciously as the captain strode to the quarterdeck rail and shouted a series of rapid orders to the crew on deck and in the rigging. The helmsman swung the wheel and the ship heeled to port. "Shall we brace for impact?" Shaa said hopefully.

"Not *this* time," Captain Luff shot back over his shoulder.

"Ah, well," said Shaa. The four-master, much of its canvas now taken in, slipped backward toward them off the starboard bow.

Roni approached, still watching him warily. "What is *wrong* with you?"

Shaa met her gaze for a moment, then deliberately looked off along the deck. "Your ward appears ripe for romance."

Tildamire Mont was down on the main deck taking in the excitement. From the direction of her attention, the more stimulating elements of the scene included the exertions of the half-clad sailors clambering along the yardarms.

"What's such a bad thing about that?" said Roni. "You could have had her interested in you if you wanted; you probably still could. Or is it something else? I wouldn't have thought you're fuddy-duddy material. You're not turning into a prude after all these years, are you?''

He shrugged. "My circumstances of late have been different from those of my youth. The Peridol lifestyle fails to translate well to that of the road.''

"In case you didn't notice, that's Peridol up there a few hours ahead. You want to recapture your youth, I'm sure Peridol will be more than happy to oblige you.''

Shaa rolled an eye in her direction. "The thought did not entirely escape my mind,'' he allowed. "The circumstances do present themselves for one terminal spree.''

"Terminal—there you go again with the fatalism.''

Shaa shrugged. "Fate is fate. Indeed, I have an advantage over others; they can merely speculate on what inevitabilities destiny may hold for them, whereas I know the tenets of my decree. Max thinks he can overturn the curse of fate, but that's Max for you; hubris up to his gills.''

"Give me excess pride any day over this giving up and waiting to die. What, is your heart acting up more?''

"Yes,'' he said testily. "My heart is acting up. You're welcome to address it directly if you like. Perhaps you can harangue it into submission. Speaking of admonitions, how is the Great one this morning?''

"Fine,'' said Roni. "Of course fine, why shouldn't he be fine?''

"I see,'' Shaa said, seeing, in fact, more than he would rather have preferred.

"What was that?'' said Roni. Captain Luff, facing away from them, had mumbled something unintelligible into his pipe.

Shaa, though, had heard the statement well enough. The captain had been muttering about dissension in the ranks.

It was no more than bald truth. They were scarcely

the happy band of days of yore. No better example presented itself than the Karlini lovebirds. Roni could barely mention Karlini without snapping at him *in absentia,* while Karlini had placed himself on permanent iceberg watch, presumably; that was the most charitable explanation for his constant sulking in the bow. A fine bunch they were turning into, the captain's remark made no mistake about that.

If these were still the old days, this would be just the time for Shaa to step in, smoothing ruffled feelings, stilling riled waters, introducing the grease of reason to the squeak of discord, knitting them all back together again. That had been one of Shaa's jobs, not that any of them had ever spelled it out quite like that, and he had done it well, too. In many ways it had perhaps been Shaa's most important job.

But what was it to him anymore anyway? He'd soon be off this particular coil, most likely, his role done if not necessarily complete. And all the plots and plans and twists and turns would still go on without him at least as smoothly as they'd done with him present on the scene. Things might even be improved—he'd be one less ramification for the rest of them to stumble over.

Indeed, after this many years of long-range plans and ultimate goals, all the agitation came to seem rather pointless. Max might never question, but then Max was Max. It wasn't only the ends one could question, either, but the means. Things were so complex and intertwined that it was a wonder any of them could sort through it and tell tail from head. They had all contributed their threads of plot, which was fine by itself except for the fact that none of them ever seemed to tie their threads off when they were finished. Not only that, they'd taken to picking up new plots off the street, too; just look at the Creeping Sword.

That other classic admonition came to mind, the one concerning the excess of cooks and their rancid soup. Of course, that maxim probably broke down under the requirements of preparing a large banquet, where the problem might be one of management and delegation rather than staffing, per se, although Shaa had to admit that his lack of background in food service left him insufficiently competent to conclude that question unambiguously one way or the other. That question, along with so many others, looked like it would just remain unanswered, at least as far as Zalzyn Shaa would ever know.

Roni, watching him sink deeper into his funk, had never seen Shaa like this before. She'd known he wasn't looking forward to the prospect of returning to his old home town. Not only was he no longer bothering to conceal his discomfort, though, he was all but wallowing in it. "Don't forget your curse isn't automatic," Roni said. "It has to be implemented. You could lie low while we do the legwork. We can head it off."

"That's not all of it," said Shaa, "you know that's not all of it at all. Even if I try to wall myself up in a basement, this is Peridol. I'm certain to encounter my brother."

"It's been a long time. Maybe you could reason with him now."

"You're wasting your time," Shaa said. "Furthermore, you *know* you're wasting your time."

"Then *kill* him," Roni spat. "Just go ahead and kill him, and be rid of him once and for all. Then go ahead and worry about his curse."

"Don't you think I'd love to do that?"

"So *do* it. Or let one of *us* do it."

Shaa abruptly turned away and strode to the starboard rail. He grasped a marlinspike and pulled himself up so that he could look over the side, into the strip of rushing water between their ship and the next one, now all of half-a-cable farther out. *He's not serious,* thought Roni. But all of a sudden serious was just exactly what Shaa *did* look like. "Get down from there," Roni said. "What do you think you're doing?"

"It would save everyone a lot of trouble," Shaa said.

The water pounded by under his gaze. It was quite hypnotic, really, when you looked at things like this. There were disciplines of the mind and will that stressed contemplation of the natural world to focus one's spirit. Perhaps he should have given them more attention; it was a remarkably honing experience, to match internal and external contemplation under—

A hand closed on the back of his coat and deposited Shaa unceremoniously back on the quarterdeck. "There will be none of this on my ship," said Captain Luff, shoving his glaring face up against Shaa's nose. "I will not stand for it. Are you clear on that?"

". . . Very well," said Shaa. "Aye."

"I'm surprised at you, Dr. Shaa." Captain Luff noted with satisfaction that Shaa's gaze, which had been sneaking back to eye the gunwales, now flickered up and met his. "Whatever you say to the contrary, your specialty is trouble. If your fate lies ahead in Peridol, man, just use your natural talent. You could be more nettlesome than ever before. Not this nonsense; no, this is not for the likes of you."

"Are you a natural philosopher now, too?" Shaa said, but it was clear his heart wasn't in it. "Just let me know when we reach the dock." He pulled clear of the captain's grip, slunk to the companionway, and vanished below.

Captain Luff and Roni watched him go. "Is this about his brother, then?" asked the captain.

Tildy Mont, who was turning out to have a gift for observation along with her other flowering talents, had mentioned to Roni that Shaa's style of speaking seemed to infect people who hung around with him too long. It hadn't happened to Karlini, but then Karlini was probably too absentminded to pay enough attention to *anyone's* words in the first place. Roni knew Shaa's patterns had affected her over the years, however, and not only his speech, either. From the way the captain was starting to talk it looked like the spell of Shaa had claimed another victim here, too. "Arznaak's a big part of it," Roni said. "Shaa hasn't been back to Peridol since his father's death and Arznaak's curse. That was part of the idea of the curse, to keep him away from his family and force him to wander the earth.''

"But his heart's going out on him now because of another part of the curse," said Captain Luff, "do I have that aright? So you all figured he didn't have anything to lose by coming back to Peridol now and defying that side of the thing?"

"Something like that."

Captain Luff clenched his unlit pipe firmly between his teeth. "If this Arznaak's the key, then, why is he still around, with your lot being as nasty as you are, begging your pardon, ma'am?"

Roni sighed. "When you said Shaa's best skill is causing trouble, you sure got that one right. Shaa won't let any of us touch his brother. He made a promise."

The captain began to shake his head. Up ahead, though, a barge was putting out from an inlet on the shoreline off to port; ships were peeling off to starboard to get out of its way. It took a good ten minutes to sort the sea lane out again after that, and by the time Captain Luff was free to look around once more, Roni had long since departed. He shook his head another time for good measure. In truth, Shaa and his lot *were* no end of trouble. Their crowning achievement, as far as Captain Luff was concerned, was just now becoming evident. He was finally on the verge of being rid of them once and for all, an event that should have filled him with a judicious sense of release and rejoicing, but here they were getting under his skin. A full kettle of trouble they were, and no mistaking.

Below decks as well, the kettle was still brewing. "Perhaps bad as they seem not are things," Haddo had told Shaa when he'd come down from the quarterdeck into the darkness of the passage below. Shaa had grunted at him to cover his momentary startlement at hearing Haddo's voice out of the blackness. He shouldn't have been surprised; Shaa knew full well how much Haddo enjoying lurking in shadows and poking his cloak into other folks' business. Haddo enjoyed it as much as they all did, it was something that linked them all together as a shared society of busybodies.

"A lid on it put," had been Shaa's only response. Haddo had faded back to wherever he'd come from, and Shaa had continued on to have a good solid grouse, adrift (as he thought of it) in the mental Sargasso. Perhaps he'd run across Karlini there.

Actually, Shaa thought the fundamentals of his funk and Karlini's might be much the same, whatever the differences in proximate causes or the binds that might be facing them. Were they just being swept along by Max's plotting because they didn't have anything better to do, because they weren't willing to exert themselves to take control over their own lives? Had Shaa's life been controlled by external forces for so long that he'd forgotten how to do anything but float along with them? Getting rid of the gods was Max's goal, not one that had excited Shaa much in some time; in fact he hadn't really had a major goal lately other than just staying alive. Now even that goal might most probably be out of reach. *That's not the real problem, though,* Shaa reflected. The real problem was that there didn't seem to be much point in trying. Shaa only realized that several hours must have passed when Haddo's voice floated again out of the shadows to announce, "Approaching are we wharves." Shaa took a few deep breaths to try to quiet his heart, which had gone into a rapid pounding run when Haddo had spoken up behind him, and climbed back to the deck, his ankles feeling particularly waterlogged. The short climb left him panting. Well, one thing Peridol always had in abundance were his fellow physicians; perhaps one among them had perfected the two things Shaa needed most, curse removal and transplantation of hearts. In the air were still the wheeling seabirds, but now stretched out around the ship was the harbor of Peridol's south port.

They had obviously passed the great moles while Shaa was still hiding in the dark. Wharves and docks, jetties, slips, quays, and embarkments surrounded them, the traffic from the channel squeezing itself into the tideways under the guiding signal flags of the out-numbered harbormasters. The main channel was already barely visible behind them. The Tongue Water would be off somewhere off to the northeast, but the cluster of warehouses and light industry on the Hook concealed even the arching bridges from view.

Rather than breaking out the sweeps, Captain Luff still had the *Not Unreasonable Profit* under judicious sail. Ahead now at the end of the current channel, just beyond a coaster careened over in dry dock, was—rarity of rarities—a wharf with an empty moorage. "How did we get so lucky?" Shaa murmured. Ships were already being forced to dock two and even three to an anchorage, tying themselves side to side out into the navigation channels.

"Steady as she goes, there," said Captain Luff. He pointed with the stem of his pipe. "Painted on that warehouse wall, can you see it? The Dooglas company crest. With the compensation for that Dooglas business we'll be repainting that, don't you know; Haalsen Traders it'll be now."

Aye, thought Shaa, and here they were indeed, heading in to the dock all open and aboveboard, hiding behind no clever incognito, their identity free and plain to the world. Now they would see if the game was once again afoot, whether Shaa's final discussion with the Creeping Sword before he'd gone over the side had predicted actual events. Had someone been trailing the ship? Was someone watching the docks? Well, even the Sword's god friends—or perhaps especially the Sword's god friends—weren't omnipotent or omniscient; if watchers there were, the Sword might have very well succeeded in giving them the slip. Of course, it might still be up to Shaa to complete the job.

"Who are those people on the dock?" asked Karlini.

While Shaa had been consumed with his musing, he realized that a small throng had gathered around him on the deck. "You see that person standing alone off there on the right?" Roni said, shielding her eyes with a hand. "It's been a long time, but . . . yes! It's Dalya!"

"Dalya Hazeel?" said Karlini. "What's she doing here?"

"She must have gotten my message."

"Your message? What message?"

"While the rest of you big-time plotters were planning what to do in Peridol," Roni told him, "none of you bothered to think about where we were going to stay."

"I figured we'd just come into town and rent some rooms or something; the usual."

"You figured that, did you. Dear. With the first Knitting in years going on, probably the biggest one in history, people streaming in from every corner of the world, on top of all the people heading into Peridol anyway looking for work, you were just planning to waltz in off the street and take lodgings. Right, dear. If I left it up to you, we'd all be sleeping in a gutter if we were lucky."

"Oh," said Karlini. "Well. Thanks, dear. Dalya, you say. Huh." The seagull on his shoulder screeched once for good measure, then looked up at the sky. With a matching wail, a smaller gull with a brown back swooped down from the flock wheeling overhead, fluffed its wings just short of Karlini's hair, and dropped to a neat landing on Karlini's other shoulder. Squirming crosswise in its beak was a fish: a sardine, perhaps, or a small herring. Leaning around the back of Karlini's neck, the visitor presented its gift to the first gull, which took it with a quick dart-and-snap and a backward flip of the head. The first gull nodded its head in apparent satisfaction, upon which the visitor screeched once more, sprang into the air, and flapped away.

Karlini had apparently ignored the whole affair. Even Shaa's attention had remained fixed on the approaching dock. Tildamire Mont wanted to ask who Dalya

Hazeel was, anyway, but from the look of things she thought it might be better to keep it for later. Maybe Haddo would know, or Wroclaw; they seemed on top of most everything. "What about those other people?" she asked instead. "Those two on the other end of the wharf, beyond the longshoremen?"

The pair in question were now clearly visible as a man and a woman. The woman was taller than the man, and wore some kind of headband around her forehead that glinted in the sun as her dark hair fell across it. The man had on the casual day-wear of the Peridol upper crust: white slacks, a light jacket of bright green, and a straw boater. In spite of his sporty outfit, although perhaps because of its slightly rumpled appearance, the man looked, in a word, tweedy.

Shaa was searching his memory. What exactly had the Sword told him? He had mentioned two gods with whom he'd interacted, in addition to Gashanatantra; a woman and a man. A "tweedy" man? *Yes,* Shaa thought, *just so.* The Sword had clearly been feeling his way through his discussion with Shaa, trying to decide where the balance point rested between keeping to himself information he wasn't sure he wanted to share and continuing to manage his balancing act solo. It was plain that the Sword knew more about these gods than he was prepared to let on. While the general rule of thumb was that the more dope you had on a god the better off you'd be, Shaa had been willing to let it ride. Who knew where this *tête-à-tête* with the Sword might lead, for one. For another, if he encountered the Sword's gods, Shaa, being his own prudent self, would never approach them, of course.

At this moment, though, Shaa was considering whether adherence to conventional wisdom wasn't exactly his major problem.

First things first, however. The *Not Unreasonable Profit* neatly edged into its moorage. Lines were tossed and secured, the gangplank was brought and placed. Captain Luff strode ashore with the logbooks and turned aside to present their papers to the local dockmaster. Shaa followed him across the gangplank, spent a short moment perched on the end of the ramp considering the wharf beyond, and then stepped over the edge. He was now officially in Peridol; he was committed.

If the curse held true, he would not be leaving again.

Nevertheless, when no electric shock traveled up from the boards to fry his body; when the wharf termites failed to spring into frantic activity and cause the circle of wood he bestrode to collapse, precipitating him into the noxious pollution of the harbor water; when his heart, though accelerated by the excitement, nonetheless continued to beat; when, in fact, no one else on the dock paid him more than a passing glance of interest, Shaa realized his mood had suddenly and disproportionately lightened. Curses being what they were, none of these divergent possibilities had been entirely out of the question. He found himself approaching, with a confident step, the man and woman at the side of the wharf.

The two of them had been examining the ship; now, as Shaa approached, their scrutiny turned to him. Shaa executed a small, formally correct bow, and addressed them. "You appear to be awaiting the arrival of this ship. Is there some matter I might assist you with? A bill of lading perhaps, or is it that you bear a competitive bid for our cargo? I am not, as you see, the captain, but I am empowered to proceed with business nonetheless."

The pair were both regarding him minutely, and not only with their eyes, either. Shaa could feel the resonant tingle of an aural probe, and a large churning spot traveling across his body in line with the woman's gaze. "Well?" said the man, but not to Shaa.

"I'd know him anywhere," said the woman, "but that's not him. I can't feel him on the ship, either. We could take this one apart; see if he knows anything, whoever he is."

The man's face was no longer frowning, or even neutral, but now instead bore an expression of dawn-

111

ing astonishment. He reached into his jacket, withdrew a slate of platinum-colored ceramic, and perused
it, jabbing at the thing with a finger while it made low
beeping sounds at him. When he looked back up, a
nasty smirk was breaking through behind the amazement. "You may not know this man, but I do. Oh,
yes, I certainly do. You are Zalzyn Shaa, the Cursed,
aren't you?"

"That's not exactly the way I'd prefer to put it if
you'd like to know the truth," said Shaa, "but in root
of fact, yes. May I help you?"

"Zalzyn Shaa," the god said, "and in Peridol. To
meet his doom."

"Yes, well, there are dooms and there are dooms,"
Shaa stated. "Foreordination often exhibits more mu-
tability than you might expect."

The god stretched out his hand, opened it, examined
the palm, then clenched his fist deliberately. "*You*
might expect changefulness; I expect none. Artistic
leeway in implementation, surely, but in the final outcome? No, certainly not."

"Don't get sidetracked," the woman told him. "We
still haven't found out what happened to my husband."

"Mr. Shaa will tell us what we want to know. Won't
you, Mr. Shaa?"

"As long as we're standing on ceremony," said
Shaa, "may I remind you that 'Doctor' is the appropriate honorific? Shall we say this is one for mutabil-
ity, hmm?"

Shaa felt the heat of the god's scrutiny break on him
like the force of a desert sun at noontime. "I shall
enjoy this," the god concluded after a moment. "I
find I don't like you." He reached out again with his
hand and extended the forefinger. Shaa watched it
come with an abstract fascination, remembering his
histrionics on the ship, languid and frozen now that
the moment might have truly arrived. The fingertip
nudged against Shaa's shirt.

His trance suddenly shattered, Shaa's head went

back and his spine arched, his teeth clenched in a rictus snarl, his eyes rolled back, and he collapsed rigidly to the deck of the wharf, his limbs jerking spasmodically.

"My," the woman said to her companion, "how powerful you are. So powerful that you render someone we were about to interrogate incapable of speech, and so surreptitiously, too. Pick him up, why don't you, so we can at least take him with us."

The god was examining his finger, his lips pursed. "No," he said. "There are regulations. I may not actually take this one into my possession. No matter; we will find your husband regardless. Here comes another one from the ship. We can take him."

"You've already caused too much of a scene," the woman said disgustedly. "This one coming has stand-off power, too, can't you feel it? We'll have to come back for them when they're not on guard." She raised her arm, made a blade of her hand, and slashed viciously down. Behind her arm the air blurred like the surface of a pond under a thrown stone. The area of disturbance rippled concentrically outward, making the figures of the two gods distort and break apart behind it. Then, as the air stilled, it became obvious that the two gods had vanished.

Or had they vanished, per se? Two rippling shadows moved quickly down the dock and disappeared around the corner of the Dooglas warehouse. Shaa continued to writhe on the ground as Karlini reached him. "They're gone," Karlini announced. "Weren't you watching the refractive edge of the misdirection field?"

Shaa abruptly ceased his writhing and straightened himself out on the boards. "It is more difficult than you might think to keep your gaze aligned when your eyeballs are rolling, especially when they are out of synchrony."

Karlini squatted down next to him as Shaa pulled himself to a sitting position. "Did he hurt you at all?"

They both looked down at the round scorch mark on Shaa's shirt. "A shock," Shaa acknowledged. "I

threw myself away before it had a chance to general-
ize. A love-tap, you might say, at least comparatively
speaking.''

''I hope Roni never tries to love *me* like that,'' said
Karlini. ''So, are you planning to tell me what this
was all about? Did you feed them one of your song-
and-dance numbers and they didn't like it? What made
you take these guys on, anyway?''

Shaa looked past the now-smooth air at the corner
where the gods had disappeared. ''You know, old
friend,'' he said slowly, ''that may just have been a
significant mistake.''

''Your brother?'' said Karlini.

''Yes,'' Shaa said, ''and no. An encounter at second
hand, from a not altogether expected quarter.''

''Gods?''

''Evidently.'' And not just any gods, either. Shaa
didn't know who the woman was, but he now had an
all-too-solid suspicion of the identity of the man.

This left no doubt that the Creeping Sword hadn't
been overreacting when he'd decided he needed help,
and had come to Shaa. In retrospect, it would have
been nice if the Sword had seen fit to give Shaa just a
little more information, like who his friends were.
Presumably the Sword *knew* who they were. Whether
he knew or not, though, didn't address the immediate
question.

Just what was the Sword doing tangled up with Jardin, the Curse Administrator, anyway?

7

"Wait a minute," said Jurtan Mont. "Isn't Peridol that way?"

They were at a crossroads; Jurtan, Max, and the remaining horse with their baggage. The east-west thoroughfare they'd been following had grown wider. It had sprouted pavement as well; clearly it had become an artery of some stature. Not only that, it had traffic, both foot and cart. Most of the traffic had been heading in the same direction, west. There was no surprise about that. The post at the corner of the intersection was dominated by a large arrow-edged sign pointing west, labeled with "PERIDOL" in half a dozen forms of script. No, there wasn't much doubt about it, not at all; Peridol *was* that way.

And it was almost in reach. Jurtan could smell the sea air. Less than an hour ago they'd even been visited by a flock of seabirds, virtually still damp, which had wheeled overhead briefly before screeching their way again west toward the ocean. If Max got a move on, they could probably reach Peridol while it was still day. The thought of not having to get up at the crack of dawn to climb on a horse ever again was almost unbearably appealing.

As cryptic as Max was, there was also little doubt that Peridol *was* their destination. It had been dangling in front of Jurtan like a strung-up carrot ever since Roosing Oolvaya, lost now in the distant pages of memory. Max couldn't weasel out on him now.

But then, this was Max under discussion. And why else would he have turned aside onto the north road, which was little more than a carriage-track, really, and be standing there with his hands on his hips glaring at Jurtan with one of his, well, *glares?* "Yeah, that's right," Max said.

"Uh," said Jurtan, "can we get to Peridol by heading north here?"

"Not unless we hire a boat."

"Are we going to hire a boat?"

"Why would we do a thing like that?"

"So we can *get—to—Peridol!*"

"Get a grip on yourself, kid," said Max. "We've got a little detour to make, that's all."

Jurtan looked north along the trail. He couldn't *see* a swamp this time, but that was scarcely reassuring.

"How about I meet you in the city?" Jurtan said. That's what he *said,* but still he found himself trudging off the main road onto the path after Max. Whenever Jurtan pointed himself north, his mental accompaniment *did* switch to something bouncy and upbeat, full of resolving major chords and an oom-pah-ing tuba off somewhere in the back, while even a glance west caused the music to modulate into something weaker and irresolutely drifting, but Jurtan was getting pretty tired of a personal oracle that thought it knew what was good for him better than he did himself. Still, how bad could it be?

"Don't *say* that," Jurtan muttered to himself.

At least the place they were aiming at this time had a name, according to the north-facing panel on the signpost. "What's Yenemsvelt, anyway?" asked Jurtan.

"The estate's just the other side of Yenemsvelt, actually," Max told him.

The 'estate'? Well, that sounded hopeful. "Is this estate in a swamp?"

Max spared him a quick glower. "First thing we do after this stop is get into the city and find accommodations, all right?"

"I thought we were going to link up with Shaa and the others."

"Linking doesn't mean we're going to stay with them. Maybe, but not necessarily. Shaa's probably already headed off on his own in any case. He grew up out here, you know."

It was news to Jurtan. "Right," he said. "He hasn't been back, though."

"Not since his father died," said Max. His lips pursed in thought. "Maybe it's time you heard a little more about that."

But that was the last Max said on the subject, or on any other subject, for that matter. They trudged north, the riderless horse behaving the most energetically of any of them. The town of Yenemsvelt soon appeared, consisting of a somewhat ramshackle half-timbered tavern, a small market square, an ecumenical multi-purpose worship-building at least as tumbledown as the tavern, and the usual assortment of tradespersons with their mixed-use dwellings and business establishments. Max took a left at the square and followed the carriage-track out between the buildings into the midst of rolling hills. Thick and bramble-ridden hedgerows lined the verge of the road, broken occasionally by stone walls and imposing iron gates. They clattered over a small stream on a sturdy open bridge. Looking over the side of the bridge into a pool just downstream, Jurtan saw a trout leap free of the water and flop back down with a good-sized splash. "Nice area, is this?" Jurtan said.

"You figure it better be, if the Peridol upper-crusters want to use it for their out-of-town playground."

Jurtan was seized suddenly by a horrible suspicion. "You're not planning to *rob* one of them, are you?" he hissed. There had been noises behind some of the walls they'd passed, the kind of noises something large might make if it hadn't been fed in a week.

"What do you take me for?" Max sniffed.

"Oh," said Jurtan. "That's good. I mean, some of those walls . . ."

117

"It's the ones without walls you really want to watch out for," Max said distractedly. "Now if I remember right, it should be just over this rise."

Sure enough, the straight stretch of road beyond the top of the hill held another gate, on the left. Max inspected the gate. Instead of a sensible lock-in-the-middle hinge-on-the-sides arrangement, what were visible were an arrangement of eccentric cranks, a windlass, and a large counterweight on a lever arm. Not visible, however, was anyone in the small watch-booth.

"Look," said Jurtan, "a bell-cord."

But Max was already up the side of the wall, new floppy hat already looking as worn as the one he'd left behind in the pit, shaggy beard and all, and then he was swinging deftly over the sharpened spikes at the top to vanish down the other side. The howl of a wolf sounded from just beyond the wall. Jurtan grasped the horse's bridle and prepared to flee.

The howl abruptly cut off and was replaced by an eager snuffling and much rapid panting. These sounds were shortly drowned under the creak and clatter of gearteeth and linkages. The gate rumbled open. "What are you waiting for?" said Max.

Jurtan edged cautiously through and peeked around the mechanism. Max was feeding their last strips of jerky to a small horse—no, it was only a large hound. An apparently *friendly* hound, however. When the beast reared back to lick Max's face, Jurtan saw a second one lolling on the ground behind it slavering onto Max's boot. "All right, all right," Max told them. "That's enough. Off with you now."

The dogs shook themselves off, licked Max's hands once more for good measure, and trotted away. Away from *Max,* at any rate.

"He's got all the food," Jurtan said nervously. One of them was almost looking him in the eye, and it still had all four feet on the ground. The other one was moving around to Jurtan's side to flank him. "Hey, stop that." He snatched his hand free of the thing's

mouth. In return, he got a low growl. "Uh, you like music?" Jurtan whistled the refrain of a hunting song he'd heard at an inn on the road.

The hound let go of his jacket and sprang back. Both of them edged away, then turned and padded off into the trees, casting glances back at him over their shoulders.

Max had done something to the mechanism, and the gate was now closing behind them. "I wish you wouldn't do things like this," Jurtan said. "Someday you're going to give somebody heart failure."

"Why make them come all the way out here just to open the gate?"

"That's not it," said Jurtan, examining the gate mechanism himself. A pull-rod ran from the gearbox into an iron conduit and down into the ground. "You can run this thing by remote control, right? If we'd rung the bell, whoever's on the other end could have opened the gate without coming out here."

"Good eyes," Max said. "This way. Bring the horse."

The gate clanged shut as they started up the long driveway. Past the belt of trees inside the wall, they entered a series of rolling lawns. The drive crossed another stream and then wound through an expanse of formal gardens. A crew of landskeepers far off to the left was pruning a hedge maze. Ahead of them on a rise, though, was the estate house; classically proportioned, with an abundance of colonnades and cornices breaking up the off-white stone facade. They skirted a fountain surrounded by a flower bed in the middle of the circular drive and Max mounted the front stairs. His yank on the bellpull brought a muffled clanging of chimes from within.

After a moment, the door swung open. "Ah," said the footman. His gaze travelled down and then up as he took in Max's travel-beaten outfit, bushy black beard, slouch hat, and generally unrecognizable yet unmistakably disreputable demeanor. "Master Maximillian, sir, won't you come in? We've been expecting you.''

Jurtan left the horse with a groom who had scurried up with just that purpose in mind and followed Max into the entry hall. ''Cleeve, isn't it?'' Max was saying. ''Did you recognize me by sight just now?''

''Purely circumstantial, sir,'' Cleeve assured him. ''You are indeed a person of indecipherable appearance unexpectedly presenting himself fresh from the road; merely a matter of context, what. Would you care for some refreshment?''

Yes! Jurtan thought. But instead, Max said, ''Is she around?''

''In the gardens, sir. The oaks.''

''Good,'' Max said. ''I'll see her first. You can take my friend off and get him fed, though.''

''I'll wait, too,'' inserted Jurtan. ''Why don't we both see 'her' first?''

''I—oh, all right, come on, then.''

Cleeve led them out through a plant-filled conservatory and out the back onto a spacious piazza. A flight of stairs took them down from the terrace onto another lawn. The lawn backed up against a sizable pond, complete with ducks, but its side margins were lined with neat rows of oak trees. ''Third back on the left when last sighted, sir,'' said Cleeve, before inclining his head politely and retreating back up the stairs.

Beneath the third oak on the left was a lawn chair, and next to it a picnic basket and a bulging gunny sack. ''Did 'she' wander off?'' asked Jurtan, looking behind the tree. They'd seen no evidence of anyone about on their stroll out from the terrace.

''It's me,'' Max called out, ''I'm here! You waiting for me to come up there after you?''

Foliage rustled overhead. Leaves parted and a dirty face appeared, upside down and craned back. ''It took you long enough,'' the face said, and only then did Jurtan realize the person was a woman. ''What was it this time, another swamp?''

''As a matter of fact, yes,'' Max said, his own head

canted back and his hands on his hips, "there was a swamp. I *told* you there'd be a swamp."

"He never could resist a swamp," the woman said to Jurtan. "Must have been some kind of deathmarch, huh, Jurtan; all the way from Roosing Oolvaya with this maniac? This is the Mont kid, right?"

"You're Eden!" Jurtan blurted. "Shaa's sister!"

Eden looked Jurtan over, then turned a frowning gaze on Max. "You haven't told him anything useful, have you? Sometimes I don't know why I bother with you." Eden's face disappeared into the branches. It was replaced by a line of rope, and then the full figure of Eden, right-side-up now, descending rapidly hand-over-hand down it. She was dressed in a leather climbing outfit, another coil of rope slung over her shoulder and a stout utility belt bearing pitons and a hammer fastened about her waist. Eden dropped free the last ten feet and landed next to the lawn chair.

Jurtan shut his eyes and ran his hand over his face. He hadn't known Zalzyn and Eden Shaa were *twins*. But what else could they be? They couldn't be just normal siblings, not when Eden could have been Shaa with a little padding here and there; even her voice sounded the same, if in a higher register, contralto to his baritone. But when she had come down the rope she had moved like *Max*.

A chair poked the back of Jurtan's knees and he sank gratefully back into it. Cleeve had returned with a small party of servants bearing between them extra chairs, a buffet table, several flagons of mineral water, and a fruit-and-cheese platter. Max finished divesting himself of hat, beard, bushy eyebrows, and nose putty while Eden, her equipment stored back in the sack, rinsed off her face in a basin. Cleeve took the basin and withdrew. "Okay," Eden declared, "now we can say hello."

Jurtan hurriedly transferred his melon plate to his other hand and wobbled to his feet for a bow. "I *am* Jurtan Mont," he confirmed.

"A pleasure," said Eden, grasping his hand firmly

for a vigorous shake. When she let go, Jurtan fell back into his chair. Eden regarded him for a moment, then turned again on Max. Max gave her a tentative hug and leaned in for a peck on the cheek. She turned her head and caught him on the lips, held it for a beat, then wrinkled her nose as he pulled back. "A bath," she told him, "definitely a bath. Then we can decide if you'd like to seduce me." Her grin widened. "I don't get many guests, after all."

"Idle flirting," Max said to no one in particular, "that's all it is."

"How would you know?" said Eden.

"Would you be serious if I took you seriously?" Max asked.

"You like intrigue so much, maybe you can figure it out. Sit down and try some of this stuff, it's good; I've been growing it in the back."

"I'm not hungry," Max told her. "What are you now, my mother?"

"I'm as close to it as you've ever gotten," said Eden, applying a slice of cheddar to an apple wedge. "When I pulled you out of the gutter—"

"Not *that* again," Max said, frowning at his mineral water. "By the time we met I hadn't been in the gutter for years, and as I recall you didn't have anything to do with me being in *or* out."

"I was speaking technically."

Technically the statement *was* correct. "That wasn't a gutter," Max said, "that was a sewer, and you may have pulled me out of it physically, but metaphorically—"

"You're getting pretty testy, you know that?"

"Never been a testy bone in my body," snapped Max. "What have *you* been up to?"

"What do you think I've been up to?"

"Probably the usual, running half the business of the western world. What's your latest triumph?"

"Houseplants."

"Houseplants?"

"That's right, houseplants," Eden repeated. She

122

tossed her plate on the table and leaned back. "Potted ferns, ficus, some succulents, the occasional flower bed."

"You worked out a way to turn plants and shrubbery into a cash crop?"

"They're all the rage," said Eden. "All I had to do was get them into the palace. The in-crowd latched onto them, and now you can't walk into an office or a bank anywhere in town without falling over a planter box. Lucky for you, I don't mind telling you. Between you and Zolly spending money hand over fist it's good *somebody's* out bringing in the bucks."

Zolly? *Zolly?* "What about Groot?" asked Jurtan.

"What about him?" said Eden.

"I thought Max was getting money from Groot, too."

"You're hanging out with a crew with expensive tastes," Eden told him.

"Am I?" Jurtan said. "It's hard to tell when you're walking all day and then sleeping in the mud."

"You want out, kid?" said Max. "You know where the door is."

I can be subtle, Jurtan thought, *or I can just go for it. But what do I have to lose?* "I still don't know what I'd be getting out *from,*" Jurtan stated, trying to keep his voice firm and reasonable, and not at all whiny. "How can I know what I'd be getting out of if I don't really know what I've gotten into? All any of you ever want to do is drop sneaky little hints."

"He's got you there, Max," Eden said.

"You want him to know something?" said Max. "You think he's ready to be a full-fledged member? Then *you* tell it to him."

"Still being touchy, are we? Okay, then, I will."

Max h'mphed and looked up into the tree.

"There's actually not much I *can* tell you," Eden went on. "There's me and Zolly, and Arznaak, too, of course, but that much I'm sure you already know. You *don't?* Well, okay, then."

"Just the high points," Max broke in. "I still want

to make it in to the city today, and there's stuff *we* need to go over.''

''Have you seen the roads? They say traffic's a total mess, the Tongue's completely jammed, and the water's even worse.''

''If the worst I ever have to face is traffic congestion I'd look forward to a long and pleasant life,'' Max said dryly. ''Don't you have anything to drink in this place besides spring water?''

Eden raised her hand and waved at the house. Cleeve appeared at the top of the stairs and hurried toward them. *More distractions,* Jurtan thought. It was going to be the same as always. They'd sit here for a while, never actually getting to the point, and then if they finally *did* start to reach any significant revelations something would tunnel out of the ground to attack them, or the tree would fall over, or somebody would come running up with an urgent message. The possibilities were endless; these people were creative, after all. The bottom line was that Jurtan would still be left knowing nothing new.

Or would he? There were certain new facts at hand, Jurtan realized. What could he deduce from them? Cleeve took Max's order, for ''something brewed, *anything,* and I don't mean tea,'' and scurried off again. When he had retreated, Jurtan said slowly, still thinking it out, ''Shaa's not the only one with a curse, is he? Eden—you're part of it, too, aren't you? Shaa can go wherever he wants except home, but home's the place you can't leave.''

''Did you tell him or is he figuring this out?'' Eden asked Max.

Max had leaned back in his chair and propped his hat over his face in conspicuous preparation for a nap. From under the hat, though, he spoke. ''It's the kid's own reasoning, if you want to glorify it by calling it that. Maybe he hasn't been asleep all the time.''

''Has Max always been like this?'' Jurtan wondered.

"As long as I've known him," Eden said. "Do you want to hear about that or about me and the family?"

"The family," said Jurtan, "please."

The "high points" account, as Max would have it, was much as Jurtan had begun to piece together. Punctuated by Max's sarcastic asides, and keeping in mind the fact that Eden might not be the most reliable of witnesses on the subject, the story of the Shaas was still well in keeping with all Jurtan had heard about the byzantine and fratricidal ways of Peridol society. The Shaa family had been prominent in Gadzura for several generations; according to Max, long enough for inbreeding to have apparently had some impact. Eden and Zalzyn Shaa had their eccentricities, but Arznaak, the first-born, had a far more intimate relationship with the borderland of sanity. As far back as Eden could recall, Arznaak had been either wonderful or miserable to be around, with little ground in between.

"It's hard to believe unless you've seen him in operation," Eden said, "but even I'll admit he can be quite charming, full of expansive good humor and flamboyant gestures, great laughter and so forth, but it's not an act, it's really genuine. The problem is his other side. That's genuine, too. He'll shift modes in the middle of a sentence, the middle of a thought."

More often, though, the elements of Arznaak's personality wouldn't switch so much as merge. For a time when Eden had been quite young, the older Arznaak had taken to giving her presents. He had given her a doll, for example, which several days later had begun to writhe on her bed until its skin burst, the stuffing having been consumed from within by maggots. In replacement, she had returned to her room after being calmed from her fit of hysterics to find, dressed in the doll's fashionable clothing, a large glassy-eyed rat. But then Arznaak had been so contrite and winsome afterward, at least publicly, that it was difficult to do anything but wonder whether the incident had happened at all.

Arznaak had not wondered, he had learned. The first conclusions he had drawn had concerned the need for secrecy and craft, the behind-the-scenes jab and the terror in the night. Each of the Shaas had their talents, and these had turned out to be Arznaak's. As Arznaak's skill at familial terrorism increased, the twins' relationship was deepened by their instinct to hang together, which in turn fed Arznaak's own tendencies. "Whether he started off just toying with us or not," said Eden, "eventually he got to where he resented us for living. Then he started to get really nasty."

"What about your parents?" Jurtan asked.

Max snorted. "Shut up," Eden instructed him. "I'm telling this."

Max pulled the hat off his face, sat up, and addressed Jurtan. "The fact that their father had been totally devoted to Arznaak and was never particularly interested in the twins gave Arznaak the perfect way to extend his nonsense permanently through their lives. Both of them are too pigheaded to admit it, but all that means is that they got it from their father in the first place. Half of this was his fault, but none of them wants to do a damn thing about it."

Eden sighed. "We go over this every time we get together, Max," she said. "You want to waste the time all over again?"

"Damn fools," Max grumbled, but he scrunched down in his chair and smashed his hat once more back over his face.

"Okay," said Eden. For someone Max was calling pigheaded, Jurtan thought she sounded pretty objective about the whole thing. Befitting the family's rank and station in Peridol's economy and society, the Shaas had received the best education and training. This had fallen on fertile ground. Eden and Zalzyn showed widespread and overlapping natural talents, but each had gravitated toward different interests. Zalzyn's high aptitude for magic and math along with the Shaas' favorable family connections had promised a brilliant career, conceivably culminating as the head of the Imperial Institute of Thaumaturgy. Eden, on the other hand, had the makings of a significant politician and businessperson. Arznaak? Well, Arznaak had the aptitudes, too, but to Eden it had been clear he wanted more.

"The throne?" asked Jurtan.

"It wouldn't surprise me for a minute," Eden stated. But whatever Arznaak wanted, he wanted it his way.

"The Shaas are a creative lot," said Max. He took another swig from the brew Cleeve had passed to him. "Arznaak's just nastier than the rest. Hurry it up, the kid and I have to get moving."

"What a guy," said Eden. "You show up every five years and the first thing you want to do is leave."

"You didn't have to let me in."

"Next time you'd better watch out for the alarm. So, Jurtan Mont, now you know the story."

I do? thought Jurtan. *No I don't, not all of it anyway.* Maybe it was another test. "Arznaak wanted to take away whatever you liked most, is that it? You can't leave this estate, Shaa can't come back to it, the only time the two of you can get together at all is when he uses magic and you're forced to attack him? He can't practice magic and you can't be out where you can do business or politics." What else had he heard from Shaa? "Neither one of you can find love, either, can you."

Eden regarded Max with a sidelong glance, which he acknowledged only by increasing the intensity of his stare off into the distance. "Sure we can," said Eden. "All we have to do is follow the rules."

"So why not just get rid of Arznaak? I mean, you hate him by now, don't you?"

"It's not that simple."

"What my good friend is referring to there," Max broke in, "is wily old Arznaak's *coup de grâce* twist-of-the-knife. As Arznaak knows full well, his siblings bind themselves by rules he doesn't even bother to sneer at."

Eden sat with her arms crossed and her face locked in a scowl, saying nothing.

" 'He's the only one of you worth a second glance,' " Max continued, "isn't that what he said? The last words of your beloved father?"

"An oath is an oath," said Eden in a low voice, her teeth gritted.

"What your mentor's sister is trying not to tell you here," Max said to Jurtan in a conversational tone, "is that Arznaak's curse keyed off the death of their father, the same father who thought Arznaak was the gods' own gift to the mortal world, the same father who made Eden and Shaa swear to support good old Arznaak and keep him safe from harm. Old Pops wanted to make sure they wouldn't attack their brother or even let anyone else go after him, and he was such a wise old guy and was so good to them all that—"

"That's enough, Max," said Eden.

"You want enough? I'll tell you what enough is. I'm out there year after year breaking my back trying to find a loophole through your curse or a way around it because neither one of you fools want to let me solve the problem at the root. Damn Peridol and its goddamned code of honor, and damn all—"

"Are you finished?"

"No, I'm not finished, I—"

"Then just shut up, why don't you," Eden snapped. "Nobody's forcing you to help us. If you can't do things the way we have to do them, we don't want your help."

"Pretty big words," said Max. "I don't think your brother would agree."

"I think he would. I may not be able to talk to him, but that doesn't mean I don't still know the way he thinks. You follow our code or get out of our lives."

"Don't give me that nonsense."

"Then get out of my house."

Max cursed under his breath. "You're stubborn as ever. You don't leave me much maneuver room."

"That's the idea."

"Fine," said Max. "So that's the way you want it. I'll think about it."

"Think fast."

". . . All right already, all right."

"Swear."

Max looked thoroughly disgusted. "I've sworn before, dammit. All right, I swear again, I'll do things your way. Are you happy? Now let me out of here."

"What," said Eden, "with no situation update, no coordination? You mean this was just a social call, just because you were in the neighborhood? I'm flattered. There must be a first time for everything."

"The world would be a lot simpler if your brother was an only child," Max muttered. "Either one of them. All right, let's coordinate, why don't we."

Eden's face conspicuously fell, except for a sardonic twist that remained in the corner of her mouth. Jurtan had seen exactly the same expression before, on Zalzyn Shaa. Seeing it here, on her, was weird, but compared to the other items on the local scale of eccentricity you had to admit it was pretty far down. "So much for the dream of sociability," Eden said. "In time perhaps I will get over the wound. The most recent update concerns the arrival of my brother and the boat this morning. Zolly had some kind of run-in at the dock, I don't have details on it yet. He'll be staying at his city house."

"And Arznaak?"

Eden shrugged. "He's around. He was here last week, but he's really living in town now."

"I brought some papers out of the swamp I want to show you while I'm here. Why don't we head back to the house?"

Jurtan fell in to his accustomed position, trailing Max as they strolled up the lawn toward the estate house. Eden and Max were speaking together in low voices ahead of him, but even if they had been talking in a normal voice and addressing Jurtan directly he wasn't certain he'd have heard anything they said. He had too much on his mind as it was. In fact, they were in the house with the Iskendarian papers spread out before them on a table, and Jurtan had a largely devoured plate of chicken at his elbow, before he began to pay attention again to what was going on around him.

"I don't know," Eden was saying, shuffling papers back into a stack. "See what Zolly has to say; he's the real scholar in the family anyway. Wait a minute—you should talk to some of the old-line religionists, too. They claim to trace their lineage back before the Dislocation; they probably have a lot of old-language stuff hidden away."

"Huh," said Max. "An interesting idea. Which group are you thinking about, the One God cultists or the God is Everywhere gang?"

"The family has some contacts with the One God people," Eden said.

"One God?" said Jurtan. "Who in their right mind would believe in only one god?"

"Some of us don't believe in *any*," Max observed.

"These cultists have a more transcendental perspective," explained Eden. "They feel that the rough-and-tumble present-day polytheism gets in the way of confronting the real issues of the divine."

"If a gang of super-powered hooligans are in your face all the time, it's difficult to get clear of the image they create," Max added. "The old-line cults think gods should be more exemplary than obviously out for their own good. More primal. As you'd imagine, there aren't a whole lot of these cult folks left."

"If they might know something, why haven't you gotten together with them before now?" said Jurtan.

"I'm only one person," said Max. "I've got limits."

"Let me go talk to them, then," Jurtan said. "Tell me what you want to know and where to find them and I'll do it."

Max looked at Jurtan, and a querulous clarinet trilled in the back of Jurtan's head. "You mean try to get some useful contribution out of you?" Max said.

"Maybe. But there's something else I want to try with you first."

Jurtan didn't know whether he liked the sound of that. He didn't like the present state of affairs either, though, and he had to acknowledge that he couldn't easily have it both ways. "Whatever you say," he said. "Let me know."

8

If nothing else, I thought I might be getting more efficient. To have the mystery of my dream present itself and almost immediately get resolved, at the same time introducing new questions of an increased level of urgency, opened new horizons of competence and high performance. There was no denying it *had* been efficient: all I'd had to do to pierce Joatal Ballista's disguise and realize he was really Fradjikan was to show up. I *was* supposed to be a detective, after all, but maybe my real contribution to the field was going to rest in figuring out how to eliminate legwork, substituting for it pure reason or the power of mind. Of course, I may have now known that Ballista was Fradjikan, but I still didn't have any idea who Fradjikan was and why he might be important.

About my traveling companion I'd discovered practically nothing. Of course, he could probably say the same thing about me. In fact, as the miles had gone past under the wheels of the carriage, the man who called himself Ballista had begun looking more than a little disgruntled. I knew I couldn't have given him much of anything to work on concerning me. The fact that he clearly *was* working on me, however, did make the situation more interesting, as if it really needed that. It was possible he was just some operator who never got out of bed in the morning without pulling on his cloak of suspicion and was, as a result, merely keeping his hand in. It *was* possible, and if it was the case, then I'd be out nothing but a little time and effort spent worrying about him and wondering what he was up to, and trying to pierce his secrets. The same would be true of him.

Unless the same *wasn't* true of him, which was plainly the safe way to bet. After all, I *had* spent my solitary dream to date visualizing him. That had to be good for something. Add to that the experience of last night, too. There had been no particular reason for Ballista to insist on stopping at the tavern and laying over to morning when we had been in sight of the lights of Peridol. His excuse concerning the danger of pressing into the city at night, what with the streets crowded with ne'er-do-wells, dangerous sorts from the hinterlands and the rough sections of town, and, well, crowds in general, was out of keeping with his forcefully projected self-image as a fear-nothing man-of-arms. The added fact that once ensconced in the tavern he had done his best to ply me with drink, an effort I had cooperated with more than not, to such an extent that even now, midway through the next morning, my memory was still patchy and my consciousness skipping in and out, implied . . . implied. . . .

Where was I? Oh, right. He was trying to find out who I was and what I knew. Whatever I knew or didn't know, I had certainly done the same thing often enough in my own work to recognize it when it was aimed at me.

That apparently hadn't been the only reason for last night's stop, though. Through the haze of spotty memory, I did remember a time when Lowell, the driver, had come in from the yard to nod pointedly at Ballista, followed a few minutes later by Ballista slipping outside himself when he thought I had passed out on top of the table. I hadn't passed out, though, at least not that time, and so I remembered him reentering the common room fifteen minutes or so later, allowing himself an expression of satisfaction which vanished as soon as I began to sputter and stir. I would have crept after him to observe his mission except that Lowell had stayed behind to keep an eye on me. That, and the fact that I thought creeping might very well have been beyond me at that point, given the quantity of reactants I had already consumed.

On his return Ballista had downed a few also, although not enough to lay him out, and not enough to loosen *his* tongue, either. I'd thought he might let something slip when he thought I was in no state to absorb it, but that hope went unfulfilled. He was being equally unforthcoming this morning. For some reason he did seem slightly more keyed-up, almost expectant, and I caught him darting a few sharp glances at me out of the corner of my eye when he thought I was looking out the window or nursing my headache. I actually wasn't hung over, not really, but I didn't see any point in telling him that.

If the truth be told, I really had been more than half hoping for another dream. The first one had taken the trouble to point Ballista/Fradjikan out, after all, so I thought it wasn't unreasonable to expect another hint, if not outright elucidation. But no. I'd woken with the residual feeling that whatever had caused the first dream was still lurking around, its feelers hanging out, but was not ready to reveal itself again. It sounds absurd to anthropomorphize the internal workings of my own mind, I know, but on the other hand whatever might be hidden there was certainly uncharted land. In any case, as much time as I'd been spending lately in self-absorption, there was coming to be even more to pay attention to in the outside world.

During my years in Roosing Oolvaya, which is to say during the only stretch of memory my mind was willing to divulge, I had left the city on a number of occasions, and several times for extended periods. I'd never made it to Peridol, though. I'd seen a few other cities, even brought a guy to ground in Edgerton, which was the biggest place anywhere at all close to Roosing Oolvaya's vicinity, but compared to Peridol any place I'd ever been was no better than second rate.

Fact is, compared to Peridol *any* place built by man is no more than second rate.

It's one thing to know that as abstract book learning, however, and another thing to see what it meant in practice. The road outside the inn had widened before we'd reached the tavern the previous afternoon, and even at night when we'd stopped there had been enough traffic to make it seem busy. This morning, though, Lowell had had to virtually force his way out of the gate and edge carefully into the flow. The sun had been up a few hours by the time we'd left, too, so we'd even missed the predawn and early morning peak influx of farm-fresh goods from the agricultural areas into the city. Judging from the cargoes still on the highway, though, it was apparent the farm trade was a day-round affair. Although we were fortunately out at the wrong time to need to tangle with sheep drivers, the cackle of chickens and the flapping of fish still fresh from the sea was prominent around us. The smell of the fish wasn't the only aroma rising in the morning sun, either. You could have distilled a pretty hearty stew from the odors alone, what with a veritable fruit and vegetable cocktail from the wagons—citrus, pears, melons; cabbage, onions, tomato; and the occasional head of beef or straggling lamb.

As we drove on at a crawl, unable to break free of knots of people on foot, on horses, in carts, leading donkeys and oxen, and jostling in carriages like ours, the road continued to widen, but the traffic kept thickening even faster than that. Where yesterday we had driven through towns and villages separated by stretches of countryside, this morning the towns had grown larger and the countryside more scarce, until now we were for all intents within the outskirts of Peridol itself.

Peridol as a whole wasn't known for its architecture; surely not, since so much of it was a warren of overgrown slums crowded with folks who'd headed for the city looking for the streets of gold. Not surprisingly, though, given the business the road traffic surely generated, the area surrounding the highway looked fairly prosperous. Befitting Peridol's southerly location and moderate, sunny climate, adobe and stucco predominated, with an excess of baked-tile roofs in shades of red and orange. The walls and courtyards were hung with banners and iconic signs advertising the wares of the businesses within. Here and there were expanses of Peridol's notorious broadsheets press-printed in rolls and rudely plastered by roving glue-gangs on the sides of anything vertical—houses, retaining walls, trees, parked carriages, even across closed gates and the doors and windows of houses. While the broadsheets themselves extolled the virtues of shops and emporiums, soap and flea-powder, nostrums and ales and patent horseshoes, emblematic of the move toward group-production in the new city manufactories, to me they spoke as much of the restless energy of people suppressed by the hand of the gods, yet still searching like the subterranean fire of the volcano for an outlet to the air.

As far as I knew, the gods hadn't yet made a ruling one way or the other on Peridol's emerging mercantilistic fervor. Because of the gods' sponsorship of the Empire and its rulers, and by extension Peridol itself, the city was enough of a special case to sometimes get away with stuff that would be flattened in a moment anywhere else. City dwellers like to push the edge of limits, though, and Peridolians were the city dwellers *par excellence;* just the sort the gods I knew would enjoy taking down. Still, if the gods were going to lay down the law, it didn't seem likely they'd do it during a Knitting. Half the point of a Knitting, after all, was its element of let-loose free-for-all, when normal restrictions didn't necessarily apply.

Not all of that assessment was purely analytical. At least a bit was due to out-and-out wishful thinking. If something was going to break loose, I was hoping it would wait until I'd left town.

Of course, if I ran into any of my god acquaintances I could ask them what was up. With the struggle going

on between the Abdicationists, those gods who wanted
to pull back and let the world screw itself up to its
heart's content without interference from them, and
the Conservationists, who figured they had such a good
deal running it would be crazy to change, it was possible that the transitions in Peridol were part of the
active debate. That much was speculation; I didn't
know enough about the politics of the gods to tell for
certain. I'd only picked up the fringes of the argument
from Zhardann and Jill, who were Conservationists of
some stripe, and I hadn't gotten any more than that
from Gash, who probably didn't have much more of a
fixed ideology than unwavering support for himself.
I'd probably learned more from my brief exchange with
Phlinn Arol, who'd seemed surprisingly Abdicationist
in sentiment, than I had in days around the others.
Whether I'd learned enough to meddle remained to be
seen.

Ballista had been wearing an increasingly annoyed
expression as the carriage lurched along in its spasmodic fits and starts. Sliding open the panel at the
front of the cab, he leaned through to commune with
Lowell, trying to convince him to lay about with his
whip. Lowell, quite intelligently I thought, had the
opinion that the crowd would be only too happy to
vent its own frustration by overturning the vehicle and
stomping it to splinters. Ballista sank back into the
cushions and regarded me. "Your first time in Peridol?" he said.

"Aye, that it is."

"Where will you go when we part?"

I shrugged. "Fortune awaits. For that matter, perhaps I'll just get out here. From the looks of it I'd
make at least as a good a time on foot."

"Afoot," he said disgustedly. "You may be right.
If Lowell—"

Just at that moment, though, Lowell spotted his opportunity, a smaller side street winding in from the
right. He veered the horses through a small knot of
people balancing fagots of wood on their heads, send-

ing branches and logs flying, and hurtled straight for the nearest wall. The coach scraped against the edge of a building just in front of my window and caromed off, but as the vehicle rocked sharply back from the impact we were through the crowd and into the alley. Hooves and rattling wheels echoed back from the close-set buildings. Winding a serpentine path, people reeling against the walls as we hurtled toward them, the street led us to another, then another. Just as I was about to wonder aloud if Lowell had any idea where he was going, the alley debouched into a wider street. The new avenue again had traffic, but this time a dedicated lane for vehicles as well.

It wasn't a street, it was a highway, in fact the main highway pointed at Peridol from the east. It was straight, too. Up ahead, several miles away to be sure, beyond the depressingly short stretch where wheeled traffic was moving forward at a solid pace, the road lifted in a broad span; that had to be one of the big Tongue Water bridges.

Beside me, Ballista snapped shut a pocket-watch and stowed it away. "Late for an appointment?" I asked.

"Possibly," he said. Then he added, apparently as an afterthought, "If they know what's good for them, they'll wait."

I turned back and looked out the window. I stared idly at the passing crowds and houses for a moment, but then when I glanced ahead again we were almost at the bridge.

Huh? I thought. We couldn't have gone that far that quickly, especially since the traffic had once more ground to a crawl. My bout with the brew of the previous night must have affected me more than I'd realized. Anyway you cut it, it was weird, though. I'd slipped out and back into consciousness so smoothly I hadn't even realized I'd nodded off.

Unless it hadn't been the aftereffect of the liquor. What if brew hadn't been the only thing I'd consumed? What if Fradjikan had slipped me some drug, too? It wouldn't be the first time for me. I didn't feel narcotized, but I had enough experience in these things to know that didn't necessarily mean anything. There were a lot of jungles out there, and in the jungles no end of herbs, shrubs, vegetables, trees, mushrooms, and assorted saprophytes just oozing with pharma-coactive sap and pollen, not to mention the legions of beetles, insects, grubs, and other chemical factories on the hoof. Folks spent their careers hunting out and distilling the stuff; there were guilds, dynasties, societies, and more freelancers than you could count.

Maybe Shaa could figure it out. Were there any other symptoms I could identify, any new impediments to my bodily functions or processes of thought, any untoward cravings, any . . . wait a minute. Did I think that? When did I start running off at the mind like some cheap paid-by-the-word potboiler poet? I tried to remember back. Could it be that my thought patterns and my trains of words were occasionally becoming more lyrical than I was used to?

But how do you pin something like that down, anyway? People change, they evolve. Unless it's blatant, how do you tell some drug's been tinkering with your mind?

"I hope you have nothing to hide," said Ballista.

"Huh?" I said. "Why's that?"

He gestured ahead. I leaned my head out the window and craned ahead, learning in the process from the stiffness in my neck and creaking in my shoulders that my skeleton, at least, had witnessed the passing of time that my consciousness had ignored. From this vantage point, though, I could now see one of the major causes of the congestion on the approach to the bridge. The highway had entered an area where warehouses and light manufactories were crammed together, elbowed apart only by irregular streets and alleys that twisted their ways off into a dark maze beyond. Foot and mounted police and highway guards had been visible in occasional knots. They were keeping the traffic orderly and in motion, I suppose, but even more than that they seemed to have their eyes on

the district behind them. I'd had the feeling they were
there to keep raiders from darting out of their lurking-
dens and harassing the highway traffic. If you were a
desperado, it looked like a perfectly good tactic. You
could strike and be gone, losing any pursuit in the
deadly tangle of what could only be the notorious
Stainside slums. That didn't mean the police deploy-
ment wasn't workable, too, but there was clearly a lot
more Stainside than there were of them. The police
forces were bolstered by numerous small forces of bul-
lyboys and toughmen apparently fielded by business
owners and local industry associations.

Any way you sliced it, though, this was clearly not
an area to stop off for the night or put your feet up for
a quiet meal and a pipe.

Nevertheless, as I saw now, leaning out the .window,
these keeping-the-peace activities were not the only
mission the greater Peridol police force was conduct-
ing in the area. "They're not seriously trying to screen
everyone heading over the bridge," I said, "are they?
They've got to be kidding."

"Perhaps they've received some particular tip," said
Ballista. "There have been reports of unrest, various
dissident groups entering the city and the like. The Empire has some sensitivity about irredentist sentiments
boiling over during the Knitting."

"If you say so." But they *couldn't* be serious. Between this bridge and the others there had to be thousands of people entering the city. And what about
boats? Yet there they were, several platoons worth of
foot and another troop of horse funneling the traffic
down and examining each entrant closely as they
waved them through. As I watched, a cart filled with
wheat in sacks was pulled aside for a more detailed
inspection. Traffic headed in the opposite direction was
much more sparse which may have had something to
do with the fact that it was clearly swimming upstream
against the cataract, but even it was meriting attention
from the authorities.

Fortunately I didn't have anything to hide, or at least

not anything that could be picked out by a frisking cop. Even the fact that the checkpoint wasn't staffed by cops alone, attested to by the slightly membranous sheen of the curtain of air hanging across the road in the midst of the squad, shouldn't make any difference to me. Most everyone seemed oblivious to the curtain's presence, even though it was rippling with constant surface waves, while each live being passing through it sparked a brief polychromatic aurora resonating from their aura. The controlling sorcerer was seated off to the side on a keg, the strands of the curtain winding into a collator matrix suspended in the air in front of her. Every so often she'd speak to the sergeant next to her or just point someone out with a finger, and that person would be stopped for additional interrogation.

From this distance, it was impossible to determine the curtain's own interrogation sensitivity or the settings of the collator. It was a surprisingly high-order construct to find in civil service, but then Peridol obviously could afford the best. Even so, I was sure I'd pass through it without a peep, which had its bad side as well as its good. At this point, I wouldn't have necessarily minded elucidation on my situation whatever its source.

As I'd expected, though, no such elucidation was forthcoming. We drew abreast of the inspection area, passed placidly through the probe curtain, and proceeded ahead up the bridge. Moving through the curtain, I'd felt a brief dancing tingle that was sort of the reverse of being pricked with tiny needles; more like a crew of invisible tailors had attached threads to my skin and clothes and were all tugging and reweaving simultaneously in an attempt to turn me into a spasmodic marionette. Fradjikan/Ballista squirmed in his seat, scratched his side with one hand and his back with the other, and muttered something about inadequate bath conditions on the road.

I hadn't figured him for a magic-user, and it didn't look like he had the kind of pipeline into one's perceptions that the metabolic link to Gashanatantra gave me, so I wasn't surprised he'd misinterpreted what had happened. It was more amazing to me that I hadn't. My ability to pull information out of Gash was apparently still getting better. Either that or the link improved at close range and Gash was somewhere in the city up ahead. I wondered what would happen when the link was finally cut. Would I retain the capabilities I'd soaked up, or would I be back to the status of a blind infant as far as my rapport with sorcery was concerned? Could I actually be getting *attached* to the idea of being magically literate?

"There is a square beyond the bridge," said Ballista. "Perhaps you would like to disembark there."

"Fine with me," I said. The central section of the bridge was a free span far enough off the high-water mark for a clipper ship to pass underneath and wide enough so the ship could probably tack while it was slipping through, too. Multiple arches sunk into caissons stretched both directions back toward the shore. To the left I could see another bridge of similar construction, and some distance off on the right a lower span with a winched-up drawbridge section. Although I'd obviously never visited the Tongue Water before, the rows of docks and wharves lining both banks south toward the Hook, the congestion in the channel (which was of a density virtually matching that of the land), and the distinct reek of sea water liberally salted with sewage certainly were everything I had imagined.

And then there was the island city of Peridol proper stretching out ahead—the hill of the Crust with its sparkling mansions, the ancient metal towers of the palace complex, everywhere the sprawl of house and hovel and temple, slum and precinct and parish, industry and business and commerce. Amidst the chimney plumes and haze of smoke from wood, coal, and wizard fires, the lakes and sward of Mathom Park adjoining the palace walls still glittered green and silver in the sun. Then we were on the downward slope of the bridge, and the buildings at the shore rose up to block from sight the view.

The traffic entered a canyon of soot-stained wood and stone. Beneath the wheels, the road surface, which had been alternating between paving slabs and the newer asphalt-and-stone, changed back to cobblestones; some of the side streets we passed, though, had no other pavement than gravel or dirt. The highway wound off and lost size to diverging tributaries like tentacles leaving the body of an octopus. We rounded another bend and debouched into Ballista's square. It was an open space only in the sense that it lacked major buildings; the din and the crush more than filled in the gap.

This was apparently the destination of many of the farmers and herders we'd joined on the road. Beyond a large sheep paddock and an adjoining area for wholesale butchering stretched a tangle of stalls and carts, each piled with produce and tenanted by gesticulating hucksters, one here waving by the neck a plucked chicken, one there brandishing a carp, another juggling apples, all yelling and arguing simultaneously as they tried to convert strollers into customers and the glint in an eye into cash. As far as the eye could imagine were throngs of dog sellers, flower girls, flypaper merchants in dilapidated top hats decorated with grimy samples of their wares, hardware dealers, tinkers, ragmen, knife grinders, gingerbeer men, apple sellers, oyster men, match vendors, lemonade hawkers mixing their vile brew on the spot in tubs, and even a few bold fellows offering oranges and other citrus fruits full in the skin and fresh from the tree, or so they were crying. The smells hit with the same impact as the sights, an assault of saddle soap, leather, brass polish, strong tobacco, wood fires, baking bread, roasting meat, fresh and rotting produce, and people whose relationship with bathing water was at best hypothetical. "I'll get out here," I said.

"I see a bit of an alcove off to the side," said Fradjikan. "Lowell can pull up there."

There *was* an alcove of sorts, but as far as I was concerned one place in this tumult seemed as good as any other. Still, I had a vague hunch tickling at the edge of my mind. If Fradjikan wanted to set the agenda, I could do worse than see where it might lead. "Thanks," I said, shoving open the door and leaning out. I elbowed aside a street urchin with his hand out for contributions and jumped down into the vacated space. "See you around."

"Oh, yes," I thought I heard him mutter under his breath, and then the carriage pulled slowly away.

I had a rendezvous address from Shaa and no idea how to get there, and no useful orientation to where I was, either. At my back was Fradjikan's alcove, a hollow between the dark brick walls of two buildings fronting on the square; the depths of the alcove were fenced off with a stout iron rail and a hedge. Ahead of me was a row of stalls arrayed around an ornate fountain with some sort of stone-and-verdigris civic monument in its center. I started for the stalls. If I could get directions from one of the sellers under the guise of negotiations for purchase that would be best, but if worse came to worse there might be an explanatory plaque on the monument.

Some kind of minor disturbance was getting underway there, I noticed then, as I made my way forward. The shouting was perhaps a little louder than the rest of the din. That much was unremarkable. The unusual part was the way a row of stalls was shuddering back and forth. Then all the stalls were more than shuddering, they were literally shaking themselves apart. Thatch and netting flew into the air, rods and boards scattered, produce went rolling. A plucked chicken went arching over my head. As the stalls fell away, the fountain was clearly revealed.

The pool was frothing with whitecaps and the water jets were wildly spraying over everything in sight. What they were spraying foamed and sizzled, though, and seemed (although this might have been an illusion) to be turning red rather than the clear of pure water or even the green of algae and scum. A wave of water, now unmistakably red, broke over the stone retaining wall and frothed over the remains of half a dozen food stalls. Under the water the wood ignited. With a < w h o o m ! > that sent me reeling back a pace the liquid boiled out in a ball of flame. Coils of fire writhed up.

But the tendrils of fire weren't random. They were forming letters.

Another word took shape partway around the fountain, rooted in the remains of a wagon. In the common script, it seemed to say "FREE KEN," and over on the other side was "RIGHTS FOR". I was trying to remember what Fradjikan had been talking about earlier, that bit about irredentist sentiments and the possibility of terrorism, when the rearing equestrian statue in the middle of the fountain began to creak and move.

This is not my problem, I thought. The upraised foreleg of the stone horse pawed the air, five feet above my head, and the regal-looking rider glanced around, brandishing his skyward-pointed sword. The sword may have been stone, but it was now showing a wicked edge and at least the gleam of steel. Beneath the horse in the center of the fountain a pulsing glow was visible through the cascading water.

I squinted through the mist. Forcelines were warping into that glow, into a spinning orb. Even from this distance, I could detect the presence of matrix programming and a catalytic power source. *It's* not *my problem,* I tried to remind myself, but no one else was stepping forward, the crowd was starting to reach that edge of panic that would convert it into a trampling mob, and that sword was starting to cut swaths out of the air as its wielder eyed the people around it with increasing interest.

I yanked my walking stick out from its perch atop my pack and dropped the pack on the ground. The urchin kid who'd accosted me getting out of the carriage was still at my heels. I dug a coin out of my belt and showed it to him. "There's two more for you if you watch this pack," I told him. "The money's worth more than anything you could get for the stuff, and anyway I'd come after you and I guarantee you wouldn't like that. Deal?"

The kid took the coin, bit it, and grinned widely, his expression missing a few of the customarily expected teeth. "What's going on, mister?"

"Stick around and watch. Damn it." A complete wall of flame-drawn words encircled the fountain. The surface of the fountain and the lashing waves were ablaze, too, the fires mounting to the belly of the prancing horse. I could have easily stood upright under the horse, or rather it would have been easy except for the fire and the water and the energy with which the horse was stomping around. The rider leaned low across the horse's neck and scythed around with the sword. The blade swished through the fires around the fountain and chopped through the remains of a stall.

When the stalls had fallen over a moment ago, they had trapped a knot of people beneath them who were now frantically trying to dig their way out. The sword lifted up and the rider leaned out further, preparing to chop.

I had the walking stick in my hand. It was humming, vibrating, virtually dragging me forward. I've always known I'm not the world's greatest swordsman. Especially after seeing Max and even Shaa I could tell what class I'm in, and it's not theirs. I'm competent, though, or enough to get by with under normal circumstances anyway, especially since detecting is a lot more brainwork than swordwork, or at least it's supposed to be if you're doing it right. But I'd already done whatever detecting was appropriate to the situation; that spinning orb was the source of this manifestation, and given that it was shielded to magic beyond my minimal level of expertise the only way to take it out would be to smash it.

The stone horse had splashed over to the edge of the fountain and looked about ready to trot out of it entirely. I took a last glance around. I thought I glimpsed Fradjikan's carriage still off to the side, but neither he nor anyone else was volunteering their services. I subvocalized the call to Monoch and stepped forward.

Immediately I was stumbling, almost falling to one knee as a vise grabbed my hand and twisted me around toward the ground. Somehow I kept my balance and came out of the almost-fall hurtling forward in a dead run. Cold flames sheathed my own hand, tearing back from the outline of the walking stick; then the outline firmed into the rune-etched metal of a very nasty sword indeed. Monoch had arrived.

I hadn't unleashed him lately. We'd had words about that, or whatever passed for words when you were communicating with a testy sword. Flaming swords are not exactly unobtrusive in the best of circumstances, and of course I'd been trying to be surreptitious rather than making a scene of myself, but the most important reason I'd kept Monoch under wraps was that I'd managed to avoid a fight. Over the same period, of course, I'd been getting my increased handle on recognizing the presence of sorcery and being able to analyze it, through the link to Gash. Monoch was also a link to Gash, though. I hadn't known whether letting him loose would enhance or degrade the other side of the link, but what I certainly hadn't expected was that Monoch would start giving me advice.

The sword was recommending tactics, or to be more precise it was taking the tactical situation completely into its own hands. We rushed forward, Monoch now low and trailing behind me, concealed by my body from the animated statue. Between us and the fountain, though, was still the billboard of flame. It was real flame, too, not an illusion, as some of the people who'd been standing close had discovered to their misfortune. Some had escaped with charred clothing or singed eyebrows, but several folks I passed on the way in were showing blisters or open red skin. I tried to aim for the space between "DOWNTRODDEN" and

''PEOPLE,'' dropped my head, and put on an extra burst of speed. As I drew up to the barrier, though, the flames on each side leaned together and wrapped their tendrils toward me.

Something went < c l i c k > in the back of my head. I heard a brief garbled mumble, as though someone's five-minute recitation had been compressed into a half-second burst, and saw a matching blur of symbols streak through my mind. The flames around me froze. I mean, they not only paused in their writhing, they went from plasma to dripping solids with arctic gusts boiling off them as the still-active fires on either side got to work vaporizing them. Remarkable as that was, there were still other things to attend to. Looking down from his twenty-foot height ahead of me straight into my eyes was the stone glare of the horse's rider.

He brought his sword around in a vast arc parallel to the ground. Monoch had anticipated this, though, and had vectored me in just barely on the same side of the horse as the rider's sword arm. I now cut to the right under the horse's neck, bent low, and scrambled along the base of the fountain.

A large splash sounded behind me as I stood back up and a wall of flaming water broke over the fountain's lip and spilled full over me. Whatever it was that was causing the water to ignite, oil or magic or aqueous camphor, all it did was hiss and crackle when it hit my body. In fact, I didn't even quite feel it hit; it was more like the fluid decided a half inch or so over my clothes that it didn't want to fall on me after all and ran down instead, as though I was wearing an invisible shell rather than the same old outfit stained from the sea and the road. Water splashed again; the rider had given up trying to reach me from his off-side with the sword, and the horse was repositioning itself while the stone guy hoisted the sword over his head and brought it down on the near side toward me. I hopped the ledge around the fountain and dropped into the water.

The horse's left foreleg was within reach and Monoch was ready. As I swung, Monoch let loose with his best beehive whine and laid a wheel of silver fire in the air. The impact rattled my joints from my wrists up to my shoulders and down my spine into my knees, but when my teeth clattered back into their sockets I saw a clean cut halfway through. Monoch had already pulled free and was urging me on. I dove ahead under the horse's belly as the rider's sword plunged down into the space I'd just left.

My dive hadn't taken me far since I'd started waist-deep in water. Monoch was already waving again in the air, though, and was dragging me back to my feet. I braced myself and did what he wanted. Both hands clenched on the hilt, I swung as hard as I could straight up in the air.

We hit stone. This time the blow was more shove than slice. I cast a quick glance over my shoulder as the shadow overhead shifted and gave way to light. With the rider still off-balance on the other side of the horse and trying to recover from his downward slash, the horse had stepped reflexively down with its damaged foreleg to try to stabilize itself. The push we'd just given had put even more pressure on that side, and now as the damaged stone shattered the horse was starting to go down.

Ahead through the flame-capped water was the controlling orb. A wave from the thrashing horse caught me from behind and washed me toward it. Then a jet of water punched into my chest and knocked me over backward. A ring of stone water jets were between me and the orb, and they were swiveling down like crossbows to take aim at me. I drew in breath and dove.

A two-footed kick and a few frantic strokes with my free arm later Monoch told me to plant my legs and swing. I broke water and let loose, and the waterjet I'd drawn within range of went flying. The others were creaking as they cranked themselves around. Behind me, the horse was lying on its belly on the bottom but had managed to remain upright, and the rider was reaching out for me. I drew Monoch back like a spear and then thrust forward, pushing off the bottom at the same time.

I had planned to let go of his hilt, too, and launch him like a javelin, but Monoch was having none of that. The sword hurtled ahead with more thrust than I'd launched it. Just as I realized Monoch was not letting my fingers let go, the pull of the sword started to try to yank my arms out of their sockets at the shoulder. Instead, my shoulders held, but my feet left the ground and then broke the surface of the water entirely. We still weren't going to make it. The band of mist was in reach, and I could feel the exact position of the control orb inside it, but even this mad lunge was going to fall short.

I didn't know what would happen if we did slice up the orb. We might set loose some booby-trap terminal defense system or cause a chain reaction between the orb's field and Monoch's own bound-in magic. The orb might even be resistant to physical attack. I knew what would happen if we didn't, though. I would go headfirst into the water, the water jets would make it into position to bear on me, and before I could get out of the way that big stone sword was going to come down on my head.

Except Monoch had another trick he hadn't mentioned. He took dead aim on the orb at the limit of our lunge and stretched. I thought the bones of my forearm had separated from the rest of my body at the elbow, but that hadn't been the purpose of his last maneuver. The middle part of the blade narrowed and squeezed another foot of rapier-stuff out the tip, spearing the orb neatly through its middle, and Monoch's silver flames flowed out to surround it. The orb cracked like a shattered egg. Its released field-lines went flailing into the air. That's when I finally *did* smash full-length into the water, and in the commotion I gave up on following exactly what happened next.

When I made it back to my feet and stopped coughing up water, the fires on the water and the flaming messages had gone out. The water jets were frozen in gnarled shapes, pointing every which-way. They had gone back to being normal stone, though, as had the looming figure of the stone general leaning in toward the center of the fountain, his sword just over my head. Although it was an unusual posture for a statue, it did project a sense of motion and the fever of action, so it was probably an improvement to the aesthetics of the monument overall.

Monoch was back to his normal sword-shape, but his hilt was still apparently bonded to my hand. "I've got to give you credit," I told him. "I figured you for just a hack-and-slash blood drinker, but those moves were pretty slick."

I had the feeling that Monoch wasn't too unhappy with me either. I spoke the words that would send him back to his stealth mode, and he didn't even complain about that. Now all I had to do was leave the area before somebody decided to do something about *me*. Whether they'd want to throw me a party or throw me in jail, attention was still the last thing I was looking for. I slogged as fast as I could toward the exit.

Out beyond the charred wreckage of the stalls, the dazed crowd was just starting to pull itself together. I spotted the kid with my pack, though; I hoped I'd held onto my pocket change. At the back of the plaza I thought I saw the top of a familiar carriage. I couldn't tell for sure but it wouldn't have surprised me in the least. Why wouldn't Fradjikan hang around to see what happened? Wasn't he the one who'd gotten me into this, after all?

9

So that was the story behind the walking stick; a flaming sword. And Fradjikan hadn't picked up the slightest hint. He *had* been interested in Spilkas, even if it had had more to do with circumstance than deductive logic, but still that had to be good for something.

Flaming swords were undetectable to the magically untrained eye, and usually (in their hidden mode) to the sorcerously cognizant as well. They *were* secret weapons, after all. Those Fradjikan had heard about, never having encountered (to his knowledge) one himself, tended to hide themselves as normal swords, though, making their magical manifestation a much less flagrant affair. By all accounts there weren't too many of the things around in any guise, however, which might make it possible to track down this one's pedigree, and through it Spilkas' own.

Spilkas himself had proved to have more surprises than merely the sword. He'd been rather impressive, in fact. Fradjikan had put the odds against Spilkas taking the initiative to involve himself in suppressing the fountain and statue's threat. As it had turned out, the element Fradjikan had put in place that would have drawn Spilkas in, whatever his will, had not even required activation.

Given the involvement of Spilkas, whether willing or not, Fradi had also doubted that the resolution of his encounter with the statue would have seen him alive, much less ambulatory. The plan would not have strictly required either. It therefore was pleasant to realize that the aesthetics would now be significantly enhanced by having Spilkas encounter his fate while still incarnate. That also meant Spilkas would remain available for use in the more advanced play that was rapidly coming up.

Lowell, from the sound of it apparently laying about with his whip, finally breached an exit from the square. The fountain area with its heroic statue now once again frozen into stone slipped around the corner and was lost to sight, even though Fradjikan craned his neck from the side window for one last glimpse. Ah, well. The next step would be to get the image to the—

He was not alone in the carriage.

"Good day," said the new figure opposite him. "That was an interesting piece of work."

The figure—probably a man, but who could really tell—sat in a pool of misty shadow, a top hat pulled low and the upturned collar of his greatcoat pulled high, arms folded across his chest. "Good day to you, sir," said Fradjikan. "What work was that?"

"Tactically quite adroit," the figure continued. "On the higher levels of discourse, though, less well chosen."

Considering the circumstances, it might be more prudent to play along with him. "Why is that?"

"Consider this," reflected the figure. "He now knows about you. Unless I miss my guess, he will also realize it was your hand that inserted him into the situation."

"That would seem unlikely," said Fradjikan. "Even if that should happen, what of it?"

The shadowed figure scrutinized him. "I have observed in you a tendency to value yourself rather more and your adversaries rather less than they deserve."

"Oh, you have observed that, have you?"

"If I were you, I might also ask myself whether I was the only operative who could possibly carry out your particular charge."

Fradjikan, who had in fact asked himself that very

question, but not recently, certainly not since things had really gotten rolling, said, "My success will be the only demonstration required. A success that is at the moment perfectly well in train."

"In a matter such as this, who can say what constitutes success? Perhaps the major issue at stake is a trial of you, yourself, rather than the obvious goal against which you have been pointed."

"My command of situational aesthetics," said Fradjikan, a bit testily, "is second to none."

"Ah, your external aesthetics perhaps, but the tenor of your own attitude and behavior?" The figure shrugged. "Who can hold a perfect mirror to himself? Take this fellow with the walking stick, for example. How often does this happen, that you meet someone against whom you bear a contract face-to-face?"

Why was this god—no, not just *a* god, apparently Fradi's *patron*—didacticizing with him this way? "He's only a bit player," Fradjikan said carefully, "at most a pawn who fancies himself a rook. A tool for leverage against Maximillian." Leverage to be applied in a most cunning manner, Fradi still had to admit to himself. Well, what of it? If you couldn't appreciate your own work, what was the point of getting up in the morning?

The god regarded him in the silence of contemplation. Then at last he spoke. "Stay away from this one. He is a wild card. His presence may lead to things you will be happier not to be involved in."

"What things? To what do you allude?"

"I," said the god, "have spoken." Vapor billowed from his greatcoat, and perhaps (although this was most likely illusion) from his mouth and eyes as well. Fog filled the compartment. Fradi felt for the side window, and then for the panel next to Lowell. Finally, with the door open and Fradjikan hanging onto it, the pea-souper began to dissipate. The god himself, of course, was long gone.

Lowell had noticed nothing, neither an entrance nor

an exit, except for the suddenly billowing fog which Fradi had brought to his attention himself. That might be a characteristic of the situation or a warning that Lowell might have collaborated in bringing it off. Either way Lowell would bear increased scrutiny.

The larger situation itself would also warrant another going-over. Either the god had misread Fradi's personality, or he hadn't. In any case, the god's admonition had served primarily to increase Spilkas' interest value. Perhaps it would be prudent to consider the better part of valor in this case, and find another stratagem, but . . . no. No, that would be foolish. Fradi had clearly been even luckier than he'd originally anticipated. Spilkas was apparently worth more than he'd seemed, and a rook mistaken for a pawn is always a valuable find.

If there was one rule in this business, it was never to throw out a usable piece.

Fradi directed Lowell to the site of the most urgent errand, and then, their business there complete, onward toward home. A horse was already in the courtyard; apparently this was Fradi's day for consultation. The visitor was already installed in the library. Fradi shut the door behind him as he entered. "Welcome, my lord," said Fradi. "I trust you find the brandy to your liking?"

"Did it come with the house or was its acquisition one of your other deals? I thought I knew the location of every cask of the '45 within the city limits."

Fradjikan moved aside the cloak that was tossed casually over the settee and seated himself, his pose one of studied ease but his senses at full alert. The man across the room from him examining the bookcases, dashing in his red and black daywear with the silver accessory highlights, was not one you wanted to let drift from your attention; Fradjikan, as one peer to another, was certainly in a position to appreciate this. "Are you running short? I'll have the extra bottle sent around to you."

"Señor Ballista is a man of refinement," the visitor

said, cocking his head to side and speaking as if from deep consideration. "Are you certain you were never a quartermaster? You succeed in unearthing the most amazing things."

"A significant compliment," said Fradjikan, "coming from you. I presume your own campaign of acquisition proceeds equally as well?"

"Ah," said the other. "The opening has been made, and all told it achieved its established goals. The final resolution will take somewhat more work. This campaign, did you call it?, will not be as simple as strolling into a shop and making a purchase from goods on hand, but then that was clear from the outset. The most worthwhile ones take time. The process will yield its own rewards, to be sure, and in any case that was to be expected."

"She suspects nothing?"

"She suspects *something,* of course," said the Scapula, "but perhaps nothing more than would be warranted by my reputation. She's particularly sharp, for a woman, yet of course she tries to deny she *is* a woman. That makes her all the riper. She'll come around easily enough, have no doubt about it." He paused, then looked off in the distance and smiled. "It may take a bit more judicious wooing."

"Without that where's the sport?"

"Indeed, so." The Scapula eyed the level of brandy in his snifter, then crossed to the sideboard to refresh it. "You have someone watching the nephew?"

"There are those who are on it," said Fradjikan, "again judiciously. The boy is guarded and apparently shielded as well. Also predictably, and it can all be handled if necessary. What did you decide to do about the brother?"

"He *is* a bit tricky," the Scapula admitted. "He's busy, though, and I've tossed a few more things his way that will keep his workload active, and in any case he's certain his sister can take care of herself. Even if he questions the situation, as he very well might somewhere down the line, his sister should be so enraptured that his freedom of action will be circumscribed. Beyond that, he can be handled, as you say, if necessary.''

Fradjikan had no doubt that the Crawfish was one of the many people who *would* be handled by the Scapula, whether that was strictly necessary or not, whether as part of the immediate sequence of events or not. The Scapula was a man on the make; in more ways than one, of course. When one's ambitions, and, to be frank, one's appetites, were as great as the Scapula's, and when one had already achieved the Scapula's level of achievement, one had to become quite adroit at identifying those who required handling, as well as implementing against them one's own plans.

Which wasn't to say that one was always successful in what one set out to do. ''What sort of past history do you have with this Crawfish?''

''This and that,'' said the Scapula dismissively. ''He's rather like me, you know. More diffuse in his objectives, more distractible, on occasion arguably more dissolute. He may be a challenge, but in the larger sense no more than an obstacle tactical in scale. Especially with the intelligence his sister will provide, yes, my colleague?''

''Just so,'' said Fradi. The Scapula *was* a valuable ally, no doubt about that, but there was equally no doubt that he couldn't be trusted for a moment. That was a general characteristic of those folks Fradi tended to end up in league with, and it, too, had always proved to be something that could be handled. Fradjikan had had a lot of experience with people occupying thrones, or those who wished to do so, so the Scapula's ambition in itself was nothing new. The Scapula might be fully as good at intrigue as Fradjikan himself, though, which *was* more unusual.

Fradi knew he himself could become a target if and when their interests diverged. Equally plausible, however, was the chance of securing more business or even a new imperial patron by demonstrating his worth. ''Not to impugn your campaign plan,'' Fradjikan ventured, "yet perhaps there is some additional force I might bring to bear on the problem."

"We shall see. It would be a mistake, I think, to lean too hard at this stage. You want your hands on her secret archives, I suspect, much more than I; after all, you do have your erstwhile master with whom to contend."

The Scapula *was* sharp. Fradi had never told him about his interest in the god-material in the Archives, or his hope of gaining insurance from the archival information against the one who'd brought him back to life for this job. "An intriguing speculation," said Fradi.

"I see you agree. With the material at her disposal, though, the Archivist could become a major player, if only she had the motivation. Acting to give her that motivation would be, you will also agree, a significant mistake. At worst she can be neutralized, at best out-and-out co-opted."

This certainly *was* the big city. It wasn't every day you turned up a pawn who might really be a rook, and yet here in the person of the Archivist was another one. The fate of all pieces, whether pawn or rook, was ultimately to be taken, but here as always the correspondence between chess and life broke down. In chess pieces don't have the option of changing sides.

10

The Scapula was doing his best to become a nuisance. The vase with the rose had been a nice little touch, as much for being unexpected and for being produced with a pleasantly offbeat flourish than because of the details of the gift itself. The message of the flower was on the way to being overwhelmed by repetition, however, and by an expansion in scale. Not only had bouquets and parcels of various sorts been arriving at the Archives, he knew where she lived, too. Leen had refused to meet with the couturier, but the fellow had obviously gotten enough of a look at her to be able to assess her coloring and estimate her size. Quite accurately, too, as it turned out. The maid had already had the ball gown out of its wrappings and hanging on the door when Leen had gotten home, and hadn't given her a moment's peace until she'd tried the damned thing on. Now the woman wouldn't let her send it back.

Once you started with this nonsense there were really no end of problems. Leen had been idly contemplating the idea of putting in an appearance at the Inauguration Ball even before the Scapula's arrival on the scene. Now he had polarized the question. If she went on her own and wore his gown, that would still be as good as walking in the door on his arm. If she left the gown out of the picture and dressed herself, he would most likely take it as a slap, and that would also still leave the maid to be contended with.

The whole situation was nothing but a mess and a bother.

With the Scapula or his agents all but camping on her door, and with his campaign obviously picking up steam, it was impossible to ignore things, either, in the hope he'd get tired of her stubbornness and would let her off the hook. There was only one thing to do. Leen had decided to appear at the Archives late and use the extra time to consult an expert.

Reentering the street after her meeting, Leen fully realized she should have known better. There was no question of her sister's expertise in assignations and *affaires de coeur,* though, and her advice in managing touchy situations was well enough known that these days she kept regular consulting hours. What Leen found she had overlooked was that clients may have been clients, but family was *always* family.

Susannah had received her in the south-facing dayroom high on the Crust. After the expected grousings about how she wouldn't be up at such an ungodly hour for just *anyone,* Susannah had finally loaded up on enough coffee to be willing to hear Leen out.

As Leen wrapped up, Susannah had frowned out the bay window at the city, her back propped against a generous cushion on her strategically placed settee. "Yes?" said Susannah. "I thought you said you had a problem. Where is it? You certainly haven't told it to *me.* "

"Obviously he's after the wrong person," Leen said. "I think he was really after *you.* "

Her sister brightened. "Do you think so?"

"Well, he couldn't have wanted *me.* That's what I *told* him."

Susannah's face was usually an open book, at least to someone who'd grown up between the same covers, so to speak. The demands of her ego vied with those of honesty, or at least those of Susannah's longer-term goal of seeing Leen prematurely ensconced in permanent domesticity. Reluctantly, she had finally acknowledged that the Scapula, rake though he was, might very well have had Leen on his mind. "I've told you and told you," Leen's sister had said, "you could be all the rage yourself if you'd only pay a little attention to things outside your books. You do come from the same stock as *me,* after all. I'm having my own little soiree in a few days, you know—you must bring him by."

This was not at all the answer Leen had hoped for. She had looked for the reassurance of her sister's usual cattiness, and so Susannah's refusal to abide by her typical rules left Leen even more confused than she had hoped to be relieved. Leen had not gone so far as to commit to anything, much less to producing the Scapula as Susannah's *pièce de résistance,* but that small victory was the only one she felt she had wrung from the encounter.

Generally speaking, Susannah was not oblivious to the political implications of personal relationships, and the manipulation of intimacy for purposes of leverage or blackmail was certainly one of her specialties. In this particular case Susannah's awareness of these factors still hadn't made her advice on the subject especially useful. "Of *course* he might be up to something," Susannah had said. "The best way to find out what that something is would be to play along with him. Just make certain you have some fun while you're doing it. Can you do that? Of course you can; you *are* my sister."

So it had clearly been a waste of time, and all the more so since she should have known it in advance. Leen's sister wasn't the right expert to visit at all. She should have started with her brother.

The Crust had its own road maintenance and sanitation brigade, but these would have been useless if the district hadn't also been equipped with walls and guards. As she wedged her way through the Tobasco Gate at the base of the hill into the press of traffic, Leen was even more shocked than she had been on the way over. She hadn't been out in the streets much at all lately, had been taking her constitutional in the park and her exercise on the practice grounds near the Reading Room in the palace complex. Rather than keep up her own residence on the Crust or bother with a flat, Leen had taken a suite of rooms in the Block. As an officer of the state she was entitled to it, of course, but in contrast to most of the others similarly eligible she was actually using the privilege. The Block was a bit dreary and rattly, and the rooms were not what you could call warm, but if you knew the right shortcuts the warren of the Block was no more than a five-minute stroll through some of the nicer palace gardens and a quick nip through the corner of the hedge maze to the side entrance of the building housing the Archives.

Her rooms in the Block were convenient, then, but since they were also on the palace grounds they, too, had kept her insulated from the scale of the influx now sweeping over the city. As she made her way west, Leen was just glad she wasn't involved in maintaining internal security. Or health and welfare, for that matter. Public hygiene had been a concern of the ancients that the Peridol government had chosen to uphold, but with all these visitors underfoot standards would be breaking down right and left. Far too many of the people around her were shabby and unwashed.

Of course, given how much—or how little—she'd been getting out in the city even before the Knitting, it was possible standards had been falling down by themselves. She'd have to talk to someone. Where was sanitation in the Corpus infrastructure? One of the Hepatic Lobes, perhaps, or more likely the First Colonic Flexure. She—

Leen stopped. Something seemed to attract her from the left. She squinted over and cocked her ear, but even as she did she realized that whatever had caught her interest wasn't something she had heard or seen. Whatever it had been, it was gone now. There was nothing remarkable on that side of the street at all. A few street vendors, a blacksmith shop, and the usual mix of passersby. A couple of grungy ne'er-do-well travelers were leading a packhorse; as early in the day as it was, the lot of them already had at least two sheets to the wind, judging by the glazed expression of the young one in the lead, and the way he appeared to be simultaneously sniffing the air and listening to it. Just then, the pair of them bent right and shouldered their way lengthwise across the traffic, dragging the reluctant horse behind them. As they crossed ahead of Leen on their way into a narrow side street, the eye of the man holding the horse's bridle swung across her from beneath the shady depths of a battered slouch hat. For an instant, they locked glances; then he was gone.

Leen shook her head to clear it. The Scapula was obviously too much on her mind. She didn't even really like him, although his physicality was certainly good for a pleasant tingle. For one random squint from a peasant on the street to give her so much of an excited shiver, though, defied rational analysis. Perhaps this was the secret of the Scapula's modus operandi, to raise appetites where there had been none and then to provide himself as the only comprehensive fulfillment. As soon as she got back to the office, she was going to get rid of the flowers and the rest of the stuff. Chances were it was spiked.

Actually, it might be better to wrap up his things and take them out for analysis. If she really was being bombarded by some aphrodisiac pheromone, it could be necessary to seek out an antidote.

Of course, if what she needed was an antidote to the ways of the flesh, the last place she should be heading now was the one she had now arrived at, and whose bell-cord she was now pulling. A small window set high in the door behind a stout barred grill slid back. "Is my brother around?" Leen asked the door.

The door swung open. "Yes he is, actually," said a man in a long tartan bathrobe. Protruding beneath the bathrobe's floor-scraping hem were a pair of purple slippers with upturned pointy toes. The man's tousled hair was the red of carrot juice on a sunny day at noon. "He wasn't expecting you," the fellow added, his tone a trifle arch, ''but I'm sure he's glad to see you anyway.''

''Is he? Would he want me to come in off the street, then?''

''As long as you bring it up, I suppose so. Come on, then.'' Leen followed the man down the hall and up a flight of stairs. ''I just put a kettle on for tea,'' he said over his shoulder. ''Would you like some?''

''I've just come from Susannah's.''

''Then you'll be tired of fending off refreshments. I won't mention it again. The way she is with food and guests, you could say she's worse than Mother, except that *our* mother never seemed to be egging us on one way or the other. *Someone's* mother, then.''

''It must have worked,'' Leen said. ''None of her children is scrawny.'' The front room on the second floor overlooked the street and had already had its shutters flung open to catch the light. Leen watched the traffic below while pots rattled in the kitchen behind her.

''I suppose it's this thing with the Scapula on your mind,'' her brother called out through the open door.

Leen fought back the temptation to ask him how he knew. The Crawfish made it his business to learn everyone else's, often before they knew it themselves. ''What do you think he's up to?''

''He's a hard one to get solid intelligence on,'' Lemon admitted, entering the room. The gouts of steam from his mug brought the smell of honey and warm milk mixed with the caress of chamomile.

''Oh, bother,'' she muttered.

''What was that?''

''I don't know what's wrong with me. All my thought patterns are mixed up. I keep thinking in, ah, physical allusions.'' The caress of chamomile, indeed. ''Just now on the way over I found myself attracted to some grubby man on the street.'' She collapsed into an armchair.

''This is not in itself necessarily a bad thing,'' the Crawfish said cautiously. ''I—what's the matter?''

There was something half-buried under the cushion. Leen finally dug it out and shook it out at arm's length in front of her. "I knew coming to see you might not be the right thing either."

"Ah, well, just toss that over there. Perhaps she'll be back for it some other time."

"The lacework is rather well done," Leen observed. "What are these ribbons for, though? And this springy bit?"

"Here, give me that." Lemon slipped the garment neatly from her grasp and made it disappear. "It's not your size anyway," he added.

It was an interesting thought, though. "Augh," said Leen, putting her head in her hands.

"The Scapula has a good sense for choosing his victims," Lemon noted. "I've actually been expecting him to go after you for some time. You *are* one of the more eligible women around, and one of the most strategically placed as well. Your reluctance to dally with the social whirl would only be an added attraction to a man like him. There may be a philosophical component, too, I should think; the battle between mind and heart, or gut, or some such, I shouldn't be surprised."

"I can't believe that's all there is to it."

"When you get right down to it, neither do I." Lemon spent a moment inhaling tea vapors. When his head had emerged again from the steam clouds, he said thoughtfully, "My Lord Scapula clearly has larger plans, layer upon layer of them. Still, we could do worse than start with the obvious, by which I mean the Archives."

"I thought about that," said Leen, "but how could he know what's there?"

"He doesn't have to *know*, all he has to do is *suspect*. It could be a move against someone else, to preempt their own access. He could merely want to control whatever the Archives *might* contain, or to have others know he has his hand on whatever *they* think might be buried in your stacks." He hesitated. "That's not where the real concern may lie, though. Did Grandpa ever tell you about an incident about, oh, ten years ago?''

"Concerning the Scapula?''

"Now I wonder. Grandpa had a suspicion—no, that's too strong, more of a hunch—that someone had gotten into the Archives.''

"*Inside* the Archives? Are you serious—and why'd he tell you? Why didn't he tell *me*?''

"He didn't want to bother you; he was very protective of you, you know. He knew he was getting a bit absentminded, too, and he thought it could have just been something he'd mislaid. And, well, if there *was* something going on, he thought my talents, such as they are, might be suited for ferreting it out.''

"Why didn't he tell me later on? Why didn't he leave some note in the journals?''

"You're getting sidetracked,'' the Crawfish said mildly. "Grandpa wouldn't like that, you know.''

Leen closed her eyes and forced herself to relax. Breathe *in,* hold, hold, then *out.* "All right,'' she said. "What made him have this hunch, and what did you find out?''

"He was researching some stuff from the equipment stacks. Mostly jewelry, but a few small appliances that he thought might have been related as well. He'd been moving a number of boxes around the way he often did, and had things spread out on his work tables, and had been rummaging around quite a lot if you want to know the truth. When he came in one morning, he thought some of the pieces might have been moved, and some might have actually gone missing.

"He said none of the defenses had been triggered, although the access log was a bit more vague about his own comings and goings than he thought it should have been. He reset the wards and never noticed anything again. I nosed around but didn't come up with a thing.''

Leen tried to make herself switch back from being appalled to being analytical. She could do it, she knew she could—even though the thought that someone could make it through the defenses and into the Archives themselves *was* appalling. It was probably worse than a typical woman would feel if she found out someone had been poking around her bedroom. "If someone *did* know how to get in and out you'd think they should be smart enough not to leave traces inside," she said.

"That's what I thought, too. Of course, if they spotted something out on the table they just *had* to have they might have just picked it up and risked the consequences. They could have wagered Grandpa *would* decide he had mislaid it, if he even realized it was missing."

"But you never found any evidence. It *could* have been Grandfather getting confused in the dark."

"It could," Lemon admitted. "Wondering why the Scapula could be interested in the Archives brought the incident back to memory, though. If there really was an intruder, the Scapula could have heard about it one way or another. And if the intruder had seen something the Scapula might want to fit into his plans . . . Anyway, it does make you wonder."

"So you think I should give him the boot."

"I didn't say that, did I? You might want to play along with him and try to figure out his game. You might even enjoy yourself while you're at it; I hear he's quite worthwhile for a girl to be around, hmm?"

"You get this from unimpeachable sources, no doubt."

The Crawfish raised his eyebrows. "How did you know? No, really, his scandals are common enough gossip."

"Scandals?"

"Affairs, anyway. Well, and a few out-and-out scandals, too. There's a family curse as well, I expect you know about that."

"Something involving an evil sister?" She did recall something of the sort. Family curses were so commonplace in their circles that it was scarcely worth considering, of course. Anyway, Lemon's suggestion was the major thing on her mind, that she go along with the Scapula. She *could* do that, but that wasn't all, by any means. She could recheck the Archive alarms. She'd supplemented the defenses herself; anyone who tried to get in now would find more to contend with than ten years ago. She could go back through Grandfather's logs. There was no chance the Scapula could have learned of her own discovery, the ancient artifact in the hidden room; her defense against mind-probe was quite adequate. It might not be a bad idea to practice her defenses anyway, and perhaps even think about an upgrade.

And she could worry. She could do quite a lot of that.

11

"Maybe we *should* have taken a boat," muttered Max.

"I don't think it would have helped," Jurtan said. He pointed over the side of the bridge toward the surface of the Tongue Water. "Look down there. We wouldn't have needed a boat at all; we could have just hopped from deck to deck."

"That's a local saying, an old wives' tale."

"That doesn't mean it couldn't be done. I mean, *look* at it."

"Look at the traffic up here instead," Max said. "If you don't keep your head down and keep pushing ahead, you're gonna get dragged backward. Watch out for the horse, too, if you don't want it stolen right out of your grasp."

"I've never seen a crowd like this in my life."

"It is pretty extreme," Max admitted. "Are you enjoying yourself now?"

"I guess," said Jurtan. But it *was* exciting—this was Peridol, after all. Even if it had taken them all day just to struggle from Yenemsvelt to this bridge. And they'd used back roads, too.

What they'd already seen of Peridol, on the landward side coming in, hadn't been too impressive, unless you liked grime and the reek of danger. Even through Max's best efforts on the road to acquaint him with these pleasures, both of them were still way down on Jurtan's list of preferences. The city so far had been impressive mainly since it was clearly *big*, though, but

not big enough by half to cope with everyone who
wanted to be there.

Then there had been the checkpoint they'd just
passed at the base of the bridge, with the police and
the search field. A modulation of Jurtan's music, and
the use of a particular trombone theme that he'd come
to associate with warnings, had alerted him to the
magical sensor system. Max had already deactivated
his own onboard defenses and countermeasures, saying they could draw too much attention, but he'd added
a comment to Jurtan about his music sense being a
handy thing to have around. For a change Max had
actually briefed Jurtan in advance, on protective col-
oration, in the course of getting them outfitted with
their disguises. "Think like the faceless crowd," Max
had said, but Jurtan hadn't had to take any special
action to accomplish that. The crowd was so big that
he felt about the size of a sand grain on a beach.

In any event, it had worked. They'd made it through
the checkpoint without incident. Of course, surely the
checkpoint hadn't had anything to do with them. Had
it? Jurtan thought it was worth braving the changeable
moods of Max to ask.

"Could be," said Max. "That's usually the best way
to plan."

"As if anything that happens is aimed specifically
at you?"

"Yeah, that's right. When you've got as many people who could be after you as I do, yeah, that's right."

Of course, Max's obvious broad streak of paranoia
wasn't news.

Even so, they were still alive, *and* they'd made it to
Peridol. And Jurtan's music was still urging him on.
More than that, Jurtan thought it was telling him some
kind of payoff might be up ahead.

What the music wasn't telling him was how to behave. It hadn't seemed to object before, though, when
he'd tried to be more assertive. Well, Max's mood
seemed as good as it got. Maybe it was time to try
being pushy again.

Jurtan cleared his throat, weaved around a farmer with a brace of flapping chickens slung over each shoulder who was following a cart similarly equipped, then launched into it. "Now that we're here, what are we going to do? What are *you* going to do? No, wait. You and Shaa have been trying to teach me to be analytic and methodical, right? Why don't we try some of that, shall we?"

To Max, what was apparent above all was that he and Shaa had succeeded in creating a monster. Of course, that wasn't to say a monster couldn't be useful to have around. The problem was one of control, and giving the creature something interesting to focus on so it didn't get bored and head off to ravage the countryside.

Something interesting to focus on was Max's immediate intention. They were nearing one. It was somewhere around here. In that neighborhood at the end of the bridge, certainly. Off to the right? No, Max decided, maybe straight ahead.

"You've got two major goals, as I see it," Jurtan was continuing. "Three, if you count driving people around you crazy because you don't want to communicate with them as a goal, instead of just a habit. But it's the other two that are more important anyway. First, you want to overthrow the gods, mainly because they want to keep on running the world and keeping people from having free will, and second, you want to get the curse off the Shaas' backs. Or should that be the other way around?"

They came off the bridge onto a street lined with middle-of-the-road shops and the occasional block-wide emporium. Street vendors were largely absent, although their lack was more than compensated for by the presence of barkers and strolling hucksters in the pay of the local merchants. None of the food purveyors or open-pit barbecues they'd seen on the other side of the bridge were visible, yet the faint aroma of roast mutton snaked down the street in front of them.

"You hoped you could pick up something from Iskendarian that would help you on both the god and the Shaa problems,'' said Jurtan. ''You did get those papers, but you haven't been able to find out what's in them. You might still get lucky, but you have to plan that you won't.

''You're running out of time, too, on Shaa anyway. Now that he's in Peridol he can't leave unless something gets done about the curse. Shaa's brother's around here somewhere, too, and he might have something new up his sleeve. But you haven't shown any sign of a plan. Now, I know better than that. Just because you haven't told me about it doesn't mean you don't have a plan. Of course you have a plan. The question is whether you're going to tell me about it.''

''That's not a bad analysis, kid,'' Max said grudgingly. ''The Iskendarian connection was always a longshot, but it's still worth playing out. The thing you got to remember, though, is that you can find most anything right here, in Peridol. That gives you a lot to work with.''

The kid *was* getting sharp. As good as he might be getting, though, he had no experience in paradigm shifts. That was more than just as well. Max didn't want anyone to get a line on the course he was considering. They might not like it. In fact, they probably wouldn't like it at all.

Which didn't mean it didn't need to be done. What *was* clear, however, was the same thing that was always clear, the importance of secrecy and misdirection. Even more than usually, it would be important not to telegraph his plans.

''What's that?'' said Jurtan. He had stopped in the middle of the street, his head cocked to one side and his eyes squinting in puzzlement.

''What's what?'' Max sniffed surreptitiously; the odor of burning lamb was still there, if you were looking for it, but there was still not a lamb in sight.

''I hear something strange. I mean, stranger than normal.'' Jurtan started forward again, haltingly.

Max followed, giving him room. ''Can you describe

what you're experiencing? Is it different in character from your typical cues, or does it seem to have some kind of unusual meaning?''

''It's like . . . it's like . . .'' Jurtan was clearly diverting so much of his attention to whatever he was concentrating on that he didn't have enough left to communicate intelligibly. It was also clear, though, that his slightly weaving path was holding precisely to the meandering aroma trail of cooking lamb. Jurtan wasn't inhaling the scent, at least on any higher than a subliminal level, but he did seem to have picked up the Track.

Not that there was anything particularly subtle about one leg of a Track. Most of the trick was in the transitions. There should be one coming up soon. And unless Max missed his guess it would be—

A cat yowled. Where was it, left or right? Neither? Both?

Jurtan had stopped. His head swiveled right. He walked in that direction, headfirst, stumbling, really, as though an invisible string were drawing him by his outthrust nose. The smell of mutton was gone now, too, another characteristic of a successful transition, as much due to the shift in attention to the next leg as anything else, Max had found, but another clue you needed to pay strict attention to. Jurtan was still tottering forward, and in another two paces was going to plow at reasonable speed into the stone wall of the ironwork shop on the corner, but then all at once an old war shield mounted on the clapboard sign of an inn a block ahead caught the setting sun in a sharp orange glint. Jurtan's head tracked around to face it, the rest of his body followed, and again he was off.

Two transitions almost on top of each other. That was a sign of a reasonably high-level Track; certainly not something a beginner should be able to traverse at all. If it held to form, the next leg might appear to submerge—and indeed, underneath the inn's sign Jurtan stalled out. Max thought he made the perfect image of a tracking hound, excepting only the long lolling tongue. "What do you think you're doing?" Max said.

"You're not going to distract me," Jurtan stated.

"Fine," said Max. "Distract you from what?"

"I thought I was, ah, following . . . you're not going to get on my case, on you?"

"Probably not," Max allowed.

"It was like a trail, then," said Jurtan. "The music was keying me onto it."

"Close your eyes and concentrate."

Jurtan turned slowly in a circle, his eyes screwed shut and his nose pointed into the air. Then his head swung back around more rapidly, swung back and forth in increasingly short arcs, and finally came to rest. He opened his eyes and squinted in confusion. "Why would I want to go back in the same direction we came from?" he asked. "What kind of sense does that make?"

"Doubleback loops are a pretty common trick."

"Oh," said Jurtan, "okay, then." He started forward, then ground to a halt, one foot in the air. "Wait a minute."

"Overlaying multiple back-and-forth legs makes it difficult to tease them apart," Max explained. "Something else that separates out beginners from the Pseudonyms on higher-order Tracks." *Except where you're concerned*, Max thought to himself, *all rules may be off*. "No, don't stop; Tracks decay, you know."

"You mean there really *is* some kind of trail here?"

Max urged the horse after Jurtan. "You've heard of the Society of Masks, right?"

"Uh, yeah, sort of. My father doesn't much hold with them. First he said it was a myth, and then he said it was nothing but a bunch of wimps skulking around in the dark trying to stay out of a fair fight."

"Your father is a man with no shortage of opinions," Max told Jurtan. "Especially, in this case, for someone who, unless I miss my guess, is at least Alias level in the Society himself."

"But I thought the Society of Masks was a secret."

"Membership is a secret," Max said, "and so are activities, for the most part. Your father's quite right, actually. Like most secret organizations, a lot of the Society is quite childish, really."

"If it's such a secret, I can understand why my father didn't want me asking questions." *And of course he is my father, after all,* Jurtan added under his voice. The Lion never wanted Jurtan to ask much of anything. Especially in public, when he usually tried as hard as possible to make people think Jurtan was certainly no offspring of his. Jurtan swerved aside, elbowed his way across the street, and plunged down a sudden alley, where the sound of an internal yaphorn harmonized intriguingly with the scent of ostentatiously baking bread. Max glanced around. Half a block up the street a woman was staring at him. Did he know her? He didn't think so, and anyway he *was* in disguise. You had to be a fool to trust a disguise, of course—but if the woman saw something in him it would be good to find out what it was. She looked—

But the kid was forging ahead; he had to follow. The other was no more than a distraction, even if—*No!* Max told himself. Business was afoot. "If this Society is a secret," the kid was saying, Max thought for the second time, "why are you telling me about it?"

"I thought I might as well, seeing as you've decided to become an initiate."

"An—oh!—really?"

"Don't stop," Max instructed. "You were quite right to tell me not to distract you; ability to focus on your intuition is a central skill. It isn't called the Intuition Track for nothing."

"But what's the point? Where do these Tracks come from? Is it just some kind of treasure hunt, or what?"

"Sometimes there's treasure, but that's pretty rare actually. Usually it's just the directions to a meeting, or some Society member showing off."

Jurtan stopped in his tracks again. "So it *is* just a waste of time. It's just some *game*. Why make all this fuss over—"

"You play chess?" Max said. "Ever seen a crossword puzzle? There's almost never such a thing as 'just some game.' Even if there is, it can still be part of something larger, or something you can *turn* into something larger. You got to be open to possibilities. Just go with it and see where it takes you."

Jurtan was moving. Actually, it had been hard for him to stay still. Max considered mentioning how addictive Track-running could be, but it would have clearly been superfluous. As Max had, well, intuited, Jurtan not only had the talent, he'd gotten the hook.

Except Jurtan's talent wasn't the straight-out typical route of intuition and instinct. However his music sense was wired, it had given him a supercharge boost straight to the upper levels.

"But what is the Society of Masks, then, anyway?" Jurtan asked. "I mean, is it just, like, a puzzle-solving club?"

"It's got its puzzle side, and its debating and wit-matching and skill-honing side, and its exclusive honorific side, but like most private clubs it's an important place to meet important people."

"People?"

"Yeah, people, gods, others, you name it."

"Is the Society why you came to Peridol?"

"It's one reason. The running for Mask Supreme should shake loose some folks I'd like to get in touch with."

Jurtan kept glancing up at the top of the buildings they were passing. They were three stories high and had peaked, ill-shingled roofs, but he had an unpleasant feeling that this Track-thing was going to try to lead him up there. What would they do with the horse? "Where does the Mask part come into it?"

"It's like this," expounded Max. "Basically we're talking about a secret society of folks who use disguises as part of their normal activities; primarily thieves, gods, and adventurers, but also spies, diplomats, and so forth. It's based primarily around the flaunting of one's ability and the courting of disaster

176

through the danger of discovery. The higher up you get, the less you really know who the true identities of any of the other members at any gathering, and since everybody typically changes their disguise or persona from time to time anyway it's also difficult to tell if you're even meeting the same person twice."

"But my father doesn't wear disguises," Jurtan protested.

"It's a loose definition; the disguise may be physical or it may not. Magical subterfuge and emotional prevarication aren't excluded. In fact, although no one really likes to come right out and admit it, anyone who can gain access to the Society of Masks is eligible for membership, ipso facto. Since no one really knows who anyone else really is, or at least each person tries to keep everyone else from finding out, what are you going to do, anyway, bar the door?"

"What about this ranking stuff, then? Is it just a pecking order?"

"It's more than that, there's a hierarchical ranking. If you get right down to it, the Society amounts to the social register of skullduggery, the who's-who's of scheming."

"All it sounds like is a place to show off," Jurtan said.

"There is that," acknowledged Max.

They rounded a corner and weaved their way down a new street. Up ahead at the end of the block was an large open space free of buildings. The Track led straight toward it—a market plaza, thronged with people. At the far side, the business of the bazaar was proceeding apparently as normal. Even though night had pretty much fallen, torches and wizard lamps gave enough illumination to keep things alive. In the area closer to them, though, the section surrounding some kind of monument had been cordoned off by police. The monument itself glowed in the harsh white glare of a high-intensity arcfire field. People were hanging back and looking on in a hum of speculative conversation.

Jurtan had ground to a halt in mid-stride. He was looking around in confusion. "It's gone," said Jurtan. "Where is it? I've lost it."

"You were right the first time," Max told him, gazing around the plaza himself. "It *is* gone, been cut. A Track that dives through a place like this is another trick to separate out the people who really know what they're doing. This kind of place—a market, a public assembly, anything big and hectic—has so many conflicting stimuli it can be next to impossible to follow a Track built on subtlety through it. This one would have been High Pseudonym class at least."

"So why are you so sure the Track was cut? Couldn't you have just lost it?"

"At my rating a High Pseudonym is a warmup exercise," Max said distractedly. "What the hell happened to that thing over there?"

"That thing" was the closed-off monument. Actually, as they approached the area, the monument had revealed itself to be a fountain, now shut off and in the process of being drained. The equestrian statue standing off-center in the pool, its horse reclining in the water and the heroically proportioned general leaning far off to one side with his sword extended, was being shored up with wood scaffolding. A section of the general's stone arm had already pulled apart from its own weight. "Kind of a strange way to build a statue, isn't it?" asked Jurtan.

"It wasn't built that way," Max told him, examining it speculatively, his fingers making passes at his side. "Somebody animated it, but it got shut down partway through its sequence. Whatever else was going on, the emanations also managed to override the Track."

"Look at this," Jurtan said, pointing to the side. A row of large posters had been flung up on the wall of a building facing the plaza. Rancid glue was still running down the wall, and a disreputable-looking landau was clattering surreptitiously away from the site.

"Broadsiders," said Max. "Another quaint local

business custom." The posters themselves, fresh off an unlicensed clairvogravure press shop, no doubt, showed the statue behind them, in the best emblematic Heroic Realism style. Around the fountain a ring of fire spelled out words of incitement and revolution. The statue was striking a pose, its sword in the air. Next to it, at its feet inside the fountain, in fact, a more human-sized figure was matching its pose. Suddenly Max gave a start. "Let's get a closer look at this," he muttered.

Jurtan trailed him to the wall. Now that the sun was down, the light reaching the posters was slim. That could have been the reason the poster-splashers had picked that spot for their handiwork; they could emplace in peace at night and have the city blanketed by the light of morning. Max glanced around, making sure they were more-or-less alone, and then made a less subtle series of passes in the air. Jurtan heard a faint strand of the melody that meant magic was being unleashed, not that he needed the extra clue. A glowing orb the size of a tennis ball spun into existence and rolled over to hover in front of the poster. The features of the man at the foot of the statue, brandishing a sword swathed in a cloud of fire, were now clearly visible.

"I guess he's in town, too," Jurtan said, eyeing the portrait of the Creeping Sword. "But what's he doing up there on that thing?"

"Damned if I know," said Max, "except no good, there's no doubt about that."

"So," said a new voice, "quite a little dust-up here, wouldn't you say?"

Another man was standing next to them, scrutinizing the poster along with them in the glow of Max's floating lamp. The man had blond hair that straggled across his forehead with a devil-may-care insouciance, and beneath it a dashing mustache. An earring glinted in his left ear. "The way the man and the statue are matching poses is rather an artistic touch, don't you think?" the fellow added.

Where have I seen this guy before? Jurtan wondered. He looked unfamiliar, but Jurtan was convinced this was not the first time he'd heard the voice. "Do you know what the story was with this?" Max asked the newcomer. "Or did you maybe have something to do with it yourself?"

"All I have is hearsay, sad to tell," said the man, making a pouting face to match. "Whatever did happen, this fellow—" he tapped the picture of the Creeping Sword "—has rather a talent for showing up in interesting spots, though, eh? Almost as much as you," he added.

"Oh, yeah?" said Max. "Has he been hanging around with you now?"

The fellow considered the question. "No," he said, "and yes. It was somewhat of a chance thing, actually, which is to say we were thrown together socially, so to speak. I went up to him and did some small talk, tried to make him feel at home."

"What kind of social occasion are we talking about here?"

"One of these conclave things. It wasn't exactly clear what he was doing there, but since the folks he was with obviously thought he was someone else I thought it best to play along with them. Who is he, really?"

"I was hoping you were going to tell *me* that, especially since he's your new pal."

"There's no need to get testy. Temperament is rather a problem for you, isn't it?"

"I'm glad you're on my side," Max said sarcastically. "But since you were on my side at last report, I'll ask you again, you weasel."

"Who he is, you mean? Someone interesting, as I said. Beyond that?" He shrugged. "More interesting all the time, though, especially now he's gotten tangled up with these terrorists. Potentially rather a dangerous lot, these terrorist chaps. Or as I like to think of them, freedom fighters. Not all that different from you, in their own way, eh?" The man sighed. "I sup-

pose it's something of an occupational hazard, me
gravitating toward this sort of bunch I mean, but what
else can I do, really? It's what I am.''

''Terrorists?'' Max said. ''Out to maim civilians?
Now *they're* your kind of people, too?''

The dapper man draped an arm over Max's shoulder. ''No, no, no, you're focusing in the wrong place.
Yes, when you put it that way, I suppose they need a
bit more discipline, more concern for niceties, but still
they're acting out in rather a swashbuckling style,
wouldn't you say? Clearly they're projecting a one-
against-the-many, individual-over-the-forces-of-the-
state attitude; you if anyone should appreciate that. It's
one of the things that drew me to *you*, after all.''

''But terrorists?'' Max said dubiously. ''Come on.
Do you have some quota to meet?''

''Nothing hard and fast. As patron of adventurers,
though, I suppose I do need to keep my hand in.''

Patron of adventurers? Jurtan thought. Wait a minute—did that mean this individual was really—

''Pardon me,'' said the man, turning his flashing
smile in Jurtan's direction. ''I haven't formally intro-
duced myself to your friend, Max.''

''Jurtan Mont,'' Max said, ''meet—''

''Phlinn Arol?'' sputtered Jurtan. ''The Adventurers' God?''

''Has someone been talking about me behind my
back?'' said Phlinn Arol. ''Charmed, I'm sure.'' He
executed a neat bow, managing to sweep his sword
neatly out of the way on the way down so that it didn't
bash against his leg, in a manner that Jurtan had thus
far totally failed to master for himself. Phlinn certainly
had the style down, at any rate, even if he did rattle
on more Jurtan had expected from the avatar of action.

But now Jurtan had remembered where he'd heard
this voice before. ''I'm charmed, too,'' Jurtan said,
popping a quick bow himself and then straightening
right up before any of them could slip away. ''But
we've met before. Almost, that is. You visited Max
while we were on the road, after we'd left Roosing

Oolvaya. In the middle of the night when you thought
I was asleep.''

Phlinn Arol raised an eyebrow at Max. "Letting
your friends sneak up on you now?" he said. "The
start of a bad habit, if you ask me. And you always
acted so concerned about perimeter security, too.''

"My mistake," said Max, glaring at Jurtan. "But
not my worst, either.''

"No," said Phlinn, "that's true. But you're working
on others. Who knows what you'll be able to come up
with?''

"I'd be happy to discuss it with you," Max said.

"Capital idea, yes, but no, not now, I'm running
late as it is, and certainly not here. Your other associate is getting rather a bit skittish, it would seem.''
The horse had been whimpering and wrinkling its nose
at the posters, and their still dripping glue, and was
now dancing nervously around at the end of its bridle.
"He has the right idea. He knows when to move on.
You're not the only one who wants my time, you
know, even if you are always one of the more stimulating. I'm at the Adventurers' Club, where else? Pop
round and see me." He coiled his cloak around and
headed off.

"What about—" Max hissed after him.

Phlinn stopped. "Oh, by the way, the Intuition Track
went off that way," he said, waving vaguely across the
plaza, "but you might as well not bother trying to pick
it up. The only Pseudonym who showed up was the
one who laid the Track, and they gave up and left after
this lot happened here.''

"Which Pseudonym?" Max said quickly. "Who
was it?''

"I hear the Pseudonym was the Table. As far as the
being behind the alias, I certainly couldn't say.''

"Couldn't or wouldn't?" Max muttered. "Well, I
suppose it was worth asking.''

"Catch you later, then," said Phlinn Arol. He
turned and began to vanish into the night, then paused
again, added, "Keep an eye on your friend," in a

cryptic over-the-shoulder remark, and strode quickly away.

"Which friend?" said Max. "Gods. Damn the bunch of them."

But Jurtan wasn't listening, Max noticed. His head was canted to one side and his face had glazed with concentration. "What is it?" Max said sharply.

"Watch out?" Jurtan mumbled. "I think."

"Where?" Max spun around, putting the wall at his back. His sword had appeared in his hand.

But no one was heading in their direction. No arrows were in flight, no spells were in progress, no creatures were on the loose. Could it be a false alarm? Only Jurtan's music sense had been reliable so far. What about—

Jurtan's head was craning upward. A dark shape was visible overhead in the murky light, a dark *expanding* shape, in fact a shape that was expanding because it was hurtling downward toward them—

Jurtan's teeth came together with a hard clack as Max thrust him away from the wall and dove after him. Jurtan sprawled on the cobblestones; Max rolled, a little more awkwardly than he liked, but came to his feet anyway, crouched and ready for further maneuvers, as the dark shape became a large chimney and then, as it plowed into the ground where they'd been standing, an exploding burst of masonry and hurtling fragments of bricks.

A brick caught Max in the chest and sent him over backward again. After a moment of judicious ground-hugging, then, and the end of the crunch and clatter of debris, he once again got up. The horse, with more foresight than either Max or Jurtan, had already edged aside away from the impact zone; now it stood eyeing Max with a look of some bemusement.

Jurtan was brushing himself off too. "I guess I'd better get used to this kind of stuff," he muttered. "Was *that* something aimed at us?"

"Don't even bother to ask," Max said disgustedly. "Damned if I know anymore."

"I mean, is dropping a chimney on someone a hall-mark of somebody you know? Like that steerhorn thing?"

"Nah, it's just sort of a classic, everybody does it occasionally. Maybe it was an accident."

"Right," said Jurtan. "Sure. I thought you told me accidents didn't just happen, they were made."

"Sometimes an accident is just an accident. There's always fate."

"Okay, fine. Have it your way."

"Don't worry," Max told him. It was just as well the kid didn't know about Ma Pitom. Ma was an absolute fiend for lurking on rooftops and shoving off decorative trim, the odd cornice and the occasional gargoyle. Of course, the local roofers' and builders' guilds loved him. He left them a lot of work to do.

But if that had been Homar Kalifa back in the woods with the steerhorn, and if this had been Ma Pitom, and knowing that that had certainly been The Hand off in Iskendarian's swamp, there was a larger question at hand. What could be bringing all these old sparring partners out of the woodwork all at once?

12

"Things are getting to be a fine muddle, there's no two ways about that," commented Zalzyn Shaa. He was speaking to no one in particular, or from a slightly different perspective to the world at large, promenading as he was down the Grand Boulevard in the heart of Peridol amidst the omnipresent crowds. As muddled as things might be, there was still a good deal of story left to run for each of his fellow players, no doubt. Shaa's main hope at the moment was that he would be around to see his full share of denouements, and not be cut short by time, space, or the action of unknowable forces. There was only so much power one had to influence the meta-plane.

And the currents of the marketplace, when it came to it, Shaa observed, eyeing the display of rich fabrics displayed beneath the wizard-lights in the shop window he was passing; linen, cashmere, angora; purple argaman and sharkskin. Come to think of it, he probably needed a new outfit, especially if he was intending to reenter the social whirl. Although it might be better to wait. Shaa hadn't yet gone through all the closets, and it was possible his sister had already provided some suitably baroque gear for the occasion.

Of course, Shaa thought, the inquiring mind might wonder why, beset as he was on all sides by curses, brothers, annoying gods, and menaces of other assorted sorts, the foremost consideration at hand was the social scene and what to wear for it. But one might equally ask what good an inquiring mind is, anyway, if all it does is bring one to such a situation in the first place.

Now that he had encountered at first hand and face-to-face the Administrator of Curses himself, of all the luck, there was clearly no purpose to be served by skulking around trying to assume an incognito, or moping around his digs either for that matter. On the other hand, he had forgotten the effect Peridol had on one's spirits and general outlook. It was probably unfair to blame Peridol for the fruitless excursions of the day, but then he was feeling in a rather unfair mood. Shaa doubted that the sect that promoted the Law of Conservation of Karma would appreciate his current application of it, where being stubborn and unfair to something in no position to fight back actually made him feel a bit better, but there it was. No one ever said the sect business was easy, either.

Not that Shaa had expected anything good to come of his earlier errands. Still, good practice required that one go through the motions. He had visited several medical practitioners, one already familiar with his case and another a specialist in magically inflicted chronic syndromes and curse-hooks. Their frustration at having no treatment for his condition, even an experimental one, was exceeded only by their pleasant expectation of being able to write up his case, and of course by the remunerative glow of his cash-on-the-table payment of fee. The cash may have been one thing, the case report was quite another; Shaa had left his own fully documented writeup among his effects. A Guide for Those Who May Follow, and all that.

On the other hand, Fah! He *would* have settled for a cure.

Those hadn't been the only practitioners he'd visited, of course. The others had exhibited a tendency to lock their doors, drop their shutters, and sneak out the back as soon as they smelled him coming. Shaa had managed to catch one in the alley making his escape, but then that didn't necessarily argue in favor of the fellow's competence either. In the event, the man had merely confirmed that Shaa was bearing a major curse before fainting dead away.

Consulting sorcerers obviously weren't what they used to be.

Not that Grand Rounds at the Thaumaturgical Guild, or even the University, had been much more of a help. No one wanted to tamper with the handiwork of a god like the Curse Administrator, especially while he was in town and had already staked out his victim face-to-face. And then there was his brother, too; no one was eager to go up against him, either.

Which left the unseen byways. And, of course, Max. Max was acting more unseen and inscrutable himself these days, enough to make one question his methods, if not his sanity. Shaa's final homily to Jurtan Mont back in Roosing Oolvaya had actually helped to focus the issue in Shaa's mind. Jurtan had slunk up to him just before setting forth with Max, as nervous as he usually was when bringing up a potentially touchy subject. Shaa could tell the thoughts going through Jurtan's mind: Shaa was supposedly Max's best buddy. Would Shaa be upset at Jurtan for complaining about him? On the other hand, Jurtan had seen Shaa argue with Max, too. "What's Max's problem, anyway?" Jurtan had opened with, tentatively.

"Which particular problem are we discussing here?"

"His attitude, I guess. He always seems mad I'm around. He treats me like I'm an idiot. He doesn't tell me what's going on or what he's doing. Okay, some of that I can take; he's trying to teach me to figure things out on my own, fine. But how am I supposed to figure out exactly what part I'm supposed to play in some plan he's cooked up when he doesn't even say there *is* a plan?"

"Max is a loner to the point of clinical pathology," Shaa had told him, a bit surprised to hear the statement coming from his own mouth. "He can be a total pain in the neck more often than even he realizes. It's

187

really quite obnoxious. He's good at what he does, though.'' *Or at least he used to be,* Shaa had added, under his voice. Max was starting to complicate things out of any bounds of rational necessity. When you thought about it, these were rather disturbing signs.

On the other hand, what did it really matter, anyway? Shaa had enough objectivity to recognize how far he was sliding into ennui, but the undertow of apathy was enough to make him not exactly care. What point was there in getting rid of the gods, after all? Max's longtime goal would just shift the problems of life onto another playing field; it wouldn't necessarily solve anything. In fact, Shaa was aware he hadn't had a major goal in some time other than just staying alive. Now, back in Peridol, in the midst of his youthful haunts, there was some question whether *that* was even a worthwhile goal.

He was passing another row of boutiques, one here for perfumes and rare scents, another there for furs, wraps, and mufflers torn from the backs of endangered species. When you thought about it, it was amazing how quickly you could sink back into old habits, even ones you'd thought you'd rejected and had deliberately fled from. The attitude of studied disdain that could make one bemoan the loss of life and natural resources involved in making a fur coat while simultaneously patronizing the nearest salon was characteristic of the Peridol aristocracy. Shaa, as a young rebel about town, had speechified in the coffeehouses against the legacy of his class, and its tendency to reduce all the excesses and pleasures of life to banality. Fine foods, rich surroundings, ostentatious dinner parties followed by bedhopping—unfortunately, it was a life he could probably slide back into without a hitch. But that would bring along with it the effete languor that shaved off the highs and lows and left one floundering mindlessly in a sybaritic haze.

What he needed was a project, a focus.

Well, there *was* the Creeping Sword. Like Shaa, the Sword had some serious problems, apparently related to magic and the gods, that Max had decided to help him with. The Sword also shared Shaa's doubts about how liberally Max might interpret his self-appointed mission. When the Sword had come to Shaa aboard ship, it had been because he wasn't sure he could talk honestly with Max; they'd never hit it off right, and furthermore the Sword thought Max might represent a threat or become an adversary once the whole story, whatever it was, began to come out. In the Sword's way of thinking, Karlini was too far out to lunch to help, and wasn't terribly well-grounded in the real world to start with. But the Sword didn't know how much longer he could manage his balancing act solo. Deciding he needed someone smart and savvy in his corner, he'd elected Shaa.

Shaa turned off the boulevard onto a tree-shaded avenue faced on both sides by elegantly colonnaded townhouses. Where was that key?—oh, there it was, just where it was supposed to be, in his pocket. The Sword had hoped for a useful slant on Max. In the course of thinking about the Sword's situation and Max's place in it, though, Shaa had ended up in a grudging reexamination of his own relationship with Max. It—hmm. Shaa eyed the key in his hand. One of Max's trademark gimmicks throughout the years they'd known each other was his habit of showing up in spots where he had no reason to be.

And Shaa could always use the exercise, especially without the caloric drain of active magic-use helping to keep his weight in line. Although it had never been quite mainstream, physical culture had long been an accepted option for the Peridol elite; this was one thing Shaa had never quarreled too much with, after shaking off the sloth of a bookish childhood. So why not?

Stowing the key, Shaa crossed light-footedly to the nearest street-adjacent tree, an oak of some stature, grabbed the lowest branch, and swung nimbly up. By the time he was ensconced in an upper branch, edging his way out over the nearest townhouse's front yard, his heart rate had accelerated dramatically, his breath had shortened to pants broken by periodic paroxysms, and he felt thoroughly rotten. As far as Shaa was concerned, though, that was no reason to lie down and give up. The branch overhung the third-floor pediment of the townhouse. Shaa carefully transferred his grasp on the branch to a perch atop the pediment and strolled off across the roof. A small flock of starlings wheeling in for a landing reconsidered and darted off as Shaa reached the edge of the building.

A running leap would have once carried him easily to the next townhouse over. Under the present circumstances he thought it might be pushing things to risk it. He never went out without a rope, however, and a judicious sling-and-swing maneuver soon had taken him across the gap, and then shortly after that to the succeeding townhouse as well. His key fit the lock on the roof door. The landing beyond was empty. A tall drink of water with an antiarrhythmic herb, followed by an overstuffed easy chair; that was the ticket.

The easy chair in the sitting room on the ground floor proved to be occupied, however. "Don't you think that was kind of a dumb stunt?" said Max. He gestured toward Shaa with a half-eaten sandwich on a large sourdough roll. "Look at you. Now you're a mess."

"Nice to see you again, Maximillian," said Shaa. "If I'm such a wreck, you could give me that chair."

"This *is* a comfortable chair," Max agreed. "Eden has good taste in furniture." He didn't move to get up, though, which seemed to indicate that the sofa would have to serve as an appropriate half-measure. Jurtan Mont appeared from the bathroom as Shaa was making himself comfortable in a full-length recline, and after pleasantries and another run to the kitchen for Shaa's antiarrhythmic, they settled down to compare notes.

Max and Jurtan proved to be fresh off the streets and an abortive Track-run. "I suppose you're planning to stay here, then," said Shaa, "seeing as it's already late."

"Lateness has nothing to do with it," said Max. "You've got plenty of room here, and anyway Eden said to make ourselves at home."

"As if you've ever needed an invitation," Shaa grumbled. Max, playing true to form, ignored his comment completely.

A perusal of the Iskendarian documents, now getting slightly ragged from the travel in which they'd recently engaged, was interesting if not ultimately productive. "Now am I crazy," Max said, waving one of the pages at Shaa, "or is that some kind of chain-reaction memory-wipe trigger?"

Shaa held the paper in front of him, wrong side out, and squinted at the transilluminated vellum. "You're thinking Spell of Namelessness, aren't you?"

"Well, aren't *you?*"

"Yes," Shaa said cautiously, "I suppose that would be a reasonable interpretation. Do you have any idea what kind of code he's using? Aside from the fact he's writing backwards, of course."

"I've been working on it," said Max, "but it could take a long time. A *long* time. You got any ideas?"

"Have you tried aiming Jurtan's music sense at it?"

"Yeah," said Max, and "Not really," said Jurtan. Max frowned at Jurtan. "You've been looking at it *here,* haven't you? You haven't had any particular insights, have you?"

"Uh, no," said Jurtan. "I guess not."

"Perhaps there are others who could help with the decipherment," Shaa tossed out.

"Maybe," Max said. "But who can we trust?"

"The Karlinis deserve a shot, of course, but of course you'll already have planned on that." Shaa kept his face furrowed in thought. Haddo might be an interesting option, and possibly the Creeping Sword, but it would perhaps be prudent not to bring them up right at the moment. Keeping information from Max was always a dicey business, Shaa reminded himself, and not to be undertaken lightly. Still, Max was not the only one around who had occasion to practice deception.

Shaa had known him a long time, too; long enough to know how his mind worked. "There is one obvious recourse at hand," Shaa ventured.

"The Iskendarian shelf in the Archives," Max stated. "With or without Iskendarian, it's time for a run to the Archives. They've been on my mind for a while."

"Things aren't the same as the last time, you know. I hear there's a new Archivist."

"Well, I'd better meet him, then."

"Hmm," said Shaa. "Indeed. Well, you know where the Archives are. It should be easy enough to discover the hours of operation."

"Right," said Max. *Why did he sound so sarcastic?* Jurtan thought. *Oh, of course. He's Max; that means he probably plans to break into the place.*

"And then there's the Inauguration Ball," Shaa was continuing. "As long as I'm here in town I wouldn't miss it for the world." In contrast to his words, Shaa sounded kind of disgusted about the whole thing, thought Jurtan. But then you couldn't necessarily tell about Shaa. "Sitting around just waiting for another shoe to drop does get a bit old. Do you want to be there?"

"I rather think so," Max said. "Don't *you* think it might be a good idea?"

"Goodness and wisdom have nothing to do with it," stated Shaa. "The fact that it's the beginning of the Season is the only fact that really matters. And what are we here for, after all, if not the Season? The investiture of the first new emperor in over a decade is a virtual footnote, a mere codicil."

"What are you doing," Max said, "trying on your old persona? All that Peridol stuff never worked for you. You're too odd."

"Fortunately," Shaa said, "you *are* my friend. I shudder to think what you might be saying about me otherwise."

"Do you think your brother will be at this Inauguration Ball?" asked Jurtan.

"*Be* there?" said Shaa. "He practically *owns* the thing."

"Oh," Jurtan said. "Well, I guess you have to run into him sometime."

Shaa frowned. "Unfortunately, that is rather the point."

13

I had arrived at the address Shaa had given me just in time to see Max and Jurtan Mont entering, after Max had done something crafty to the door. That meant link-up with Shaa was out of the question for the moment; the one person I was least interested in dealing with right then was Maximillian the Vaguely Disreputable. Unless it was Zhardann or Jill, or for that matter Gashanatantra, and let's not forget Joatal Ballista, aka Fradjikan, which I guess was just another way of saying that I had more trouble than I knew what to do with any direction I turned.

Shaa was sure staying in a hoity-toity section of town, I had to give him that. Me, I was basically on the streets. I'd had the vague idea of renting an office and setting up shop, but the more I thought about it the more potential drawbacks kept surfacing, even aside from the fact that with so many people in town real estate was one of the commodities in shortest supply. Staying mobile might help keep me ahead of the folks on my tail, too. When you got right down to it, too, the whole office idea was a distraction. I wasn't here to be a detective-for-hire, I was here to find answers and solutions to my own problems.

Well, I'd lurked behind this tree long enough. Night might have firmly fallen, but here in the midst of Peridol it didn't seem to much matter. The streets had more lamps than anyplace I'd seen before, and every other carriage or walker seemed to be carrying another one of their own. Lanterns weren't the half of it, either. Radiant globs of magic and out-and-out sculptures were perched in the intersections, and others were floating freely along the boulevards. Over to the south, too, in the part of town where I'd heard the sorcerers congregated in their rows of lofts, manufacturing plants, academies, and colleges, occasional sprays of fireworks erupted into the sky, and a large precessing pinwheel had been hanging for the last half hour firing aquamarine sparks.

As I pried myself loose from my perch and strolled toward the end of the block, splashes of light from near and far washing over the scene, a man turned the corner ahead of me, glanced around him, and then launched himself into the nearest tree. Leaves rustled gently but quickly fell still; the guy was good. An indistinct form reappeared a moment later out on a branch. The man swung himself onto the adjacent roof and into the glow of a dying starshell, and only then did I realize I'd been watching Zalzyn Shaa. He was too far out of earshot to call to and I'd never catch him going up the tree either; he was moving at a surprisingly good clip considering his health problems. I shrugged and headed on toward the boulevard. I'd check back with him later.

The question of the office kept nagging at me. A large part of my mind was pulling me in the direction of familiar instinct, as though it was following some kind of built-in track and didn't want me to head off on my own. It probably wouldn't make much difference one way or the other—if the gods were going to come after me they'd find me sooner or later regardless, although I might be able to make it later rather than sooner, and on my terms. Maybe what I really needed was some genuine training in magic. I seemed stuck with these abilities I'd sucked out of Gash, and I kept running into these sorcery-based situations to boot, so I might be better off if I learned more about what I really could be doing.

That wouldn't be a bad idea to add to my plan. Not

that it was much of a plan in the first place, but you had to start somewhere. Distancing myself from Max felt like a reasonable first step. It would be even better if I could take advantage of any information Max might feed me through Shaa while staying out of Max's immediate grasp, at least until I knew more about what was going on.

There were other possibilities on my list. Learning how to more convincingly play the role of a god would be nice. If I could do that, I might be able to use or otherwise deal with the ring containing the trapped Pod Dall. The Karlinis had had the ring the last time I checked, but if I had to I could probably get it away from them. Then again, they might even let me borrow it. I am—or I was—a detective; that kind of thing should have been right up my line.

That wasn't the only thing up my line. What about detecting, itself? My own backtrail apparently didn't exist before I'd shown up in Roosing Oolvaya, but that didn't mean I might not still uncover somebody who'd known me earlier or some evidence about what I might have been doing. A list of people who'd been affected by the Spell of Namelessness over the years would be nice. Did any such list exist? If it did, could it be short enough to be of any use? Maybe there was documentation about gods who'd had the Spell used on them. That should be a shorter list—how many gods would ever have been in that situation, after all?

The Peridol library was supposed to have all kinds of interesting stuff. I could do worse than stopping in to ask the librarian. But then, that wasn't the only individual it might be useful to consult. The street wouldn't be the most likely place to find him, however. I put my head down and pushed forward.

Like most other places I'd seen in Peridol so far the boulevard was crowded, even though it was going on the middle of the evening. The folks in the crowd were better dressed and altogether more kempt than those I'd encountered earlier. Given the high-class appearance of the district, and its location at the foot of the

Crust not far outside the gates, that wasn't surprising. The street was free and clear of scum and garbage and the walls were clear of the otherwise omnipresent posters and slogans.

For all their show of gentility, though, the passersby were acting a touch strangely. Not in general, just toward me. Whenever I entered a patch of decent lighting, people started to stare. More than one or two of them even did a full-scale double take on catching sight of my face, and all around others were nudging their companions and pointing in my direction and stopping to whisper among themselves. When I glanced back, I discovered a small gang of kids dogging my steps.

I may have been from out-of-town, but I wasn't exactly a bumpkin. There was no straw in *my* hair, and I wasn't wearing hand-me-down homespun or walking around in some costume of equatorial minimalism. The last time I checked no one was going to find on me an unusual number of arms or eyes or some other major divergence in physiognomy. Monoch wasn't making a nuisance of himself. So what was going on?

An alleyway appeared on the right and I darted into it. A few twists later I paused long enough to unwrap my overcloak and slip it over my head. Unfortunately, the cloak wasn't designed with the head-covering in mind; if I ran across a monk, maybe I could try to grab his hood. Until then, I'd probably look like an itinerant ragpicker or someone preparing for rain, but I could live with that. I've lived with worse.

I kept to the shadows and finally ended up back in a decent-sized street, in a less exalted but hopefully more mind-your-own-business neighborhood. As I stepped out of the alley, I passed a tall brick wall liberally plastered with generation atop generation of messy posters. I had already gone past it when some tickle in the back of my mind made me stop, turn around, and give the broadsides my real attention.

So *that* was it. Damn! It was a good likeness, too, or at least good enough. There was Monoch flaming away, and the animated statue and the words of fire and the whole bit, but the greatest care had gone into rendering me, posing me like a real honest-to-gods hero, of all things. So much for being anonymous and melting into crowds; any of my god pals who wanted to track me down only had to listen for the murmurs and follow the stares. The next time I saw Fradjikan I just might try to wring his neck. No lie, he was turning out to be a pretty tricky customer indeed.

On the other hand, being turned into an icon of advertising probably did solve another problem. From my casing the city on the way over to Shaa's place, and the map I'd picked up from a street vendor, I knew pretty much where I was; almost at my destination of the moment. Ten minutes of brisk walking interspersed with slinking from one shadow to the next brought me to the nearest entrance.

The entrance itself was nothing dramatic. It had instead the studied nonchalance of someone who knows they're cool and wants to underline the point by pretending they took it for granted. Characteristically, the obvious entrance that you came into off the street was a well-stocked bar, with the real entrance being a staircase leading down from an unmarked alcove to the left through the door to the kitchen. I had to wait at the top for a party of guys with swords to exit, and close on their heels an ax-toting dwarf, before I got my own chance to descend.

A sign of glowing words hung in the air on the landing halfway down, curling from one language and script-form to the next in wisps of orange and green while an unseen voice pronounced their message directly into your ear. I heard a skirl of gibberish, and then the voice said softly in Peridol common, "Adventurers' Club. Members and qualified guests only. Turn back now or risk consequences." I went through the message and down the stairs to the lobby.

The lobby proved to be as small and chummy as I'd imagined, with a lot of dark panels of wood promoting the shadowed gloom and a few burgundy-cushioned armchairs trying to elbow it back. One wall was hung with shredded battle pennants stained with grass and mud and other authentic-looking substances. A trophy case faced it, the most prominent of its exhibits being a pair of thong sandals and a throwing knife. I was bending over to read the exhibit card next to the shoes when a throat cleared itself at me from behind the reception desk.

"Good day, sir," the clerk said as I ambled the three steps toward him across the room. "I don't believe you've been with us before. May I help you? If you wish to give an offering, the worship area is upstairs."

I rested an elbow on the counter. "I need a room."

The clerk's tone remained noncommittal. "Are you certified, or do you have tokens of accreditation?"

I pushed the cloak back off my head. The clerk looked up from his register and squinted, then one eyebrow went up, followed by the other. "Ah," he said, "I see. I will put down 'obvious current notoriety.' Accommodations for . . . how many in your party? Do you wish flagrant or anonymous?"

"One, anonymous," I told him.

"Do you plan to lecture or otherwise hold forth?"

"I'll let you know."

"Very good, sir. Here is your key, the map shows the hidden exits to your suite, and here is your certificate of active adventurer status. Just follow the commotion to the bar of your choice. Do you have baggage, or will you be needing to restock or equip?"

This was all I'd heard, and more. "Every Facility for the Discriminating Adventurer," indeed. "Stocking up would be nice," I said.

"Shall I send the chandler or the armorer around first?"

"Whichever. It can wait till morning, but what you could get me tonight is some food."

We went back and forth a few more times on the question of the night menu before he finally let me find my way to the room. The halls snaked along in short straight-line segments broken by acute-angle jogs and lateral offsets, the result being you could hear if someone was approaching along the hardwood floors before they hove into sight. With the number of dark alcoves, tall potted plants and ceiling-height trees, and not a few coats of armor, there were plenty of places to hide if you didn't want whoever-it-was to see you. My suite proved to have a sitting room, its own bathroom with functioning internal plumbing, and a bed fit for quite a few adventures itself, I didn't doubt. I dropped the pack and slipped off my boots and settled back on top of the covers to study the brochure. Of most immediate interest was the list of hidden passages and doors, but I'd kick myself forever if I'd been in a place like this and didn't find out about the other amenities.

I'd been examining the documentation and kicking a few other odd things around in my mind for a moment or two when a voice spoke in front of me. "You have been causing a lot of people a lot of trouble," it said.

Standing there at the side of the bed was someone I'd seen before. He'd been at the gathering of gods I'd attended courtesy of Zhardann and Jill and Gash (in his disguise of Soaf Pasook). Or at least someone who looked exactly like the figure facing me now had been at that meeting, which wasn't at all the same thing as being able to conclude they were in fact the same personage, as I had now come to understand more deeply. Nevertheless, the mustache, the impossibly wavy blond hair, the neat scar, and the single jeweled earring that confronted me at the moment in the flickering lamplight were exactly as I remembered them.

How they had snuck up on me was another question. For all I knew I'd had another blackout. Seeing as who this was, though, I wouldn't have put it past him in the least to have catfooted it into the room with me fully conscious, and looking in his direction all the time to boot. "Phlinn Arol," I said. "Nice of you to drop by." But then, where better to encounter the Adventurers' God but at the Adventurers' Club?

"I thought I'd bring your dinner round myself," said Phlinn. He indicated the tray next to me on the end table. "The personal touch, you know. Now that I'm here, I find I don't seem to have eaten lately either. Do you mind if I join you?"

"Be my guest," I told him. "If the master of the house wants to spend his time hanging out with a customer, it's a dumb customer indeed who'll tell him to get lost."

Phlinn seated himself at the chair next to the end table and set to work carving hearty slices off the roast. "You're not a vegetarian, then, I take it?"

He *had* popped in to see *me*, which I suppose gave him the right to choose the elements of conversation. Still, this was one of the stranger opening gambits I could easily recall, and remember I'd been spending time with some world masters of the disputationally bizarre. "Not the last time I checked," I said. "If you're looking for vices I'm afraid you'll be disappointed. I don't smoke, but I have been known to drink on occasion." From the look of the flagon on the tray it was a reasonable hope this occasion would be one of them.

Phlinn Arol took a sidelong glance at me, then returned his attention to the roast. "I see," he said. "I rather like diversity in adventurers, you know. Not to mention the adventurers themselves, mind you; that goes without saying. Horseradish sauce?"

"A small dollop on the side."

"It's excellent stuff. They grow the roots out back. Considering how far the Club meanders, though, you won't find that information very useful if you think you can raid the garden, I'll warn you right now."

I had a feeling there was some local allusion going on here I wasn't tuned into. The Treasure of the Secret Herb Garden of the Adventurers' Club? But then the world was a strange place. I settled for saying, "I'm not in town looking for treasures," and let him take that whichever way he wanted.

"No," said Phlinn Arol, "no, I didn't suppose you

were. Treasures of the material sort at any rate, hmm?''

"Why can't anybody ever have a straightforward starts-here ends-up-there kind of talk?" I muttered. "This stuff gets a little old."

"Complained like a true adventurer," Phlinn commented approvingly. "I presume you will unbend your feelings about vegetables sufficiently to accept some of these peas on the side, and perhaps a spear of broccoli? The local chef makes a specialty out of scalloping these potatoes, too, I'd best warn you."

"Everything but the broccoli," I said. "I hate broccoli."

"Do you now," he said, almost to himself. "I wouldn't have thought broccoli would be invariant, of all things."

"Wait a minute," I said, taking the plate from his hand and setting it right down again. "What are you talking about? What's the big deal about broccoli?"

Phlinn eyed me consideringly. "I once knew someone who hated broccoli. He wasn't anything else like you, though."

Hated broccoli? What kind of useless coincidence was that? On the other hand, maybe this broccoli-hater had been my father. Maybe my brother. Hell, maybe he'd been *me*. "Broccoli, eh? Sounds interesting. How long ago did you know this friend?"

"Forget about it," Phlinn said, waving his hand dismissively. "I'm sure it's not relevant."

"Relevant? To what?"

"To our conversation, of course."

"To *what* conversation? You waltz in here, say I've been causing a lot of trouble, and then the only thing you talk about is *vegetables*. Look, I was coming here to see you because I was hoping to get some answers, and I wouldn't mind maybe a little help either. I've been paying dues to you all these years, I figure I should be able to ask for *something*. And then there were those cryptic little comments you dropped the last time we met, when we were all ganging up on old Sapriel.''

''Cryptic comments?''

''Yeah, that's right, about how we should get together, about how our interests are congruent, I think you said, about how you'd been in contact with a friend of mine named Max.''

''Oh,'' he said, in a *pro forma* sort of way, *''those* cryptic comments. If you recall, there were others around at the time. Speaking plainly was plainly unwise.''

''Yeah,'' I said, ''right. But there aren't others around now.'' The statements I'd reminded him of weren't all, either. There had been his remarks about his association with the long-dead god who had started Abdicationism, a guy called Byron, remarks that had implied that Phlinn Arol might now be the main keeper of the flame. And Gash had told me to stay away from Phlinn because he was a subversive radical, too.

All of which had bounced Phlinn Arol to the number-one slot on my list of folks I *should* be talking to.

Except now I *was* talking to him, and it was about as rewarding as interrogating the broccoli he'd included, after all, on my plate.

''You *are* a lot of trouble,'' Phlinn Arol told me.

''Why, because when I ask somebody a question and they don't want to answer, I ask it again? You must hang out in a pretty quiet section of town.''

He set down his fork and raised his arm. It occurred to me then that for all his cozy exterior, he *was* a god, and probably one of the more powerful I'd run across. Phlinn gestured at me, but it was Monoch, resting on the bed at my far side, who stirred. Monoch made a low whine and rolled over against my leg. He was hot and vibrating.

''That is a particularly dangerous implement to be carrying around,'' Phlinn Arol informed me. ''Especially if one is not its owner.''

"Who says I'm not its owner? Gashanatantra gave it to me."

"If you believe that you're not the person I take you for."

"Okay," I said, "then you tell me. Who *do* you take me for?"

Phlinn hesitated, then lowered his hand. Monoch continued to make the buzz of an aggravated beehive. I wanted to take Monoch in my *own* hand, but what was I going to do then? Attack the broccoli? I wanted information out of Phlinn Arol, not a battle royal. Finally he spoke. "You are not who you seem to be, you know."

"That's not exactly news."

"You are also not who you think you are."

"Seeing as I don't even have the slightest idea who I think I am any more, that also isn't hard. If you know so much, who am I, then?"

"That's a very good question."

"Yeah," I said, "more news. Maybe I'd better phrase it a different way. Who do you think I am?"

"Perhaps no one," said Phlinn Arol. "On the other hand, perhaps someone. I'm not being evasive, I really don't know."

I gave him a dirty look. "Let's start with the basics, then. I'm not Gashanatantra, you know that. You knew that the other time we met. You knew I wasn't Gash even though nobody else except Gash seemed to. Gash had a good excuse; he was the one who'd set me up, and he was there in his own disguise as Soaf Pasook. So how did you know? And how did you know I had some connection with Max, and why was that something we needed to talk about?"

"Simple enough," Phlinn said, taking another bite of roast. He swallowed and thumped himself on the chest. "I love that horseradish. There's a story behind that horseradish, in fact—" He eyed me, and must have caught the flavor of my expression and its clear message of rapidly dwindling patience. "But perhaps that story should wait for later. Max mentioned you to me, so I know about the Spell of Namelessness, of course. Max thought I might know who you were. When I saw you, it was easy enough to determine who you were *supposed* to be, what with the aural interleave from Gashanatantra and the camouflage field being put out by your friend, there.'' He nodded at Monoch.

''Is Monoch transmitting to Gash?''

''Not at the moment,'' he said with certainty. ''But in general it's quite likely. I'd be surprised if Gashanatantra wasn't rather interested in the question of your identity himself. I assume he stumbled across you by accident and only later discovered what he'd stirred up. You've been making significant use of his magical resources, haven't you?''

''Not in a real controlled way,'' I said, ''but yeah, I have. I haven't exactly been efficient at it, though. It might help if I had a better idea what I'm doing.''

''We can look into that. From what one hears, you've been particularly lucky, you know.''

''That hasn't escaped my notice either, and don't bother to tell me luck doesn't last forever because I know *that*, too. Magic isn't the only area where I don't know the score. As long as all these other gods think I'm a god just like them and I've got to keep up the fancy footwork—well, you know what kind of loser's game that is.'' If I couldn't get dancing lessons, at least I might get a look at the dance card.

''Oh, you've got the attitude down just right, don't worry about that.''

I didn't know whether that was supposed to be a compliment or not. Since I wasn't after praise or approval, though, I'd take the information content of his remark at face value and ignore the tone. ''Are you waiting for me to tell you how much I already know so you won't have to reveal too much new to me? Fine, if that's the way you're going to make it.'' Under normal circumstances I would have held out and played with him a while longer; the less you seemed to want, the more you could usually end up with. I had the feeling his patience would outlast mine, though. He was interested in me, but he was also just fishing; if he had a particular goal in mind I couldn't sense what it was. I took a deep breath. "I know about the Conservationists and the Abdicationists; the Conservationists wanting to keep the status quo and the Abdicationists fighting to make the gods phase out of meddling with the world. That's oversimplified, but okay. I know about Pod Dall holding a balance of power that kept too much from happening. Then he wound up trapped in a ring and the balance started to break down. Gash helped put him in the ring, and now Gash is doing his best to ride with his plot and stay a winner while cleaning up against his enemies while he's at it. Using me as his broom."

"You have a particularly vibrant way of putting things, do you know that? But let that pass. You've been out of touch since Oolsmouth, haven't you?"

"Yeah, I suppose you could say that."

"Then you don't know what your pal Zhardann kicked loose by his little stunt, do you."

"I can guess," I said.

"Can you?" said Phlinn Arol. "Since Zhardann convened that gathering to put the seal of mass approval on his move against Sapriel, it's been a veritable madhouse out there. It's gone far beyond politics. Every grudge and petty vendetta anyone's ever harbored is out in the open. How long has it been in real time, a few weeks? At least three gods have been decorporealized, *three*, and there are rumors of another two more. *Decorporealized*. That's more than in most *decades*. Yes, they were minors, but *still*. It's an absolute mess."

"And you're just sitting on the sidelines? Trying to quiet things down?"

"What do you take me for? If I don't uphold my image, *I'm* a target."

"I see," I told him. And maybe I did, or at least maybe I was starting to. The situation might have gone far beyond politics, but I bet it wasn't ignoring them either. The issue of Abdicationism was a question of existence to the gods, and under what (and whose) terms. "Are you telling me it's open warfare among the gods? Every god for himself?"

"It's not quite that bad," Phlinn acknowledged, mopping his brow with his napkin and trying to calm himself down, "not yet, anyway. The only way we've been able to live together all these years in some degree of harmony has been though our traditions, our customs and protocols and rituals, our ways of adjudicating disputes and battles and so forth *without* spilling into general warfare."

"I don't understand something. How did Zhardann's little ploy upset all of that, then? By stacking the deck against Sapriel? Was that what was against the rules?"

"No," he said. "Yes. Zhardann was the trigger. The fuse was there, he provided the match."

The fuse, I thought. But that's not all I thought. "Pod Dall," I said. "But I thought he was a Death."

"Death is such a relative term," Phlinn Arol said, a little impatiently, I thought. Phlinn took another look at the roast and then pushed his plate away from him, scowling at it. "All of us can be Deaths, if you think about things in that sort of way. The Death part was the least important side to Pod Dall. He was one of the Checks and Balances. He was the Referee. A strange fellow, Pod Dall." Phlinn shook his head. "To be willing to stand outside, to backpedal his own aggrandizement, to neglect scheming and plotting, to be *evenhanded*—well, it's certainly not *godlike,* I can assure you of that."

I'd seen enough on my own to agree with him. "So no one else wants to do his job and the system's breaking down."

Phlinn glanced up at me, squinted, and looked away across the room. "I wish Byron were still around. He's the only one who could have made heads or tails of this and brought things back under control. Any of the rest of us who try will most likely just add to the confusion.''

Like I said, I'd heard about Byron before; Byron, Phlinn Arol's old pal; Byron, founder of Abdicationism; Byron, creator of the gods' communication and meeting system, and, by inference, the larger infrastructure Phlinn had just been alluding to; Byron, described by Phlinn as ''the trickiest of us all, but not always the most prudent;'' Byron, purged by the gods—by Jardin himself, in fact—and dead-and-gone these several centuries. Byron, whom Phlinn had connected with what he'd called ''the genesis thing.'' ''If Byron was so smart, why didn't he deal with a contingency like this? Wouldn't he figure something might happen to your Referee?''

''At the end he might not have cared,'' Phlinn said slowly. It looked like I'd started a thought in his mind, though.

''Byron knew the innards of what made you gods tick, right?'' I continued. ''Why would he bother with Abdicationism in the first place? Why not shut the system down himself? Why bother spinning things out this way?''

''He liked the system, thought it could be reformed.'' But Phlinn sounded a bit uncertain of himself.

''And what happened to Bryon's stuff? His records, his papers, any equipment? Who else was he friendly with? Maybe he *did* leave something helpful around. Where would it be? Who would have it?''

Phlinn said something, but I couldn't hear it. I knew it wasn't important, really, it was only something vague about looking through his own records, and maybe there were a few other places for him to check, too. I couldn't hear him directly, but I caught the sense of what he was saying. I hadn't realized I was concentrating so much on my own questions, focusing myself so much that I was digging into Gash's data link again, but obviously I was because all of a sudden my vision blurred, the sounds of the room faded out, the world of mist I'd seen in my dream descended, and I could see another realer-than-real face, and had on the tip of my tongue another name. I couldn't quite get at the name yet, but I knew whose name it was; Byron's last protégé close to the end. A wizard of some sort, a human wizard.

Phlinn was looking at me strangely—he was on his feet, too. I blinked. At the moment I'd noticed Phlinn again, it was because the mist had suddenly disappeared. "Why was I saying all that to you?" Phlinn muttered. "I wasn't—I didn't—I, ah." He had his hand pointed in my direction again, his head tilted quizzically to one side. "There may be more that makes you a detective than just your training, I think," he said to himself, still mumbling.

There was too much going on here, far too much. I needed to catch my thoughts. I still needed to ask about— "The Spell of Namelessness," I said. "Maybe there's some compensating effect; you lost your memory, you become a detective. Tell me this—who knows the most about the spell? How many people have been hit by it—is there a list? Is there—"

The stand-up closet against the wall behind Phlinn had pivoted open, revealing a dark opening that hadn't been listed in the brochure I'd been reading about the room, and Phlinn was backing toward it. "Far too many for a list," Phlinn said, "far too many. Perhaps Jardin has records, you know he likes that spell of course, don't you? But still there would be far too many. Jardin's not the only one wielding that spell, you know, although he does have it by right of office. But you know that already, too, don't you. I'm afraid there's no help for you there."

"Wait a minute! I still have a lot to—"

"I've spent far too long—I have other business, pressing business. I'll be back in contact. I'm on your side, you know."

"It's good to know that," I told him. "That's reassuring, but—"

Apparently satisfied, he continued through the bureau and vanished through the wall. The furniture wheeled shut behind him. Slowly, I shut my mouth, bottling up the questions I'd never gotten to ask, not to mention the ones he'd never answered.

Some detective *I* was.

He'd left me with the remains of the roast. He'd also left the broccoli. The broccoli wasn't the largest problem he'd left behind, though.

I don't know why I hadn't expected it. After all, everybody else seemed to be lying to each other, or at best passing around half-truths. Why should Phlinn Arol be any different? That he knew more than he was willing to admit seemed certain, or at least if he didn't know for sure he had some strong suspicions.

What was he afraid I'd find out? Even more, why had he seemed to fall apart there at the end? He was Phlinn Arol, for gods' sake. Why was he afraid of *me*?

The link to Gash had shut down again, now that I had a *real* question for it. I mean, how much use would it be for me to know that good old Byron, gone for centuries, had palled around with a human? A mere human would have been dead a long time by now. Well, maybe someone else had heard of him. Or maybe I'd find something about *him* in my research, this wizard called . . . called? Iskendarian, that's what his name was. Big deal. In Peridol you could buy a dozen wizards with a good-sized carp.

14

As had been his habit since his youth, Svin closed his
eyes, turned his face to the heavens, threw wide his
arms, and began to draw a deep, forceful breath in
through his nose. He had managed no more than a
moderate sniff before the air launched a full-scale assault on his nostrils and lungs—there was smoke in it,
and soot, and rancid cooking grease, and some type
of acrid brew that made his chest seize in its expansion
as though slapped suddenly around by bands of iron,
and—but it was too disgusting to even contemplate.
Svin exhaled with a convulsive wheeze-and-gasp that
far outstripped the effort he'd put into bringing the vile
stuff in in the first place.

He was far from the pure frozen nectar of his youth
in the north, as if he needed yet another reminder of
how much his path had taken him away from . . . from
what? Harmony and oneness with nature? Well, yes,
that had been part of it, and the way of the warrior
born, too, and the other traditions of his fathers. But
then new experiences were not necessarily a bad thing
either, nor (as he was gradually coming to acknowledge) was personal change or growth. Now if only—

"Isn't this great, Svin—I mean just look at it!"

Svin opened his eyes. Tildamire Mont, freshly
scrubbed and with her hair still damp from the morning Karlini wash ritual, had joined him on the stoop
in front of the facility. Svin had heard her approach,
of course, and had identified her by the sound of her

211

step. Of course he had, he told himself. After all, that was no more than his job. But— "Great?" he said.

"Sure it is!" Tildy bubbled. "Here we are at last in a real city—I mean it moves, it bustles, things are happening everywhere, and it's all going on all day and all night—it *is* great!"

"Great," repeated Svin, with less enthusiasm and no little skepticism. It *did* move, it did bustle, and so forth; these things were undeniable. The narrow street in front of the small building the Karlini party had taken over hadn't been empty for a moment since they'd arrived, night or day. If anything, there were more carts, people, animals, familiars, and things rattling along its twisty maze the later the hour became, reaching a climax only toward midnight. That, too, was to be expected. Where else would the Karlinis set up shop but in the heart of the Conjurers' Quarter?

Fortunately Svin had gotten a lot of rest on the boat. After they'd finished hauling all the gear from the ship through the tangled streets and their congested traffic, Roni would settle for nothing but that they immediately unpack and set things up. This operation had taken them all the better part of the day and well into the night. Svin's short sleep had started then, only to terminate some unknown distance into the new day when several crowds of shouting students from some of the nearby schools or academies had lurched along, shouting spells and imprecations at each other. They had stopped to launch into a mass duel right underneath Svin's second-story open-window guard-perch. Pinwheels and sprays of multicolored firebeams were lancing outside the window when he'd cranked open his eyes, dying embers raining their sooty fallout in the low breeze directly through the casement and onto his chest.

There was nothing to be done about it, though; nothing practical, anyway. The neighbors on either side and across the street were obviously old hands at this sort of entertainment. After making sure their buildings were not actually burning, they leaned out their own windows and proceeded to yell at each other or the academicians below in running commentary, place the occasional side bet, dodge the nastier-looking constructs from below, and rain a few tricks down in return. Svin had watched silently, his sword at the ready, but the Great Karlini had gone further, rousing himself to spin out a swarm of animated pink mosquito-things that had gone swooping down into the crowd. Judging from the reaction below, the pink things had acted like real mosquitoes, setting loose a wave of frenzied swatting broken by ouches and squeals of pain. For this, Karlini's wife had taken the time to chide him, reminding him that they were not here to attract attention but to work. Karlini had turned away, his frown once again intact.

But how much attention would one more magic-user bring around here? The only normal people Svin had found within the three-block radius he'd scoured when he'd been out scouting the terrain had been the proprietors of the carpet factory down the block, another warehouse of dry goods, and the row of food stands lining the larger avenue their street opened into, although some of the foodstuffs they'd had available for sale had made Svin avert his eyes and stride quickly past. Everyone else seemed to be involved in sorcery, one way or another. Either they were doing it, or manufacturing it, or advertising it, or soliciting it, or (as the Karlinis were) studying and researching it. Or they were *themselves* magic, in one way or another.

One thing few of them seemed to like was being up in the early morning. This wasn't a surprise either, of course; it was virtually a standard of magical practice. Prior to his attempt at breathing, Svin had been watching as several knots of weaving folks stumbled home from their taverns or study sessions, jostling against the tradespeople coming in to restock, provision, or clean house.

"It's not just the city itself," Tildamire added. "It's got real people and everything."

That was clearly more to the heart of the matter than

her earlier, more sweeping remarks. Svin didn't think she was referring to people in general now, either. She was now surely talking about something Svin *did* know about. "You mean real *men*," said Svin.

Tildy gave a start, began to glance at him, then collected herself and turned deliberately away. "Well, so what if I do? What's wrong with a little fun? This is a real town, and I want to go out on it."

"So you shall," Svin rumbled.

"What do you mean by that? *You're* not planning to take me. Are you?"

If that was how she was going to be, so be it. "That is part of my job," he told her. "I am to be your escort."

Tildy frowned. "My guard, you mean. They want you to make sure I don't have any real fun."

It was more the other way around, as far as Svin saw it. "Say what you like. My people are not dour all the time. We also live for fun."

"Huh?" she said, with a look of thorough disbelief. Whatever her full-scale retort would have been, though, was never to be known, for amidst the clatter of wheels on the cobblestones, the beating of an area rug out the upper-story window of the potion factory across the street, and the general hubbub of morning commerce, was heard suddenly a familiar voice. The voice of Zalzyn Shaa, in fact.

"I *told* you, Maximillian," Shaa was saying. "The Wraith District near Sheepsend, *that* was where we would find them. Did you listen to me? No, of course not. You never listen to me, you never listen to *anyone*. Hodgetown, you said, so Hodgetown it had to be, halfway across the city."

But where *was* Shaa? There, behind the milk wagon rattling past behind its shuffling dray horse. For all his downbeat words, Tildy thought Shaa cut a natty figure in his yellow slacks and a rakishly tailored jacket with bold red and blue stripes. Next to him was her brother Jurtan. It *was* Jurtan, wasn't it? But who else could it be? Surely it was her imagination, but Jurtan looked a good inch or two taller than he had when they'd parted in Roosing Oolvaya, and more wiry, too; in fact his whole upper body had filled out, and his face had traded the pasty white of candlelit rooms for the darker glow of the outdoors. It was strange—for an instant Tildy had looked at Jurtan and seen their father, the former Lion of the Oolvaan Plain, which had certainly never happened before. As far as had ever been evident, Jurtan might as well have been a foundling adopted in infancy. Certainly no one would have mistaken him for a blood relative to the Lion. Now, though—but she'd never tell that to Jurtan, of course.

That was two of them. But where was Max? Shaa had been talking to him, but where was he? There was a shabby, road-beaten, comprehensively disreputable figure slouching along beside Jurtan, its whiskery face virtually invisible beneath a drooping wide-brimmed hat, but . . . Wait a minute—Max *was* called the Vaguely Disreputable, wasn't he?

Jurtan was muttering, "We could have saved ourselves that whole detour and stayed in bed past the crack of dawn for once. At least no one tried to kill us on the way over, although there *was* that greasy stuff you bought us from that food vendor."

"I thought you wanted to be scenic," said Max's voice from beneath the slouch hat.

Either he was throwing his voice, or . . . it *was* him, though. "I thought you were only supposed to be *vaguely* disreputable," Tildy told Max as the trio drew to a halt in front of the building. "But there's nothing vague about you—you're a total mess."

"He even had a bath at Shaa's," added Jurtan.

"Birds of a feather, the lot of them," Max said to Shaa. "I wash my hands of them all, and high time, too. They're all yours. *You* take care of them now."

"And your promise to the Lion?" Shaa drawled.

"If he shows up, he'd be on *my* side."

"Max?" said Svin, eyeing the unrecognizable character in front of him. "You *are* the Maximillian who—"

"Yeah. Hey, Svin," Max said, punching him on the arm. "I'm glad Groot found you. How's it been—more interesting than guarding a caravan, right?"

"It has been educational," Svin admitted.

"Is Roni here?" asked Max.

They went inside. Behind a short entry hall was a large open room with a two-story warehouse ceiling. A long straight staircase headed up to the right along the wall. Beneath the staircase, a row of person-tall wooden vats caulked with tar marched toward the rear. An elevated catwalk hung over the vats, and over that a traveling block-and-tackle was suspended from a track on the ceiling. An assortment of tables, book-cases, and blackboards were scattered around the well-lit area in the back. Ronibet Karlini was standing in front of one of the blackboards, her hands thrust in the pockets of a white smock and her face furrowed in concentrated thought, watching a piece of chalk scratch a new series of equations in the midst of the maze of symbols already festooning the board. "That classification has to be wrong," the voice of the Great Karlini was saying from the depths of a high-backed armchair also facing the blackboard.

"Why's that?" said Roni.

"Read your own observations." The top of one of Roni's laboratory logbooks waved beyond the chair's armrest, the edge of a finger visible at its base. "You've looked at enough of these free-living animal-cules to have plenty of comparisons. I really think you should concentrate on the paramecium model rather than the—"

"What do I have to do to get noticed around here," said Max, "break a chair over somebody's head?"

"Yes, here he is, ladies and gentlemen, courteous as ever," muttered Shaa.

Max continued to ignore him, which (as Shaa had already pointed out) was normal. Shaa (also quite routinely) continued to offer side comments and the occasional suggestion of dubious though intriguing merit, but somehow they still made it quickly through the basic catching-up and recounting of stories. Haddo and Wroclaw circulated with coffee and morning refreshments, having already made a run to the bakery on the corner. The Iskendarian manuscripts were again produced and perused, still without significant useful results.

"There is something familiar about these, though," Roni said, pointing to one block of equations on the third Iskendarian sheet. Actually, she was pointing at the mirror they'd set up for increased ease in viewing; one of Iskendarian's tricks had been writing in reverse, with certain characters shaved off or twisted additionally to make it less obvious what was going on. Which is to say the characters themselves were recognizable, when put back through the right transformations. The language and the meaning of the text were not.

But equations are still equations. "But those are not equations," Shaa said, peering over Roni's shoulder. "They appear to represent a descendance hierarchy, this begat that or some such, or perhaps a synthetic pathway."

"These aren't spellwork," added Karlini. "Unless Iskendarian was using his own really strange notation. I mean, obviously he was using his own strange notation, we can see that, but you understand what I mean."

Roni was rummaging through a stack of her own papers filed neatly on a shelf near the worktable. "Look at this," she said, selecting a loose page. "Here." She smoothed the sheet down next to the Iskendarian.

"Similar," commented Shaa. "Not exact, but clearly similar."

"My page shows what I think are the relationships between some of the different animalcules I've been studying," explained Roni. "You can see the drawings I made of what these microorganisms look like under the microscope. As you know, we've discovered that some of these animalcules exhibit rudimentary magical behavior. That is, with the right filters they can be seen giving off disorganized spell-packets; they look like little bright flashes under magnification. These organisms aren't actually spell-casting, of course, and they don't seem to be using this release of magical energy for any particular purpose. Nevertheless, they *are* somehow generating magic.''

She stood back and frowned in concentration. "Not all animalcules show this characteristic, though. Even species that look to be closely related may be dramatically different in the amount of magic they're giving off. I thought by classifying them I could determine what other features might set the Thaumaturgia apart and—''

"Thaumaturgia?" said Shaa.

"One-cell magic-using organisms.''

"Of course," Shaa said under his breath. "How silly of me.''

"And then when you've studied them, you're going to breed them, right?" said Tildamire.

"Of course," said Karlini. But he didn't sound too happy about it. "Why do you think we've got all those vats? We'll breed them as a power source. Breed them so they can do real magic, then teach them some spells and set a flask of them loose as weapons. Breed them so people can drink them down and—''

"You sound like you've got some problem," said Max. With the slouch hat and the scraggly beard both off and resting on the table next to him he was now recognizably himself, which only made the warning tone in his voice and the glint of caution in his eye all the more apparent. "All the study and politicking and fancy footwork won't mean a thing if we can't meet the gods head-to-head and overpower them. You know all about that. So what's your problem?''

"I barely know from day to day what my name is, let alone where your research is going," Karlini said, looking from Max to Roni. "I want to keep up on things, that's all.'' He shrugged. "I just want to be able to tell when it's time to head for the next county.''

"Oh, yeah?" said Max. "Why would you want to do that? When's that going to be?"

"When you let these things you're breeding *out*. You know of course, once you let them out you're never going to get them back in. I've been watching them. They'll keep breeding by themselves, mutating, gaining their own powers and—"

"They're so small you can't even see them," Max protested. "They're going to be under our control, they'll—"

"You can see them when there's a *lot* of them piled up together," Karlini told him. "Look over there in that basin behind you."

"You're missing the point entirely," said Roni. "Dear. In planning our own Arcanocytes—engineered magic-using organisms—" she inserted, seeing Shaa's uplifted eyebrow, "—there's always been the question whether this is original work or not."

"Original work?" said Karlini. "Of course it's original—we've been all through the journals and Encyclopedia Necromantica and—"

"And now the unpublished papers of Iskendarian, too," finished Roni. "Don't you think these change the story? Look here, and here, and *here*. Iskendarian studied the same things, I'd bet on it. And unless I miss my guess, he figured out how to do the same stuff we're working on."

"You wouldn't expect to find all this spread out in the literature if it's as powerful as we think," Max added. "Anybody who developed anything that heavy would keep it for themselves."

"So maybe Iskendarian did the same stuff a hundred years ago," said Karlini. "Where did it get *him?*"

A very good question, thought Shaa. It was not the only one, either. Was *Iskendarian* even the first?

According to the old documentary sources Max unearthed from time to time, and other material they had viewed over the years, there had clearly been a time when magic did not exist. If that was true, and Shaa saw no reason to doubt it, it was equally clear that something had changed.

Introduction of magic to a world that had none would have been a cataclysmic event. An event that fit that description had in fact taken place in historical times. While the circumstances were obscure and a subject of scholarly debate, it seemed quite likely that the Dislocation and the appearance of magic in the world had been one and the same.

Fine, that was the story in broad-brush. But what lay behind the macro-event? What *had* changed to bring magic to life? And had it changed by itself, or had someone changed it?

These one-celled microorganisms were most likely involved, but they could only be part of it. The Karlini bodies Roni was now describing were another, more interesting step on the road. She had discovered the Karlini bodies within *human* cells—indeed in her *own* cells, and those of her husband. They were analogous to the free-living Thaumaturgia; quite similar in many features but at least a step beyond. In fact, the Karlini bodies were apparently the organelles at the root of the human ability to wield magic. If one was of an anthropomorphic bent, one could speculate that the Thaumaturgia were rough drafts; experiments done to work out the basic concepts. The Karlini bodies were what the Thaumaturgia had given birth to.

Okay, discovering the cellular raw materials at the source of magic was a nice piece of work, but it presented a much more central problem than Roni's Thaumaturgia did. It seemed unlikely that such a powerful and complicated system could have appeared by accident. To have happened *overnight*—or at least quickly enough to cause a quick revolution such as the Dislocation—accident was all but impossible. One had to presume somewhere behind the scene a designing hand.

So who *had* caused it?

And where were they *now?*

Max had followed Roni over to a work area near the

vats. A chalk circle had been marked off on the floor surrounding a fence with a locked gate; within the fence were the interlaced green and pink tracers that indicated an active defense matrix. Within the matrix field was a membranous tent; inside *that,* completely enclosed, was the actual workspace. Overhead, an array of nozzles led up to a cylindrical tank hung from the ceiling. As he watched Roni lead Max into the central tent area, Shaa was morosely pleased to note that the safeguards did appear, in fact, to be adequate. The acid- and flame-bath system overhead should be thoroughly adequate to scorch anything unlikely enough to emerge under its own power from the multilevel quarantine.

Of course, the quarantine measures were really designed to contain something migrating by random chance on air currents or flowing along the floor, or the products of explosion or other accident; bulk processes, in other words. But what if that assumption was inadequate? What if something was trying to escape because it was *smart?*

That wasn't beyond the bounds of reason either. After all, Roni had the ring from Roosing Oolvaya inside the sealed workspace; she'd said she was using its emanations and fields for a template and power source. But the ring wasn't merely a generator. It had a *Death* trapped inside it. The Death hadn't been acting too intelligently when it had gotten out in Roosing Oolvaya, and look at the damage it had still caused. It—huh?

"What was that?" Shaa called out. His chair had shaken. No, more than that—he had heard a dull < w h o o m ! > sound. And it hadn't been merely his chair. The *building* had rattled.

"Well, it's not us," Roni yelled back, emerging from the quarantine tent to glance around the lab. Glassware was still clattering and liquid could be heard sloshing in the sealed vats, but nothing had broken.

"Something like that's happened at least once a day

since we've been here," Tildamire said to no one in particular.

"You got to get used to it living in a neighborhood like this," said Max from Roni's side. "All these magic users around, and students, too. Somebody's always blowing something—"

<WHOOM!> The floor lurched. Everyone staggered. A heavy bookcase leaned out from the wall, then smashed back. "The street," said Shaa, leading the way.

The smell of smoke was unmistakable before they reached the front door. Clouds of black were billowing from the carriage entry in the building across the street. The building's double stable-sized doors were lying in the street, fractured and shredded. Through the opening the doors had left, flashes of green were illuminating the smoke from within. The flashes were coming off an angular green latticework, warped and jagged and growing as it fed on itself.

That wasn't the only glow in sight, either: magenta was radiating from beneath Max's slouch hat as well. "What is that place?" he said. "There're active re-action products in there shedding magic like crazy. Something's going toxic, can you feel it?"

"It's a potion factory," said Karlini. "Looks like they've been operating on a shoestring; not enough safeguards. Typical."

"I thought you scouted the neighborhood before you set up here?"

"We did," said Roni. "There's at least one of these shops on every block everywhere in the district."

Something in the factory was going <clunk—WHINE>, <clunk—WHINE>. With each whine, static crackled, hair stood on end, and clothes leapt out from the body. "Feel that?" Shaa inserted. "There *is* still an active containment field."

The inner recesses of the smoke column were consolidating, too; crystallizing, in fact. A few humanoid shapes in bulky all-body overgarments could be glimpsed circling around inside the mess. One worker was making passes in the air, others were spraying ropy foam over everything in sight from large bladders slung over their backs. A loud bell was clanging somewhere off to the right down the street. "It sounds like the subscription fire brigade's heading in this direction, anyway," said Max. "Have you signed up yet?"

"Yes, Max," Roni told him. "It's all set."

Haddo had led Wroclaw off to the side. "Dangerous business see you how much?" Haddo hissed at him.

"Anyone can fall victim to an industrial accident," said Wroclaw. He was watching the declining fire carefully, though.

"Danger is not so much from single batch of potion," Haddo continued. "When is released energy from fire, does not potion merely destroy. Can change into something else; new can be powers, unstable can be results. If combine also different brews into one, interact can whole, mutate and transform can together they. If escape into air do they—"

A billow of smoke suddenly separated itself from the column and fell to the ground in front of them with a distinct clunk. Looking more like a hunk of aerated coal than a wisp of smoke, the thing broke in pieces. Vapors coiled up from the exposed center, but the pieces themselves sizzled and foamed, apparently melting their way into the cobblestones. "The results can be totally unpredictable," said Wroclaw. "Yes, Haddo, that is certainly clear."

Haddo pointed apocalyptically at the factory. "Potion batch this was for construction, for automatic alignment of bricks and walls, for cement and mortar. If escape it had, created it would have fallout. Glued together would have fallout whatever it touched. Or maybe even worse could have been. To predict is impossible." He jerked his black-cloaked arm up to point back over his shoulder. "In building behind us more dangerous is potential by ten. By hundred? Who can say? Problem here is—can size of danger say no one!"

Wroclaw had his arms folded behind his back, which considering the arrangement of his joints was a rather disconcerting sight, and was whistling an atonal tune as he watched the newly arrived fire brigade lay down an extra band of containment spells while a pair of burly black-clad bruisers unlimbered a long coiled hose that ran back to the large water tank strapped to their wagon. "So what are you getting at, Haddo? What is your point?"

"Have known you now long time, have I. Know you rash am I not." Haddo took a deep breath, or whatever it was he actually did underneath that cloak. "Must ensure we that research of Ronibet proceed does not."

"Indeed. Are you proposing this as Haddo the individual, sorcerer-at-large?" asked Wroclaw, with his typically dry manner. "Or is something larger at work here?"

"Haddo alone am I. What mean you—"

"In that case," Wroclaw said in a clear note of finality, "we have nothing further to discuss. Seeing as how that is plainly not the truth," he added.

"Of you speak what?"

"You might reconsider that aggrieved tone, my cloaked friend," suggested Wroclaw. "Especially when you are trying to win someone to your point of view. Much evidence indicates you are up to far more than you are willing to admit. There was, for example, your other friend hiding in the hold of the ship. There is also our employer Karlini's present miserable state, which owes much to you. Unless I am gravely mistaken?"

"Down keep your voice," grumbled Haddo. "Mistaken are you not. If be that way will you, tell you must I. In cabal involved am I. In league of not-humans. Danger to not-humans fight we; resist we gods of humans."

"That much has been clear for some time. Yet only now you say this is a matter for 'we,' in which you now include me? And now in your dangers to non-humans you include our employers?"

"Speak you to Favored should you," Haddo muttered.

"Your friend from the hold, is that? Yet at the moment I am speaking to you. I'm afraid you will have to make your own points."

Down the block, the knot of onlookers was beginning to break up along with the fire. Roni, having had had her fill of near-disasters for the morning, was gazing in another direction. "What do you suppose Wroclaw and Haddo are talking about over there?" she asked.

"Plotting insurrection no doubt, dear," said the Great Karlini.

Max gave him a sharp glance, then turned to scrutinize the pair down the block as well. "If that's what you think, you'd better get rid of them."

"Whatever happened to your sense of humor?" Karlini said quickly. "You never used to be this bad. Now you've got that quiet steely tone of voice all the time. You're getting positively too deadly for me."

"It's a deadly business," Max told him. "Haddo and Wroclaw, eh? Hmm. I'd better put them on my list."

"Max—" said Roni.

"They're on a *break*, Max," said Karlini. "They're adults, they're entitled to shoot the breeze if they want to. Well, *Wroclaw's* an adult. Who knows *what* Haddo is."

Max was now clearly ignoring him. "You concentrate on your research and leave this other stuff to me. I'd better get moving. See you all later." Without a glance back he headed off down the street.

"He's starting to scare me," said Karlini.

"He needs to be in love," Roni pronounced.

"Yep, you're right," said her husband. "That solves everything, you bet."

Roni glared at him, looked for a moment as though she were about to punch him in the stomach, then turned and stalked through the door.

"Breaking up the old gang," said Zalzyn Shaa, "are we, then?"

"Not you, too," Karlini muttered. "I—oh, forget

225

it." He made his own glowering exit, punctuating the gesture by slamming the door behind him.

"Let this be a lesson to you," Shaa told the Monts, staring in matched slack-jaw amazement at the shaking door, "on the limitations of promised panaceas."

"I thought they loved each other," said Jurtan.

"Karlini and Ronibet? Oh, they do, they do; you can tell by the level of annoyance. As you can see, that's the problem, or part of it, at least. Now if you'll excuse me, it appears to be the time for timely exits. I—"

"What was that?" Tildy asked, staring down the street in the direction Max had taken. "It sounded like a building fell over. And look—a cloud of dust rising up over the roof there, around the corner. What kind of place is this?"

Shaa had a discerning ear cocked. "Not an entire building; more like a cornice, or perhaps an upper-story facade. I will investigate on my way out. As I started to say before, I believe I have a ball to prepare for."

"Wait!" said Tildy. "You just—" But Shaa was already strolling away up the street in the direction of Wroclaw and Haddo.

They watched him go. "Okay," Jurtan said, "so what *was* the lesson?"

"I think we'll know when it's already happened. Are you going to run off now, too?"

"If I don't it means I've probably failed some test, but who cares? How about we go try to grab a decent meal?"

"Are you sure you're really my brother?" Tildy murmured.

"What do you mean by that?"

"I—oh, forget it."

Shaa, on his slow amble down the street, had drawn abreast of Haddo and Wroclaw. They had fallen silent as he approached. Shaa paused, turned to inspect once more the remains of the fire, and said, out of the corner of his mouth, "Whether or not you two are plotting insurrection—which is not, if you want to know my feelings, a necessarily bad idea—you might want to take prudent precautions. Maximillian seems to have developed a certain unhealthy suspicion of anyone who chooses to stay around him." Without waiting for a response, he turned again and continued on along the street.

"What was that about?" said Wroclaw.

"Of plots have we surplus," Haddo told him. "Of which speaking, me excuse please."

Svin was now standing alone in front of the building. Haddo scuttled up next to him and hissed, "Remember you conversation had we on ship, in hold?"

Svin continued gazing across the street at the fire brigade. "Yes. I remember," he said. "We talked about Dortonn. We talked about Haddo, Fist of Dortonn."

"Old history about worry not," Haddo told him. "Important only are current events. Important is that—"

"Do not tell me new stories," Svin rumbled conversationally. "Do not try to confound me. Do not try to trick me. First tell me this. When you escaped from Dortonn, why did you not return to fight for the freedom of your people?"

"Did not say same Haddo am I, but—"

"There is no but. I will not listen to you."

"Wait!" Haddo spat. "Go not inside. Extortionists are becoming everyone." He took a breath. "Things are the way things are; the only sane philosophy this is. No point there is to fight power structure that stronger than you is."

"I see," said Svin. "This makes you a mere creature of fate. It is an interesting attitude, but one I reject. The way is not destined. It is the duty of a true warrior to challenge fate, to fight these power structures of yours. Whether you fail is not the point. The point is to challenge."

"Very nice. Not of us all warriors born are. Now—"

"As I am learning," Svin said thoughtfully, "there

are many more kinds of warriors than just barbarians with swords."

"To me listen!" croaked Haddo. "Suspect I in town is Dortonn."

"In Peridol? Now?"

"In or coming soon is. On river attacked Dortonn the boat. After me he is."

"I see," said Svin.

"Complete you your quest can you. Prepare you Dortonn to face you must. Plan must we for him."

Svin's gaze didn't waver from the now-departing fire fighters across the street. "I am ready now. But we can plan. Planning is good. If what you say is true, a plan will be valuable. Dortonn is strong."

"True it is," Haddo told him. "True it is." *Well,* he thought to himself, *went that well enough.* And it hadn't even been a complete deceit. What was Max's favorite word? Misdirection, that was it.

15

I could have been up and out at the crack of dawn, but I wasn't sure there was much point. The streets were as crowded at dawn as any other time of the day or night so I wouldn't exactly be beating the rush, and anyway my first stop of the morning wouldn't be open until later. I'd end up hanging around either way, on one end or the other. I figured I'd take advantage of some of the amenities the Adventurers' Club provided for just this sort of slack time.

Not surprisingly, the gymnasium and sparring rooms sprawled over a significant slice of ground. I teased out some of my kinks from the road and then went a few rounds with a sword-trainer. Monoch wasn't too pleased when I chose a blade from the practice rack rather than him, but I wanted to work out, not dismantle the trainer and demolish the facility. I also wanted to see if my blackouts were random enough to incapacitate me in the middle of a fight. If I didn't lose consciousness while sparring that wouldn't necessarily tell me anything, but it still seemed like an exercise worth running.

In the event, the whole session was routine. The practice grounds were crowded, but everyone there was pretty serious; I couldn't spot a single entourage or idle hanger-on. Some were a bit the worse for wear, thanks to various injuries in some cases or one of the Club's bars the night before in others. I could have been out carousing myself, but after my session with

Phlinn Arol and the earlier events of the day it seemed wiser to lie low and meditate on the situation. Looking at the bleary-eyed faces around me reinforced the validity of the lying low part, if not necessarily the meditation. Not everyone around me was human, of course, and the number of apparent free-lancers seemed roughly balanced by those in some official capacity. At least a half dozen of the men and women I saw at the gym displayed the characteristic dress of someone in the Imperial hierarchy. Here a finger, there a shin, on someone else the line of a rib were picked on their clothing in silver against black or some other contrasting color combination. Without a guidebook or a long careful study it was next to impossible to tell exactly who outranked whom or what the function of their office might actually be, but you could still make a rough guess; especially here, where they were mostly Bones, Muscles, or Ligaments.

The conceptual structure of Imperial officialdom made sense, it was the implementation that got confusing. As the structure of their body characterizes the individual, so civilization is given structure through the body of the State. That's the way the official credo ran, anyway, according to the guidebooks that had been provided with my room. The Muscles were military, the Bones administration, Ligaments handled interior affairs and civic services, Nerves and Liver were thinkers of various sorts, and so forth. After as many generations as the system had had to evolve and twist around on itself, though, the organization resembled more of an overgrown bramble hedge that hadn't been pruned in a few decades than a neat hierarchy. Some positions had become hereditary, some were tied to particular functional posts—the administrator of Roosing Oolvaya's province, for example, was always a Femur—and some had correspondences with a real body that could only be fulfilled if that body was a serious mutant. The listings of office in the guidebook had included at least four other Femurs but at least twice that number of Patellas. The closer in to the torso you got, though, and the higher up toward the head, the better you were doing.

Since a Knitting generally resulted in a wholesale shuffle of officeholders, filled with promotions and purges both, everyone who was smart brought themselves and as much of their power base as was mobile to Peridol for the season; that was part of what helped to feed the crowds outside. I didn't see any reason to get involved and was hoping no one would find one for me. I had my hands full just trying to keep up with the politics of the gods.

After a while I had clearly spent enough time, so I got cleaned up and put together and hit the street. The guidebook had also contained a good set of maps, filled with landmarks, sights to see, and shortcuts. The landmarks were a mixture of the straightforward and the idiosyncratic. At the end of Temple Row in the Edifice Quarter, for instance, the Temple of Jab-Bonita was noted as the site of the most spectacular ecclesiastical theft in modern times, when a lone freebooter had succeeded in traversing the Moat of Whirling Octopuses and the distortion fields to reach the effigy of Jab-Bonita itself, had somehow made it up the inverted incline of polished marble at the effigy's base, through the ring of smoke, and through the ceaselessly writhing ramifications of the god's tentacular seat to reach the door, hidden from sight from below, through which the acolytes emerged to conduct Jab-Bonita's characteristic ritual. The interloper had proceeded to follow the acolytes' passage back down through the interior of the effigy and the root of the marble base to the secret quarters beneath the temple, had eluded the acolytes while making his way through the maze of passages to the vault containing Jab-Bonita's staff of office, had obtained (in a manner nicely glossed over) the staff and other accoutrements of office, and had finally used these tokens to unseat Jab-Bonita himself and steal his godhood. To me, it all sounded more like misdirection; it had probably been an inside job. On the other hand, I guess the new Jab-Bonita was entitled to spread whatever myths he wanted to about himself. It came with the territory.

If I ran into him, I could ask him.

Another area clearly marked by the guidebook was the public area of the palace complex. The road to the recommended gate passed through the wide meadow that encircled the outer wall. The tall panels of the gate themselves had been thrown wide, leaving an opening high enough for a large giraffe to have strolled in fully upright and sufficiently broad for a good ten elephants to have marched through comfortably abreast. Even this outer wall was so thick that it could easily accommodate the matching set of gate panels on the inner surface. Of course, the wall had been built at a time when symbolism was the last thing on anyone's mind; the practicality of repelling attack had been the foremost concern.

According to the guidebook, however, the palace never had been assaulted. The other sets of walls along the banks of the Tongue Water, combined with Peridol's fortunate island geography, had proved the key defenses. In allowing Peridol the chance to pull itself from the mess left by the Dislocation before anyone else on the continent, they had directly paved the way for Peridol's march to its present world mastery. The Tongue Water defenses were long since dismantled, but the palace remained, its symbolism now unmistakable.

But symbols were scarcely the morning's business, or sightseeing either. I made my way through the public gardens, skirted the dour warrens of the bureaucracy, where even now new construction was appending an additional three-story wing, and followed the signposts into a much grander building and down a polished corridor hung with unrecognizable portraits and a tasteful array of statuary. Another set of double-height doors beckoned; this was obviously the place. Through the doorway was a hall with a high domed ceiling faced around with windows, the marble floor arrayed with chairs and wide tables, and the walls lined with books. Books in the thousands, at least, or tens of thousands, or quite possibly the millions. I had never seen so many books—and scrolls, and screen-writings, and periodicals, and on and on—in my life. But then this was the library, or the Library, to give it its proper due. Or the Archives? Anyway, here I was. And the only thing I could think, detective or not, was that I'd better get some help.

Well, the desk in the middle of the room was obviously the librarian's. As I ambled over, I saw I wouldn't have to wait long. The woman in the chair had only a single customer before me, another Imperial functionary in fact, so I figured I'd hang around obviously enough so she could see I was next.

The librarian didn't seem all that happy with the guy, actually, based on the sour expression that kept breaking through on her face. She kept taking her spectacles off and putting them on, and had edged back in her chair as the guy persisted in leaning closer across the desk. The guy obviously took his own workouts seriously and had the costume to show off the results, a flashy number in black and red with the silver emblem of his office spread across his shoulder blade. As I surreptitiously watched them, though, the figure he cut was more that of a masher than a seeker of knowledge and reference materials. I edged closer, trying to decide if there was any good reason to intervene.

While purring into her ear, the guy made a grab for one of the librarian's hands. She managed to elude him, though, and slid her chair back with a loud screech against the floor. The man straightened and started to move around the desk himself, which is when my own boot made a prominent squeak on the floor itself. I coughed once or twice, and was prepared to clear my throat a few times or even gargle, for good measure, but the man did stop. He unhooded his striking blue eyes and cast a sharp look at me, but apparently could draw no serious information from the gloom under the hood of the overcloak I'd acquired from the supplier back at the club. "Until tonight, then, my dear,'' he murmured to the librarian, and glided off.

With that expression on her face she sure didn't look like she was happy being that guy's dear, or more probably anyone's. He'd looked vaguely familiar, like I might have seen him someplace, but unless I'd had another dream where he'd shown up that I'd otherwise forgotten I couldn't think of where it might have been. The librarian shook her head and transferred her attention to me. "How can I help you?" she asked.

"I'm a detective. In fact, that's what brings me here in the first place. I'm doing some research for a case."

"A detective?" She was squinting at me as though she might have seen *me* somewhere, too, only in her case she probably had; striking a heroic pose on a wall no doubt.

"Yeah," I said, "that's right. Maybe I should be asking *you* how *I* can help."

"I wish I knew what he was up to," she said, almost to herself.

I'd been concentrating on my own business far too much lately, anyway. I needed to clear my head. I needed somebody else's totally unrelated problem to worry about. This *was* sort of my kind of job, after all. "If you like, I could keep an eye on him. Maybe I can find out."

"No, no, I'm sure there's no need. Anyway, he's powerful. He's dangerous. He's the Scapula."

"I'm not exactly a sheet of dough myself, ma'am. It would be a pleasure."

She looked at me while obviously considering the situation. "Well," she said finally, "perhaps. Thank you for your offer regardless."

"You're welcome," I told her. I was considering some things myself. What had come over me? What was I doing drumming up business at a time like this? It did feel comfortable, *right*, somehow, the same way I'd reacted when I'd thought about getting an office. Something in me was much happier when I was following what it thought my role in life should be. That didn't necessarily make the rest of me feel better, though. Again it felt like something was trying to reattach me to a hook that I'd somehow been designed to fit. Another side effect of the Spell of Namelessness? Well, maybe the material in this library would help me find out. "Excuse me?"

"Your research," she said. "For a case."

"Right. I've got a client under the Spell of Namelessness. I need to find out whatever I can about this thing and how it works, and especially if there's a list of folks who've had it directed at them."

Her expression turned dubious. "I doubt the holdings have anything that will help you. Gods and sorcerers aren't known for documenting their intrigues, especially if the loser isn't around any more."

I spread my hands. "Whatever."

"I'll show you to to the stacks," the librarian said, getting up. I trailed her toward the maze of tall shelves. "Have you visited the Temple of the Curse? That *is* the Curse Masters' primary contact-spot. If you tell them you're thinking of commissioning a Curse of Namelessness against someone, perhaps they'd give you information on past employment."

"That's an idea." The thought of seeking Jardin out under my own power had the virtue of audacity, but somehow its overall wisdom seemed questionable. She didn't have to know that, though.

She was frowning at shelves as we passed. Then she nodded up ahead, at an area in a cage, with a locked grillwork door. "The magic and god-related material is restricted access. You'll have to ring for me to let you out so perhaps you'll tell me then whether you've found what you need. I'll think about it, too; maybe rummage around a bit. Perhaps there's something more I can turn up."

"I'd really appreciate that." As she unlocked the door and led me in, pointing the way to the shelf she thought would be of greatest relevance, I had a new question to turn over in my mind. If this was a restricted access area, why was she letting *me* in, and so easily, too? What made me an approved researcher? It couldn't be just my claim to be a detective. Could it?

Well, probably I was just starting to see plots around each corner and under every bed. As the door shut behind me with a muffled clang, I turned my attention to the books. Then I turned my attention back from the books, to the almost imperceptible scuff of a foot I heard behind me down the row to my right. The man who had been hidden down the aisle was just looking up at me as I looked around at him.

Although he tried to conceal it, he was clearly a lot more surprised than I was, but then it took an ever-more-remarkable occasion to get me astonished these days. "That was a pretty cute trick you pulled on me," I told him.

"Shh," said Fradjikan, sliding his book back onto the shelf. "This is a library. One must behave with decorum. What trick is that?"

"Setting me up to fight that animated statue and then getting my face plastered all over town as a result, and don't tell me it was a coincidence because we both know it wasn't."

"How could I—"

"Look, Ballista," I began; but then, seeing the confusion ebb and the expression of calm mastery begin to settle back on his face at the sound of that name, I decided to change tack. "You've been lying to me since you picked me up out there on the road, starting with who you are, Fradjikan."

He blinked, his hand snaking as if by reflex to the hilt of his sword. "Why do you call me that?" he said unconvincingly.

"The usual reason," I said. "Because it's your name." That wasn't the only thing I realized I knew about Fradjikan. Assassin, subversive-at-large, kingpin and kingmaker, one-time Grand Shroud of the Society of Masks—no wonder Gash had this information to pass me. Fradjikan sounded like just his kind of guy. "What are you doing here?"

"Leaving," he replied.

I moved to put my back at the door and hefted the walking stick. Fradjikan walked toward me with his controlled sword-master's glide. His sword was still slung, but I knew there was only a half-second difference between having it on his hip and having it in his hand entering my chest. On the other hand, he'd seen Monoch in action; that had to give him pause. On the *other* hand, a library was the last place I'd want to get into a fight wielding a demolisher like Monoch. All those dry pages mixed up with a flaming sword wouldn't be pretty. "We should discuss your game," I stated.

"Perhaps we should, but this is scarcely the place."

"Can you think of a better neutral ground?"

"Most probably," he whispered.

"Yet the here and now has its advantages."

"Whatever those may be, they certainly pale." He continued moving ahead, showing every intent of strolling straight through my body if it happened to still be there when he arrived.

I wasn't about to attack and he wasn't about to talk, so we could either stand there at an impasse or get about our own businesses. I shrugged and stepped aside. Instead of pulling the call-bell cord, Fradjikan did something to the lock and swung open the door. He grinned an uneasy grin at me through the grillwork as he eased the door shut again, making sure the lock engaged, and then turned and strode quickly out of sight through the stacks.

Somehow I didn't think he'd come into the restricted-stack area the same way I had, either, with the assistance of the librarian; the air about him had been just a little too furtive even before we'd started sparring. Also, the librarian might have mentioned that someone was already in here, or she might have glanced around when we'd entered to see where he was. Of course, she could have just been a touch absent-minded. More plots under the bed? I'd ask her about him on the way out.

But first things first. I was torn between following Fradjikan right away or doing the research I'd come there for. Actually, there wasn't much of a choice. I'd better do the research; who knew when I'd get back to it otherwise? Too bad I didn't know any operatives here in Peridol. It would be nice to hire somebody to help with the legwork. Maybe the Adventurers' place could get me a referral.

Before my own research, however, there was still something new worth investigating. I went down the aisle to the spot Fradjikan had been standing. Which book had he been looking at? Here was one still partially out-of-line. I withdrew it and puzzled out the title. The language was . . . Chafreshi, a tongue I didn't recall a prior familiarity with, but what else was new. *Arundi's Weapons and Armor?*

Then I realized what the book was. A text and encyclopedia of magical weaponry. Unless I missed my guess, Fradi had been trying to look up Monoch.

That wasn't a bad idea. I flipped the pages. The text was fairly dense; Arundi apparently enjoyed watching himself write, but was less concerned with anyone else's ability to read. The first part of the book was theoretical rather than descriptive. Arundi presented a long discussion on the design tradeoffs in embedding magic in an implement. On the simplest level was the sheer infusion of power, or power feeding a simple onboard spell (such as an edge-maintainer or an active saw effect or even the odd flame-burst), but such power boosts were only good for a limited amount of activity. The first real trick came in when you added a recharger, I learned. Vampire-mode recharging, for example, worked by siphoning life-energy out of the weapon's victim. This was powerful but not too versatile, and without surge cutouts you could suck up too much too fast and have a blowout. On the other hand, low-intensity modes could renew themselves in a whole host of ways. Even leaving the weapon out in the sun for awhile would sometimes do it.

And then there was the topic of active versus passive. The more helpful you wanted an instrument to be, the more of your own smarts you had to program into it, and the more you gave it the better the chance it had of developing its own. Once that happened, the implement was as much its own as its creator's. This could be a good thing or a bad thing. In introducing the possibility that the object might come up with its own goals in life, and an agenda that might differ from that of its wielder, a serious element of negotiation entered the relationship. Arundi devoted several chapters to the question of how to convince a magical device to do what you wanted it to, and of how to protect yourself against it if you couldn't.

According to Arundi the association between complexity and intelligence was a topic of major debate. Whether complexity produced actual intelligence and true self-awareness or merely a simulation thereof did sound interesting, from a purely philosophical standpoint, and for all I knew it could have some practical significance, but darned if I could think at the moment just where that would be; and anyway I had a lot more to do than time to do it in. The stuff on How to Relate to Your Weapon, though, did seem to smack of relevance. I settled in to read.

After a few pages I was seriously wondering if Arundi had ever been in the same room as a creature like Monoch. He had anecdotes, sure, but I already had my own share of those myself. I also had a lot more practical information on what worked and what didn't. I flipped ahead to the long appendix. I was greeted by panel after panel of illustrated halberds, buskirks, shields, hand-axes, saddles, self-aiming grappling irons, and swords, swords, swords. After a few pages of metallurgical analyses I never wanted to hear about tin content again, or forging descriptions, or where Famous Weapon X had picked up this nick or'd gotten that chunk removed. The details of the engravings included as reference plates had their worthwhile parts, though. Between the narrative walkthroughs of the holdings of this museum's collection, or that armory's, and the armamentarium wielded by this or the other legendary ravager of continents, it was hard to remember that this stuff was supposed to be *interesting*.

I could add Arundi to my list of folks I'd have some words for if I ever caught up with them.

There was no sign of Monoch, though. There was a section on paraphernalia hidden in various parts of the scenery, staffs in trees, swords in anvils, and whatnot, but these were accompanied by literal illustrations that made it clear that these were not cases of cloaks or disguises but rather riddles or curses or traps of one sort or another. Arundi did prove to have a section on transubstantiations, but it was uncharacteristically short and elliptical. I shoved the book back on the shelf. I could stand around reading all day and still never come across anything useful except by luck. This wasn't the way to do it at all. What I needed to find was somebody who'd *already* read all this stuff, and had some experience under their belt to boot. What I needed wasn't only a legman, I needed a research assistant. I should ask Shaa, or Karlini. They knew these kinds of folks. The way things had been going lately maybe one of *them* wanted the job.

I made my way back around the shelves to the location the librarian had shown me and started going through the volumes I found there. I quickly discovered a disappointing similarity to Arundi. Where Arundi had been long on picayune facts, these histories of the gods were heavy with what sounded suspiciously like gossip; unfortunately, neither of them seemed concerned at telling the reader what they actually might want to know. The Spell of Namelessness did pop up here and there. It was clearly just another tool, though, traditionally favored by the Curse Administrator but used more widely than that. One writer thought that the sorcerer Iskendarian had developed it, but since another book mentioned its use a hundred years before the earliest date quoted for Iskendarian's activity perhaps he'd just made it popular.

As far as lists went, it looked like Phlinn Arol was right. There were too many documented or suspected victims of Namelessness to make it anything like convenient. Don't get me wrong, I wrote them down. Forty-eight gods spread out over three hundred years, and maybe another hundred others, magicians and politicians and heroes-on-quest, mostly, but quite a few of them just names, or even flat statements like "another half dozen victims during Holito's sweep through the South"—how was I supposed to know if one of those was *me* mixed in there? None of the names sounded familiar.

Well, maybe I'd get an insight while I was off doing something else. I rang for the librarian, and soon I was back on the street with directions to the Scapula's major haunts. I'd slung my cloak back over my head, of course, and tried to stay as far away from those damned broadsheets as possible, so it took me a while before I realized that the posters up this morning were not identical to the ones I'd seen before. I had to come around a blind corner and almost walk straight into the one plastered on the facing wall to notice the difference.

I was still there fighting off the statue with Monoch; that much was still the same. Now, strings ran upward from the horse's limbs, and the big sword and the rider, to a set of outstretched hands rendered jerking and bobbing in a dance of control. Hanging in the air between them, right above the stone general, its expression captured in a moment of devilish glee, was the face of my erstwhile pal, Maximillian the Vaguely Disreputable.

I stopped in the middle of my step to stare. Passersby weaved around me and merely cursed under their breaths, but no one actually tried to shove me out of the way. Perhaps there was something about me at that moment that warned them off. If so, I hoped I could recapture it later on, when I'd certainly need all the help I could get. Against Max? Against Fradjikan? Against Jardin? Against Phlinn Arol? Who knew any more who I'd end up fighting and who'd actually turn out on my side?

But the outline of what Fradjikan was up to might be coming clearer. If he was the one behind the posters, and there was no reason to doubt it, his plot involved not only me but Max; or perhaps his plot had always been aimed at Max and I'd only gotten in the way. Max had powerful enemies, among them at least some of the gods themselves, or so he'd maintained. It looked like Fradjikan was one of them. I'd been trying to stay clear of Max, but this changed things. I'd better get word to him. Max would see the broadsheets, too—he couldn't miss them unless he was asleep—so he'd know something was going on. But *I* knew about Fradjikan.

Of course, Max would see *me* on the poster, too. He might think I was part of the plot. It looked like I *was*, too, one way or another, but Max might decide it was deliberate on my part. And he might decide the best course was to take me apart to find out what I knew. . . .

Shaa; again, Shaa. I'd tell him and let *him* tell Max. I'd been in the library longer than I'd thought, though, and I didn't know how long I'd stood around thinking in the street either. It looked to be midafternoon already. I'd probably be too late to catch Shaa at home before he left. On the other hand, I wasn't that far from the Scapula's address, and I *had* told the librarian I'd check into him. I got myself moving again.

The librarian, Leen, in telling me how to find the Scapula's principal residence, had concluded by saying I couldn't miss it. Arriving at the location she'd described, I understood more fully what she'd meant. He had a walled compound that occupied an entire block. It wasn't a very large block, but it was a pretty intimidating wall, stout with neatly laid stones and topped with spikes and radiating the telltale glow of active magic. Vegetation was pruned back and no trees grew close enough to drape themselves over the top. The broad driveway gate in the front was hung with sheeting, too, keeping the inside courtyard free from prying eyes, and whatever buildings the compound contained were set back far enough to be out of sight from the street as well. The only outward sign that connected this place with the Scapula were the twin flagpoles setting off each side of the gate, one with the ensign of Peridol and the other showing a silver shoulder blade against a background of black and red.

As I circled the block, looking for a decent vantage point to stake things out, an even more telling observation became apparent. The walls weren't only clean of vines and shrubbery, they were unblemished by posters. True, the palace complex had been lacking the broadsheets as well, but out here in the city this was the first location I'd seen free of their otherwise omnipresent blare. The message was clear. Even the anonymous free-lance street propagandists and fly-by-nighters didn't dare cross this guy.

But I was different, right? I'd stroll in where wimps feared to tread, which said something about either my common sense or my intelligence, if not both, and I was certain neither comment would be all that complimentary. Of course, I wasn't actually strolling *in* anywhere, either, so maybe it would balance out, or so I was thinking as I rounded the corner into the alley at the back of the Scapula's block. As I'd surmised, there was a back door as well, a smaller one, suited for individuals afoot or horsed, or possibly even a compact carriage. At the moment it was open, and in the process of admitting a single man alone and on foot. He finished slinking in and the gate closed quickly behind him, but I was standing in a muddle at the corner with my mouth agape.

I shut my mouth; that part at least was easy enough to handle. The muddle was a more difficult matter. Which one of them had I been tailing? No, it was the Scapula; there was no doubt about that. I'd only *thought* about following Fradjikan. So why was he making things convenient for me? What business did *he* have with the Scapula?

Could I overhear their conversation? Something—Gash's senses operating through the metabolic link, I guess—was warning me it would be dangerous, *very* dangerous, to try to sneak inside. But what else might I be able to do with those same senses? I closed my eyes and concentrated. *Focus,* I told myself, *focus on sounds,* and indeed after a moment I did start to become more fully aware of the activity around me, of the cawing of a crow overhead, of the rattlings and mutterings of a man in his rough lean-to of sticks and castoff burlap in the alley across from the Scapula's wall, of the yapping of a dog pattering along behind a ragpicker toting his sack-o'-cloths, of a troop of horsepeople on the main street at the front of the compound. . . . Then I realized I wasn't only hearing all this bustle, I was *seeing* it, too, as though through a roving eye that jumped and zoomed from spot to spot, bobbing and weaving through the air.

Even though my real eyes were closed, this roving vision was still murky, indistinct. It wasn't seeing so much as visualizing, if you will; it was too schematic for out-and-out sight. But that didn't mean it wasn't timely. Could I send my new vantage point over the wall? The roaming eye darted up and arched over.

Crackle—BLAMM! Blinding light flashed behind my eyelids as something the size of an ox kicked me in the head, only from the inside out. . . .

For all I know I lost consciousness; probably I did. Gradually I remembered who I was, I mean as much as I ever did, although the roar of the ox in my ears and its continuous stamping on my forehead didn't help matters any. The ox was growing smaller, though, maybe shrinking to the size of a goat, but its access to my head was facilitated by the fact that I seemed to be lying full-length on my back in the mud.

Obviously the Scapula's defenses could go after something like my roving eye. I'd better get out of there; I might have set off an alarm, too. I still had Monoch, I could feel the stick in my hand, but a fat lot of good he'd done me this time. If Arundi had been right, an implement of his caliber should be giving warnings and advice, and should have helped to blunt the damage from attacks as an extension of his personal protection field. Monoch hadn't been doing any of that. Arundi had suggested techniques for making your magical assistants earn their keep, but for some reason I didn't seem to be able to think of any right at the moment. In fact—

"Taking a nap, are we?"

There was a woman standing over me. I cracked open my eyes, squinted against the stab of pain from the alley's low light, and said, "What, is it time to get up already?"

The woman snorted. Had we met? I didn't think so, but I thought I might be on the verge of knowing who she was anyway. Maybe another one of those dreams was trying to break through. "There is danger to us all, and you waste your time wallowing in mud?"

"There's always danger," I told her. "What else is new? To which danger are you referring at the moment?"

"Breakdown of the social contract," she said, "for one. For another, folks who sit on the sidelines while others are smashing down the boundaries of good sense."

I had a feeling she was including reclining on the ground in her definition of sitting on the sidelines. Well, perhaps my head would stand letting me get to my feet now. I put Monoch's tip on the ground, snarled at him mentally to "Help out, dammit!" and felt myself unroll from the mud and jerk up into the air. My feet even left the ground in a small hop, stretching my joints with a chorus of snaps, but when I settled back down to the ground everything popped back into place and my balance held. My head was still pounding. As I'd said, though, what else was new? "So what would you have these 'folks' do?" I asked. "If they happen to get off the sidelines and stand up?"

"Make themselves presentable, for a first step.

We've got enough problems with loss of legitimacy without becoming a laughingstock, too. Here, let me.''

I gave off my looking around for a clean cloth or a source of running water as she stretched her hand out toward me and passed it slowly down from my head toward my feet. Aquamarine coils wound out around me like a small tornado. I felt like something was scouring my skin with a stiff brush, but the grime and mud were lifting free of my clothes and spinning off into the tornado and showering onto the ground. In a moment I was cleaner than I'd been in, well, a while. "Thanks," I said. "That was certainly timely, as well as handy."

It also wasn't the first hint I'd had she was a god. "The last time I saw you weren't you a palm tree?" I went on, falling in step with her as she began walking along the lane toward the main street.

"Why, didn't you like it?"

"No, no, not at all," I said. "I thought it was clever. Well executed, too—I liked what you found to do with the coconuts.'' It had been a palm tree with a man's voice, too, but what did that matter? At the conclave of the gods I'd attended from Oolsmouth, courtesy of Zhardann and the disguised Gashanatantra, most everyone but me had worn some persona or another. Since the conclave had taken place in an artificial environment that didn't really exist anyway, and since the attendees were represented not in the flesh but as projected constructs, those constructs could take any form their projectors pleased. I was happy the gods had that outlet, at least. Playing dress-up and masquerade gave them a way to posture and show off without anyone getting hurt.

Of course, there *had* been Sapriel.

"Yeah, well," she continued, "when you're supposed to be Protector of Nature, you have to spend some time representing your constituency."

"I'd feel the same way," I told her, "if I had a constituency myself, of course."

"Don't take that abstract air with *me,*" she said.

"We all have a constituency, and more than that we have the needs of our own community. It's not Conservationist/Abdicationist at this point. If this goes on, it's whether there'll be anything left at all."

"I think that's a little apocalyptic," I said.

"Well, I don't," she snapped. "You may think you can keep playing your usual games and pulling your strings and end up on top of whatever heap is left, but this time you're wrong. Things are getting completely out of control. Abdicationism may have started this, but it's not the only destabilizing factor now by a long shot."

She was Protector of Nature, right? Nature had done pretty well under the gods, all things told, if you left off things like the continent of Zinarctica; and if you believed what you heard even Zinarctica was starting to come back. If "ground-huggers," as she'd called them before, got control of their own destiny again, they'd probably mess up the land the same way they had before the Dislocation. So she was Conservationist. She thought her constituency would be better off under the status quo than under any other arrangement. "But what power do *I* have?" I said. "What do you expect *me* to do about anything?"

"You know something incriminating about everybody, and don't say you don't." She didn't pause at the corner. No, she stalked around the turn in the Scapula's wall without breaking stride and charged straight into a knot of women loaded down with baskets and wrapped parcels of fish, her elbows flying as she cleared herself a path. The women cursed as they dodged out of the way, and then muttered again as they began chasing after stray loaves of bread and a few errant turnips. I skirted the mess, not wanting the turnips aimed at me, and hurried to catch up with her. "If you called in your markers and used what you know," she continued, "you could stop things dead in their tracks."

"You're exaggerating again."

"Damned if I am. There's been enough of this an-

247

archy and checks and balances and never getting anything done. It *is* time for a change, but Abdication's
not the one to bet on. We need a leader to step in and
take charge.''

"An interesting concept," I commented. "I take it
you're not alone in this thought?''

In following her along the avenue, I had now drawn
abreast of the Scapula's main gate. What I had missed
by casing the joint from across the street, I now discovered, was a small brass address-plaque affixed to
the wall next to the gate's hinge-post, and as soon as
I saw the engraving on the plaque I realized I had
forgotten to ask the Scapula's original given name.

So *that's* why he looked familiar.

It was only about the two-hundredth time that day,
but I had to ask it again. What was going on? What
had I stumbled into? What—

Maybe I'd better try to see Shaa now after all.

But the Protector of Nature wasn't finished with me
yet. "Of course I'm not alone," she declared. "But
if you want us to back you as a leader you have to take
an active role. You have to demonstrate your willingness to commit yourself.''

"Indeed. And did you have by any chance a particular demonstration in mind?''

She scowled at me. "There is a threat present here
in Peridol, an external threat, even a significant threat;
a threat that has the potential for totally blowing up in
all of our faces. We need more assurance that this
threat will be removed from the scene. Unfortunately,
he's under the protection of Phlinn Arol, that's what
makes it tricky.''

"He?''

"A human," she said. "Named Maximillian.''

16

"Very well. Now, the skyrockets. Have you emplaced the skyrockets? What are the specifications?"

Favored-of-the-Gods pushed back from the table, leaned back in his chair, and looked up. He spread out a hand, indicating the graphs, charts, and lists arrayed along the work area between them. The large page at the top of the pile at the moment showed an artist's conception of a pavilion shaped like a half-barrel lying on its side in the midst of a lawn garden, its gold ribs glowing against the deep indigo of a romantic night sky. Multicolored sparklers were going off overhead. "They're there," Favored said. "The skyrockets are there. Twenty-two batteries, all along the perimeter, just like I promised you." He swept the rendering aside and dug through the heap, coming up with an overhead terrain map. "Here and here, see, and all these other spots marked with the starburst symbol."

"Yes . . ." mused a voice in the shudder of distant thunder. A shadow gathered itself out of the larger darkness across from Favored and loomed over the table, stretched out a black hand-shaped something, and retrieved the painting Favored had moved away. "I have inspected the new hall. The catering facilities are most intriguing."

Favored had set part of the kitchen out on one edge of the promenade floor itself, on a raised dais. "I've jazzed up those open-pit ovens to spew fire," explained Favored. ''Should be like a cross between a volcano and caged lightning.''

''A nice touch,'' agreed the voice. ''And the earth-rumbler?''

Favored drew a deep breath. ''Look, boss,'' he said deferentially. ''We can either sit here another hour, me going back over all the details for you again, or I can be out at the site fine-tuning things and supervising the crew. I'm not omnipresent like you; I can't do both.''

''I do not employ you for your effrontery.''

''No, you keep me around because I'm good at what I do and I don't let you down. So let me get to it, huh?''

The shadow extended itself over Favored, wrapped him in a clammy fog with a temperature straight from the icebox. The voice shuddered through his bones. ''Very well. Fail me and your flesh will be food for beasts and your eyes a treat for wild crows; your soul will be kindling for fire.'' Then the shadow shrank away. The gloom retreated; somewhere a door slammed.

''Don't I know it,'' Favored muttered. But it had gone well. Zimrat Yaw, Lord of Storms, was a tough customer to please. However, Favored was no push-over himself, and had worked for Zimrat Yaw long enough to know how to play him. Fortunately there weren't many of the old-line fundamentalists left. As far as Favored was concerned, all that fear, trembling, and terror stuff—plus the total obedience and the rigid lifestyle—came back to bite you in the long run. Not that he'd say that to Zimrat Yaw, of course. The program was to keep his head down and wait for a new Storm Lord, and maybe give the old one a judicious push when the timing was right.

Of course, what with one thing and another the timing was never *entirely* right. On the other hand there were many periods when the timing was absolutely wrong. Take the present, for example. Which was un-doubtedly why, of course, Maximillian and that wife of Karlini's had chosen the moment to get as close as they were to causing real trouble.

Favored swept the documents together into a neater pile, selected a few and rolled them up under his arm, but left the others on the table. He'd produced them for the Storm Lord's consumption and as orders for the crew, not as working papers; all the important information Favored kept in his memory system, anyway. Zimrat Yaw, fundamentalist that he was, would be displeased to the point of launching an eradication if he discovered the memory system's existence, but then virtually everything Favored was really up to would have the same effect on any number of gods. Flotarobolis, Favored's sphere-vehicle, sitting off to the side under a drop cloth, was an exception through special dispensation. Flotarobolis *was* under a cloth, though—even dispensations had a way of being suddenly revoked, especially if they were waved around one time too many or a tad too ostentatiously.

At a sharp knock from the door, Favored, who had been turning in that direction already, said, "Yeah!" The door opened, admitting the light of day and a husky man in coveralls, his face the beaten mahogany that came from a lifetime working in the sun. As the daylight dispelled the last shreds of Zimrat Yaw's habitual gloom, it was clear that the building was basically a shack, and that if not for the worktable and an assortment of chairs, the shrouded Flotarobolis, some wall charts, and a paraffin hotplate, it would have been an abandoned and derelict shack as well.

"Rolf needs to see you about the mortars," the crew chief said. "Hagbard's spotted another wagonload of food coming in and the access road's still jammed where the pavement shifted. Hamper Lo and the gang testing the roof think one of the bearings needs to be replaced. Then there's the caterers. . . ."

Favored followed his assistant out of the headquarters shack, up the embankment, and out of the copse of trees, the shack disappearing utterly behind them. At their left the shoreline of the lake swooped pleasantly along; ahead and back from the bank on the right glittered the new pavilion. The scaffolding was almost all down, and not a moment too soon. A swarm of workers were doing everything from tidying the flower beds and polishing the brass to stringing the police barricade along the path at the margin of the meadow. Beyond the pavilion and its wide contoured lawn rose the gray mass of the palace wall. The lake swelled as it approached the wall, wrapped itself along the stones, and coiled off into the distance, forming the decorative moat. A few swells were out on the water sculling in punts and families had begun staking out choice spots on the opposite shore of the lake. If Favored had his way, he'd be there with them; the reflections of the fireworks in the water would be a spiffy sight indeed.

"Hagbard first," instructed Favored, seeing as Hagbard was the closest of the ones hanging around at the foot of the pavilion waiting for him anyway. "Then—what was that?"

"Sounded like a hiss," said the construction chief.

A hiss it had been, from behind, in the trees. Beneath one of the trees a small black shrub appeared to be waving. The shrub shifted position, and they noticed its glowing red eyes.

"I'll be there in a minute," Favored said. "Tell the antsiest ones what we talked about or just make up whatever'll work. You know the drill."

The man went on without a word. Favored put his head down and charged back to the trees. "This is a bad time," he muttered to the shrub.

"Right have you it," agreed Haddo, brushing a stray branch off his cloak. "Yet never will be time good."

Favored scowled at the retreating back of his crew chief. "I never should have taken that slow boat to get back here. If Zimrat Yaw knew how big a mess things were here, they'd be serving *me* tonight."

"In command through long distance were you. Deputies on site you had."

"Yeah," said Favored, "and I was here right until the moment I left for that little jaunt to Oolsmouth, too, but that excursion took time I never should have spent.''

"Perfectionist are you,'' Haddo said dismissively. "Important was in Oolsmouth the task.''

"Yeah, yeah, right, tell me something I don't already know. Any sign of Dortonn?''

"Of signs none, yet feel him I do. Around is he. But with us is now Svin. Prepared is he.''

"No, he isn't,'' Favored observed. "He may think he is but he isn't.''

"Matters not. Matters only his resolve. Matters not that knows he not about the ring.''

Favored hesitated. "Okay,'' he said. "Okay. And Wroclaw?''

"Help us he will. Reluctant is he, but help us he will.''

"They all start off reluctant, but when they find out how deep they're in, they realize it doesn't matter because by then they've got no choice. Like Karlini, too. It's time for another push on him.''

"Think I not,'' Haddo said slowly.

"You going sentimental on me again? We can't have him out there waffling back and forth. We either cement him in our camp or get him off the board.''

"No need is there for muscle.''

"Time gets shorter the further along his wife gets with her work. You said there's a limit to how much you can slow them down yourself. So we need Karlini, right?''

"Right.''

"You *are* going soft again,'' Favored muttered. "You can't win this one by just grumbling and complaining, or half measures you don't follow through. I'm not gonna bail you out this time. I can't. You got it?''

"Urr,'' grumbled Haddo. "Time will have you for Dortonn to search?''

"After we're finished here, maybe late tonight if I'm not too beat. Tomorrow more likely. See if you can dig up any more leads first. And figure out what we're going to do about Karlini.''

Favored pursed his lips. Should he tell him? It could compromise his sources and methods. Actually, it could be more dangerous than that. Acting the way he was, Haddo might just feel he had to tell somebody about it. That wouldn't do; especially not if this other agent might end up taking care of their problem with Maximillian for them. "Look, I've got to go. You watch out. If Dortonn's around, who knows who else could be hanging around, too.''

That felt like a good compromise, thought Favored, watching Haddo scuttle away. It was generic enough not to let on he had specific information but had still come out sounding emphatic. In truth, how much more specific could he be? This other guy he'd heard about was slipperiness on the hoof. How could you watch out for someone like that?

Well, maybe he could find out more. Until then he'd just have to keep alert for this Fradjikan himself.

"Goals diverging, are?'' grumbled Haddo, scurrying his way out of Mathom Park. The park would surely be full tonight, and for the rest of the upcoming Knitting festival as well. The festival as well as the park would mean ongoing work for Favored, which in turn meant that it would be hard to pin Favored down long enough to figure out what he really knew, much less what he was really up to.

After that last enigmatic warning it was obvious Favored did know *something*. Who knew how deep his connections went? Further than just what he could find out by talking to gods, that was certain. Haddo had his suspicions. Although Favored played his capabilities close to the chest, things Haddo had observed over the years could best be explained by assuming that Favored could eavesdrop on conversations the gods held secretly among themselves.

Perhaps it was time to confront Favored with it. If he—

"Sassa kachanta,'' spat Haddo, skidding to a halt.

What a mess. He had followed the most direct route out of the park and onto a main street winding south. Things being what they were at the moment in Peridol, one more half-height figure in a black cloak was thoroughly unremarkable, so why not take a straight shot, why even bother to lurk in the shadows? Well, traffic was one reason, or in a larger sense the myriad obstacles a big city threw up to make life challenging to everyone, in its thoroughly ecumenical and equal-opportunity manner. Such a complication had indeed presented itself here.

Among the modern innovations for which Peridol was famous were its plumbing, its waterworks, and its desalination utility. Applied sorcery might have motivated the purification and pumping systems, but there was nothing magical about getting water out of an indoor tap. All the water had to do was flow. This it did through the maze of water mains buried beneath the streets. Except, of course, when the water decided to flow somewhere else, or the water mains refused to remain in their assigned places underground.

Which in a nutshell described the scene Haddo had rounded a corner and marched straight into.

A carriage horse was rearing and pawing the air. The carriage itself had overturned on a milk cart. People were alternately craning for a view or shoving their path backward out of the way. Rain was falling and wetting down everything in sight—no, not rain at all, but a geyser erupting from the middle of the avenue, the tall column being torn to shreds at its top by the breeze. Somewhere up ahead, Haddo caught a glimpse of a work crew struggling to set up orange barricades.

Obviously another route was indicated. Haddo turned to go . . . turned . . . why weren't his feet moving?

Like everyone else in the area, he was standing in a puddle. Up ahead there was a veritable lake, but back here the pavement was merely awash. From the looks of it, one of the street-cleaning detachments had been through not long before the problem had broken out.

That was fortunate; if the street had still been filled with the usual mix of mud, refuse, and offal, the water would have churned the arena into a sewer. Perhaps Haddo had caught his foot on some sticky residue the sweeping crew had missed? But then why would his feet be *cold?*

Cold?

Ice. Haddo's spot of the puddle had frozen solid as he stood there, trapping his feet in the frost. Could this be a strange freak of nature, a spurious microclimate?

Of course not. "Yourself show," Haddo called out. "Know I that there are you."

Behind him he heard a chuckle. "A guilty conscience is it, then, O Fist?"

"Of elimination the process," Haddo muttered, feeling a frigid breeze move across his back. Damned if he'd give him the satisfaction of twisting around with his feet still trapped to look him in the eye. It felt like a sending anyway. "South do not you usually come."

"If it were merely to visit you, my wandering Fist, I most likely would not have made the effort, much thought I regretted the circumstances of our parting."

"Bet I just did you," said Haddo under his breath.

"You are as feisty and even-tempered as ever, I see. The tendency of time to mellow has scarcely—"

"To the point come. Chilly are feet."

"You always were too much the serious one, weren't you. Very well. The point is this. In return for his favor, my lord Pod Dall has bound me to certain obligations. I now extend these obligations to you."

"Reject I your obligations. Finished are we."

"Oh, no, we are scarcely finished, are we, Fist? *Loyal* Fist? Straightforward Fist? Fist who, if he was going to league himself with his master's enemies, was unwise enough not to complete the job, and was further unwise to leave behind certain friends and relations? No, we are scarcely finished. But first things first. And who knows, but that first things handled well may not moderate a stern decree otherwise to follow?''

He always *had* liked to hear himself talk too much, thought Haddo. Haddo wasn't quite fool enough to say *that*, though. "State your task," he said.

"The situation is simple. I have come south seeking the ring that imprisons my own master. A ring that is within your reach. You will obtain the ring and give it to me."

"I—"

"Please don't try to tell me your principles won't allow you to betray your employer. We both know that too is scarcely the case, don't we?"

"Difficult would it be," Haddo protested. "Guarded is ring, trapped and by wards protected. If careful were I not, to Pod Dall greater hazard caused would be."

A touch of ice patted Haddo companionably on the shoulder. "Then revenge would be my obligation, rather than rescue and release. I know you will take all necessary care. Still, I am reasonable, and there is the good of my lord at stake. I give you three days." A swirl of cold wind tore at Haddo's back, followed by a *schlurp*-POP.

So much for the sending, and now the ice at his feet was turning the barest bit mushy to boot. Making nasty sounds under his breath, Haddo grabbed his leg with both hands and pulled, kicked, squirmed . . . ice creaked and crackled, and finally his foot began to move, hung up, and then slipped smoothly free. He got to work on the other one.

Damn Dortonn. Damn Favored, damn Max, damn Karlini, damn the whole damned bunch of them. He was really in a corner. It only made it worse to realize how obvious it was in retrospect. He should have expected a direct approach from Dortonn. But he'd already pointed Svin at Dortonn, too. Svin was no dummy, either; it wouldn't be easy to swerve him from *his* course now, and he clearly wouldn't settle for being sent on a wild-goose chase.

Dortonn would expect some kind of doublecross.

His taunt about failing to finish the job was an obvious cue. But would he expect Svin, or Favored? Or Karlini? *Damn.* The situation held nothing but hazard.

On the other hand, Dortonn hadn't been that bad a boss. Savage and brutal to be sure, and all the other typical elements of that kind of job description, but he did get things done. They'd had a decent working relationship.

Maybe it was time to consider again another position of employment.

17

It promised to be a pleasant evening—weather-wise, at least. Socially, it might prove to be quite another matter. Leen adjusted those useless shoulder flounces again, fluffed out the chiffon, and glanced out the window a final time as her hired carriage rolled up the grand drive and turned into the portico. Her invitation had gotten her smoothly through the barricade at the edge of the lawn where the waiting crowds had craned for a glimpse of the celebrity she might happen to be. She had thought of telling them to visit her at the library, why didn't they, but in the event she had maintained her decorum and let the crowd rush up to the pair of Bones on horseback who'd been coming up after her.

From the outside, the pavilion certainly seemed to live up to its advance billing, and to the word of mouth that had accompanied it around town. It was traditional to inaugurate the first night of the Knitting season with the Inauguration Ball, of course, and the tradition included the dedication of a new commemorative piece of architecture for the ball to be held in; the tradition had been one of the few excesses of Abyssinia the Moot to have survived the test of time. As excesses went, this one had actually done a relatively significant amount of good. A number of the most useful public works projects had been Inauguration legacies, Carstairs' Symphonic Hall, for example, and even the Grand Vestibule of her own Reading Room.

Leen would have liked to have been around for the extravaganza held *there,* sure enough.

But this pavilion wasn't bad. The great metal ribs, the interlacing superstructure, the staggered levels and balconies above the wide promenade floor, and of course the broad sheets of glass that covered the surface now all glittered gold shading toward ruby in the last moments of the setting sun. Inside through the glass, lamps, lanterns, trendy floating light sculptures, and roving spotlights were becoming visible, and over at the far end what appeared to be the roaring flame of an open fire. Alighting from the carriage, the hubbub of voices broke in on her, mingled with the merry sounds of a seriously sprightly band. Leen handed off her wrap to an attendant, accepted a claim ticket in return, shook out the chiffon once more, squared her shoulders, and marched resolutely through into the din.

Fortunately they'd proved to have abandoned that other annoying custom, of formally announcing arrivals complete with their tokens of renown or notoriety. Especially under the circumstances, she would much rather make herself apparent under her own terms. Leen grabbed a wide-mouthed glass of some bubbling liquid from the nearest person in livery and set out to find a safe vantage point from which to observe the crowd. One of those upper platforms, perhaps—*that* one, with all the foliage—

"Not so fast," said a voice as an arm hooked itself through hers. But it wasn't the Scapula, or even a man. No, it was her sister, Susannah, already strategically placed for spotting whomever came through the door. Leen forced her pulse and her breathing, which had both taken a quick lurch, to begin quieting themselves.

"My dear, *look* at that dress," Susannah was saying. "Look at *you.* I've been saying it for years but who could have known it would be so true? You are quite a ravishing creature, quite respectable indeed."

As always, her sister was speaking in a loud enough

voice to easily address her whole circle, and to cause surrounding groups to stop and glance over as well. "Really, Susannah, there's no point in making such a fuss over—"

"*Au contraire,* dear sister," Susannah said, this time in a low yet pointed voice, and this time directly to her. "If you think I'm going to let you sneak off to hide in some corner you'd better think again. I've been waiting for this forever and I don't intend to miss a moment. Where is that beau of yours anyway? Why isn't he with you?"

"If you're talking about the Scapula, he's not with me because I'm not with *him.* I came on my own."

"You—you what? But what about the dress?"

"Murgatroyd and Walmark's boutique on Best Street," Leen said.

"Oh, my dear. What could you have been thinking? That was scarcely wise, scarcely wise at all."

Actually, for a change Leen wasn't sure she didn't agree with her sister. What *had* gotten into her? Cussedness, certainly, but it had been more than that. Feeling sure the Scapula was up to something and not knowing what it was had made her uncomfortable, a sensation that had only deepened as the Scapula's campaign to woo her had intensified. He obviously saw her as a challenge. Well, she could do the same thing right back. She'd see how he behaved this evening. Even the Scapula would have to be somewhat inhibited by the massed presence of the entire upper crust of Peridol, along with the city's most inventive gate crashers.

And he didn't have to take her rejection of his dress as a declaration of war, either. It was a statement of independence, that's all it was, a refusal to be bought. At least by gifts of that magnitude. Knowing him, he might even be amused at her spunk. Of course, knowing *about* him, it could equally well tip the scales toward vendetta.

Unless whatever he needed her for was more important than his feelings.

Or unless he needed her at a specific time, which was running out. . . .

Well, whatever would happen would happen. Anyway, the ball didn't have to be a total loss even if he did decide to be unpleasant. She was intelligent. She could hold up a conversation. She might even meet someone else. *Perhaps,* she thought sarcastically, *I'll run across that ragman who caught my eye on the street.*

But whatever the evening held for her, it hopefully didn't involve hanging around indefinitely with her sister. "Oh, look," Leen said, "there's Lemon," and taking advantage of the fact that Susannah had turned to address another dignitary she'd snared, she slipped away.

Once out of reach Leen decided to make a swing past the food. Lemon had to be around *somewhere,* so she'd spot him for real eventually. Who else might be here that she actually might want to see? She murmured greetings to a few acquaintances as she passed, and couldn't escape being drawn momentarily into eddies of conversations with people she recognized or who claimed to recognize her. She wasn't particularly trying to be aloof or distracted, really she wasn't, but given the circumstances it was just naturally the result. It seemed to be working, too, and she didn't especially mind leaving people more confused than satisfied by their encounter with her.

The place was filling up rapidly, but not with anyone she might have liked to talk to. Who was on her list? There was that detective fellow she'd spoken with in the library, but even if he'd been honest about who he was and his intent to help her, he surely wouldn't have discovered anything of use in the few hours since they'd met, and certainly he wasn't likely to show up here tonight if he had. Unless he'd found out something that couldn't wait.

Well, her list didn't have to be *realistic.*

But then there *was* her brother, finally, off across the floor from her on a balcony. She started toward him, balancing a plate of canapes and a chicken concoction dusted with powdered sugar as she plotted a route up the interconnecting stairs and landings. Perhaps *he'd* managed to uncover something about the Scapula.

It took the better part of five minutes of squirming through the press to reach Lemon's position. Or what had *been* his position, damn him. He'd circulated on. Leen deposited her empty plate on a service table and leaned on the balcony railing, scanning the crowd below. If she—

Huh?

What was *wrong* with her?

She'd made eye contact with yet another random stranger who was standing on the main floor making his own survey of the occupants of the upper landings. Maybe it was the fact that that street vagabond had crossed her mind again that had made her receptive. It couldn't be the *same* man, of course—this one was well-groomed and fashionably dressed, complete with cravat and shirt ruffles and tailored over-jacket, a ceremonial sword (as with most of the men and some of the women) slung at his side. But the slug of electricity that had shivered its way down her back into the pit of her stomach—*that* had been the same, all right.

When she'd had a chance to blink and recover her bearings he was gone. Had she imagined the whole thing? Could waiting for the Scapula's reaction be preying on her mind more than she'd thought? Perhaps it would be better to sit down for a moment.

No, damn it. She'd never been weak-kneed in her life, and damned if she was going to start now. Even if she rarely used it, she was a member of her class. This gave her a certain background, and certain skills. What better time to use it all than now?

The best way to decide how much was imagination was to find this guy.

"Where the hell is that Archivist anyway?"

Max had worked a finger into his tight collar and

263

was hauling away at it, trying to force the unyielding material to stretch, no doubt. "Or is it the collar button you hope to pop?" Shaa asked.

"Stop being so goddamned urbane," Max told him.

Shaa's face grew mournful. "I can't help it, especially in a place like this. I was raised this way. It must be in my blood."

"That's not the *only* thing in your blood, and you'd better not forget it."

"Oh, I wager the context won't entirely slip my mind." Shaa eyed the contents of a plate whose owner was drifting by. "What is *that,* do you think? It rather looked like a sauteed kumquat. I can't remember the last time I've seen a kumquat this far north. But that sauce—would the chef have dared to use *salsa?*"

"With help like this," Max muttered, "I might as well have brought the kid."

"Be patient, Maximillian. We've barely just walked through the door. How do you intend to spot the Archivist anyway? You didn't bother to get a description."

"Give me a minute with him and I'll pick him out."

"You could save yourself some effort and *ask* someone," Shaa suggested. "But no, that wouldn't be underhanded enough, would it."

Max favored Shaa with a momentary scowl. "It's the aura I'm after, you know that; that's what's characteristic. Okay, so I never made it over to the Reading Room to reconnoiter. I've been busy; you know that, too, and anyway the Archivist has to be around here somewhere tonight."

"Yet from your busy-ness, what have you to show?"

"Precious little, damn it all. Okay, we might as well grab some food anyway. Come on."

Max, as he strolled through the crowd, was the very picture of hair-trigger alertness, his eyes tracking, his stance taut, contained energy in his sinews. *Compared to him,* Shaa thought, *I portray the essence of lounge-lizard languor.* But then it was, as he'd remarked, in the breeding. And it was also true that Max was taking, as always, matters close to heart. A good part of Max's activities had involved running down experts and leads on Shaa's own situation. *Always has to do things his way, wouldn't take my word I'd already been over it.*

That was Max. Although he appeared to be growing, if anything, more intense.

But perhaps that had something to do with the other activities surrounding him. "You're still having that problem with loose pieces of architecture in your immediate vicinity?" Shaa asked him, as they entered the line for a large table festooned with vegetable appetizers and a steam table.

Max's head snapped up and he quickly scanned the arched roof. Nothing was cascading toward him. "Don't—"

"It was only a question," said Shaa, "that obviously contained its own answer. You suspect Ma Pitom?"

"Yeah. I do, but what I don't understand is why all of a sudden it's old home week. I know about the Hand for sure, and now there's this indication of Ma Pitom, and the steerhorn I told you about from the road makes you think about Homar Kalifa, and there's been some other stuff too. . . . Makes you wonder if there's some one force behind it all."

"I'll take some of that, please," Shaa told the server, "and a few of those—what *are* those?—battered cauliflower, yes, fine, and perhaps a slice of that garlic concoction as well. Why bother with speculation? You are who you are; you might as well presume."

"Thanks for the reassurance," Max said, ignoring the server and helping himself.

"I was meaning to ask, why did you decide to dispense with your cloaks and camouflage? Merely the obvious, or some other nefarious purpose? That's quite enough, thank you, although . . . yes, I believe I will hazard one of those kumquats. They *are* kumquats? How remarkable."

"Which obvious is that?" muttered Max, adding a bow-tied sour roll to his spoils.

"The fact that your disguises obviously haven't been doing much good, since Ma Pitom and the Hand and whoever else haven't been deterred by them for a moment."

"Yeah," Max admitted, "that's obvious, all right." As they turned away from the table, they could scarcely miss the white-haired gentleman in the purple of a high-level Nerve who was goggling, jaw dropped, at Shaa.

"A pleasant evening," Shaa greeted him, "who could deny it? I recommend the skewered salmon."

If anything, the man's mouth opened wider. "Good lord, it *is* young Shaa!" he said out loud.

Shaa squinted at him. "The senior Hargreaves-Hedge, I hope I'm not mistaken?"

Hargreaves-Hedge grasped Shaa by the shoulder. "But the curse, boy, what about the curse?"

"Catch you later," said Max. It was time to get serious about the evening, and Shaa would obviously be tied down for the time being. Max made his way to the edge of the main dance floor next to the band, finished inhaling the contents of his plate, and began to scan the crowd.

Well, maybe he'd *better* ask someone for directions to the Archivist, Max considered after a few moments. There was no shortage of recognizable faces; he'd even spotted the woman he'd noticed on the street, the one who'd been staring at him as though she'd seen something in his face that lit him up like a beacon. In his brief glimpse just now, the woman had seemed almost as astonishingly transformed as he was himself. On him the transmutation was from unrecognizably, well, *disreputable,* to something approaching an all-around gentleman, if he didn't mind saying so himself. That was nothing compared to the change in her. On her it was from mundane to extraordinary.

Although that wasn't quite true. The woman *hadn't* been mundane. There had been something exceptional about her that had leapt out at him even in that brief instant in the midst of traffic. If it wasn't time for business and things weren't so much on edge, he might try to find her and figure out what it was.

But as it was, he had to find the Archivist. It was fairly much night outside now, which meant he might not have long before the entertainment. What time were the fireworks supposed to start? Max looked at around at the folks nearest to him. Which one of them seemed the type who'd be able to describe the Archivist? There was something about the woman with the excessive tiara . . . no, it was the tiara itself, it was a node-point for some wag's Track. There were no shortage of Tracks around tonight, spread around as liberally as calling cards, but this was not the time for them, either. Perhaps one of the majors-domo?

"Good evening," said a smooth contralto at his elbow.

"Good—" Max said, but as he turned, his voice trailed off as a frog lodged unaccountably in his throat.

It was that woman.

Well, he could always talk to her for a moment and then find the Archivist.

Except—

"Excuse me," the woman was saying. "Is this a bad time? I don't think you've been hearing a word since I came up."

"Perfect time," said Max. "Perfect. I'm sorry. I've had a lot on my mind, and then you—I mean, you . . ."

She was looking at him now as though wondering if she'd entered the effective radius of some virulent contagion. "It must have been my imagination," the woman muttered, half to herself. "Only—could I have seen you on the street? Looking like a refugee from a rubbish heap? Oh, pardon me, I know this is horridly rude. Of course, it could scarcely have been you—your face, what I could see of it, was different, and . . . But your aura . . ."

Tell me about auras, Max thought. To his surprise,

267

though, he found himself saying, "This is what I really look like. When I'm on good behavior and there's a point in spiffing up, that is." What had gotten into him? Why was he telling her that? Shaa would be amazed. *Max* was amazed. Or was appalled a better word?

Especially since he had come seeking the Archivist, and had a rather nasty bit of business in mind for the Archivist once he'd been found. Except it was suddenly clear that the Archivist wasn't a he.

Tell me about auras, he thought again. But auras didn't lie, at least in other hands. And he was in close enough range to fully size up this one. "Madame Archivist?"

The Archivist frowned. "Please call me Leen, why don't you."

It was surprising how quickly this stuff came back. Or not so surprising, really; it was a characteristic of really useless skills that they remain indefinitely intact long past the decay of other, fully essential capabilities. There was context to consider, too. His background in social etiquette was getting its current airing merely because of his hovering miasma of impending doom.

On the other hand, there were scenarios that were probably worse. It would be worthwhile to contemplate them, as a counterweight to his current train of thought, except he would have to think of a few of them first.

"Please excuse me," Shaa told his current companion. "I believe those pickled mahi curls are calling to me."

"You just watch yourself, now, Zolly," the fellow said, his handlebar mustache flapping.

"Indeed," said Shaa. "That's just as good advice for you, seeing as you've been imprudent enough to be seen with me, Chew."

Chew Andrews, an old friend of his mother's and still one of Eden's representatives here in town, squinted at him. "Why the hell not? Damn curse isn't catching, is it?"

"No," Shaa said, "but my brother very well might be." Reflection returned with a vengeance on his way back to the refreshments. It really was tempting fate for him to even be here, but as Chew had said, what the hell. He'd already met the Curse Administrator. What more could his brother do to him, after subcontracting the curse in the first place, other than humiliate him publicly? That would be no picnic, but it was still not in the same league at all as progressive eradication.

Of course, where restoratives were concerned, the evening's caterers were more than adequately stocked. His plate liberally replenished, Shaa popped one of the mahi-mahi twists into his mouth and considered his next move. It would be wise to check Max's status; who knew what kind of situation he might have gotten himself into by now.

And there he was, too, half-concealed behind a line of potted dwarf palms and a statue of some Emperor past. Talking. With a woman. One tended to forget it because of his usual frenetic level of activity, but Max was not particularly tall; the woman topped him by at least an inch or so. The woman had a no-nonsense air that complemented Max's own. In contrast to the elaborate coiffures that predominated among the other celebrants, of both sexes, her short black hair artfully streaked with gray had merely the look of a natural curl to it. Her—

Then Shaa noticed that the two of them weren't merely talking, they were strikingly engrossed.

That was unlike Max, especially while he was on a self-set mission, and when was he not? Max had made a career out of avoiding potential new entanglements and complaining about the ones he already had, such as Shaa himself, for example. Max's behavior at the moment seemed scarcely typical. Even better, it might be a hopeful sign.

Shaa drifted closer and lounged back against the old

stone Emperor's chest. Eventually Max would acknowledge his presence or he'd force his own entry
into the conversation, or on the other hand perhaps he
wouldn't. Max had noticed him, certainly he had, but
it was true that Max's manners, not being ingrained
in him from birth, sometimes showed a tendency to
disappear under pressure.

Where was the pressure *here*, however?

If Max was taking something seriously here, that
could be pressure enough.

Leen was confused. What had come over her? Where
were all the social skills that had been pounded into
her reluctant mind throughout her childhood? What
had happened to the guile that was supposed to shield
any true feeling from public view, the defense of re-
serve, the aloof unconcern?

Where, indeed?

But then why was she still feeling these curls of
electricity? Why, although she didn't particularly like
cats or cat-based metaphors, did she feel like nothing
other than *purring*, of all things? Nothing was tickling
her belly in any objective sense . . . but it still felt like
it, anyway. She'd better find Lemon; *he'd* know.

On second thought, she'd better *not* find Lemon. For
exactly the same reason.

And why was she sure these feelings weren't just
hers alone? For the radiation of sheer competence and
force of personality, this Maximillian was right up
there with the Scapula, clearly. Like the Scapula, he
was most likely out on some secret errand or another,
or why would he have been out in the street in that
disguise?

But at the moment Max looked as woozy as she felt.
As though something had walloped him upside the
head, knocking his perceptions and reactions completely out of whack.

These weren't the most confusing things of all. The
most confusing thing of all was that, deranged though
her senses felt, she found she rather liked it.

"Understatement of the year," Leen mumbled under her breath.

"Excuse me?" said Max. "Would you like some more food? Would you like to leave? Would you like to sit down?"

"No, no thank you. No." She broke her gaze away again and quickly scanned the room.

"Who are you looking for?"

"There's someone probably here I probably don't want to see."

"I shouldn't have asked anyway," Max said, with some confusion. "It's none of my business. I—I apologize." A throat cleared itself in a familiar way behind him. "Oh, here's somebody for you to meet. Zalzyn Shaa, Doctor Shaa actually but most everyone just calls him Shaa; Leen. The Archivist."

"Charmed," said Shaa, bowing over her hand. "Completely and absolutely."

Shaa? She knew that name, of course, but not this particular person. "Are you—"

But then her gaze, which had lit on this Shaa only for a moment before resuming its ongoing inspection, found the object of its search. "Oh, damn," Leen said. Max glanced over his shoulder and followed her stare.

He was not actually that far away, only thirty feet or so, and he too had apparently been looking for her. Or them. The Scapula paused in the middle of the sentence he was saying to the man next to him, like himself garbed in the dress costume of a Bone, and his eyes grew wide. His smile became more of a smirk, and then an open gleeful grin. He inclined his head in greeting across the intervening partyers, then broke with his partner and embarked on a leisurely but deliberate stroll toward them.

"*That's* who you probably don't want to meet?" Max sputtered. "Shaa—"

"I see him, Maximillian. Unless I miss a sucker-bet guess, he has just spotted me, too."

Leen looked between them. "Oh, you know the Scapula?"

"Yes," Shaa acknowledged, "you could say so. After all, he *is* my brother."

"Your. . . ?" Wait a minute—what was that Lemon had said about the Scapula having a family curse, that she'd brushed off without thinking twice about it, that she'd actually remembered something about herself? There were curses, but . . . wait a . . . *Holy*—Leen almost muttered something highly inappropriate to her office. This was *that* Shaa! This was *that* curse, *that* was who this fellow was—the one who could never set foot in Peridol again. And he was *here*. Oh, my lord—

And then Shaa was not the only Shaa who was here; *right* here. "Arznaak," Max said.

"What a *nice* surprise," said the Scapula. "Not only Maximillian, but Zal, too. I heard you were in town and hoped I'd have a chance to see you."

"I'm sure you did," Shaa said evenly.

"So you did come back, did you."

"Yes, well, you know how it is."

"Do I? Why don't you tell me. In any case, how *are* you? We should get together more often, being siblings that is."

"Oh," said Shaa, "is that how siblings are supposed to behave? I wouldn't know."

"Come now, dear brother, be affable. You are on public display. And Arleen, my dear—just having a pleasant little conversation, I suppose?"

"As a matter of fact that's right," said Leen, trying for evenness herself.

"I didn't know you'd become an exemplar of the arts," Shaa said suddenly to his brother.

"Oh?" said Arznaak. Something sharp seemed to glint in his eyes, something scarcely affable at all. "Why do you say I have?"

"This scene is a signal example of surrealism as performance. Wouldn't you say?"

"Actually, I wouldn't. It seems perfectly straightforward to me. And just because you can cloud the minds of others, dear brother Zal, don't think you can do that to me." Arznaak directed his gaze at Leen. "Arleen and I had been conversing just this afternoon, if you recall, and the topic was not finished, my brother's attempt at distraction or misdirection or whatever you choose to call it notwithstanding. No, not finished at all."

"I rather think we were," said Leen.

"I rather think not," the Scapula told her. "Do you stand with me or do you stand with them?"

Leen stuck her jaw out. "Neither one. I'm just standing, that's all. That's what people do at parties." *Normal* people, anyway, in whose company none of those around here at the moment could obviously be counted.

"An interesting attitude, if an untenable one," pronounced the Scapula. "Now Maximillian, or shall I call you Max?, what—"

"You can call me fed up," said Max, "that's what you can call me. This has all gone far enough. Once and for all, will you drop this ridiculous vendetta and cancel the curse?"

Arznaak looked amused. "No, of course not. What do you propose to do about it?"

To Leen's eye, Max was clearly athletic. He didn't project the overwhelming material power of bulging muscles or the raw intimidation of an aggressive stance, but the controlled glide when he moved and the way he stood balanced on the balls of his feet and the sheer physical competence about him said this was clearly a man who knew how to manage more than his mind and his tongue. He did know how to manage *them*, that was plain, even if they had seemed somewhat askew during the time the two of them had been talking together; no one would have given *her* clarity of conversation high marks from that period either. But had she seen a hint that Max was capable of the world-class skill that would let him move between one eye-blink and the next from a position of studied if

273

watchful rest to a full *en garde,* a sword that was anything *but* ceremonial in his right hand, with nothing
but an afterimage of blurs and streaks to attest to the
transition that must have taken place in the middle?
She had not, yet that was apparently exactly what had
just unfolded in front of her. And what was unfolding
still, as the *en garde* continued without pause into a
full-force and maximum-speed lunge directly toward
the Scapula's chest.

The Scapula was in motion, too, his own hand snaking to the hilt of his weapon and the weapon itself
starting to come free. He would never make it, though,
he would barely get his sword halfway to position, he
was about to be—

But then all of a sudden Max's right foot, which had
been planted in a step while his other foot propelled
him forward, flew out to the side, the rest of his body
began to turn a lateral cartwheel, and he hit the floor
hard with his right shoulder and the whole edge of his
head. His sword clattered to the floor next to him.

"No," said Zalzyn Shaa, breathing hard. But that
was to be expected from someone whose own abrupt
display of unexpected dexterity had thrown Max to the
ground in the first place, with a carefully timed kick
against Max's vulnerable ankle.

Max glared up at him from the floor. "You *idiot!*"
he snarled. "I would have had him—this time I would
have had him, and we could've all been done with this
garbage once and for all. Get your foot off that sword."

"No," Shaa said again.

"Come now, Max," said the Scapula. "You
couldn't even *hold* a sword at the moment. Look at
your right arm—it's numb." The Scapula's own sword,
however, was still in *his* hand. His sharp smile was
still in place, with perhaps a few additional barbs dangling from the corners, and his attitude of mocking
nonchalance was fully active, but he too was breathing
with more than a hint of a pant. "You may be right,
you know," he went on, waving his blade in Max's
direction, if from a great enough distance to keep Max

from catapulting himself from the floor to snatch it from his grasp. "You might have gotten me. Fortunately, my dear brother Zal has my welfare at heart. Don't you, dear brother?"

"Obviously so," said Shaa.

"You idiot," Max was still muttering. "You'll never get him off your back with a sharp tone and snide remarks. Why should I do all this work for you when you don't give a damn?"

"Why indeed? But the answer is still no," Shaa told him. "That's final." And his tone certainly sounded that way. He looked around, at the hushed crowd ringing them, its breath drawn in a collective gasp, said "Excuse me" to the person nearest him and to the mass at large, pushed the fellow aside, and swam away across the floor.

"And we were just starting to have such fun, too," stated the Scapula.

"You want fun?" said Max, getting slowly to his feet. "I'll give you fun." *Damn* Shaa. He'd even taken his weapon away with him.

Leen's own head was spinning, but one thing still seemed to be clear. "You're going to have real trouble in a minute if you don't both cut this out."

Above them, on the highest balcony, a slender figure had emerged, bathed in a wash of white light; a figure that appeared to be staring directly down at them. Max wrapped up his scowl, lowered his head, and dropped down on one knee. Out of the corner of his eye, the Scapula more slowly did the same thing.

The wave of obeisance spread. The Emperor-Designate's direction of gaze, however, never wavered. Yet neither did he beckon to the small entourage at his back. Instead, he raised a hand, outstretched toward the roof. "Let the festivities begin," he called in a strong, projective tenor.

A rapid series of < c r u m p s > sounded from outside. Trails of sparks streaked into the sky. Overhead at the roof's long apex, with a large mechanical groan, a line of sky appeared, unfiltered by the tint of the glass panes. The line widened to a bar and kept increasing; the two sections of the roof were folding back. Then, in a massive coordinated barrage clearly visible beyond, the first six skyrockets went off together.

To Leen, however, the more significant pyrotechnics were those taking place in her immediate vicinity. The Scapula, his gaze turned up past smoldering to incandescent, had moved in on her as the lamps and fires inside the pavilion went down and the show in the sky kicked off, putting her and Max and him shoulder to shoulder in a potentially more than metaphorical triangle. The way the Scapula—Arznaak Shaa—flipped his personal magnetism off and on was starting to annoy her more than a bit, though. Knowing it was just as much a tool to him as his sword or his henchmen made it easier to resist.

Whatever it was about Max, on the other hand, clearly wasn't indiscriminate, and she didn't think it was planned, either. It was new and different, but she wasn't necessarily *looking* for new and different. From the context of things, too, whatever Max might have to offer was situated in the middle of a plain of booby traps and broken glass. "This all has nothing to do with us," the Scapula murmured to her beneath the explosions of the air-shells.

"What *does* it have to do with, then?"

The Scapula shrugged. "Families are unaccountable, hmm?"

Max was watching from the side, his arms folded. His stance seemed calm, though, or as calm as she'd seen him earlier, anyway, rather than displaying the full force of the frustration he undoubtedly still felt; only his eyes showed that. In contrast to the circle of onlookers still hanging around in case of any new outbreak, Max was close enough to hear the words between them, and the Scapula plainly didn't care if he did or not. "Are they?" Leen said. "I'd say sometimes an accounting is *exactly* what's needed. Hmm?"

"No matter," he told her. "Come with me now, Arleen. Nothing else is important." The force of his gaze *was* intense, but its meaning was inscrutable. He made her uneasy. He'd always made her uneasy, but it had taken meeting Max to really make her realize that. There were similarities, true, but when you got right down to it there was truly no comparison between the feelings she got from the two of them.

Of course, at the moment the Scapula was *trying* to make her feel uneasy. "No," said Leen, "I don't think so. Not now."

"If you decide to come with me later the terms will not be the same."

"That's just a risk I'll have to take."

Arznaak shifted, and for a moment she thought he was about to lean in to kiss her or perhaps to make a grab, and maybe he had had that in mind, too, but then out of the corner of her eye she saw Max adjust his stance as well, not blatantly or with any explicit move toward her on his part, and the Scapula paused. He looked deliberately at Max, then at Leen, and then turned abruptly away with a swish of his jacket. The crowd around them exhaled as if in unison and began to break up.

"I've got things to do that won't wait," Max said. "I'm not like Arznaak, but—hell." The expression in his face seemed to be going in about half-a-dozen directions at once, which only made it an accurate mirror of the way *she* felt. "I—damn." He shook his head. "When can I meet you again? I don't mean to muscle you like him, but—" he swallowed some comment she thought it was just as well she hadn't heard. Then, with a note of what sounded strangely like *despair* in his voice, he said, "I *need* to see you again."

"I'm at the Archives most days," Leen said.

"Right," he muttered. "I—right." With a strange imitation of someone tearing himself loose from a piece of flypaper, he twisted and moved away. His head jerked once to the side, as though he was catching himself before he'd actually turned back around to face her, but then he put his head down and disap-

277

peared behind a clump of people craning upward at the aerial pageant.

What is wrong with me? Leen thought. Why, her pulse was racing and she was more short of breath than on her periodic runs around the park. She was even shivering, although the banked fires and space heaters kept the chill of the evening air from penetrating the assembly on the floor. And—

Someone clasped her around the shoulders. She broke the grip, wheeled, and was about to pummel whatever she found there with her bare hands when she recognized her own brother, Lemon. "You're an idiot—" she sputtered, "don't you know I've had attack training—I could have—"

"It is time," Lemon told her, "to sit down."

Damn, Max thought. This changed everything. But he didn't *want* everything to change. A life of discipline and artifice, of practice in masking your feelings because you knew damn well they cause nothing but trouble, and then when it really matters, when the situation comes that all that training was geared for, out the window, that's where it goes. He'd better pull himself together and get back to the job or he'd be out to lunch, and it might be a lunch he'd be the guest-of-honor entree at, too.

And these other things had to come first; he had to settle things one way or another, once and for all. The backup plan was now essential. Whoever the Archivist was was beside the point. Whatever his own feelings were or might be was immaterial. A plan is a plan. And this wasn't just any plan, either. It was now the plan that had to be run.

If he'd only thought to pick the material up the last time he'd been in the Archives he wouldn't have this problem now. But how much could he carry? He hadn't had a cart, and things being what they were he hadn't had an assistant either. He also hadn't had an opportunity to go back, or (to be honest) a real reason. How could he have known he'd ever need it?

But all these after-the-fact squirmings were just futility and empty wind. He needed to concentrate, to focus—he'd never pick up a trainer course, let alone a high-order Track, with a mind as cluttered and whirling as his. He did the breathing control, the progressive relaxation wave starting at his toes and working up, and even though he usually detested chants he did the core visualization mantra, too. The external noises of crowd and fireworks and his internal jumble both gradually receded; slowly the traces of Tracks began to tune in. Not that one, no, or that other one across the room with its node in the wineglass left in the hand of another stone Emperor, or—

Wait.

The gods operated on magic's second quantum level; naturally a full-scale God-Track would have a second quantum component to it. The Tracks Phlinn Arol sometimes used to bring Max to him were the kind an unaugmented human could follow, but then so far Max thought he'd managed to keep Phlinn from the knowledge of how far into the technical arcana of the gods he'd actually been able to penetrate. Max spoke the right trigger words and adjusted the calibration with a small sweep-and-wriggle of his fingers. A pink haze spun across his vision; his hearing shifted tone values, and then clear as day beside him was the buzz of normal conversation.

The conversation of the *people* around him was muted and thin, however. Max edged to his left until the seemingly normal sounds were most distinct, then strolled ahead. There were no bodies attached to the conversation, not yet anyway, and no intelligible meaning, but the Track characteristics were present nevertheless.

There it went, now, up into the terraces. In the multicolored phosphorus glare of the skyrockets and the twirlers and fixed jets on the lawn around the pavilion and even now spouting from the lake, a pale pink hood across his face shouldn't be worth a glance. Waltzing into the midst of the gods with it on was another matter, even if they had been heavily partying. For that matter, meeting the gods with *himself* on wasn't exactly the smartest way to go either.

This new nonsense was affecting him more than was healthy. At least he hadn't out-and-out screwed up. He *had* made certain preparations, too. A different trigger-phrase launched the false aura he'd whipped up earlier in the day, and a few moments' work behind a portable azalea with his paint-and-putty kit took care of his face.

The stairway to the final terrace proved to be hidden by a wall. At least, to mundane perception it was a wall; on the second quantum level, however, it was nothing but a screen of mist. Max squared his shoulders and ambled through.

With luck this wouldn't take long. Even with all the precautions the gambit was a significant risk; the quicker he could be out the better. On the other hand, Max did have the amulet from the Archives, and anyway he didn't know a better way to quickly contact the one he was after, if he happened to be at the ball in the first place. That seemed a reasonable bet since Max knew he was in town and had a recent description to boot. Otherwise Max would have to wait in line at the temple.

But he *was* in luck. Not fifteen feet from the top of the short stair behind the mist-wall, standing by himself and staring pensively up at rolling green fireballs, was the one he'd come to see. Max had a window of opportunity; he wouldn't even use the note-in-the-guy's-pocket ruse. Max sidled up next to him. "I think we have business to do together," he murmured.

The other lowered his face from the sky and looked Max up and down as though he were a person-sized insect. "And why is that? Who are you, and what do I have that you want?"

Max ignored the sneer; this was business. "It's what *I* have that *you* want that's more to the point."

It had been well done, Fradjikan thought. A little histrionic, perhaps, but then that was what the situation had required. His associate, the Scapula, had even handled the unexpected collapse of his plot involving the Archivist into that of Max with reasonable aplomb. Now the next step could proceed. Tomorrow, when the next wave of posters would show Max challenging (if allegorically) the authority of the new Emperor himself . . . But first, there was another pawn to pursue. That promised no end of fun.

Then again, there was this Spilkas fellow. They were keeping the refreshment tables open while the show of illuminations went on, so Fradi helped himself to another slice of braised lamb; the chefs had done a superb job with that cabernet sauce and it was important to show one's appreciation. Fradi was also willing to admit it might be appropriate to revise his original impression of Spilkas. It was starting to appear that Spilkas might indeed be a potent adversary—or a potentially powerful ally—who had insinuated himself into Max's camp for his own reasons. He was clearly a force to be tiptoed warily around. How *had* Spilkas learned Fradi's identity? From the Scapula? Doubtful in the extreme. One of the players Fradi had set loose against Max? But *they* didn't know. That left a limited range of possibilities, all of them sufficient to give a sane man pause.

According to his sources, Max's potential as a destabilizing factor was a growing worry to certain of the gods, and no longer only Fradi's patron, either. Perhaps Spilkas was really another operative on the same mission as Fradi himself. Given that Fradi's long-term self-interest was not necessarily the same as the mission he had been assigned, perhaps there was a basis for collaboration.

The Scapula had implied he would be generous with his own assistance to Fradi in the future. Hopefully the Scapula's promise would in fact be redeemed. In any case, though, it was essential to have backup plans.

For that matter, Fradi could also reinterpret his instructions. Might he be bold enough to try shopping his services around to other, competing gods, too, if such there really were? Spilkas might know. Spilkas might be able to help. Spilkas might—

But anyway, there was that other more immediate pawn, and the other step that could now proceed. First things first.

It was just another party. Nothing ever really happens at a party, so I was sure I wasn't missing anything. On the other hand, I'd gotten here just in time to see Shaa and Max go in, and a bit later Shaa's brother Arznaak, the Scapula, making his own grand entrance. I was back with the rabble behind a police line; comes from not planning ahead and getting an invitation. Well, I'd never been fond of parties anyway, and in any case I had enough thinking going on to hold my own party in my own head.

My life had gone through some strange gyrations lately. I couldn't remember the last time I'd climbed in a window or threatened someone with a sword or gotten hit over the head, and as for shaking down clues and getting paid for it, well, I might as well have done that in another incarnation for all the familiarity it had for me now. Most of my activities had come to consist of wandering around and talking to folks who came up to me on the street. There *had* been that setup with the fountain and the statue, but that scarcely counted in my favor. How many grown men outside of a lunatic retreat spend their time fighting stone monuments?

But the talking hadn't exactly been idle chatter either. This latest salvo from the Protector of Nature was the screwiest yet. What kind of sap did she and her cronies think I was anyway? Suppose I did take care of Max, not what you'd call a cakewalk itself. The Protector couldn't know that by striking against Max I'd set myself against the only group that was anything approaching friendly to me. In exchange, though, the Protector's gang would make me leader of the gods, she'd said, which meant I'd be the front man for their cabal until they'd swept the opposition out of the way, and then they'd stab me in the back, or I'd outsmart them by doing my own doublecross first, or—

I didn't want to think about it.

Why was I bothering to spend time on it, anyway? The Protector thought I was a god, probably Gashanatantra, but as far as I knew I wasn't anything of the sort, or if I was, it sure hadn't done me much good so far. I'd better remember that before I decided to take her up on her offer.

That wasn't the only possibility, though. If she'd gotten wind of the fact that there was something strange about me, the Protector could have been using her story as a cover to check me out at closer range. Maybe she was trying to figure out who I was, too. Or perhaps the real center of interest was Max. Could she be more interested in finding out the full scope of Max's own contacts with the gods, and using that information against the gods in question?

I may not have wanted to think about this all, but I seemed to be getting as far with that desire as with any of my others.

Even with all my mental activity, I tried not to lose track of the comings and goings in the crystal ballroom across the lawn. With Arznaak, Shaa, and Max, and probably Fradjikan lurking around, too, for all I knew, I'd have my choice of targets. Well, I'd follow whichever one of them showed first.

Actually, the first significant change in the situation was when the fireworks let loose. As the big top roof of the pavilion started to crank open, a bunch of long trailers of fire jumped off the ground from the fenced-off area around it. The folks around me starting in to "ooh"ing and "aah"ing feverishly. After the first barrage, a raft out on the pond let loose with its own display of animated sparklers, here the old Emperor's profile nodding sagely in fire, there the face of the new Emperor receiving the symbolic accolade with sober acknowledgement. A wizard-light display of Bones and other constituent parts of the Corpus Politick began to rise from the far ground. That was when I noticed that someone had approached me from the crowd and was standing in front of me, eyeing me with a familiar glare.

He seemed a few inches taller than the last time we'd met, just before my departure from Oolsmouth. He could have been wearing special shoes but somehow that didn't seem quite his style. His face had also flowed a bit, enough for him to no longer be the spitting double of Jardin, although he still had something like a second cousin's relationship, or perhaps a stepbrother once removed. His hand was out for me to shake.

I braced myself and gritted my teeth. The last time we'd shaken hands, when Jardin had taken him into our little band of conspirators, thinking him to be Soaf Pasook, I'd gotten a shock about on a level with what I'd expect if someone with a large mallet was suddenly using it to pound a not-particularly-sharp stake through my palm. Nevertheless, it wouldn't do to just stick my hand in my pocket and refuse to be baited. If I'd learned anything from my dealings with him, Gashanatantra was not a god to be toyed with. So I bit down on my molars and slapped my palm against his.

He didn't seem surprised, but I sure was. What I felt was . . . a hand, and nothing else. No bolts of lightning, no surreptitious attacks, no sucking at my life force, just . . . a hand. "How you doing?" I said.

"Well," he informed me. "And yourself?"

"Sure a nice night for fireworks." Maybe I was just getting used to my contacts with him, because there were some other odd things about the way this encounter was shaping up. For one, I was not feeling the vague ghost of Gash's own sensations. Maybe that was a side effect of the metabolic link that you built up a tolerance to. I'd been fairly much distracted at that last meeting in Oolsmouth, but as I thought back on it now I didn't recall feeling his perceptions then either. I had no idea what if anything that meant. Maybe now I could punch Gash in the stomach without laying myself out, too, but it scarcely seemed worthwhile to try. Throwing a fist at him that other time had probably been valuable once, if only to learn that I really did pack a pretty hefty right, but that was the kind of lesson that seemed worth learning the first time and never having to take again.

But all that was subsidiary. Our relationship was clearly not founded on small talk, so what did he want from me this time?

"You are an interesting young man," he observed.

"Plenty of people like fireworks," I said, not because it was a particularly witty comeback but merely to feed him something to move him on to his real gambit. I had an idea of what his first definite move might be.

"May I visit with Monoch, please?"

I hesitated. I'd been right, he wanted Monoch in his hand so Monoch could give his spy report on my activities. But if something had shifted in the metabolic link, perhaps something had shifted as well in the balance between us. "Actually, no, not at the moment," I told him, and held my breath as I waited for his retribution.

Gash stared at me, but as I stared back it became apparent that my blood was not in fact boiling or the skin melting from my face. I'd won this bet, at least.

But then he'd said "please." He'd never done *that* before, either.

Monoch, in his walking stick form, was vibrating in my hand; *he* wanted to talk to *Gash,* too. *You heard me, now shut up!* I thought at him. Monoch gave a last limp quiver and subsided.

"It is unimportant," Gash stated. "There are other matters for us to discuss."

"Yeah," I said, "you're right. There's a lot of strange stuff going on, and folks thinking I'm you has landed me right in the middle of it. I'm getting a little tired of you setting me up all the time to draw your fire."

"Have you ever had an angry ex-wife after you? No, I'm sure you haven't."

That's what he said, but all of a sudden I realized he'd told me something else entirely. When I made that last remark, I'd been thinking of my interview with the Protector of Nature. As far as Gash was concerned, that had seemed to me to be the biggest plot element on the table at the moment. I figured Gash would know about that gambit; he'd have to. But he didn't. I'd bet he didn't.

What was still on *his* mind was my experience with his wife Jill and the stuff he'd been stage-managing in Oolsmouth.

"Sure I have," I told him, shifting my bearings. "I've had yours. I've managed to avoid her since I got out of Oolsmouth, but that can't last forever. I'm not gonna let her eradicate me, either, so don't think you can get off the hook with her *that* way. She might even be warming up to you again."

"To *you*, do you mean?"

"Don't start *that*. *I* don't want her, and I don't know whether you do or don't yourself. So do us both a favor. Decide what you want to do about her, and then do it."

"It's not that simple."

"Nothing's that simple. But maybe it could be. Or maybe you could treat it that way anyway and make some progress before complicating things up again. You guys with the complex plots—if you don't watch out, you're gonna trip over your own tangles."

"There may be some truth to that," Gash admitted.

He seemed to be in an uncharacteristically mellow mood, not that I'd ever had the slightest hint before that Gash and that adjective might ever find themselves mentioned in the same sentence. Was it an opening? "Look, I've got some information for you I'm willing to trade."

"Trade?"

"That's right, trade. Here's what I've got. I was approached this afternoon by someone who wants my help in straightening out the political mess you guys have gotten yourselves into. In return they were gonna make me Dictator of the Gods. For some reason I thought they might not really have had *me* in mind.''

I'd captured his interest, all right. It looked like I *was* telling him news he hadn't already heard. ''That may be,'' said Gash. ''Who was this who contacted you?''

''I'm not sure,'' I told him. ''I don't know all of you the way you all know each other. It seemed to be a woman, but we all know how much that means.''

''What was your response? Did you turn her down?''

''I never turn *anybody* down. I seem to be living longer that way.''

''You are no fool,'' he observed. ''But then that is self-evident, or I would not continue to treat with you. Very well, what do you propose in trade, for this information and for the next contact?''

''With this metabolic link thing and all, I'm sure you know I have a certain problem.''

Gash hesitated. ''The Curse of Namelessness.''

''Yeah, that's right.'' Gash had more than paused, he'd seemed as off-balance as I'd ever seen him. That was saying a lot, since I'd never seen him anything close to fazed before either. ''How much do you know about it?''

A particularly loud and flashy barrage of star-shells lit up over the lake, and Gash turned to observe them. He waited for the echoes to die out before informing me, ''I don't know who you are, if that's what you're asking, and I assume it is. When one encounters a victim of that Curse, however, the wisest course of action is to investigate further to make certain they are not a trap.''

''A trap?''

Gash looked at me with a clinical gaze. ''Certain nefarious individuals have been known to use deep-level programming beneath the Curse of Namelessness to create a weapon. I do not now believe that is the case with you. You may be the damaged byproduct of some earlier magical conflict, that is a possibility. Plainly, though, the most likely case is still the most straightforward one.''

Those were intriguing ideas. They gave me new things to think about, as though I really needed that, but one of the new things was centered in what he *didn't* say. I had the feeling there was a concept he'd left off his list. ''Okay, but—''

''For now that is all,'' he stated. ''Have Monoch contact me when you have your next meeting.'' He swirled his cape around and seemed to melt back into the crowd.

I looked back over at the fireworks. I had to admit this was getting interesting. I wasn't thinking only of the way I was even starting to get used to the abrupt entrances and exits the folks I was dealing with always liked to make; that was merely window dressing. On the other hand, this talk with Gash was strikingly reminiscent of my interview with Phlinn Arol. The key similarity was the strong feeling they'd each left me with that both of them were lying. Perhaps they didn't out-and-out know who I was, but they had some pretty good suspicions.

How far back might that really go? Had Gash sought me out in Roosing Oolvaya because of who he thought I'd been? That was probably going a bit far. There was no reason to assume our first encounter had been anything but happenstance. Once he'd roped me into his plot involving the Pod Dall ring and the necromancer Oskin Yahlei, though, and pinned me with the metabolic link, he'd have realized I presented my own mystery, too.

The way I understood it, Gash had been teamed with Soaf Pasook on the play that put Pod Dall into the ring. I thought Gash was nominally on the Conservationist side, but his real interest was in improving his position and playing off one side against the other for his own benefit; this was the reason he'd put Pod Dall in play in the first place. Maybe he didn't anticipate the other things he'd stirred up, though.

If I was willing to run the risk of possibly elevating my own importance, it wasn't outside the bounds of credibility to speculate that Gash had set his plans for Oolsmouth with me in mind, and not just as a tool, either. In the way he'd hung back behind the curtains he'd been able to monitor the situation, and to monitor *me*. He'd also been seeing if he could get things to cut loose or to clarify a bit by arranging for extra pressure to be applied.

So just who the hell *was* I?

More to the point, I was getting a very uncomfortable feeling. All these major heavy hitters wouldn't be interested in me if I wasn't at least potentially part of their league, either as pawn or player myself. But I didn't like their league, and I wasn't too fond of them either.

What if I *was* one of them anyway?

In the red glare of the flame pillars and the drifting green of the latest overhead burster, I noticed a familiar figure stalking down the drive from the pavilion, hands in his pockets and head thrust forward aggressively. I angled to intercept him and caught up just as he pushed past the guards at the roadblock and headed off down the street. "Hey," I said.

Shaa glanced at me, looking clearly the worse for some kind of wear. I offered him my handkerchief; he took it and mopped his brow. "I don't want to talk about it," he told me.

"To hell with plots," I agreed. "How about getting drunk?"

"That," said Shaa, "is the best idea I've heard in a week."

18

"Now this is more like it," said Tildy Mont.

"I don't know," said Jurtan. "I don't know if this is such a good idea."

"What would you know about it?"

"I was just out on the road with Max, remember. I—"

"Don't take that tone with *me*. And what would being on the road have taught you that's of any use to anybody anyway?"

Jurtan probably *had* been speaking a little too haughtily for his own good, he thought. He wasn't about to admit it, though, and on top of that there was clearly no point in making the effort when he had his sister around to do it for him. "It sure made me learn how to watch out for myself in a place like this."

"Great, so then do that. Watch out for *yourself.*"

Not that this place bore any more than a generic resemblance to those Jurtan had encountered on the road, either. This didn't seem to be a bar, per se, and it sure wasn't an inn; it was more of . . . of . . . a nightclub? That flashy cursive-scroll lettering spelling the name of the establishment across its front wall in fiery green wizard scrawl, for one example, and the dapper doorman, for another, and even the carefully arranged shrubs and small trees decorating the entrance bespoke a facility with aspirations, at least. "What are you looking for here anyway?" Jurtan said, putting a hand on his sister's shoulder to hold her back from her obstinate charge through the door. "You've changed a *lot*. What happened? What happened on that *boat*? Were you getting, uh, *friendly* with the sailors? What about Shaa? Were you—"

There was a difference between learning something in the more-or-less abstract of a place like the road, Jurtan was discovering, and being able to put the lesson into practice automatically in whatever other situations it might warrant, which was to say at any time and any place. But then who would expect that his own sister would haul off without warning or provocation and sock him in the stomach?

That was obviously the message, Jurtan thought, bending over with both arms folded over his belly, trying not to throw up on the neat tiled walk. Tidy had quite a punch on her. Well, who needed *her* anyway, and good riddance—

Not quite. She was still standing over him. When she was satisfied Jurtan had noticed her again, she told him, "That's none of your business. Why are you asking me? You trying to cover up something on your own conscience? Was Maximillian being *friendly* with *you?*"

Jurtan again considered the option of vomiting. "Watch your mouth," he said weakly.

"Watch your own mouth. They're all too obsessed with their plots and their plans anyway."

I really should let well enough alone, Jurtan thought vaguely. "Oh, you mean Shaa wasn't *interested* in you?"

Tidy's new shade of facial red was quite striking. Interestingly enough, Jurtan had the feeling the flush had not come out of anger, or at least not *totally* out of anger. This time she *did* wheel, though, and stalked away from him through the double-height doors.

Which just went to prove his point. His sister did need someone to keep on eye on her. *Somebody* had to be concerned for her well-being here in the big city where she was so obviously out of her depth. She might have rejected him now, but she'd certainly thank him later. He creaked to his feet and wobbled in after her through the door.

Inside in the main room, Tildy had spotted the Karlinis holding on to a small table off in a side booth. She wasn't in a mood to tangle with them again just yet. They hadn't been going at each other on the walk over, and when it had appeared for a moment that they might be getting ready to start, the fireworks had taken off over on the other side of the city. The pyrotechnical storm was no more than a background rumble and boom from their position, but its message was clear; the Knitting had officially begun. A whistling yellow cloud had arched down the street overhead, a small mob of gowned figures stampeding after it with wine bottles held high, music had burst free from a building down the block—in a word, utter pandemonium had cut loose, all around them and undoubtedly all across Peridol, as the thousand-and-one celebrations that had been awaiting the traditional signal to get themselves underway had jumped on the good news.

In the midst of all that, for Roni and Karlini to have launched into their evening argument would have been gratuitous as well as useless since you could barely hear yourself think, much less listen to someone standing next to you. Karlini had put an arm around his wife's waist. She had merely ignored it, until the arm seemed to give up on its own and slide off.

But the Karlinis weren't the only role models around tonight. Standing with her hands on her hips surveying the main room from a position next to the reception station was Dalya Hazeel, iridescent in a slinky gown that picked up the green of her eyes. "Hi again," Tildy greeted her.

"Hey," said Dalya, not taking her gaze off the crowd. "What kept you?"

"Nothing," said Tildy, with a meaning-filled glare back up the entry hall at her brother staggering in.

"Yeah, right, I know *that* kind of nothing, too. I got a candidate already picked out for you—see that guy with the black hair and the biceps over by the edge of the stage?''

"Not bad, I guess." Tildy hesitated. "What am I going to do about Svin?"

"Leave him to me." Dalya flipped her head, making her long black hair coil out like a cloud. "Why do you think I didn't tell you who I spotted for *me?*"

"I don't know about Svin. He's sort of a drag."

"You just have to know how to treat them, honey. Take the time Roni and I . . ."

The Great Karlini gazed morosely out across this waste-of-time joint and toyed with his glass. What *was* Dalya telling the Mont kid? Dalya had always been a bad influence, and if—

"How's your drink, dear?"

True, Karlini thought, *it might be prudent to give some attention to my wife.* "Oh, it's fine, I guess. I don't know where they'd be getting strawberries this time of year so they're probably frozen, but the ice maker seems to be working, anyway. What did Dalya tell you about this place? Seeing how she seems to own it and all?"

"I don't know that she *owns* it—"

Karlini gestured across the room. "She greets people at the door, she tells the waiters where to go and even bosses the maitre d', she's the only one who goes in the little room behind the bar in the corner—she's sure not the hat-check girl, you can bet on that."

"As long as you finally seem to be waking up and taking an interest in the world," Roni said, "and since we can hear each other over the din from outside, I think it's about time to have a talk, dear."

Waking up, thought Karlini. *So that was my mistake.* "I always love to talk with you, dear."

"So I've seen. So you won't mind talking about whatever's been eating you."

"What? What are you talking about?"

"You've never been very convincing when you try

to lie, dear. What I don't understand is why you're doing it? What is it you don't want to tell me?"

Karlini felt like he had been blindsided by a runaway elephant, and was even now subsiding into the large circular footprint it had left behind it in the mud. "Uh, well, it's—it's Haddo. I'm thinking we may have to let him go."

"Haddo? Whatever is the matter with Haddo? And why is *that* something you're keeping from me?"

"You've been busy," said Karlini, doing his best to sound sincere. "I didn't think it was worth distracting you over. You've been doing all the work around the family, after all, and I haven't been doing anything of consequence, so I figured the least I could do was take care of this little problem."

"But Haddo's been with us since—"

"All the more reason for a change."

She wasn't going to let this go; he knew her. If this kept up, Karlini was sure he'd end up spilling the whole thing, dribble by drop, which was exactly what he knew he shouldn't do. Why was there never a diversion handy when you—

What was the *other* Mont kid up to? "What's Jurtan doing over there with the *band?*" Karlini said.

"He's getting much better at dealing with his problems," Roni stated, "which is more than I can say for some of the other men around tonight."

"That's not fair, dear."

"You want to discuss fair? Well, I'll tell you what's fair. . . ."

Was it a Track? Jurtan was wondering. *Or just some instinct?* Not that it mattered what you called it, or if there was really any difference between them. All he knew was that he'd been wandering aimlessly into the club, still thinking about his sister when he could spare the time from concentrating on the pain in his stomach, when all of a sudden he'd discovered himself at the edge of the drawn-back curtain at the foot of the circular thrust stage. On the stage, a small instrumental combo staffed by men in dark glasses had been playing something in a haze of smoke. Maybe it wasn't anything magical, maybe it was just the music the band was playing, the way it was unreeling in a hypnotic coil, limp and cool and brassy and sharp all at the same time.

So then what had brought Jurtan back to awareness? One of the instrumentalists was addressing him, that's what it must have been. "My man," the fellow was saying out of the side of his mouth, the other side being occupied by a thin cigarette trailing a matching line of blue exhaust. The smoke wound its way upward around the neck of the tall string bass the man was plunking. "You look to be grooving there goodly. What's your instrument?"

"I, ah, I sort of play a bunch of stuff," Jurtan was surprised to hear himself saying.

"You want to get on up here, then, pick up that saxophone. It's Ploord's, but he ain't here yet anyhow. Show us what you got."

And then Jurtan found himself on the stage, holding the saxophone and blowing a tune that seemed to go along with the line the others were laying down. Had he ever just let his music sense go off on its own like this without any particular goal in mind? No, of course not—but it still felt like it made sense, like it . . .

But then Jurtan decided to just quit thinking about it. Like the bassist was telling him, there was a groove going.

"Music," muttered Svin. And modern music at that. Civilization had so many wrinkles to get accustomed to it was amazing that anyone ever got anything done.

"Are you sure I can't buy you a drink? A *real* drink, I mean?"

Svin was leaning against the low wall that separated the bar from the step-down floor with the tables and dance area surrounding the stage. The vantage point allowed him to keep his various charges in sight, not that any of them were showing any signs of *wanting* to be in sight. The same could scarcely be said of this Hazeel woman. She was obviously trying not to be *out* of his sight.

Of course, that was one wrinkle on which civilization had nothing new to teach him. "You may have heard I was recently ill," Svin told her. "While I was recovering, these juices made from fruits and vegetables were very helpful. Also, I am on duty."

"Can't I get you something decent?"

"Do you have any more carrots? Grated, not stirred. A splash of rhubarb would be tasty."

Dalya Hazeel shook her head. "I don't know about you. You're a hunk, no question about that, but you're weird."

"I used to be a barbarian."

She grinned. "Some people used to say the same thing about me. You want to arm wrestle?"

Jurtan was still getting a strange feeling; stranger than before, in fact. He was having fun, he felt good—that was strange enough by itself, but that wasn't the crux of it. As his senses seemed to float free on top of the music he'd been having the same sensation as he'd gotten from the Track, with Max. Only it was different. It was like—it was like . . .

He watched another odd character come in off the street, pause at the top of the four-step entrance leading down to the ringside floor, and eye him deliberately across the room. This character was a dwarf wearing a black satin evening jacket that matched his eyepatch, and a trimmed pointy-tipped beard. The dwarf had his head cocked slightly to the side as he considered the music; then, as Jurtan's riff came to an end and the guy with the cornet launched into his own bit, the dwarf seemed to reach a decision. He straightened his shoulders and walked briskly across the floor to the swinging door to the kitchen, pushed through, and vanished into the curl of steam that met him coming out.

Just the same as the veiled woman and the guy in the burnoose.

What had he done?

But Jurtan knew. It wasn't coincidence, and it wasn't his imagination, except indirectly. He could feel the Track himself. It was there now even though it hadn't been when he'd come in. But the thing that was different about this Track was that it ran through *him*.

Jurtan had shanghaied someone else's Track in off the street. That was assuming he hadn't actually laid down his own.

The guy with the biceps might be an athlete, a swordsman, an up-and-coming beat patroller for the police, and good with the women (all by his own admission, unasked for but torrentially provided), and he might genuinely like this interminable music her brother (of all people) had decided he could play, but if the man had an inkling of brains they could fit inside a peanut or, if you wanted to give him the benefit of the doubt, possibly a hulled-out filbert. "Uh-huh," said Tildy; it seemed about time to say something again, not that she had the slightest idea what he was talking about. But then why bother at all? "Excuse me," she stated, getting to her feet and then strolling off.

Maybe in a minute or two he'd notice she was gone. Or maybe not, but either way it wasn't her affair. She'd go talk to Dalya. . . .

But Dalya was trying her best to be occupied with Svin. *Huh!* Tildy thought. Well, maybe ex-barbarians were her taste.

If Dalya was busy with Svin, though, she might not be watching what Tildy ordered at the bar. "Ale," Tildy told the bartender.

"Ale it is, then, miss."

Or maybe Dalya didn't really care, despite her pronouncement earlier in the evening. Tildy put an elbow on the bar and watched the barman fiddle with his taps.

"Excuse me," a man murmured next to her. "That oaf—" the man jerked his head back in the direction of the table she'd just left "—obviously doesn't appreciate the treasure he's letting escape. Will his mistake be my gain?"

"I don't—" she began as she turned to get a better look, "I—And then she got her look, at a head of hair so blond that it looked a mere half-step from the light metal of a shined-up sword; and at those eyes, those clear blue eyes. . . .

"Would you care to dance?" asked the man.

The number came to an end. They'd done at least three, and probably more than six, but exactly how many beyond that Jurtan had no idea. Sweat was still running down his face and the rest of him was soaked, his eyes stung from the smoke, and now that the mouthpiece had left his lips he kept coughing and clearing his throat and half-gargling the contents of the glass the cornetist had passed him—so why did he feel so good?

The bassist clapped Jurtan on the back. "That was one cool set," he told him, drawing out the long vowel sound like another smooth horn note. "We the Underlings, man. You just set in with us anytime; Ploord gonna be out himself one gig. You hear?"

"All right," said Jurtan. "Sounds good. Uh, cool."

"We make a real cat out of you yet, eh man?"

"Sure," Jurtan agreed, hoping he'd understood what the musician had said. "I got to check something else out now."

"Like you say, then. Don't forget now."

Jurtan let himself into the small backstage area and peered out through the peephole that overlooked the room. His lips were tingling and his fingers, too, but at least they weren't worn down and bloody the way his music sense had ground him up in the past. Maybe it thought fun was supposed to be, well, *fun*. But there was fun and there was fun; there was music and then there was what his sister had been up to out on the floor, and now out at that small side table. Her and that tall dangerous-looking blond guy.

Jurtan's internal music had honked at him when the man had come in the door. Floating along over the plunk of the bass and the wail of the clarinet, Jurtan had watched the man check out the room. The light was low and the air was murky, and to be frank Jurtan knew he wasn't quite all there himself, but he'd thought that perhaps the man's gaze had lingered for a bit longer than happenstance on Svin and Dalya, on the Karlinis arguing off in their booth, on Jurtan himself. And on his sister.

And now here the two of them were, Tildy and the guy, bent low across the table's candle in its red glass jar, hands resting near each other on the cloth. Any way you sliced it, it wasn't just an innocent conversation.

But then what *did* he know about it? *He'd* been complaining about Max's instruction, not Tildy, after all. *Had* he picked up Max's paranoia, too?

But she was his sister. Either she'd be in his debt or she'd never forgive him.

Well, he'd keep an eye on things and see what developed.

"Dear," said Roni, "I still love you, you know that. I just can't live this way, knowing there's something important you won't talk to me about. I can't do it, that's all. Until you can straighten out your mind, I'm going to have to ask you to leave."

19

Drat. And damn! And—

This was getting her nowhere. Leen kicked back
from her desk and glared at the holograph logbooks
spread out across it. This was work, damn it, it needed
to be done, and she was the one who needed to do it.
But to do this kind of work you generally needed a
mind, too. So where was hers?

From the evidence, nowhere in the vicinity, that
much was sure.

She was fast acquiring an unexpected appreciation
for the ways of the monastic sects. The attraction of
the ivory tower approach was that it removed distractions. If you forswore social niceties and personal at-
tachments, you were clearly better off when trying to
apply yourself to anything beyond—

"Aunt Leen! Aunt Leen!"

Grateful for the distraction, Leen left her desk behind and made her way through the book rows to the
storage room she'd set aside as a nest for Robin. She
had set him up with one of the ancient spell-operated
vision-viewers. He was sitting rapt on a rug she'd
spread out on the floor in front of the thing. "Aunt
Leen!" he was babbling. "Look at this! Look at this!"

In a dark space like a miniature stage in the thing's
front, schematized images were flickering back and
forth, accompanied by tinny sounds. Sometimes the
viewer's language was recognizably one extinct dialect
or another, sometimes the sounds were totally unin-

telligible, and sometimes (as now) there was no language to need interpretation, rather just a sequence of accent music and sounds that counterpointed the action. Such as it was; Leen had given the thing up herself when she'd been not much older than Robin since its repertoire had limited appeal to someone who preferred to use her mind.

Or *had* she given it up? To be honest, the thing had remained a guilty pleasure for . . . well, longer. She'd been hoping its programming would improve, but—

No, actually, she'd enjoyed it. Until—

Why was she wasting time on useless old reminiscences? Was it the sight of the vision-story Robin was engrossed in at the moment, possibly a morality tale of some sort played out against a desert backdrop of harsh buttes and precipitous gorges, with its sole actors a slavering wolf and its prey, an ambulatory bird of some sort? Leen had watched the same characters often enough herself, she was horrified to realize, but she had buried the memory for years. Was her mind breaking down now?

Or to be more precise—or just more honest—*why* was her mind breaking down now?

"Not too much more of this," Leen told him. "Then it's time for your reading." Robin was already back in his trance, though. The viewer-thing was definitely addictive. Whether it was actively harmful, however, remained to be proven.

The sounds of the loony contraption faded behind her as Leen traced her steps reluctantly back to her own work area. She had to remember to take Susannah to task. If Robin were Leen's child, she'd certainly have taken him to the Ball last night, for a short time anyway, so he could at least get the flavor of things. Susannah's housekeeper had let Robin stay up so he could watch the fireworks from afar, but it was scarcely the same. It was too bad. Robin was a charmer; he'd have fit right in. Maybe Leen's sister just hadn't wanted the competition.

Competition—*double* damn! How could she of all

people have let herself be sucked into a morass like this? The longstanding enmity between the Scapula on one hand and his brother and Max on the other was clear, now that it was too late for her to see it coming. And too late for her to deny to herself that she was more than casually interested in at least one of the principals, and more than casually wary of at least one of the others.

Why couldn't she leave it alone? If all of a sudden she wanted sex, there was no shortage of opportunities. If she wanted someone to talk to, she could probably even find that. She loved Robin; wasn't that enough? Why did she suddenly have to have everything all wrapped up in a single person? Why was it important that she might have *found* it all in one?

But work still needed to be done, regardless. Lord Farnsbrother had been back again needing some research for the final scrollwork for his barge, and needing it *now;* after all, the Running of the Squids was coming up in . . . in . . . the next few days, wasn't it? Already? Then there was her own research into the old secret room, too, research which had led to these heaps of old Archivist-ledgers out on her desk. Why was this all happening at once?

These independent elements couldn't be connected, could they?

Only by the barest threads; to presume more would be to plunge into the depths of abject paranoia, seeing conspiracies behind every door.

Unless she tried to associate the pieces herself. . . .

Maybe she *should* share the puzzle of the hidden room. Perhaps what she needed was another perspective. She'd gotten the feeling that Max might know quite a bit about the nooks and crannies of the extinct world. There had been something about that unusual amulet around his neck, for example, something familiar, as though she might have once seen it pictured in an old book. . . . That could be an excuse for meeting him again, to probe whether he might be able to help her—

What *was* she thinking? Why was she looking for *excuses,* of all things? Why—

Augh!

A softly chiming bell brought Leen's thoughts out of their endless circle. Her pocket watch, right, reminding her it was time to get ready for that ridiculous luncheon. Why had she ever agreed to make an appearance? But she had, and now there was no time to waste. There was the Farnsbrother stack, and here was her bag, and she'd set the watch alarm to let her make the next neutral cycle on the Front Door and speed up her exit traverse—there, the Front Door even saw her coming and was creaking itself open in advance. Leen tried to clear her mind. It would be a muddy traverse unless she could concentrate. She felt for the currents and set her feet. Except—

Damn! Something was still nagging at her mind. Something she'd forgotten? Leen inhaled deeply. Her mind was undeniably a mess.

But now it was time to *concentrate*. Whatever it was she couldn't think of, she'd worry about it later.

This was worse than bad form, it was just *bad.* But there was nothing to do except go ahead. Max adjusted his hood again, leaving no more skin exposed along his body than the thin slit across his eyes, and hung back in the shadows. His trace on the Archive monitors said she was still on the Front Door path on her way out. The Back Door in its hidden alcove was down the hall and around the bend from his current position, in one of the doorless cells in this derelict section of the dungeon, but Max had learned last time that the guard systems made a habit of examining passersby even before they approached a door with the goal of passing through. He didn't want to risk confusing the defenses; they were bright enough for *that,* anyway.

The monitors weren't the only thing around that might be confused. Max felt confused enough for everyone. What damnfool rotten luck—here he was running out a plan he'd had in process for who knew how long and he had to go get interested in his target as a *person*. The way to do this kind of thing right was for a target to *be* a target; you couldn't worry about their feelings or whether they'd hate you if they found out or even if there'd be enough left of them to mop off the floor afterward, much less feel anything one way or the other. You couldn't care.

And he never had.

Not for a long time, anyway. Not since he'd gotten good at this.

Not until now.

Damn.

But he was still going through with it. He *had* to go through with it.

And if he worked things right, there was no reason Leen would ever know. Then he could find out just what he felt about her without business hanging over his head.

Not that he should feel anything in the first place, but that looked like just about a lost cause at the moment. The only thing to do was to try to contain the damage. Maybe he could still talk himself out of it. It would make things a lot simpler. It would put things back the way he'd always liked them to be—clean, slick, with no grease to slow him down and no entanglement to limit his options—

Fat chance.

What had *happened* to him?

Concentrate on the job, Max told himself. *That's what you're here for, after all.*

That was no more than the truth. And since Leen had cleared the far end of the path and was exiting the matrix's sensing range, it was time to move.

The first step was the most critical. Max invoked the trigger phrase for the aural cloak and felt the thing began to unfold. His vision went gray, sounds faded, a prickly wave ran hot and cold down his body, but the real dislocation was the wrenching twist of his sense of self. A blur of sensory memories riffled through his mind. He was—*she* was?—they were thinking that—

But then Max's reflexes began to reassert themselves, and his own aura damped itself down and encapsulated itself, and the cloak began to withdraw its interdigitations from his core and to become at last merely . . . a cloak. Max did his deep breathing focus exercise and felt himself start to even out.

Disguising yourself in someone else's aura was sometimes an indispensable technique, but it did have its costs. From Max's experience, those spellworkers who favored the procedure still liked to use nonsentients as their cloak-models. With good reason—the more defined a self-image the subject had, the more you had to be careful not to be absorbed into their personality field rather than wearing it as a shell. It was a far cry from a muskrat to a human.

It was also another jump to move from just any human to one with whom you had some personal relationship. But how could he have known? At the same time as his preprogrammed aural probe had been interrogating Leen during their meeting at the ball, reading her standing waves and soaking up those spiking energy gradients, fulfilling the purpose that had caused Max to seek her out in the first place, Max himself had been—

Had been . . .

No, dammit, Max thought. *I won't accept that. I gave all that up.*

And so he had. But it appeared, as Shaa would have it, that fate had intervened.

Better to sort it out later; now was clearly not the time.

Max pulled the goggles with the dark-vision field down over his eyes, left his hiding place, and made his way through the dust, leakage from the aural cloak helping him to achieve the right gait. The corridor was dark; when you put that together with the dust, it made a good sign that no one had bothered to come around lately. Perhaps the palace administrators were conserving on candles. Through the goggles, though, the way stood out under a flat pink light. The illumination faded twenty or thirty feet out, becoming even more spectral and ghostly, but all he really needed was—

There, around the corner, keeping to its own pool of shadow even in the goggle-enhanced perception, that's where it should be. An unbroken expanse of stone wall? No, of course not. Max let loose the second-order perception spell, and was rewarded by a dancing green line that snaked its way up and around the stones. Max held out his hand and approached the Back Door.

This was clearly the first moment of hazard. Max felt the door interrogating his aura like blunt thorns denting the surface of a balloon. Something riffled through the surface layers of his mind . . . or Leen's mind, rather, as captured by his recording device. Max caught a sideglow from her thoughts wafting past him like the old scent from a pressed flower.

So she thought she might like him, too, did she?

Max had told himself he wouldn't tap into her thoughts. That was perilously close to the kind of violation he'd always drawn the line at, and that was with subjects he never planned to see again. But you couldn't totally seal yourself from the damp when you were working underwater, either.

What a mess, thought Max.

The guard systems were obviously thinking something over, perhaps trying to understand how Leen had made it from the Front Door to the Back Door so quickly. It was a potential flaw in Max's plan, true, but there had been no evidence that the path guardians worked with that kind of contextual and historical information. With timing presenting the problems it did, it had seemed a risk worth taking. After all, Max had the advantage of having done this before, too. It had been years before, admittedly, and the subject then had been a different Archivist, Leen's grandfather apparently, but as long as the same systems were still in place there was no reason for it not to work again.

With the rumble of rock on rock, an opening appeared. All his sensor-augmented perceptions stretching, Max carefully placed his foot in what appeared to be the right place on the threshold and went through.

The Back Door ground itself shut behind him. Ahead was the Three-Floored Room, and after that Creeley's labyrinth. If Creeley hadn't enjoyed a habit of bragging a little too freely about his creations to a diary-keeping confidant, and if Max hadn't had his own habit of compulsively reading everything he unearthed, Max would have had *no* idea of what to expect going in. He might still have made it the other time, but the labyrinth in particular, and then the Water Gate, could have potentially—

Concentrate, Max told himself. And indeed there was much to concentrate *on*. He was already through the vestibule and into the room shaped like an inverted pyramid with the tip lopped off. Straight ahead was the obvious exit—and an immediate one-way trip to doom. Creeley didn't let you make a mistake twice. Instead, Max put one foot up on the steep inclined wall in what felt like the right place, pushed off with the other leg, and propelled himself up in a quick sprint. Two steps, three, now feeling as though gravity would coax him into the inevitable backflip any instant—but then instead, there he was pounding upside down into the ceiling. One more step—where was it?

There. The ceiling, in another play of shadow on shadow, concealed an inverted pit. Max fell up into the hole, rolled forward away from the lip, and came back in a crouch to his feet.

The Three-Floored Room, indeed. Well, it was only illusion anyway, that's all, and Creeley hadn't wanted his Archivists to turn into desk-bound slugs, either, but *really*.

There were clearly walls close around, but for all the world it felt like Max had emerged onto an endless windswept plain covered with head-high grass. Last time it had been a forest. The pits would still be the same, though, even if they felt like quagmire bogs this go-around. This was where the incantations would start, too.

Max lost track of time. Pace after pace, step after step, each one precise even if it meant serious contortions to achieve. Into the Walk of Glass, climbing apparently unsupported into the air, then the Pirouette Gate, then that live guardian—

It was sure a lot of trouble for a pile of books.

You had to respect someone who did this for a living, though.

In fact, if you—

Max wrenched his thoughts back. One of those floating distraction zones, no doubt. His aural cloak was under interrogation again, too. Had anything out-of-kilter leaked through?

Tunnel walls closed in again. Bobbing and weaving through the tracery of the field matrix, Max had already slid past the bend gates before he realized he'd even come that far. Were the guardians giving him a break because they figured he—or she—had just gone through a traverse a few moments before? Had he found a shortcut? Scenes from a life he hadn't lived were flashing through the air an inch in front of his eyes—stacks of books and piles of papers, people he didn't know but felt quick twinges of emotion for, here a jolt of anger, there a bubble of warmth, a cock-eyed parrot. . . .

Another step forward and the blizzard stopped. Something tried to push him forward, off-balance; he resisted, carefully took the next deliberate step. The floor seemed to crumble beneath his foot. *No, it isn't,* Max thought firmly, and indeed the sliding gravel *did* firm up and decide to support his weight. Ahead was nothing but blank wall. Max narrowed his eyes and glared at it in a way that felt like authentic Leen.

A line of light appeared at the level of the floor, widened into a rectangle, and elongated itself upward. Max bent and stepped through while it was still moving.

The dim light came from a guttering lantern on a

stand next to a cluttered desk. Beyond the desk were books, endless and infinite. The Back Door creaked down again behind him and seated itself with a dull boom.

Well, that hadn't been too bad. He'd rest for a moment or two and then—

No, he wouldn't. Why bother with all that physical conditioning if not to keep moving at a time like this? Leen might be at her luncheon for hours, but then again she might not, and anyway if he wasn't lucky it could take days to find the stuff he was after. So there wasn't a moment to lose.

What was that?

Sounds. A low tinny flickering sound at the borders of hearing, and atop that a bubbly laugh. Down to the right and along the aisle. Max crept along, up to a closed door. The sounds were coming from behind it.

Max put himself at the ready, manipulated the door catch, eased the door open a crack, and slipped noiselessly through.

A low boxy contraption was contributing the tinny sounds, and a flickering light of illusion spreading out before it across a shaggy area rug. The laughter was coming from the rug, or more precisely from the small tousle-haired boy sprawled in the middle of it.

This was nothing to panic over. It was *never* worth panicking.

Max knew that, and he'd trained his body to know that, too, except that one by one various organs, starting with his stomach, seemed to be tossing their lessons out wholesale.

"Hi," said the boy. "Who are you?"

At least the kid wasn't going to throw a tantrum. What had Leen taught him? Enough not to be spooked by a sneaky-looking guy dressed in black with a black face-hood that covered everything from his eyebrows on up and his eye-sockets on down. "You're Robin, right?"

The boy nodded vigorously. "Who are you?" he repeated.

Max hesitated. If he told Robin his name was Max, Robin would tell Leen and there would go his plan of sneaking into the Archives with Leen never the wiser. But if he told Robin something else he'd *still* tell Leen, and she'd still know someone had been creeping around behind her back. Maybe she could figure it out; Max thought *he* could, given the right clues, and it was always a bad idea to underestimate your adversaries.

Except Leen *wasn't* an adversary.

Or more to the point, she *hadn't* been an adversary. Now who knew what might happen.

Of course, if Robin told Leen someone had been visiting, Max could happen to worm that fact out of her and then volunteer to help her find the culprit while upgrading the Archival defenses. It was a tricky plan, but it might work. The start was to give Robin a false story. "I'm—" began Max.

What was *that?*

Had the wall rippled? Had something creaked, was someone sneaking up behind him? Then Max realized what had tugged at his attention. He was still attuned to the rhythms of the Archive entry-path patterns. They had been quiescent since he'd finished his traverse, but they were quiet no longer. There was something strange going on back there.

Oh, Leen thought. *Damn!* Her mind was worse than a mess, it was a complete disaster area. How could she have forgotten *Robin,* of all things?

She was already late for the luncheon, too, and she *had* promised to be there. She couldn't just leave Robin alone in the depths of the . . .

Could she?

He did have a hamper of snacks, and he did have things to play with, and the Doors wouldn't let him wander into the traversal hazards, and she could just bounce in quickly to the luncheon, make her greetings and show herself around, and then sneak back out. She could . . . but on the other hand she couldn't. Not to

Robin. She'd most likely never forgive herself, even if Robin was still in the same position on his rug when she returned as he'd been when she'd left.

There was Susannah, too. *She'd* never let Leen forget it either. If she found out.

Damn, damn, damn—

"Archivist?" It was Vellum. Leen realized she had paused halfway through the Reading Room, an undoubtedly blank expression on her face, in the same spot where the realization had hit her.

"Nothing, Vellum," she said. "It's nothing. I just remembered I forgot something downstairs I need to go back and get. You take care of Lord Farnsbrother."

"Are you certain you're . . . ."

But she was already leaving him behind. She had, she realized, apparently made up her mind. If she was going back down, there was no time to waste.

She had already touched up her face on her way out of the anteroom; if she had a quick passage in and out this time she might not need to do it again. That could save a minute or two. The path might still be at the same calibration levels as well; that would save additional time on the traverse. She should be able to make it to lunch while they were still on the appetizer, or at worst, the salad.

Susannah would never know, Leen thought on her way through the stacks heading toward this terminus of the Front Door route. Robin would never stir, either. It might be smarter just to go to the luncheon first and *leave* when they reached the salad.

If people found out, they could just add the anecdote to her reputation.

Max, though . . . what would *he* think of her? She had the impression that how someone dealt with responsibility was important to him. Robin *was* her responsibility, at least at the moment, and she'd walked away from it.

Leen was tired of standing back from herself and asking why Max's possible reaction made any difference at all to her in the first place. It just did, that's all. She took a deep breath, tried to compose her mind, and rested her hand on the Front Door.

It stuck.

Come on, now! she emoted at it.

The door creaked indecisively. What was wrong with it, anyway?

"You know me," Leen said out loud.

That did it. With another reluctant squeal, the door rolled open. She stepped through into the launch chamber, felt for the matrix, and set her feet in the start position.

The matrix, though, was reacting sluggishly, indecisively. Of all the times to have the thing act up, of course this had to be it. Leen gritted her teeth and moved ahead.

It was as if she were doing the breaststroke in a pool filled with molasses. Actually, the situation suddenly became stranger than that. She had been pushing forward against resistance when the resistance suddenly vanished. The first time this happened she almost flung herself forward, propelled by the extra force she was applying to each step. Almost, but not quite; she managed to catch herself. It *was* strange. Nothing like this had ever happened before.

It might be better to spend a moment catching her bearings again, but on the other hand it might not. Stopping in the middle of a traverse could be dangerous. Going out of control or off the path, however, could be even worse. She did have momentum, though, and that decided it. Leen forged ahead, reaching the downward spiral.

The second time the traverse flopped on her she was ready; she handled it without even breaking stride. The guard fields were still radiating confusion, a confusion Leen certainly shared. The third time around, then, when the matrix seemed to crystallize around some sudden decision, perhaps she should have expected it more than she actually did. Leen was braced for the same drop in resistance followed by an incremental ratchet back up. Indeed, the drop *did* follow. That wasn't the problem. The real problem was that that wasn't the *only* shift it brought with it.

Leen had reduced the force of her own pressure against the retarding force so that she wouldn't catapult ahead out of control; that's what had worked the earlier times. Instead, she took a small easy step ahead and to the right. Under the pattern that had been established, she'd now have a moment to recapture her strength as the next obstruction slowly built. Leen carefully shifted her weight into the next step, and froze.

It took her a moment to understand that her dead stop wasn't discretionary. There had been no slow increase in drag. It had happened all at once, and to a much greater level. So great, in fact, she discovered as she threw her full force into it, that she was completely immobilized. As stuck as an ancient fly in a chunk of amber.

20

"What's that?" Zalzyn Shaa said brightly. "Over there?"

"There" turned out to be a park, and in the park a meadow. A small crowd of revelers still going strong from the previous night had spread out just inside of the tree line, surrounding a group of half a dozen brown-skinned men wearing white shirts decorated with geometric embroidery in various primary colors. The men were playing rhythmically on underarm drums, a whistle, and assorted bells, while another half-dozen similarly garbed fellows ran back and forth across the meadow in front of them in crisscrossing groups of three. In each threesome, one pair had suspended between them a line of cowbells. The third member of the trio wore on his head a papier-mâché effigy of a large shark.

"No, a swordfish, I believe," said Shaa. "Observe the serrated nasal attachment."

"I suppose," said the Great Karlini. "But isn't that dorsal fin hooked on with rivets?"

"Be careful," Shaa advised. "You don't want to profane someone's ritual or, worse yet, antagonize their ancestor."

Ahead of them, the trios had now broken up and the bell-carriers were pursuing the fish-heads, with obviously serious intent. Karlini, however, had become once more intent himself on an intensive study of the ground. In the midst of a city breaking out in festivities, Karlini had been parked on Shaa's doorstep when Shaa had staggered home in the early hours. Shaa had been somewhat the worse for wear himself at that point, but his spirits were by no means in the basement. The same could scarcely be said for Karlini. Shaa could not recall ever seeing one of his circle looking as bedraggled and woebegone. He couldn't think of anyone he'd encountered projecting quite as complete an image of morose dejection, in fact.

So if Shaa had been looking for something new to occupy his attention, that something had clearly arrived. Not that Shaa would admit it, but seeing Karlini so totally miserable had served to elevate his own mood, at least by comparison. And at least so far. It was unclear how much of this he could take without being sucked down by the undertow.

Obviously it was better for Karlini to be out rather than vegetating in a closed room; hence this midday constitutional. Perhaps the surroundings would help to moderate the blow when they discussed what needed to be discussed, perhaps not. Still, regardless of the surroundings, there was no point in putting off the discussion any longer. "So what do you propose to do?" Shaa asked idly, looking away from Karlini at the revelers to soften the opening blow.

"I don't know," said the Great Karlini. "I never thought it would come to this."

"I still have only the roughest concept of what 'it' is," commented Shaa. "Being thrown out by Roni is obviously a cardinal feature, but I'm sure it is scarcely the only one. Hmm? Very well, keep your peace if you must. Shall we discuss this another way? To what do you attribute your present impasse?"

"I can't talk about it."

"I see," Shaa said. "That would explain some part of the issue, certainly. I take it there is also a self-referential component to the situation? Which is to say, the fact that you can't discuss this with your wife, either, is related to the fact that it *concerns* your wife?"

"You always did like listening at keyholes, didn't you?"

"My superior insight only makes it seem that way," Shaa said, with his own nod at self-referentiality; a typically auto-sarcastic lip contortion too ironic to be called a grin. "And are you in this bind by yourself and of your own volition?"

"Yes. Yes, I am."

"From the totally unconvincing nature of that response, I will take that as a firm 'no.' So, what does that leave us with?"

"Don't worry about me. I've got some ideas. I can get the baggage out of the way and then talk Roni out of—"

Shaa raised a hand. "Stop. This situation has clearly gone beyond business into the personal. More subterfuge will not point the way toward resolution."

"You got something else to recommend? Oh, who cares anyway," Karlini said heavily. "I love my wife. We had a fine life. Now everything's falling apart. What did I do wrong? What happened?"

"How far back do you want to go?"

"You don't have to sound so . . . *clinical* about the whole thing," Karlini grumbled. "Why don't you tell me what you're planning to do about *your* problems?"

A ticklish question. Fortunately he had a deflective answer. "Lunch," Shaa said promptly.

"Lunch? You think you can eat your way out of your mess? Anyway I'm not hungry."

That was just as well, since it saved a subterfuge to deal with the fact that Karlini wasn't invited. "Suit yourself," Shaa told him. "You don't intend to jump off a bridge while you're out of my sight, do you?"

"I could just as well ask you the same thing. *You* were the one who almost flung himself off a boat."

"It remains a recourse of last resort," acknowledged Shaa. "I don't see it being required today, however. It's Haddo, isn't it?"

Karlini started. "Haddo? What do you mean, Haddo?"

"Who's enmeshed you in whatever it is you're enmeshed in. Who's been sneaking around even more than usual. Who's been holding side consultations with everyone else in your household except your wife, so who through the principle of logical completeness had to be in touch with you as well. Who has an interesting history in the far frozen north, along with a repertoire of talents that are equally interesting, if not more so. *That* Haddo."

"Have you been talking with that detective guy again?"

"Yes," Shaa said, "but not about this."

Karlini looked up at the sky. A flock of seagulls had been circling, evaluating the edibility of the papier-mâché fish helmets no doubt, but now one of them separated from the mass and swooped down. "Great," Karlini said, bracing himself. "That's all I need. The one member of my entourage who's willing to be seen with me is—OWP! Watch those claws!"

The seagull screeched at him, batting his face with an outstretched wing. Then, apparently considering its point made, the seagull fluffed itself and settled down atop Karlini's left shoulder.

"You could go to sea and become a pirate," suggested Shaa.

"Arr!" screeched the seagull.

"I don't need your opinion," Karlini told the bird. "Who are you, anyway? Why do you keep following me around?" But the gull had ostentatiously closed its eyes in a show of going presumably to sleep.

"Perhaps it just likes you," Shaa said.

"Do you really think so?" said Karlini, his mood brightening for a moment. He glanced at the bird and his face fell again. "No, of course not. This isn't coincidence; nothing's coincidence anymore. The thing's somebody's agent. Just because I haven't turned up any gods who use seagulls as their avatar doesn't mean they're not around."

"Could it be a friend of Haddo's?"

"Haddo again—why do you keep harping on Haddo?"

Shaa was watching the sky himself, on the off chance that the seagull might really have taken a shine to Karlini, and might further be acting as a trendsetter for its flock. "I have been making certain inquiries concerning Haddo. Enough to underline the desirability of learning more. There is more to him than meets the eye."

"You could say that about any of us."

"If anything, that only underscores my point. Ask him sometime about a fellow called Dortonn. You might as well ensure that that 'sometime' happens soon, too. On the other hand, you might consult with Wroclaw."

"Roni wants me to stay away."

"What does that have to do with it? Wroclaw isn't restricted to his room. Indeed, behold."

Karlini followed the line of Shaa's outstretched arm. Coming toward them across the lawn was, in fact, Wroclaw. "Maybe he followed the seagull," Karlini muttered.

"Good morning, sir," Wroclaw said to Karlini, as he approached to within conversational range. "I dropped your things at Dr. Shaa's, and—"

"Wroclaw," said Shaa.

"Yes, sir?"

"How long have we know each other? Decades, most likely?"

Wroclaw looked a bit nonplussed. "Quite possibly so, sir."

"How many times have I tried to convince you not to call me by those honorifics? How often have we talked about the extent to which they perpetuate a class-stratified society?"

"Many, doubtlessly."

"So do you persist in doing it out of contrariness, or is there some other reason rooted in ideology?"

"Has your encounter with your brother put you off your mood, sir?" suggested Wroclaw.

Shaa took over the role of nonplussed recipient of a conversational lob. "As you say," he said after a moment, "quite possibly."

"Just so, then," Wroclaw said, "sir. If I may be so bold, you'd best be off or no doubt you'll miss your lunch date."

Shaa's expression changed to one implying a good deal of sudden mental activity. "I see," he stated. "Quite right. You have your key, Great One? Good; I'll see you back at the house later, no doubt." After another quick sharp glance at Wroclaw, Shaa added, "I'm off, then," turned, and headed for the street.

Karlini, watching him go, said, "Nice to see you, Wroclaw. What do *you* think I should do now?"

"Not that it would be my place to advise you, sir, yet it might be appropriate for you and me to discuss our colleague Haddo, his plans, and our places in them."

"Let's take a walk," Karlini proposed. "I think there's a pond around here somewhere. Unless you have to get right back?"

"You've always encouraged me to manage my own time, sir."

"Yeah," said Karlini, his hands sunk back in his pockets as he trudged along, "but everything's changed now."

"Not necessarily everything, sir."

"Huh. Tell me this, then. How *did* you find me, Wroclaw?"

"Why, just as you suggested, sir."

"Me? What did *I* suggest?"

"I followed the seagull," Wroclaw said. "You see, my people have rather a long relationship with waterfowl."

So, Shaa was thinking as he made his way back into traffic, *yet another player whose role needs reinterpretation.* Was no one the person they appeared to be? Was their world merely a seething mass of counterplots and intrigues? What ever happened to an honest day's work and a spot of theater in the evenings?

Perhaps it *would* be just as well to stop fighting, to make a stand in the street and let the oncoming carriage traffic compress him into the dust. If your friends no longer seemed to be what you'd thought they were, and your goals seemed to shift and vanish in the fog, and the day-to-day was—

Lunch; perhaps that would be the ticket. "I knew I never should have read that article on moral relativism," Shaa muttered to no one in particular. Especially before bed last night, with his head—and his mind—in the shape they'd been in. If the firm anchor of certainty in one's position and its underlying rationale was swept away in the recognition of the equal validity of multiple interchangeable frames of reference, it certainly didn't help one find solid reasons for hanging around. . . .

Away from Karlini and his distracting distress, it was clear to Shaa that his mood was starting to seriously slip. Yet there *was* still lunch. The food by itself was scarcely the attraction, although the branch of the Adventurers' Club up ahead was justly famed for the products of its kitchen, at least among the adventurous. Rather, the potential of the invitation itself was the main draw.

An older stone building amply colonnaded beckoned, and within an ascending staircase. A betweenfloors alcove—ah, here was the reception gauntlet. Shaa displayed the crested envelope, then withdrew the folded invitation to display that, too. The message was merely a brief scrawl with date, time, and place. The signature below, for such it obviously was even though it was graphical instead of alphabetic, had the desired effect. Shaa examined it again as he followed the maitre d' into the dining room. Although one could argue that Shaa and the letter writer were in the same line of work, they had never officially met; still, the signature was unambiguous in context. The maitre d' indicated a side table with a very good window view over the street and a corner of the park beyond; the table was set for two. One place was already occupied by an extremely red-headed fellow squinting out at the bright scene beneath a somewhat overhung expression. Shaa slipped into the other seat. "The Crawfish, I presume?"

"What's going on with my sister, that's what I want to know," the man said, not diverting his gaze from the window.

"Arleen the Archivist?" Shaa said. "That sister? Or perhaps Susannah, the well-known socialite, not that there's much to figure out there beyond the obvious interpersonal intrigues?"

"Been doing your homework, then, have you?"

Shaa inclined his head. "A pleasure to make your acquaintance as well." He extended the inclination into an outright craning of the neck to match the Crawfish's angle of view. "Am I missing something of interest? To my inadequate eye it looks to be a straightforward street scene."

"Habit, I suppose," said the Crawfish, continuing his stare. "What do you suppose your brother is up to?"

"Aside from no good? Of course you realize I may be biased."

"Of course. Don't bother to ask me if I've asked *him*, either. I'm on his list."

"You're not short of company. I imagine you've already ordered?"

"I'm having the squab with chilies and various steamed vegetables; I thought you'd like the turbot in citrus."

"We shall see," Shaa stated. Two pots of tea had arrived, one at Shaa's elbow. Shaa sniffed at the vapors and raised an eyebrow.

"They'll bring more without the herbs if you'd rather," the Crawfish told him.

"No reason for that, as long as the dosage is accurately calibrated." He took a sip.

"You can understand my reason for asking."

"Certainly," Shaa agreed. "Your sister and my brother, and now my associate Maximillian as well—who else would you want to consult with? How long have you been working with *my* sister?"

"Is that deduction or did you have some evidence?" said the Crawfish. "No matter, I suppose."

"Obviously Eden would need someone to keep my brother under scrutiny, seeing as neither she nor I have been in a position to do it directly." Shaa shrugged. "You would clearly be a leading candidate, even if it weren't for your mother."

The Crawfish turned from the window to eye Shaa directly. "Don't you think some things should remain unspoken?"

"Do you?"

"I'm actually more worried about your brother than I told Leen. He *is* up to something, there's no question about that, and it seems like something major. You don't think he'd outflank the new Emperor and slip into his place before the Knitting, do you?"

"I wouldn't put anything past him, but that would sound a tad egregious even for Arznaak. He'd rather spin a plan out over years."

"Just my point," said the Crawfish. "Here you are back in Peridol at last. Some type of end-game *must* be at hand. But how does it link to my sister?"

"There will be at least two levels," Shaa observed, "or my brother is seriously off his game. Access to the Archives would be an obvious place to start."

"Is that your Max's goal? Or is he on multiple levels, too?"

"Always," drawled Shaa. "Yet in this case Maximillian seems to have been taken significantly aback. I believe he has a genuine feeling for your sister, and she for him; and I suspect furthermore that neither of them is very pleased with that state of affairs. So to speak."

"There was an incursion into the Archives some years back," the Crawfish said. "A one-shot that was never repeated. I've always been on the lookout for whoever was behind it. Until I caught a glimpse of that amulet Max had around his neck last night, that is.''

Perhaps they had arrived at the crux of the matter. Well, perhaps they would still be sitting cordially at the table when the entrees arrived, and perhaps not. "Is that where that amulet came from? Max has spent time with some shady customers, you know; he could have acquired it from one of them.''

"*You* know,'' the Crawfish said conversationally, "after that little contretemps last night I might be asking myself how closely I wanted to cleave to Maximillian, should I have happened to be his partner, given the divergence of means that appeared to be in evidence.''

"Might you,'' Shaa said in an equally even tone.

"Of course. I also might be reconsidering my own position, but for *myself* that would clearly be a short and fruitless exercise. With a brother like the Scapula, though, the exercise might deserve more attention.'' The Crawfish leaned back in his chair and regarded Shaa directly. "But there is yet another possibility to consider. Given that the various players on this stage are mostly known quantities, whose reactions within basic parameters might be reasonably well anticipated, *could* your brother be anticipating them?''

"I don't think we're as predictable as all that,'' said Shaa, but not without a noticeable pause. Arznaak wasn't a god; he couldn't possibly have a plan *that* intricate. Could he?

What gods might he be working with?

This Crawfish was rather clever, at that. "An intriguing thesis,'' Shaa told him. "Farfetched, but intriguing.''

"Well, I try. Now, on the other hand . . .''

After all that Shaa *was* still here and the turbot *had* arrived, citrus garnish and all. At this point he was not surprised to find the citrus sauce surprisingly appropriate. The Crawfish indeed was looking to be a usefully substantive fellow.

Clearly, Shaa thought, the cure for his ennui would need more than some new faces and a change of scene. But that didn't mean they might not be a fruitful start.

21

Was I asleep or awake? Awake, I decided; even those nightmare dreams I'd heard about couldn't possibly make a body quite as miserable as I was feeling right at the moment. If I was awake, then, I'd better get up. Maybe the front desk had some witch-doctor remedy that could boost me back into the ranks of the glad-to-be-alive. I hoisted an eyelid. Bright lights slammed through the gap with an icepick slash. My eyes slapped shut and I fell back, thinking about other options—most of which involved throwing up—and listening to someone moaning loudly in my own voice.

I'd never had a hangover like this in my life. It must have meant I was out of practice in *something*. I hadn't actually consumed that much when I'd been out with Shaa, really I hadn't, but here it had to be already the middle of the morning and I could barely bear to lie still, let alone struggle up and set about doing whatever it was I had to do. Still, given that at some point I must have regained consciousness, by the inexorable logic of things that meant, in turn, that at some other point I would have to get out of bed, if only to try to hunt down a cure. Or if not a curative to restore me to health, then something to put me out of my misery. For the time being, however, I figured that trying not to move and hoping the world would go away was probably the most appropriate strategy.

"So," said a voice from the side of the bed, "you *are* here, after all."

A voice? *Not again,* I thought, but sure enough it was. And not just any voice, either. This was a voice I recognized.

As if I'd been encountering any other kind since I'd arrived in town.

There was no question but that I'd have to speak to the management. I had a suite that was supposed to be guarded against incursions, where I was supposedly registered under a cloak of incognito—as though I ever traveled under any other kind—and yet here anyone who pleased had no problem in popping up as close to me as the nearest end table.

"Even I was surprised at how low you've sunk," said a second voice, from the other side. "Crawling through gutters no less. This is not a sign of personality, you know, not a sign of character. In Oolsmouth I even thought—"

I figured I might as well deal with her first. "If you were thoughtful enough to bring a pitcher of water with you," I told her, "you might as well go ahead and pour it over my head now."

"As I said," Jill responded, "a clear denizen of the slums."

I gritted my teeth and opened my eyes. If she didn't have a restorative, I seemed to recall I might have my own. There it was, on the end table next to her; a brimming flask. But there *she* was, too, putting out a hand to stop me, assuming no doubt that my debilitated state would keep me from resisting even that feeble effort.

Actually, if I'd had a chance to think about it, I'd have probably assumed the same thing.

Except I didn't think twice. I sat up and reached out, and as I did a small blue lightning bolt lanced sharply out of my reaching fingertips into Jill's hand, hit, and clung. She straightened and took an involuntary step back, trailing a billow of dark smoke and a gust of sulfur from her wrist; then the cloud and the residual arcing sparks slid off her hand and fell to the floor in a messy clump.

"That stung," she said in an accusing voice, but I had reached the flagon of water and was pouring it refreshingly over my hair and face.

"How did you find me this time?" I asked through the shower.

"It wasn't very hard to pick up your trail last night, yours and your cronies'."

I'd figured that much out for myself, I just wanted to hold off the moment when I'd have to engage in substantive confrontation as long as possible. "It's good to know you can pick up a clue when it's thrown in your face, at least," I said.

Pink did begin to spread up Jill's face and across her cheeks, but the spoken response came from the other side of the bed. "You think you're clever, don't you, you and that last bit of trickery in Oolsmouth."

"Not particularly," I said. "Only by comparison, you could say." The pitcher empty, I was on a roll of sorts, so I swung my legs over the edge of the bed and used the momentum to pull myself to my feet. I'm not the sort for dressing gowns, and after I'd arrived back at the room last night or this morning I'd had little choice but to collapse still fully clothed. These were decisions that appeared particularly fortuitous right at the moment. Monoch had collapsed along with me, too, which put him in my hand now as well. If I only had a working brain, I'd be prepared for anything.

"I still want the ring," Jardin continued. "It is clear, however, that you do not have it, nor did your confederate in Oolsmouth, the hapless Sapriel. I use 'confederate' here in the loosest sense only, of course."

"Of course," I agreed. "I never said I had the ring. I—"

He clearly wasn't listening. "What was rather clever was how you let us continue to draw our own conclusions, adding very little of your own. Your other confederate—I now use the term somewhat more precisely—was much more a driving force than you, yourself, if one goes back to analyze the flow of events.''

"To say that would be only fair," I acknowledged. The question on the table at the moment, after his last statement, was whether he'd figured out that that other confederate, whom they'd known as Soaf Pasook, was really the god they thought was me, Jill's ex-or-current husband Gashanatantra.

"A certain amount of this one can accept as the cost of doing business," Jardin stated. "Eventually, however, all bills must come due."

I was finding it a little hard to keep my full attention on what he was saying, considering that Jill was doing her best to probe me at the same time and considering that taking into account the effects of the toxic by-products in my system I didn't seem to have very much attention to spread around anyhow. "Must they?"

"Don't start with that again," Jill snapped. "Don't change the subject. If—"

"Why not?" I inserted. "As you both said, it's not a topic that's given any of us any satisfaction this far. Why don't we just say our little partnership has been dissolved and go back to our other fun? Why—"

This time they weren't the ones who interrupted me. You could say I interrupted myself. I suddenly had the strong sensation that someone was looking over my shoulder. I had Jardin and Jill both in view at the same time as I edged back against the end table and toward the wall, to keep them from flanking me, so the only thing behind me should have been the wall, but of course the walls in this room had so far proven to be nothing more than decorative cloaks for the passages and secret doors that my assorted visitors had been utilizing. The feeling was strong, though—I could almost feel a breath on the back of my neck. So I turned my head rapidly for a quick scan.

There was nothing behind me except wall. Unadorned wall, unbroken by even a portrait with the chance of mobile eyes.

Okay, so I was losing contact with reality. I twisted

back to face my visitors again. As I did this, however, I realized that the sensation of something perched just behind my head had not actually gone away. Was I imagining it? That would be the logical explanation; too much introspection and too little sleep, and chemical stress on top of it to boot.

But what if I wasn't? Logic hadn't exactly ruled my life lately. Why would it start now?

That was when it occurred to me that perhaps my pounding head and sluggish paths of thought were not due totally to the previous night's binge.

Jill was eyeing me strangely. She had her hand up gesturing toward me, and I could feel the renewed force of her probe somewhere out in front of my chest where it was sliding off the defenses I evidently now possessed. Jardin, too, had a wary cast to his eye. "What was that?" he said.

"You saw me out carousing," I reminded him. "Wastrels like me are always jittery in the morning. Don't you know it's pretty crowded in here—you want me to count the elephants?"

"Jardin," Jill said uncertainly. "I'm building a strange picture here."

"I—"

"Shut up," snapped Jardin. "Tell me."

"That's him," said Jill, now openly staring in my direction. "I mean, that's not him. I mean that's *him*, the one we were with in Oolsmouth, but he's not who we thought he was. The sword is the sword of my husband, but this man who bears it is not. I mean, not my husband."

Jardin pursed his lips. "Yes," said Jardin. "That is clear to me now. You are not Gashanatantra."

For myself, I felt like a butterfly on a pin. Or a butterfly in the net, with the pin descending toward it, when it probably had a similar suspicion that events were moving out of its control. "I never said I was."

"You lied to me," Jardin said thoughtfully. "If you are not Gashanatantra, you have no deterrent capability."

"That's not entirely true," I began. "Actually, that's not true at all." This would be a good time to tell him about the metabolic link that let me draw on Gash's abilities and powers. "Gash—"

His hand was outstretched toward me, and I was feeling the remote tingle that meant he was doing his own interrogation of my aura beyond my shield or running some other kind of probe. Perhaps he'd pick up the metabolic link himself. I didn't understand how he was missing it, or Jill either for that matter, except for the fact that my experiences with Jardin hadn't given me a very high impression of his intelligence. "I see now," he said. "That wily scum Gashanatantra gave you a disguise, didn't he. That reckoning will come, but it can wait. Now that he has withdrawn his protection from you I will deal with you first. I can crush you like a bug." He clenched his fist. "In fact, that bears every promise of being a fulfilling exercise."

"Now wait a minute," I said. Obviously Jardin's probing ability was completely on the fritz at the moment; on a par with his creativity in conversational metaphors. Gash hadn't withdrawn the metabolic link at all. I'd still been drawing knowledge and skills from him ever since the last time we'd met; what about that little lightning bolt I'd zapped Jill with, for example? Gash was just sneakier than Jardin was, that had to be the explanation, not that it was any news, of course. Gash had been running plot circles around everyone in sight since our paths had crossed the first time; around me, too, if the truth be told. No, I still had Gash's power at my fingertips and the front of my mind. If Jardin couldn't see that and came after me, the surprise he'd get would be—

But that's just when he did exactly that; come after me, that is. A force grabbed my arms and tried to pull them out of my shoulder sockets, grabbed each finger and tried to separate them from my hands, grabbed my legs, my teeth—

The pain was extreme. The attack was also classic, aimed at making it impossible to cast gesture- or speech-based spells since the victim couldn't waggle his hands or control his vocal chords. Beside me, Monoch was still upright, balanced on his walking-stick tip, rapidly turning into a stalagmite from the ice sheet forming around him; that part was Jill's casting, I could tell. I tried to focus my mind and call on my inner reserves. . . .

But I might have still been the most surprised one in the room when the bed lifted up off the floor, flipped end-over-end, and slammed squarely into Jardin, carrying him over on his back beneath the hurled mass of the board-backed mattress and the heavy wooden frame.

The sound of shattering glass filled the air around me. I was free; I staggered and almost fell, and I felt like I'd just spent a long afternoon on the rack under the care of a very diligent operator, but I was free. I cleared my throat to propose something like a truce, with a return to our earlier standoff of armed neutrality, but what emerged instead was a word that blistered my lips as it passed and snapped at my face like ten days staked out in the high desert sun. Air curdling behind it, the power word looped into the overturned bed and burst into clinging flame.

A vortex appeared over the bed. Loose things around the room flung themselves toward it—the water pitcher, my folded towels, a basket of fruit I'd picked up on the street for snacks. My clothes lashing my body in the sudden gale, I felt myself being dragged across the room, too. Jill, arms flailing, was trying to dig her heels into the floorboards, but then the whole flaming bed took a hop off the floor, twirled once, breaking apart, folded itself through the vortex, and vanished. The vortex made a loud slurp, fell in about itself, and followed the bed into nothingness.

Jardin was lying on his back on the smoldering floorboards covered with soot. He looked up at me with a somewhat cock-eyed expression. "The Spell of Namelessness," Jardin said dazedly. "Why didn't I feel it before? But not one of mine. You're not Gas-hanatantra. Who *are* you?''

I couldn't recall doing anything to bring this about, but Monoch was in my hand, flaming and hoping for lunch. I had never appreciated before how compli-cated a construction he was. Monoch wasn't actually steel, he was some sort of phase-changing composite material with carbon fibers and diamond whiskers held in place by a crystal matrix; that's what allowed spell-work to take place around him without the inductive backlash magical field currents caused in conductive metals. This also allowed a much higher level of bound-in energy and—

Something gnawed at my forehead and tried to chew its way into my brain. It had materialized partway in-side my protection field, courtesy of Jill, and one scrabbling claw-appendage was trying to hook its way into my eye. I flicked Monoch up and slashed across my face, carving off a dangling chunk of hair and a thin slice of integument but dragging loose the con-struct as well. It burst into flame and fell into ash, and as I readied my next offensive stroke I—

I suddenly realized how strange this whole thing was. I was as aloof and placid as if I'd been reading about it in a book rather than being in the middle of what looked to be a fight for my life. Even in a book you'd expect to get more involved with what was hap-pening than I was here. In fact, even the fact that I was taking this time to think about what I was doing even while I was doing it was enough to—

A counterattack was apparently underway: my own. Whatever automatic protection facilities I was inher-iting from Gash seemed to have the situation well in hand. Why not sit back and watch? Why should I bother to try to run things? I hadn't succeeded very well during those times in the past when I'd done my best to exert conscious control. Sure, I had volition, I *knew* I did, but part of intelligence is knowing when to stand aside out of the way. So what if the aftereffects of the evening's brew left me feeling sedated, like I'd quaffed down some potion of anxiety suppression? Who cared if time seemed to flowing in stops and starts? Who—

Wait a minute. Wait a *minute*. *I* did. At least, I *should*, anyway. I clenched my jaw. The scene swam back into focus, or my attention returned to focus on *it*, I couldn't tell which, and if my jaw was still following its own agenda rather than tightening up as I'd ordered I was willing to ignore that for the moment since I seemed nevertheless to be back in some sort of control.

A patch of wall across the room was steaming, but beneath the vapor the surface had fused into something reflective as silvered glass. Some kind of slime was dripping from the ceiling. Jardin's left arm was twisted awkwardly, as though it had tried to turn into a tree but had decided to settle for just breaking in a few strategic places instead. Clouds of glowing and whining things were whipping back and forth through the air. The floor beneath my feet had also peeled partially back, leaving me perched over an open chasm on a narrow bridge of wood. "There really is no need for this," I tried to say over the tumult.

What came out was slurred and twisted, and would have been unrecognizable I was sure if anyone else had actually been able to hear it. The fact that something *had* come out, though, had to count as some sort of victory for me. But against whom? Against myself? I—

I was starting to slip back into that same narcissistic reverie. Again I pushed it away. This time I heard someone else speaking. "Stop it, whoever you are!" Jill was yelling. "Get back!"

"Fine with me," I said, but at the same time I was spreading my arms wide to hit them with some new sending. I could feel subroutines clicking on and meshing together in their terrible symmetry, and in a brief moment I would understand what construct they were building to—

Which was when the remaining floor underneath me disintegrated completely and dropped me into the pit.

It wasn't a very deep pit, and the opening wasn't all that wide, either, so my outstretched arms landing on either edge kept me from falling completely into the earth. When I saw the large bureau grinding toward me from the side wall, and after it the tall free-standing closet cabinet, I started to consider whether I might be better off taking my chances with the earth and rock caving in around my legs, but then again someone seemed to have that stuff under control even if I wasn't sure it was me. Through the dust and smoke I could see a shaky Jardin back on his feet, looking at me with a frankly incredulous expression on his battered face. He was muttering something to himself under his breath, and if anything more could surprise me at the moment it would have been the realization that I could actually sort of hear what he was saying; something about having to deal with some human after all.

The wood in the bureau had been aging and crumbling as the thing tumbled toward me, so the piece of furniture that tottered onto my head then wasn't much more than a loose pile of rotted sticks. The closet, however, had shed less mass in its journey across the floor. I actually felt the impact when it smashed down on top of the chest of drawers. It didn't break my arm, although my arm did subside into the long crack in the floor where the protection field had transferred the force of the blow, but it hurt when it hit and it was clear the bruises would remind me of it for days to come, too.

For that matter, I was abruptly realizing just how battered the rest of me was, on top of the fact that all my energy seemed to have just drained out of my feet into the earth. Whoever was running the show had either knocked off for the day or had come to the end of their ability. Leaving me to clean up.

Me, all I felt like doing was going back to sleep.

At the same time as I'd started feeling exhausted and the pain started creeping through, though, it occurred to me that something else had changed. I didn't feel like an indifferent bystander anymore. I was aghast at the damage I'd helped to cause but happy to be alive, amazed at the cool expertise I'd shown but plenty worried about the abandon I'd used in slinging it around. It felt—

It felt like I'd just moved back from another county into my own body.

That was ridiculous, of course.

As ridiculous as still feeling like someone was sitting just behind me looking over my shoulder.

Well, maybe Shaa had some ideas. Or even Max. As my own strangeness kept mounting I was getting less squeamish about consulting him for advice. The first thing I had to do, though, was dig myself out of the floor and from under the debris. Then I'd probably have to vacate these rooms. I tugged on my arm and got to work.

I could have called for help on whatever faculties had just waged battle for me, I suppose, but my ingrained distrust of magic was resurfacing with a large vengeance. Maybe I'd been calling for help too much as it was. Maybe that's what was playing games with my mind. Use of power can be addictive—

Just a second. What *about* calling for help? Where was the staff of this place? Why wasn't anyone banging on the door to investigate what was after all a significant uproar? Did they just ignore this kind of stuff here?

Well, that probably wasn't unreasonable if they did. I hadn't been too distracted to notice Jardin and Jill making their exit through the same secret door Phlinn Arol had used, but since they'd pulled part of the ceiling down in front of that wall as they'd left, that exit clearly wasn't going to be used again any time soon. For whatever reason, no one was pounding at the regular door either, but it could only be a matter of moments. It might be best if I wasn't waiting whenever they *did* decide to check up.

Especially since what did I really know about the

staff here? They were beholden on some level to Phlinn Arol, weren't they? How *had* Jardin tracked me down in the first place? Peridol was a big place and there were a lot of folks out on the town—how *had* he gotten on my trail? Had someone fingered me? What was Jardin's relation to Phlinn Arol?

I'd gotten free of the better part of the debris now, and had squirmed my lower body out of the dirt. If it wasn't my imagination, I thought I'd dropped weight since I'd woken up, too; maybe as much as five pounds I hadn't particularly wanted to lose. Since I needed food and needed sleep and wasn't sure which was more urgent, it was just as well I'd lost weight, I suppose; that way I didn't have to consider whether I might be pregnant. Instead—

"It is almost time," I told myself.

Wait a minute. Time for what? Why would I think something like that, and in such a forbidding tone, too? Was it another one of those dreams, except sneaking up on me in a waking moment rather than while I was asleep?

Could it have been Gash, speaking to me directly through the metabolic link? Or perhaps Monoch?

I thought I heard myself chuckling at myself. That was ridiculous, too; of course it was ridiculous; I knew it was ridiculous. So why was I still hearing it? Gray was creeping across my vision. Gray, fading to black, fading to that mist I'd seen in my dreams.

22

Damn, damn, damn. Damn! There was no question what had happened. It had the inexorable logic of a bad dream. Max understood that not everyone's dreams *were* logical, being characterized by a singular lack of causality and a distinct loss of contact with reality, but that had never been his own habit. He *did* dream, of course, but his own dreams typically unfolded like the operation of clockwork, or at least that was how the progression appeared to him (as spectator or participant) at the time. Events occurred in sequence, plots unreeled, mysteries unraveled; indeed, Max often thought he got some of his best thinking done while he was asleep.

Every so often, though, a dream would go sour. That was unpleasant. Seeing a sequence begin to proceed down the wrong road, foreseeing how things would continue as they went from bad to worse, being powerless to do anything but watch, or more annoyingly yet, be caught up by the inexorable gears of a grinding fate—that *was* unpleasant. And that was what was happening now. Except he wasn't watching, he was involved. And it was a *very* bad dream.

Except he wasn't asleep, either. Without question he was awake; there was nothing vicarious about it. For that matter, he could never have assembled such a mess in his sleep. No, he'd had to roll up his sleeves and work at it.

Come to think of it, he hadn't *been* dreaming lately,

or at least not in the lucid manner he could recollect upon regaining consciousness. Was that his subconscious' way of washing its hands of the whole matter, of trying to tell him he was headed this time for serious problems?

No, it couldn't have been. This plot was no more risky or convoluted than any number of exercises he'd run in the past. Things had just gone wrong, that was all. The die had fallen against him, random chance was sour today, fate had intervened; you could pick your metaphor of choice.

On the other hand, a critic might say this only proved he'd been unreasonably lucky this far.

The critic might also say he was retreating from the problem at hand to indulge in useless philosophizing. Philosophizing, as always, wouldn't solve a thing, and there were things that *had* to be solved. Or addressed, anyway. The leading one at the moment was Leen.

He could tell what had happened. In her hurry to get to her social obligation Leen had rushed out of the Archives, forgetting about Robin. She *had* exited through the Front Door, Max had felt that quite clearly. That had also been borne out by events, in particular by the ease of his own passage through the Back Door path disguised as Leen. Once he'd gotten inside, though, Leen had remembered Robin. Being the responsible person she obviously was, she'd resolved to go back in after him. The problem was that the path guardians knew she was *already* inside.

The guardians weren't particularly intelligent, but they weren't exactly dumb, either. They knew there should only be one Leen, and that if that Leen had gone inside the Archives she couldn't go inside again until she'd gone out first. But when she showed up again they'd recognized her. Being the original, she'd probably been more recognizable than had the disguised Max. She'd known what she was doing, too. So the guardians had allowed her to start down the path.

But that hadn't solved the problem. There were still

two Leens apparently roaming the vicinity. The guardian systems had surely waffled back and forth trying to decide what to do. Finally, though, they had obviously fallen back on an underlying principle: when in doubt, immobilize. That would allow the guardians to wait, and hope that perhaps an answer would present itself.

So Leen was out there, frozen, waiting for the guard systems to make up their minds, which they would now be in no particular hurry to do. In theory that was fine; Max could finish his business and depart at his leisure. Or finish his business, anyway. He wouldn't be able to leave for the same reason Leen couldn't finish entering. *He* was the other Leen that had caused the problem. If he tried to set foot on the recessional path the guardians would put him on ice, too. Once they had the two of them on hand for comparison, they might be able to reach a decision after all. Max had a nasty suspicion who'd be the loser in that process. After all, *he* knew who the real Leen was. Most likely the guard systems would, too.

Of course, Max *had* tried to look more like Leen than Leen herself. . . .

But the fact that remained was that *one* of them would end up on the short end, liable for immediate eradication in some traditional manner. Unless the guards decided the best thing to do was just wipe the slate across the board, and got rid of them both.

He *could* wait; maybe the guards would break their deadlock on their own. Either they'd let Leen through, or they wouldn't. If they got rid of Leen that would solve things, sure enough.

Unless it wouldn't. Damn! Was he really ready to sacrifice Leen? Was he ready to even risk it? And he *couldn't* wait, either. The guard systems were getting old, which meant they weren't necessarily stable. They could slip up, through inattention, or malfunction, or sheer crotchetiness—and any of those could convert a temporary immobilization into permanence.

Perhaps he could outwit the guardians to make his

own escape. But could he abandon Leen? And Robin, for that matter.

Could he sacrifice another bystander, whoever it was?

If Roni found out, she'd never forgive him. Worse, she'd never let him forget it.

"Mister?" It was Robin. No doubt wondering why Max had suddenly turned into a statue in the middle of their conversation.

"Excuse me," Max said to Robin. "We'll talk later. I just thought of something I have to do."

"Okay," said Robin. "See you later. Bye."

"Bye," said Max. He eased the door shut and then took off down the aisle. The Front Door terminus was ahead. Could he just bludgeon his way through? No, it would never work; even the second quantum level force levels he could bring to bear would never overpower the Archives' generators. Creeley had wanted to keep out gods just as much as he'd wanted to keep out ordinary people. If not more. Finesse was what was indicated here. In fact—

You gotta pay attention, Max muttered to himself. This would be tricky, *extremely* tricky. But what was expertise for, if not to face challenges?

Sure, Max thought. Right.

This was certainly a fine mess. As much as Leen hadn't wanted to attend the luncheon, it was paradoxical how annoyed she now found herself at being delayed in getting there. And Robin—well, Robin.

Which of course was all just a way of not thinking about the real situation.

Physically, it was clearly a lost cause. The guardians were a lot stronger than she was, and they didn't have to eat. Mentally she wasn't having any better luck. The guard systems were refusing to listen to her, and they weren't leaving themselves open to her attempts to worm into their mechanisms to run diagnostics or overrides either. What could have gone wrong with them?

Maybe that was the wrong question to ask. What if *nothing* had gone wrong? What situation could have caused them to respond as they were currently doing? What—

Hmm.

If it hadn't been for that story her brother had told her, she wouldn't even consider the possibility. But if you accepted the idea that someone could have gained entrance into the Archives once before, and proceeded to ask how, then, well, perhaps . . . but it also meant that the intruder was still *inside* the Archives. With Robin.

Leen clenched her teeth and probed again. Again nothing . . . but no, wait. Something *was* different. Fields were fluxing, forcelines circulating. *She* was being probed again, too. Probed by what from the backscatter appeared to be a very confused set of guardians. Creeley hadn't designed the guard systems to be verbal, unfortunately, which made it difficult to interrogate them, not to mention virtually impossible for them to ask for guidance. They never *had* asked for anything of the sort before, but that only made it all the more surprising to begin to suspect that they wouldn't at all mind an appropriate contribution from her now. "Why don't you show me what the problem is?" she emoted.

And then she was free. It was as simple as that, which of course meant that it could scarcely be that simple at all, or in other words some juxtaposition of events had occurred into which her message had slid, possibly tilting a balance one way rather than another. She wasn't *free,* actually, merely remobilized, released from the web to continue her inward traverse. Not only free, either; she was being actively urged onward, as though the guardians had placed a wind at her back.

There *had* been another presence on the door path recently, she realized, and that presence was now back. She could feel it ahead and below, or wherever the geometry of the inner end of the path really translated into. Not only another presence. It was another . . . *her*. She'd been right, then. But what had happened? Anyone tricky enough to sneak into the Archives by impersonating her probably knew more about the workings of the guard systems than she did, herself. They'd have had to be monitoring her own comings and goings, too, to perfect their own timing. So they must have known that she had reentered the path and gotten stuck. If they'd known, though, why had they revealed themselves? They had to know that faced with a head-to-head choice between the two of them the systems would recognize her as the original. There was one possible reason. . . .

But that couldn't be right. Why would whoever-they-were go to so much trouble to sneak around and then throw it all away merely to rescue her? It didn't make sense.

Which might have been what the guardians thought, too. Why they wanted her advice.

There *had* been another presence—but all of a sudden there wasn't anymore. The intruder had now entered the Front Door path, showing themselves at least through the antechamber and even into the Watermark's eddy-point, the Stain. The intruder had entered, made sure the guardians had had a full chance to probe her or it, and then . . . vanished. Leen had almost reached the Watermark herself, that was obviously how she was now able to feel the situation so clearly. The ripples of the intruder's escapades were still washing back and forth.

When one was traversing the Archive paths, there was a tendency to rely primarily on the inner eye. So many of the cues and dangers were not directly visualizable, so many sights were mere tricks of perception, that something as mundane as eye-vision could lead one more into hazard than toward help. The partial trance state that was the traditional tool of the Archivist also fostered a mode of neglect of exterior phenomena. This wasn't accidental, but then what was? It was clear to the initiate that the guard systems themselves functioned on that inner level, having rudimentary or no capabilities of sight themselves.

Maybe what they wanted now were her eyes.

The Watermark was a midair maelstrom, a ball of whipping vapor so tangled it might as well have been a rather confused waterspout or an errant floating pond. The usual traversal trick involved the use of its lashing wind as a crack-the-whip boost to spin yourself around and past it. The Stain surrounding the Watermark on the jagged floor-path usually had the appearance of a shoreline trough after a passing tidal surge or flood wave, being strewn with kelp and other seaweeds, sucking sands, the occasional lashing flounder, and residual pools of salt water. None of these things were actually *there*, of course, which only served to bear out the distinction between the perceptions of outer and inner eyes. The guardians (and Creeley before them) had been big on verisimilitude.

As she neared the Watermark now herself, nothing appeared out of place. The churning water-wind or wind-water, the flotsam, the force that tugged at her clothes and wanted to spin her around the room, all were as they usually were. There were no residual energy clouds, no soot stains on the rocks; there was no hint that someone had discovered the permanently elusive secret of teleportation. Yet someone *had* been here, very recently. Or had they? Could it have been a sending, a red-herring decoy? No, the guardians were quite certain.

So where had the intruder gone, then?

Oh. Of course. Leen planted her feet and stopped, secure in the knowledge that the guardians were giving her quite a lot of leeway at the moment; she should have no problem getting started again. "You might as well come out," she yelled over the Watermark's howl. "I know you're in there."

There was no ripple in the field-lines, none of the usual indications that someone with an active aura was present or passing through. But there was still something out of place, something moving—a darkness beneath the surface of the Watermark, that was it, something physical spinning and tumbling in the midst of the winds, something heaving at the agitated surface—

Something popping free of the Watermark and tottering and toppling to splash squarely into one of the larger puddles on the path. Something? No, a person, completely garbed in form-fitting black, now considerably the worse for wear through close acquaintance with the Watermark's core. The person wasn't dead, though, he was spinning to his feet with surprising control and grace for one who must have been bruised and pummeled to an extreme, spinning first to his feet and then around to face her.

"Hello there," said Max.

He was trying to brace himself. It was proving to be the hardest thing he'd done all day, harder by far than merely traversing the path. That damned Watermark had been no fun at all—his ears were still howling and his balance was shot, and his body felt like he'd just been rolled down a tall mountain and off a cliff into a cataract trapped in a poorly cushioned barrel; he should know. But when you got right down to it, the episode had been primarily physical, and in any case he hadn't gone into this expecting a picnic. If his stay in the Watermark had been the nastiest thing he'd had to deal with, in fact, there would have been no question that he'd gotten off easily. Instead, on top of the Watermark he was facing . . . well, what he was facing.

It had been worth a try. If she hadn't realized what was happening, as she obviously had, Leen might have continued straight on through to the end of the path without detecting him. She might have written the affair off as a malfunction. He hadn't *expected* that, but it had been worth a try. He hadn't even been certain that collapsing the Leen-aura and trying to shift his emanations immediately to the profile of something on the order of magnitude of a fly would succeed in dropping him below the guard systems' threshold of detection. *That* had worked, anyway. He'd had to use the cloaking effect of the Watermark to help, though, and whether he would have been able to continue to use stealth to make his way out of the Watermark and then out of the maze had been even more hypothetical. It looked like it would stay that way, too.

"Hello," Leen said. "Nice to see you again."

"Is it?" said Max.

"Why not?" she said, folding her arms. "Last time all you seemed able to think about was seeing *me* again, so I'd suppose you're happy you've gotten your wish."

"You must be right, of course," said Max, trying not to scowl. "I wouldn't lie about a thing like that."

"Wouldn't you?" Leen stated. "I wouldn't know."

"I doubt that saying 'take my word for it' would have much of an impact."

"Actions speak louder."

"So they say," agreed Max. "But actions themselves are subject to interpretation."

"I suppose they are. Also to tests of plausibility, and while we're at it we might as well throw in veracity, too, wouldn't you say?"

"A slippery topic, or at least it has a tendency in that direction, but you're certainly right there again, too. Your nephew is perfectly safe and happy, by the way."

"No other possibility ever crossed my mind," said Leen.

"You're going to be late to your luncheon. I'm sorry if I'm helping to delay you."

"I'm sure there will be other luncheons," Leen said. "Since you're keeping such a close eye on my calendar, perhaps you can schedule me for one. Unless people get fed up one time too many and stop inviting me, so I suppose there's a chance some good will come of this yet."

"It might be easier to hold a discussion if we moved out of this area," Max suggested. "This wind howling in my ear makes it hard to think, not to mention having to shout.''

Leen regarded him. ''On the other hand, it might be just as well to stay right here. I rather think the guard systems are waiting for me to help them with a decision about you. Right at the moment they might take movement on your part the wrong way.''

''It's your call,'' Max said, forcing a shrug. ''It's your turf.''

''Is it?''

''Could you ever doubt it?''

'' 'Doubt' is as good a word as any, I suppose.''

Max cleared his throat. ''This has turned into a messy business,'' he muttered. ''I've always hated messes; it's always a lot harder to clean them up and put things back in order than if you hadn't messed up in the first place.''

''That's the truth, at least, but it doesn't mean it isn't worth a try.''

Max sighed and cleared his throat again. ''My first problem was trying to mix business with—well, something that wasn't business. No, that's not true. The real problem was . . .''

Leen gave him a moment. ''Was what?'' she prodded.

''Letting myself forget the main rule,'' Max said disgustedly. ''Being weak enough to think I could get involved in anything that wouldn't come back and bite me.''

''Such as?''

Max looked away. ''You probably won't believe anything I say, but I like you, fool that I am. A lot. It's weak of me, but I do. It's also not smart. Every time I, uh, start to like someone, something nasty ends up happening.''

''One of those messes you mentioned, I suppose. But a mess isn't the end of the world, or at least it isn't to most people. Is it a reason to stop trying?''

''Isn't it?'' Max growled something under his breath that even *he* was glad he couldn't hear. ''If only you didn't turn out to be the *Archivist*. I needed to get into the Archives and this trick was the best way to do it."

"A proven way, too. You picked up that amulet around your neck when you were doing your 'trick' with my grandfather."

Max met her eyes for a moment, then glanced back at the Watermark again. "I was more rambunctious when I was younger."

"From the look of things you're still proficient. Your technique's not bad."

"Only my luck is sour."

"Not only your luck," Leen told him. "One could question your judgment. Didn't it occur to you to ask me for my help? That might have avoided a fair amount of deceit and at least some sneaking around."

Max opened his mouth, but when no sound emerged he closed it again.

"With the time the Back Door traverse must have taken you," Leen said thoughtfully, "you couldn't have been inside the Archives for more than a minute or two, so you couldn't possibly have accomplished whatever you'd set out to do there."

"I seem to have accomplished things I didn't set out to do instead," Max muttered, "things I'd rather I'd never started."

"I don't know," said Leen. "That remains to be seen. Are you after the same goals as the Scapula?"

"I'm sure I'm not. Whatever they are."

"Don't you know?"

"Aside from the obvious?" Max said. "Arznaak wants to rise as far and as fast as he can, getting whatever he wants to along the way and stepping on as many other people as possible, starting with his family. Beyond that? More specifically? Your guess is as good as mine. I hope you don't think I'm like him," he added.

"The Scapula seems to specialize in making people nervous," commented Leen. "You seem better at making them aggravated."

"You're not the first one to say that. Arznaak makes

me nervous, all right. Especially when I don't know what he's up to.''

''Yes, well, you're not the only one around with that point of view.'' What would her brother do with this situation? Leave Max to his fate or string him along? ''How much do you know about the Archives?''

''Not as much as I'd like to.''

''Your immediate reflex is to be evasive, do you know that? That's a habit you might want to try to fight.''

To Leen's satisfaction, Max looked thoroughly disgruntled. Then he seemed to change his mind about something. ''I know about Creeley, of course,'' he said. ''I've read some of his stuff.''

''Creeley? Not the *lost* papers?'' Darn, it had come out before she'd even had a chance to think.

''Nothing's lost if you know the right place to look,'' Max said. ''I may be able to get hold of them for you, but anyway I remember most of the interesting stuff. Let's see, I know about—''

''What do you know about the foundation of the Archives?'' Leen interrupted.

Max's response was a slow, calculating, speculative glance from beneath an upraised eyebrow. *Uh-oh,* Leen thought. *I may have overstepped on that one.* ''How much does anyone know about that?'' he said.

Leen paused. She was thinking about motivation. Not just anyone off the street would want to get into the Archives. Even if they knew the real Archives existed, which you could say about few enough people in the first place. What was really going on here? What *was* he after?

Well, she hadn't exactly *asked* him. So she did.

To his own surprise, Max found himself telling her. Not everything, more than he expected, certainly, but not the details of his current scheme—although Leen was enough of an outsider that he might actually be able to tell her that, too, and maybe get some useful comments in return; still, he was spouting enough to—

''You *are* right, there,'' Leen said. ''There *is* Archival material on some of the gods, and possibly even some vulnerability data, too.''

What *had* he been talking about? What kind of spell was he under here? Finding material on the gods, of course, right. "I'm particularly looking for loopholes or weaknesses I can exploit," added Max. "At the moment concerning this one in particular."

"I stand a better chance of finding it more quickly than you would, blundering around without knowing where anything is . . . unless you *do* know where things are, I suppose."

"Not the way you do, I'm sure."

Leen regarded him. "I don't know about you, I think you should know that. I don't know whether—well, let's just say I don't know. But whatever you're really doing here, whether I trust you or not, there's something you still may be able to help me with. What's a little subterfuge between friends, I guess?" Leen shook her head, more to clear it than for effect. *Stop lollygagging,* she thought. "Look, you're an antiquarian, a technologist, an artifact specialist, right?"

"I try."

"Okay, then. I want you to look at something." She had already gotten moving again on the path. "Well, come on. What are you waiting for?"

This is not what I expected, Max was thinking. He didn't know what he'd expected, not really, but this certainly wasn't it. When you're used to interpersonal relationships characterized by distrust and stabbing in the back you—

"Come *on*. Or would rather I feed you to the guardians right now instead of maybe later?"

The guardians were clearly withholding their own final judgment, too, but as Max launched himself again into motion as well he could feel their willingness to follow Leen's lead, at least for the moment. With Leen blazing the trail and the guard systems contenting themselves with an occasional querulous jab to remind him who was really in charge, the short trip back to the Archival terminus was the easiest of the several passages he'd experienced. Max knew that was just as well. Between the pummeling from the Watermark and his equally unbalancing encounter with Leen, he was not exactly at his prime.

Once through the door, Leen made the expected beeline to check on Robin. Max was lagging behind. "What's the matter now?" Leen said. "Afraid what I'll find?"

"Of course I'm not afraid what you'll find," Max growled. "I'm not fond of kids, that's all."

Leen now had the door to Robin's room open. "You can't hate *Robin,*" she said, smiling at the occupant. "Look at him—you can't hate him."

"Is the man in the funny black suit still there?" Robin said.

"Come on," Leen ordered, "say hello to Robin."

"Yes," Max said under his breath, so that Leen wasn't quite sure he was actually speaking, "I do. Especially right at the moment." Then, in his full voice, Max said with convincing sincerity, "Hi there, Robin. How you doing?"

"I think he likes you," Leen told Max as they retreated into the Archives a few moments later, leaving Robin again to his pursuits.

"I guess that's a good start," Max said. "Isn't it? Or maybe it's a question of whether Robin's judgment becomes a generalized response."

"You want to wedge your own foot deeper down your throat, be my guest. Turn here."

Max, continuing to trail Leen, pulled off his eye-slit mask and stuffed it roughly in one oversized pocket. This was certainly not the sort of situation he'd ever imagined he'd even be entertaining the question of whether he might have met his match. He—

What was Leen doing, down on her knees in front of that bookcase?

Oh. Oh! "You found this?" Max said.

"Yes. No; actually Robin found it."

"I thought he showed potential," Max muttered. "It's not a trap."

"Is that a question or—"

"It was a gratuitous remark," he said, moving slowly down the tight circular stair. "Sometimes I think out loud. . . . Obviously you've been through here, you've cleaned the place up, if there'd been a trap you would have . . . look at this, look at this." Max approached the alloy wall and the thick dark window. "A metal detector would go berserk in here. You tried probes and got nothing?"

"Nothing," Leen said. she had seated herself a half-turn above him on the staircase and was watching him prowl the compact room. "Seems like a total null, a blank. Like what you tried to pull on the guardians and me."

"So you're hoping it'll take one to know one? Well, could be. What did this glass panel look like when you first broke in here?"

"Like it does now, except dustier."

Max had his face scrunched up against the panel in question, apparently to bring his eye as close to the surface as possible. "If you want my ideas," he said, in a muffled voice, "you'd be better off telling me whatever you can. There were lights, right? Little round glowing lights?"

"How did you—you weren't in here the other time you broke—"

"Hold on a second, hold on. I heard about one of these things once, that's all."

"There's *another* one of these somewhere?"

"That would seem to be the case," Max stated. "You hear stories like this, you have to figure they're a myth, except sometimes they're not. This other one was supposed to be in the tower of one of the gods. There's so much garbage out there about the gods, I figured, well, who cares anyway, right? It's not like I was planning to burgle another god, especially one who was probably mythical himself."

Another? thought Leen. "Who was this other mythical god?"

Max stood back and considered the wall. "Now that

I think about it, that story might be making more and more sense after all. This is Dislocation stuff, you realize that.''

"Of course."

"And according to the stories, Byron was the one who caused the Dislocation and the birth of the gods in the first place."

It was just as well she was sitting down. "Byron?"

"You haven't heard of him? Byron the Artificer?"

"What do *you* know about him?"

Max shrugged. "How much does anyone know? He was the father of the gods in some allegorical way, created the magic that overthrew technology, turned against his creations and was swallowed up by them. How mythical can you get? No real person could be that much of an archetype. Maybe there *was* a real Byron and he just had a lot of creation legends hung on him, who knows? But this thing's no legend, sure enough.'' Then Max started spouting gibberish.

Leen jerked upright. *Was* there a curse after all, and had it just stricken Max? But suddenly as abruptly as he'd begun Max had fallen silent. "Are you all right? What was that?''

"I'm trying to remember what extinct language Byron might have used,'' Max said, his hands on his hips and a glare on his face toward the wall. "Drooze ya?'' he demanded of the wall. "No, huh?''

"You actually speak pre-Dislocation languages?''

"What good is grubbing around in the past if you can't understand what you find? My accent's probably wrong, though. The only folks around who really know the right pronunciation are the gods, and of course they're not talking.'' He said something else bizarre to the wall.

"You don't think something might really be listening to you, do you?'' But she was the one who'd first thought that something was alive back there, so why not?''

"It worth a—what's this?''

A small green disk of light had appeared at the upper left corner of the dark glass slab and somewhere in its interior. It was slowly blinking—on, off, on, off.

"What did you say to it?" Leen asked, with no little amazement.

"Hello, I think. Good morning, something like that. Let's try this." Max spoke another phrase, a longer one this time, from the sound of it in the same language.

The green dot hesitated, stopped blinking, disappeared; then suddenly leapt back to life and raced across the panel, leaving letters glowing in its wake. That was the only thing they could be, letters. Only what did they—

"The hell you say," Max sputtered, squinting at the display. "Goddamned oracle."

"What?" said Leen.

Max scowled at the green scrawl. "The worthless thing's being cryptic. I asked it what it had to tell us, but it's gone into some kind of riddle mode. Either that or it just likes non sequiturs. 'If it's advanced enough, you can't tell technology from magic.' What am I supposed to say to that?"

"Huh?"

"Yeah," said Max. "I—oh, great. Now it's gone away."

The letters had vanished again, leaving the blinking green dot. "That's it? That's all?"

But apparently it was. Though Max cajoled it for the next fifteen minutes, the thing now totally ignored him; whatever riddle-answer it had been expecting it obviously hadn't gotten. Max cast an eye back at Leen. He would have to trust her to do his research for him. *He* certainly hadn't accomplished his mission in the Archives and it was already getting to be time to go. He had his appointment with his contact from the Inauguration Ball, to get the god's answer to the proposal Max had made. It was a tricky enough gambit already without running the risk of being late as well. But if the god did accept the deal, that's when Max would need the insight the research should provide, and he'd need it pretty damn fast. "Let me explain some more about what I'm up to . . ." Max began.

23

One certainly had to give credit where credit was due. Maximillian the Vaguely Disreputable, in the course of his career, had managed to run afoul of quite an impressive list of talents. It was really quite neighborly of him, Fradjikan thought. It had made it so convenient to recruit forces for his own plan. Not every major job gave one the luxury to pick and choose.

Not that any of those he'd recruited were up to his own level, of course. There *was* the Scapula, whose precise level remained to be determined but was certainly high. Fradi hadn't exactly recruited the Scapula himself, however; there had been some amount of solicitation on each side. That clearly had planted the roots of the current situation, with its questions and uncertainties. Which was not to say that the Scapula's additions and modifications to the plan weren't well-chosen, and rather clever, too, in the sneakily underhanded manner that gave the best plans their revelatory character. Still, the Scapula's motivations and ultimate goals remained cryptic. There wasn't anything particularly wrong with that, either, since Fradjikan obviously was facilitator and not target, but it was always better to be on the safe side. Safety, as always, rested with greater knowledge. He would just have to keep his eyes—

''Is that it?''

Fradjikan recollected himself smoothly from his brief reverie. Standing across from him next to the

355

refreshments he'd set out in the dayroom were the three other participants in this final preparatory meeting. "That is the plan," Fradi restated.

"You're sure he'll be in the right place?"

"He will be there," Fradi assured them. "There will undoubtedly be some last-minute improvising required, but that is what distinguishes professionals such as yourselves from the rabble, does it not?"

The man stroked his curled black beard with the hand that was not holding a goblet, then ran it through the rakishly wild hair over his forehead. "Max can be a pretty slippery guy," he remarked. "It's never been an easy matter keeping him in sight. He's always changing himself around and climbing up on roofs and letting off decoys, who knows what-all."

"It's about time somebody turned that against him, too," said the robed fellow at his side. His own head was shaved clean, except for a residual fringe that ran in a circle above his ears. "You've done a solid job, I'll give you that. Using Kalifa and Ma Pitom to keep the pressure on—and us, too—I bet Max doesn't know if he's coming or going."

"Never hinge an operation on a bet," the third man said darkly, glowering at the titles on the bookcase.

The first one eyed him with an expression of some surprise. "You're awful talkative today, Romm. You got a problem?"

Romm V'Nisa turned to face them, his arms folded across his chest. "Maximillian is always a problem," he intoned. Then he added, "Problems are my job."

"If there weren't problems to solve we'd *all* be out of a job," said the man in the robe. "Max has always been so suspicious it's been hard to pull anything on him; show him a *picture* of a bed and he'll think somebody with a dagger's gonna jump out from under it at him. The idea of playing to his suspicions by burying him up to his eyebrows in plots was a master stroke. All these traps, menaces, ambushes falling on him from every which way, and then the subversion of the irredentists, and linking Max to them with that scandal-poster campaign, well, it's—''

Romm grunted. "Were you raised by magpies? If you compromise operational security with your chatter, I will cut out your tongue.''

Their leader sighed. "Is there some particular detail you still want to discuss, Romm? I'm satisfied that Señor Ballista's plan is as solid as we can ask for.''

"As you say,'' Romm told him in a dour tone.

Were they deliberately trying to butter him up? If he was in their place, he might do the same. After all, they had to suspect there was more to the plot than had been shared with them; this was a reasonably non-confrontational probing gambit to see what other information they might easily glean. Chas V'Halila, the talkative one, had just stated more than they'd officially been told, subtly underlining their own capabilities and resources while at the same time seeming to praise Fradi himself. They clearly understood the role of the smokescreen in shielding the central thrust.

It was most likely just habit. An endemic symptom of plotters was their desire to understand the full scope of a scheme in which they might be merely supporting players. "Just be certain you wait for the signal,'' Fradi reminded them. The most complicated element here—and consequently the one most worth worrying about—was the sequencing of events.

"Shall we maintain our guard detail?'' Gadol, the leader, ventured.

"Why not?'' said Fradi. "It gives your people practice.''

"Just so,'' agreed Gadol. Casting a last reluctant glance at it, he set down his glass. "Well, I suppose we should check in with the civic authorities. Especially since we're officially under their command.''

"We've never worked for this branch of Peridol before,'' Chas reminded him. "If we play things off right, we could be in for some serious long-term employment. Replenish the coffers and all that.''

"It is possible that we might have occasion to work

together in the future as well," suggested Fradjikan. "One does not come across a resource such as the Hand every day."

On that note of mutual congratulation, the threesome departed. Things *had* been developing remarkably well, and at a lively pace. When mapping things out originally, there had been an outside chance that events would move rapidly enough to stage this denouement at the Running of the Squids; he *had* hoped, but it had still been no better than a tossup. It was indeed gratifying that this would now be the case. The appropriate canvas would set this act off with that extra flair of memorability.

There was still the issue of his patron. At least he had been able to program in *some* insurance. Not as much as he liked, granted, but it should be enough. And then there was the Scapula. . . .

Perhaps Fradi should have lined up more insurance against him, too. Well, at this stage it couldn't be helped. His greatest hedge was that of nonthreatening future utility. Although . . .

What about that woman, the librarian? She had obviously become to the Scapula a thorn. Perhaps there was some move to be played there. Yes, perhaps there was.

On the other hand, there was a danger of overbooking. Fradi was already up to his neck managing his female-related intrigues. Did he want to add another? Some thought was called for here. Perhaps it would be better to ride with events; a target of opportunity might present itself.

Thinking of events, what time was it? Oh!—later than he'd expected. It was time to be out and about. Plots or no plots, one had to keep one's hand in.

24

"You got to keep your ears open to what these sects are talking about," Max had admitted. "Sometimes they get on to something." So here Jurtan was with these loonies.

It was turning out to be a waste of a good day. He could be out jamming with the Underlings or checking out one of the other clubs the guys had told him about, or practicing on his own for that matter, but instead he'd wanted to be part of the plan that had dragged him halfway across the world.

So here he was. He hadn't thought streets could get any more crowded than they'd already been, but regardless of his attitude they'd accomplished that anyway, and as if that wasn't bad enough, the temple Eden had arranged for him to visit wasn't located in the district of the gods at all. No, it was down by the Tongue waterfront. The address had been off along a lane of warehouses, of all things, their whitewashed walls glistening with salt-spray mist and the street cobbles scarred from the passage of overladen wagons. These streets were jammed also, filled with overflow from the banks of the Tongue. Even though the traditional squid spectacular wasn't supposed to start until tomorrow, revelers and vendors of everything from refreshments to choice bleacher seats were jockeying for position wherever there was a space big enough to plant a foot. Jurtan had clearly been in the wrong place, since the street number on his note proved to yield just another anonymous warehouse door, but he'd knocked anyway, and a bearded man had arrived to let him in. The man had led him through a small entry hall into the warehouse proper, which indeed turned out to be a temple, pointed out a place for him in an empty pew, and returned to his station by the door.

The interior was given over to a high-ceilinged chamber of assembly more stylishly appointed than the shabby outside facade had implied. It wasn't the appointments that fostered the image of refinement; in fact, the temple was strikingly clear of the usual fetishes and effigies and altars. Aside from a few stained-glass windows on abstract themes which he thought mainly involved fire and trees, with here and there a recognizable chicken or sheep or fish, and a raised presentation area in front, the chamber was undecorated. The ranks of pews in a dark polished wood, and the similarly paneled floor, however, were set off dramatically against the cream-colored walls, contoured into a cunning series of setbacks and alcoves beneath the undulating ceiling. As far as Jurtan could remember, this was his first experience of architecture motivated by deliberate tact and restraint, but he found he rather liked it.

The religionists and their mysterious service already in progress, though, were a different matter. As soon as he'd come through the door, his internal music had begun imitating their ongoing ritual, a sort of a wailing minor-key chant built out of repeating melodic units. Up in the front on the podium, a line of four or five readers were eschewing the comfortable chairs behind them for a cross-legged position sitting on the floor, from which they were singing aloud in turn from a text, chapter by chapter. The congregation, matching them privation for privation, were also arrayed on the floor in the aisles, occasionally humming along with the reader of the moment for a choice passage or two. Everyone sounded thoroughly miserable.

But what was the point? Mass hypnosis, maybe—if all this kept up much longer he'd probably be humming along, too. Jurtan had tipped his head back to better study the way the skylights were tucked into the folds of the roof, and to watch through them the declining light of evening, when he realized that someone had slipped into the pew next to him. The man was alternately paying attention to the keening from the stage and twisting in the pew to scrutinize Jurtan.

"Blessed be those who join with us," the man whispered after a moment.

"I'm not joining anything," Jurtan said. "I'm only here because my friends thought you might be able to help us."

The fellow adjusted his headdress, a sort of flat turban, before responding. "Within a traditional greeting may still be a message of deeper truth."

Creeps and kooks, what other kind of person did the world contain? "Look, I'm sorry if I've showed up at a bad time. Why don't I come back when you're not in the middle of a service?" Or better yet, maybe he'd manage not to come back at all. In fact—

"Eden is not one to watch her calendar too closely," the man commented. "Yet any request from her is one we are only too happy to rush to fulfill. This has nothing to do with her endowment of this building, you understand."

"Of course," said Jurtan, who indeed suddenly felt as though he did have some greater idea of *something* that was going on. He fished around in his pack and came up with the Iskendarian page Max had let him take. "We wanted to know what you could make of this document."

The religionist perused it with pursed lip. "Tarfon should see this," he allowed after a moment. "That section of the lamentation will be finished momentarily."

The high-pitched guy currently wailing up on the stage? Oh, great. "Uh, excuse me, but do you do this stuff all the time?"

The man rocked back and forth a few times in apparent consideration. "This is a day of commemoration, a fast day, a day of meditation on the state of the world. This is the day when we remember the calamities of the past, ours and the world's, when we learn from what we have lost what our task is for today. We acknowledge that God, for our sins, has cast us out of our land, our age, our—''

"God?''

"We worship the One God,'' the man confirmed.

"The One God? *Which* one? Gashanatantra, Slugan Kaporis—''

"The Ineffable One, the One who can neither be seen nor heard, the—''

"What good is that? Isn't the whole reason you want to tie yourself to a god because of the stuff they can do for you?''

The man made an expression that was more smile than rictus, but shared an appreciable amount of both. "That is indeed the current sentiment. We are certainly behind the times, but what can we do? We believe what we believe. Some consider it a curse to bear witness to the truth. We think it is a blessing, but I will grant you it is often a fairly problematic one. Our history is not pleasant.''

And there was a whole temple full of people as crazy as this guy was? Or half full, anyway? "Why don't the gods you don't believe in wipe you out, then? They don't like to be ignored, not to mention disbelieved.''

"The world is full of cranks who remain beneath notice,'' the man said with a thoroughly straight face. "But, no, I didn't say we don't believe in them; that would be denying empirical reality. We just don't think they're gods. Ah, here's Tarfon.''

As the new person, his chanting complete, came stalking up the aisle, it occurred to Jurtan that this was in fact just the kind of loony organization the Shaas might hang around with. They were, after all, more than a little loopy themselves. Was Eden just a supporter or an out-and-out believer? Zalzyn Shaa's attitude of sardonic disdain also might owe more than a chance amount to this sort of variant ideology. There were obviously more people running around off the beaten track than he'd suspected.

Even if they were crazy, that didn't mean they might not know something. Maybe this Tarfon guy . . . or rather, this Tarfon woman. Or girl? The contralto had thrown him off, and he clearly hadn't been paying enough attention anyway. "Mirror writing," Tarfon said immediately on being handed the document. "Distorted script, too." She perused it for a few moments in silence. "The letters belong to another language than the one this is written in. The writer's using the letters to make a phonetic transcript."

"So you can't read it?" Jurtan said.

She glanced briefly up at him. "Sure I can read it. I know this script system from a few book fragments in my father's library, and I can piece together the meaning in the other language as I go along. Both of those languages are pre-Dislocation, but this page here is a good few hundred years post."

"How can you tell?"

"Look here." Tarfon indicated a section of text at the top of the page. Max had given him one of the pages that contained only line after line of unbroken writing, without any of the drawings or equations featured in some of the other material. "It's context. The writer refers to the God of Curses, and then here's a mention of something called the Steadfast Spell. The modern gods came in with the Dislocation, and magic, too, of course; so that immediately tells us this had to be written after that time. Then here's an aside about Abyssinia the Moot." Tarfon stared at the passage, then suddenly blushed. "Uh, it looks like old gossip, actually. I can't make it all out."

"What about your father?" Jurtan said. "You learned from him? Maybe he could help more."

"I learned from his library," Tarfon told him evenly. "That's all he left me. He died when I was a child."

"Sorry," Jurtan muttered. Maybe he should work more on learning when to keep his mouth shut, or at least on practicing a better way to phrase things.

''That's all right,'' said Tarfon. ''Aki, why couldn't you read this? I know you know—''

The first man stroked his beard and merely raised an eyebrow.

''Oh, another one of your practical lessons, right?'' Tarfon put on an expression of deliberate bemusement. ''One of these days . . .''

''One of these days Tarfon will take my place,'' Aki said to Jurtan.

Tarfon was ignoring him, or perhaps she was only engrossed back in the document. ''This isn't the only page,'' she stated.

''No,'' Jurtan said. ''That's right.'' His authorization from Max had extended far enough to admit that. ''There's enough stuff to fill a sack.''

''I'm not surprised. The writer seems to be writing notes to himself. Or herself, that's not clear. More than notes, really—more of a complete personal history. Look, here the writer refers back to an incident he's apparently already discussed, and here he talks about Formula 138.''

''You mean this is a book of memoirs?''

''I don't know,'' said Tarfon. ''I'm not sure. Maybe I just don't have enough of a command of the language. It sounds less like storytelling, though, and more like . . . how would you describe it?''

''Lessons,'' said Aki. ''Instructions. Very curious; it does have a didactic style. Would you like us to review the rest of this material?''

''Yeah,'' Jurtan said. ''We sure would, except you've got to come to where it is.''

''A reasonable precaution, the streets being what they are,'' allowed Aki.

Jurtan gave the address and they set an appointment for after the congestion from the Running let up. Jurtan didn't forget to thank them both; he thought he even managed to do that without punching himself in the mouth. As he was exiting back onto the road outside, though, thinking how nice it was to get away from that weird sect and out from under their mournful chanting, no matter how helpful they might or might not have been, he realized that that had not actually happened. His mind was still playing that damn chant at him.

"Stop it," he muttered. "What's gotten into you?" That's all he needed, a built-in torture squad. The music wasn't giving him any particular message, either; it was just loping along driving him up the wall.

He broke free of the warehouse row onto a major street. To the right toward the Tongue Water, the boulevard fed into one of the big bridges. As it crossed the center of the channel it sprouted a second level, an observation deck, now a focus of the attention of a crew of workers hanging bunting and scrubbing down surfaces, and another crew of toughs mounting guard. The last thing Jurtan wanted at the moment was to fight the throng to look at a grandstand, though, so he turned his back on the scene and began to fight his way in the other direction. Next to him, the middle of the boulevard was still being kept clear for a single lane of vehicle and mounted traffic in each direction. He had been considering hitching a ride when it occurred to him that his internal music had indeed finally changed.

On top of the chant was a new horn theme. A *new?*— no, he'd heard it before . . . with the Underlings. No, not *with* the Underlings, but while he'd been playing with them. It was . . . oh. Oh! It was the melody that had come with that man who'd been paying a little too much attention to Tildy.

Where was it coming from now? A closed carriage, clattering away from the bridge toward him along the road. Jurtan didn't think twice. He slipped through a gap in the traffic behind the tailboard of a water wagon and a party of horsemen heading toward the bridge just behind it, teetered for a brief moment at the shifting boundary between the east and west lanes, and then launched himself with a rapid sprint at the rear of the carriage as it rattled past. A narrow footboard protruded beyond the hamper trunk strapped to the hindmost part of the vehicle. Was it too narrow? Running just behind, Jurtan managed to slip a hand around one of the trunk straps and swing himself up.

The perch was precarious but not impossible. With his arm tucked through the strap he could maintain his seat, with his legs dangling and his feet a good foot off the roadbed. As long as the driver didn't accelerate . . . but then there was just about no place in Peridol at the moment where you could move faster than a trot. Jurtan settled himself back for the duration.

Except . . . what was he really doing here, anyway? It was sort of a damn fool stunt, when you thought about it. What if he *was* following the person who'd been pursuing his sister, and what if he actually *did* have some nefarious intent? What would he do about it? More likely he'd just get yelled at by some complete bystander. It *was* a fool stunt—it was exactly the sort of thing Jurtan thought Max would be likely to pull.

Of course, on the other hand—

A sliding of wood just above his head caught Jurtan's attention. He craned around just as the sliding rear window in the carriage's landau top slammed shut again. Jurtan hadn't caught the slightest glimpse of whoever might be inside, and the angle was awkward—perhaps they hadn't seen him either. Perhaps—

A powerful whistle pierced the air from virtually overhead, from within the carriage. Jurtan went to slip his arm free from the strap . . . slip his arm free—his arm was *stuck,* dammit! Behind the carriage, three horsemen had broken loose from the press of following traffic and were bashing their way toward him, their eyes clearly locked on one thing and one thing only. Belatedly, Jurtan's internal music was warning him of something dangerous in his immediate surroundings. *Thanks a lot,* he thought, and just then his hand *did* come free, a metal buckle on the strap gouging a nice chunk out of his forearm in facilitation. Jurtan spun free and slid off his perch, staggered as he hit the ground, still moving with the momentum of the carriage, and then hit a patch of fresh sewage not yet considered by the sanitation crews; his legs flew out from under him and he smashed full-on into the pavement.

Ahead was a team of oxen, behind was the carriage, rolling to a sudden halt, and to the side were the converging horsemen. Jurtan scrambled toward the center of the street, away from the nearest ox and the guys on the horses, and from whoever had jumped clear of the carriage and was now coming around its corner in his direction. As he stumbled ahead while looking over his shoulder, Jurtan abruptly caught his foot on yet another obstacle and tripped again—the low curb dividing the two directions of traffic; that was it, he thought dazedly, as the pavement came up at him once more.

This time he caught himself on his hands, grinding skin off his palms and knuckles but keeping his face intact. The first swordsman was trying to maneuver his horse around the now interposing oxen and a chorus of angry shouting had broken out. Jurtan got himself to his feet and launched himself weaving back through the opposing traffic—a blast of discordant trumpets hit him at the same moment as something massive walloped him across the side of his head. He'd straightened too much, Jurtan realized in a dull haze, and one of the horsemen had managed to sweep across over the oxen with a long sword or a spear and catch him a good solid blow.

Somehow he made it across the street. Beyond the churned ditch, a knot of people were hooting and yelling at him. Someone clobbered him with a market basket as he plowed through them, ''all in good fun, no doubt,'' he found himself muttering, ''but if it's all the same to you I'd—''

With that, something round and squishy and extremely foul smelling hit him right on the nose. A rotten cabbage? He needed an alley—where was an alley? There! Jurtan was a good half-block down it away from the street before he heard pounding feet behind him. What had he stirred up? All this over hitching a ride? It was—

The alley jogged again and split. He had no idea of the tricks of the neighborhood, where he was or where he was going, and for that matter why wasn't his music being more helpful too? Actually, it was trying, Jurtan realized as he staggered to the left, he was just too dazed to pay enough attention. He risked another glance back over his shoulder—he couldn't see anyone, but he could hear them, and his music seemed to think that letting them catch up with him might not be a very good idea at all. That didn't seem to be the music's only concern, though. What else was it—

The ground, unpaved since he'd entered the first alley, had been growing progressively more filth-heaped and decrepit as he'd gone along. People in the surrounding buildings were clearly used to dumping their trash and offal into it and then moving away to another neighborhood, but even so, the surface was distinctly more boggy than it had been. Jurtan scrambled over a fall of construction stones where the side of a building had subsided into the alley and slid down the other end, slid down . . . down? The surface wasn't merely yielding beneath his feet, it was *sucking,* and then the ground was sliding, too, sliding down, collapsing!

Jurtan flailed with both arms. But there was no purchase—he was only dragging more muck in on top of him. What was a sinkhole doing in the middle of a city, in the middle of *Peridol,* for gods' sake? Goo slimed into his mouth, covered his eyes. He was kicking, thrashing, writhing, but there was no air, there was a terrible pounding in his head, there was. . . .

There was movement. He was slipping, rolling, upside down now, wallowing down a chute or a hillside or—one clawing hand tore free. Jurtan lurched up, caught a gasp mixed half of disgusting air and half of mud before feeling himself bowled over again. Rotted pilings glimmered above, then, as he went head over heels into the mire, ahead and below there was a glint and splash of water.

25

"What ever happened to Jurtan Mont?" Shaa asked, surveying the street full of people ahead.

"Damned if I know," said Max. He rubbed an extra-bristly eyebrow; today was a day of full disguise. "He went out to see the One God people yesterday and never came back."

"You don't suppose he could have gotten lost?"

"Overnight? Anyway, he had directions. From what Svin said about his performance the other night he probably stopped in at some music club and got turned out into the gutter when they closed. He'll wash up eventually, I'm sure."

"Yet whatever the results of his mission might have been," Shaa observed, "they remain unreported."

"I didn't really expect anything useful, but you're right, it would have been nice to know." Max snorted. "What did we drag the kid along for, then, anyway?"

"An exercise in education, wasn't it? Although you did mutter something about him being a secret weapon, as I recall."

"All I can say is he's sure been a pretty *effective* secret." Jurtan Mont was purely a side issue, but Max was perfectly happy to be discussing him, rather than have Shaa focus again on something more central, such as where they were going and what they were going to do there. You couldn't ask for a better cover story than the Running of the Squids, of course, but Shaa had an uncanny talent for sniffing out the presence of one of

370

Max's stratagems. Especially when it might directly involve Shaa himself.

Fortunately Shaa was off his game. "Actually, I was giving serious consideration to taking to my bed," Shaa had said grumpily when Max had arrived to roust him out, asking heartily what he had planned for the day.

"Nonsense!" Max had told him. "And miss the Running of the Squids? Now that you're back in Peridol and all? That's not the Shaa I know."

"You said it," groused Shaa, "I didn't. Do you know your tone of voice is far too light for credibility?"

In the event Max had won out, and so here they were; the two of them and what appeared to be the entire population of Peridol, if not the western world.

"It is a pleasant day for it," Shaa allowed. "If one likes sunshine, that is. I'm not going to have to watch you compete, am I?"

"Why would I want to do something like that? What's to gain? I seem to have all the notoriety I need at the moment."

"Too many of our activities lately have seemed to culminate with someone ending up in a body of water," said Shaa. "I was only asking."

"I'm staying on dry land," Max stated. "That other Running was quite enough to last me a longer time than this."

Up ahead now as they bashed and elbowed their way along was the main Tongue Water bridge decked out with its event marshal's reviewing stand. "Did your plans extend so far as to involve a vantage point with a field of view?" inquired Shaa.

"You mean watching the spectators isn't enough for you?"

Indeed, the spectators were a show-and-a-half all by themselves. Fish and other sea creatures were the order of the day, but that was only an aid to inspiration rather than any sort of restraint. There were the food vendors, of course, slinging fish fried, sauteed, pickled, and raw along their portable service counters or through the air at their customers; there were fish balls, fish broths, fish sculptures; catfish, pike, perch, trout, flounder, bass, salmon, halibut, mackerel, cod, carp, eel, swordfish, tuna, pompano, sardine, haddock—and those were only a selection of the sea creatures with scales and fins. Mounds of shells awaiting preparation or already consumed lined the gutters and crunched underfoot, and off to the side a gang of urchins were playing pitch-and-catch with what appeared to be the remains of an entire bed of clams. Next to the game, a juggling troupe wearing on their chests the emblem of a startled grouper, complete with animated pop eyes, were tossing and twirling small octopuses, or at least their stuffed effigies. Tentacles whirled in the air, entwining in artful pinwheels and whirlpools of color. Overhead flew long stylized banners, taking the air in through gaping mouths and gill slits and puffing out their red and bright orange bodies.

And then there was the crowd itself, or at least the minor part without a particular scheme or profit-making goal. Plainly not everyone was costumed, but the riot of odd sights parading past made the more typical majority fade into obscurity like sun-bleached wallpaper. Headdresses were the most common, some purchased from the tall waving stacks artfully balanced by the omnipresent hat hucksters, with the result that waving eyestalks and drooping flagellae and gape-lipped mackerel assaulted the eye in every direction. Here though, too, was a proudly promenading school of two-footed herring, and trailing behind them two crisscrossing sharks, their dorsal fins cruising above the head level of the throng. At the bridge rail—

A vast shout had broken out on the bridge, and was even now rippling out as spectators turned and craned and gaped. Atop the reviewing stand, a human figure, radiating a golden glow even in the sunlight, had stepped up on a platform and was waving at the multitude. "What, Maximillian," said Shaa, "not even the barest yelp from you of communal approval? No acknowledgment of the presence of a great one in our midst?''

''It'll take a lot more than a personal appearance by Phlinn Arol to make me stand up and holler,'' Max said. Phlinn's advent did mean that they might be drawing close to getting officially underway, though. It was time to start looking out for the one Max was there to meet. He'd been on guard all morning, of course; even more so than usually. Once he'd taken the thing from the lab into his possession again late the previous night extreme prudence had been indicated. It had taken until almost morning to make the other preparations after Leen had messengered over the scanty results of her research the night before, but who needed sleep at a time like this. He'd napped before the stuff from Leen had arrived, anyway.

The god was probably already around. He'd have to reveal himself eventually, hopefully in the manner they'd agreed upon in their exchange of messages yesterday evening. Still, some sort of preemptive strike couldn't be entirely ruled out. The amulet gave Max the benefit of anonymity, although the thing in his pocket might have something to say about that, too. When it came right down to it, there was no substitute for old-fashioned vigilance.

''As long as we're here,'' said Shaa, ''I would just as soon have something worthwhile to look at.''

''Right,'' Max said. ''Sure. Let's go over here.''

How had he talked her into this? Perhaps this was what being swept off your feet really involved. If so, Leen could certainly understand why it had never held any appeal for her. The question was why she was letting herself be sucked into it now.

It defied belief. After Max had (after all) put her in significant danger as part of his own nefarious plot, after she had found herself wanting to cosh him over his head and write him out of her life, whatever she might have thought she could be growing to feel about him, she had simultaneously and to her great surprise listened when he proposed a favor she could do for him, and then to her total astonishment discovered she was entertaining the notion of doing what he'd asked. True, he had all but stated that he was putting himself on the line and changing the habits of a lifetime in trusting someone he barely knew, and he had apparently put himself back into hazard to extricate her from a nasty situation of his own devising there in the Archives. But it was increasingly clear that ''apparently'' and ''from the looks of things'' were not only appropriate modifiers to apply to Max's activities, they were (if anything) far too weak. Max clearly couldn't do something simply if he could rather, with a little thought, complicate it beyond understanding. So who knew what he was really up to? For that matter, who knew who he really was, and not as a matter of surface identity, either? It was questionable if he even knew himself.

Only the problem plainly wasn't Max. It was her. She'd held the power to squash him, probably. Certainly she still had the choice to walk away. She kept telling herself she was explicitly undecided about what to do about him, right? So what was she doing here?

Maybe he reminded her of her brother.

Still, it was developing into a nice day, if you liked this sort of thing, and if you liked mobs, of course. Leen was finding she didn't mind the excuse to be out for the Running. It might be overwrought and it might be garish, and the whole idea was without a doubt more than vaguely ridiculous, but there was certainly nothing else like it. It wouldn't be anything like the time she'd gone with her grandfather, the famous year that a full score of celebrants had run the oars of a galley in center channel while being flanked by a pod of killer whales. The whales had been preoccupied with keeping an eye on the pair of cuttlefish ahead of them, jockeying for position for the moment when the restraints came off at the exit of the Tongue, so several of the people who'd missed their footing or had gotten smacked by oars and had fallen in had actually survived unscathed, and most of the others had made it through with the loss of only minor parts of their anatomy to the whales' distracted snacking.

Her grandfather had disapproved of the bloodletting, of course, but had been quite open with her afterwards about its soporific effect on the masses and its consequent value as a tool of state. And no one could deny that, in the context of the Running at least, the actual carnage was not the central point of the celebration. The spectacle of the massed creatures of the sea proceeding in solemn panoply to pay homage to the new Emperor, as one of the several ritualized manifestations of his power and majesty, was a sight in the wonders-of-the-world class. At least in the better years. Who knew how it would turn out this time around? Advances in sanitation and sewage disposal since the last Knitting had reduced the miasma from the Tongue, so perhaps not as many of the sea creatures would sicken or pass out before completing their transit, but the water was still not a place any sane person would willingly dunk themselves. Even putting yourself in a barge at ringside was hazardous enough, prestige notwithstanding.

No, Leen would have surely drawn the line at that, if that was what Max had asked of her. It was just as well he'd suggested she do what she'd been considering anyway, use her pass to the Emperor's grandstand. She'd have as good a view of the Tongue Water as anyone, she'd be up away from the vapors, and she'd be able to keep an eye out for Max himself on the bridge level below. When Max appeared, or when, more precisely (if she was really going to align herself with his instructions) Shaa appeared, she would be positioned to try to join them.

What she hadn't considered, scanning the crowd below yet again, was how difficult it would be to spot Max in the first place, even though he'd told her where they'd be standing. Was this fated to be her life? Searching for Max in various venues? She might as well circulate again, spend some time nodding at the other guests and picking one or two she knew better than others to make approving remarks with about the weather. At least the Scapula didn't seem to be around. He was another complication she surely didn't need right at the present. Although as focused as he was on climbing the ladder of power, it was a bit surprising he wasn't here at its momentary center. Well, perhaps he had some grand entrance scheduled for later.

"What do you think this is, anyway?" Favored-of-the-Gods demanded, staring at the bird on the Great Karlini's shoulder. "What are you supposed to be disguised as, a pirate?"

"This would need to be a parrot," Karlini said testily. "But it's not a parrot. It's a seagull."

"I can *see* it's a seagull. You don't have an eyepatch either, but—"

"Nervous are you, Favored one?" said Haddo, appearing suddenly from between the traces of a stalled wagon to rejoin them. "Not fidgety am I."

Favored wheeled on him, his hands planted on his hips and his jaw protruding. "Oh, yeah? Which one of us has been scuttling back and forth for the last half hour, doing his best to wear a groove in the pavement?"

"I have cleared the way," announced Svin from ahead of them.

And so he had. The other three filed and skittered up behind him into the aisle he was leaving through the press. This was scarcely, Svin had been reflecting, the acme of realized potential for a warrior born. It was becoming ever more clear, though, that birth had very little to do with how one actually lived out his life. Here he was, after all, in the big city for the big festival; a thief's paradise, a reaver's playground, a brawler's delight. But what was he doing? Holding down a regular job.

It was a perversion of his heritage.

On the other hand, it was not only comfortable, it was habit-forming.

Which was to say, Svin understood he was having a crisis of identity.

He also had before him the example of where all this civilization might lead. Up to his neck in plots and schemes, that was where. To be honest, though, that was a simplistic argument. There was plenty of plotting back home in the lands of the frozen north, even on such a basic level as trying to outwit the animal one happened to be hunting for dinner. Was plotting the natural tendency of sentience? Even more so, was intricacy of plots perhaps a measure of one's level of intelligence?

A new thought occurred to Svin with a twinge of dread. Perhaps what he was really becoming was a philosopher.

"Here stop," hissed Haddo. "Scatter should we now. Proceed to rendezvous will I, while—"

"We've got the plan," snapped Favored. "Just let's go ahead and do it already."

Haddo spat something back in Lower Pocklish and vanished down the intersecting street. By Karlini's estimation they were several blocks from the waterfront, in the midst of a throng that was thinning somewhat as folks jostled closer to the bank of the Tongue Water for the festivities getting underway. "Just as well you didn't try to fly your floater-module," Karlini said to Favored. "You'd still never make it halfway down the block."

"Then what the hell am I doing here? Don't tell me, dammit, I know, I know."

Svin was back in motion drifting after Haddo along the street. He cast a quick glance of disgusted reproach over his shoulder at Karlini. Karlini grunted and resumed his own meandering path as Favored turned back to rejoin Wroclaw with the equipment wagon stalled somewhere back behind them in the traffic. *I really need to get up some enthusiasm for this job,* Karlini thought. If he was going to be haphazard about it, he might as well have stayed at home.

Except he didn't really *have* a home at the moment. So what was there to lose?

Aside from the obvious, of course.

It had been a surprise when Wroclaw and Haddo had opened up with the story about Dortonn, the ice sorcerer, and his quest for revenge here in the south. The episode of the icebergs on the River Oolvaan had now come clearer, in retrospect, but the subtlety of craft Dortonn had displayed there did not diminish through now having a specific culprit to tie the incident to. Was it a good sign that Karlini *had* been the one to triumph in that engagement? Not necessarily. It had clearly been a shot across the bow, an announcement of Dortonn's presence to those who knew how to read the message. Even Karlini's victory had been accomplished through main strength rather than any particular cleverness on his part.

Forewarned this time Dortonn should be significantly better equipped.

Karlini could hear Haddo's voice muttering in a low tinny tone in his ear, courtesy of Favored's short-range transmission device. Haddo had almost balked at that part of the plan, but with the crowds likely to be as congested as they in fact had turned out to be the problem of keeping in visual contact had begun to weigh on him. The fact that Favored's gadget, with no magical emanations, should be invisible to Dortonn's inevitable security probe had been the deciding factor.

"Nearing am I site of message," Haddo whispered. "Back from waterfront by block it is, with boards covered are windows."

Karlini could see the place also, although Haddo with his short stature was not in evidence. Favored should be moving into position in whatever passed for an alley behind the building, or on the roof if no alley was available, and Svin—there Svin was, loitering across the street having a deep conversation with his sword. Karlini strolled ahead down the block paying no attention to any of them. In fact, he *wasn't* paying much attention to them, at least not directly. Sifting the cryptic information from a battery of passive probes was enough to keep him busy.

"Ow—there, watch where you're going!" said someone in front of Karlini, or perhaps partially underfoot. Karlini grunted and maintained stride.

"Inside am I now," reported Haddo. "Derelict is interior, decrepit and with cobwebs hung. No sign see I of Dortonn."

Dortonn's instructions, arriving earlier that morning by an anonymous messenger hired off the street, had been clear, however. Haddo moved in from the doorway. Like the windows, the door had been boarded shut, but the promised loose board and the gap at the lower edge of the sprung frame had allowed entry, although even for Haddo it had been a tight fit. No doubt this was all part of whatever clever plan Dortonn had coined for keeping himself safe while still getting his hands on—

Something creaked loudly in the gloom. "Come, come, Fist of Dortonn," said an echoing voice. "Straight ahead."

"Always had you nasty sense of humor," Haddo called out. Haddo's night vision was certainly good enough to show him the blank wall he would have plowed into had he followed the instruction. Even if he'd had his eyes closed, there were still his instincts, too. Still, as Dortonn cackled to himself over his own attempt at amusement, Haddo dodged a pile of waste provided by an earlier occupant and edged through a sagging doorway.

Dortonn was wearing a short-sleeved tunic tucked into loose traveling pants. His arms were bare, which should be helpful. Of course, Dortonn was used to the frozen north, so even the seasonal climate this distance south would seem tropically sultry. "Meet now do we at last face-to-face," Haddo stated.

Dortonn ended his laughter with a choke and a cough and a sparkling gesture toward Haddo. "I am not in a mood for banter," he said, stepping closer across the small inner room. "Where is Pod Dall? Give the ring to me now."

Haddo noted that ice had once again encased his feet. Well, that was not exactly unexpected. Still, his hand was free. Haddo reached into his cloak and felt for the ring.

"No, get away, get away," said Tildamire Mont, trying to dodge the attentions of another street vendor waving yet another appalling treat-on-a-stick in her direction. She didn't even *like* fish. So why had she bothered to go out for this Festival of All Fish thing in the first place? True, Roni had told her not to miss it. But if it was such a big deal, why hadn't Roni wanted to be there?

She hadn't wanted to leave Roni alone either, with everyone else having disappeared on their mysterious errands or heading out to the waterfront for the festivities. Who knew *what* they were really up to—no one seemed to be communicating any more these days. But Roni had brushed off her arguments, reminding Tildy that she'd been at this business long enough that nothing surprised her. Roni also wanted to have enough peace and quiet to concentrate on some serious work for a change. She'd been talking about a new unifying hypothesis, something she was calling the Mediator mechanism. "Intermediary agents that translate your command into the smaller bits the magic organelles can actually handle; somewhat similar to translating a language," that's what Roni had said, anyway. True, it did sound all by itself like something that needed translation from a foreign language, but that wasn't really the point. The point was that Roni was responsible for herself, and if she wanted to stay and work what did Tildy have to say about it?

The deciding factor, though, had been her brother. Or more precisely, the *lack* of her brother. He certainly wasn't responsible for himself, not if he'd gone off on a simple errand and never come back. Tildy could do two things at once—track him down at whatever club he'd disappeared to, and take in the sights of today's spectacular while she as at it. Except it hadn't been that simple.

Tildy had stopped first to pick up Dalya Hazeel at her establishment, but the place had been closed for the Running and Dalya was nowhere to be found. Of the other clubs on the way to the waterfront Dalya had mentioned to her earlier, most were closed as well, and those that weren't professed to know nothing. Tildy had finally found herself close to the Tongue Water with nothing to show for it but the exercise. She had gone ahead and found the address Jurtan had been sent to, and the door hadn't even been locked, but the only person in the place had been an old caretaker who hadn't been of much help. Yes, he thought he might have seen somebody like Jurtan around in the afternoon yesterday, but he didn't know for certain and anyway he was sure this possibly mythical person would have left.

Maybe he'd hung around to get a good position for the festival. Some of the prime sites were on the big bridge nearby, the one with the Emperor's grandstand. As long as she was in the vicinity, Tildy thought it was worth a try. She dodged another street hawker and began forcing her way up the boulevard toward the bridge rising a block ahead.

The grandstand did indeed offer a commanding view. If it served virtually all of the time as a harbormaster's lookout and command center, it had still been transformed quite effectively for the present into a gala spectator gallery in the sky. The bunting and festive effigies of sea creatures that adorned the walls and pylons also helped to conceal the detachment of troops and sorcerers deployed around the margin and on the subdeck under the floor. Another party of invited guests appeared at the top of the staircase from the main level of the bridge below, having made it through the cordon and the checkpoints, and headed with relief toward the refreshment tables.

But he was here to observe the niceties and to show the flag, of course, not to lollygag. Phlinn Arol again raised a hand and waved at the crowd. From this height, and his position at the center of the bridge and accordingly above the midpoint of the Tongue Water, his perspective of the scene below was that of an endless carpet of massed spectators interrupted only by the surface of the water itself, and not even entirely by that. There were the ranks of festive barges at the banks, moored carefully off the navigation channel, and then the much more daring vessels, coracles to two-masters to racing galleys, that were darting back and forth through the open channel itself. None of the swimmers had obviously entered the water, although it wasn't certain he'd be able to spot them from this vantage point.

He had picked out two of the lure-boats and was scouting for a third, as a way of giving himself something to concentrate on in the midst of the endless roar of the crowd, when he became aware of someone else at his elbow watching along with him. Was it time for his traditional empowerment of the Emperor?

No, not yet. "Enjoying the spectacle, cousin?" inquired Phlinn Arol.

"I suppose," said the other. "It's a nice day for it, at least. Someone's dealt away with the coastal fog."

"Not you, I take it?"

"Weather is scarcely my forte." The fellow rested his hands on the rail and gazed out at the throng. "You, though, are certainly fulfilling your civic duty, I must say. At least as far as our relationship with the power structure of the mundane world is concerned."

"We *did* make a pact," Phlinn observed. "Someone has to keep it going."

"Your dedication to the public good is admirable."

"No more than any of us should be doing, hmm?"

"Bravo," the man said conversationally. "You'll pardon me if I infer an implied comment between your remark and the actual state of affairs?"

"Infer to your content," said Phlinn. "Even for

those of us who know where we stand the world seems increasingly a muddle. Perhaps especially for those who know where they stand. In a breakdown of order, stances, no matter how principled or well-founded, can start to seem rather beside the point.''

''There are some who agitate for a turn to a strong central leadership.''

''There are some who point out a decided lack of strong leaders. The days of the giants among us are gone.''

''Not necessarily,'' said Gashanatantra. ''Atsing and her crowd may be burnt out and retired, but that isn't to say there aren't some in the current generation who might not be up to the job, given a chance to grow into it. Neither of us are exactly youngsters. Did you know that Byron recruited *me?* No, I didn't think you did.''

Phlinn raised the other arm for a change, and was rewarded by a new surging bellow from the multitude. ''That *is* interesting,'' he allowed after a moment, ''but scarcely germane. As close as I was to him, and as much as I try to keep his legacy alive, Byron was not exactly a great leader himself. He was rather a bit too much given to acting on impulse, and when he did pause for consideration in advance he had a tendency toward convolution over clarity. Perhaps that's why he liked *you.* Anyway it's all moot.''

''We need Byron,'' Gashanatantra stated. ''He designed the infrastructure, he may be the only one who could still disentangle the state it's grown into.''

Gash was still leaning on the guardrail with his eyes fixed on the display below, but Phlinn Arol knew better than to assume that he wasn't still watching *his* reaction as well. ''Byron's dead,'' Phlinn said. ''He's been dead for a long time.''

''No,'' said Gash. ''No, I'm not so certain he is.''

''Is that librarian woman around?'' Shaa asked.

''Why,'' said Max, glancing around, ''do you see her?''

"Noo," Shaa drawled. "But since you are obviously up to something, I was nibbling about for hints concerning its nature."

Max opened his mouth to respond, but just then the volume of sound jumped again. Above them and down at the center of the bridge, the Emperor-Designate had mounted his podium of state. Another figure was with him: Phlinn Arol. Together they raised their arms. A nimbus of golden light settled over them in a blare of trumpets, the multitude roared, and then far away down the Tongue Water another wave of commotion began to roll toward them, given by its magnitude and distance the character of an approaching storm. Around the far bend and beyond the next major bridge to the south, in the center of the channel, the water began to mound up and drift toward them. Behind the mound a wave curled toward each shore.

"Look at that," said Max. "I guess they're not extinct after all."

A spray of mist and water erupted into the air from the fore-point of the traveling bulge. "The lure-masters will be the toast of some serious festivities tonight," Shaa agreed.

"They won't be the only ones. Can you believe those idiots?"

"They *will* be the only ones," Shaa said, "unless these guys are better than they look and somehow manage to survive." On either side of the huge whale, a small pack of people had appeared, trying to mount the crest of the wave on swim-boards. On the left, two of them collided and went over, sweeping away a third. Several knots of furiously paddling celebrants were attaining the churning wave-top, however, and rising to their feet atop their boards. Then the leviathan passed under the center span of the south bridge.

The wave riders were frantically scattering to avoid the bridge pilings and the few bottom-protruding elements of architectural substructure. As the head of the whale appeared from the bridge's shadow, though, something separated itself from the edge of the deck and hurtled toward it. A person? Yes, indeed. He or she landed on the whale's back behind the blowhole and scrabbled frantically, but somehow managed to hold on.

Behind the leviathan a devilfish broke the surface, its wide leathery wings flapping, and quickly nosed back under. It was followed into view, however, by a pair of breaching swordfish. The swordfish seemed to hang glistening in the air free of the water for an exceptional length of time, before abruptly reversing end-for-end and disappearing again into the water. Behind them now, even farther out, were the first of the cuttlefish. "This does have the potential of being a reasonable outing at that," Shaa acknowledged. "I—Maximillian?"

Max had given him the slip.

Shaa forced his way away from the rail. Four or five people back the crowd thinned out considerably; after all, folks wanted to see, not just hear the cheers of others. Damn Max!—where was he? Or, more to the point, what was he up to? He—what?

Out of the corner of his eye, Shaa spotted someone hurrying toward him from the stairs to the viewing platform, someone not only hurrying but waving. Shaa turned and inclined an eyebrow in lieu of an actual wave back. Well, he *had* had a hunch she'd be around. Why was it not reassuring to find he'd been right? "Are you enjoying yourself, Madame Archivist?" he greeted her.

"I—" said Leen, but just then the bridge rocked, the roadbed shuddering underfoot. The spectators at the rails hooted wildly at the arrival at their station of the leviathan.

"Yes," said Shaa, "indeed it is a spectacle. A sorry one to miss, too, seeing as one is already here in the first place. Which is to say, to what do I owe the pleasure of your company at the moment?"

Leen stared at him. "I can't believe he talked me into this," she muttered.

"I assume we're discussing Maximillian? Many's the

time I've had that same thought. Just what is it he *has* talked you into?''

''It didn't seem like much,'' she said, resting her hand on his shoulder. ''He wanted me to stay with you while he went off to meet someone else.''

In point of fact, Max was barely fifty feet away, but was concealed from Shaa's view by one of the grandstand level's support pylons. He was, however, not alone. ''Here it is,'' Max said.

The other clenched and unclenched his good hand. The other arm was encased in a cast and splint. ''Give it to me.''

''You should be able to feel it from where you are, right?'' Max told him. ''You can tell it's the real article. And don't think about doublecrossing me and taking it off my body, because I've got the safeguards bound to me, just like we said. No, you do your part and I'll release it.''

The other guy was sweating and appeared clearly the worse for recent wear that extended significantly beyond the busted arm; not at all the sort of picture gods liked to cut, in Max's experience. Max wasn't complaining. Whatever had happened to him had apparently pushed him over the edge into agreeing to Max's proposed deal.

The guy's teeth snapped shut with a clack. ''Very well,'' he said, with obvious reluctance. He withdrew a small slate from his jacket, jabbed at it with his finger while consulting it closely, made a few final passes, and then shoved the thing back in his pocket. ''There, it's done. The curse is removed.''

''What's the matter?'' Leen said.

''All of a sudden I confess I feel rather strange.'' The world was reeling, Shaa's insides were rippling, his heart was—what *was* his heart doing? Shaa bent over and put his hands on his knees.

''*Is* it your heart?''

His head was hurting now, too; he felt drunk. Overloaded with excess oxygen? Leen still had him by the shoulder, but the site of her grip was tingling. Some sort of probe? "Damn you, Max," Shaa breathed. "What *are* you up to?"

Leen wasn't looking at him, though, she was gazing away up the bridge toward the grandstand. And not just gazing, either. Now she was nodding.

"Okay," said Max. Leen's gesture toward him should have meant that she'd run the probe he'd given her and had confirmed the status of the curse. He subvocalized his own trigger-word. A small whirlwind and a swirl of heat danced on his palm, then subsided. "Here it is," he said, and handed it over.

"I should blast you now," said Jardin, shoving the ring in his pocket.

"I could have let loose against you, too," Max reminded him, "which was the whole reason for doing this thing under the feet of the Emperor and all your lollygagging god-pals in the first place. I—"

But Jardin was already striding away. Just as well. This wasn't the time for gabbing, it was time to get back to Shaa and have it out. Max darted out from behind the pylon and began making his way back along the bridge.

There was no warning, only a flicker of light over his shoulder and a quick fluorescence in his detection field. Then a massive <WHOOM!> burst out from behind, and a gust of flaming hellfire slammed into him and lifted him off his feet and sent him hurtling in a long dive toward the rippling surface of the bridge.

Haddo withdrew his hand from the cloak and extended the small plain ring to Dortonn. Dortonn snatched it away and clenched his fist over it. He allowed himself a quick supercilious smirk. "Once a loyal flunky, always the same, is it not so, O my Fist?"

"As say you must it be, Great Dortonn."

"We must speak again," Dortonn said. He took a single step back and vanished. Vanished? No, Haddo realized, as a trapdoor in the floor slammed shut behind Dortonn's falling head. Just as well, since the ice encasing Haddo's own feet still had him locked solidly to the floorboards, even though the boots Favored had equipped with the internal heating coils were now radiating for all they were worth. And Haddo had reached the end of his mental count of ten.

The dark room suddenly lit. Slices of glaring white lashed up from the gaps in the floorboards and sprayed up through the dusty air and laid a fiery grid across the ceiling. The expected shriek of pain from below was simultaneous. Haddo had never doubted Favored, not really, but it was always remarkable when one of his tricky devices did its act. With Karlini's magical camouflage radiating the signature of the entrapped Pod Dall, the false ring had obviously felt right to Dortonn. It wouldn't have held up to serious probing for long, but it hadn't had to. It had been long enough. Favored's quick fuse had now run to its end and ignited the white phosphorus band itself, and the capsule of clinging fire.

Dortonn was wailing from below as the light source began to whip back and forth. Haddo yanked again and this time one foot came free, then the other. The sound of Dortonn was suddenly joined by the sound of splintering wood from behind Haddo at the front of the building. The front door exploded inward, and then standing next to Haddo was Svin. But now Haddo could hear churning water, too—too much water for a single swimmer. He waved his hand at the floor. The noise from below was swamped by the quick grind of an invisible saw against wood and the trapdoor and a chunk of floorboards an arm's span across converted themselves into shavings.

Through the new hole under the building were tarred pilings and lapping water and a murky bank of mud—obviously an old pier. In the center between the pilings, a twenty or thirty foot drop down, Haddo could see in the phosphorus glow a stretch of frothing water, but no Dortonn. The glow was coming from just out of sight, and it was receding. Haddo poked his head down and craned his neck. A boat—a small house-boat—was just moving out of the hiding place and breaking through a concealing mat of woven netting into the sunlit Tongue Water channel beyond. A bub-bling wake led to the houseboat's stern. "To the wa-terfront," said Haddo. "Head him off we must."

But Svin was already gone. Or at least going—a serious leap took him over the crater in the floor, a huge sword-swing bashed out the wall into the next room, and then there was nothing to see but a new cloud of swirling dust. Haddo wheeled and made for the street through the first gap Svin had left in the front wall and door.

Karlini swung another elbow and the seagull batted its wings, and the people in front of him reluctantly parted again. One more row and he'd be at the edge of the wharf. As nearly as he could determine, he'd gone straight from the rendezvous location toward the Tongue Water. The sides of the channel below were lined with decorated barges and other small craft, but they were obviously not what he was looking for. Where was—

A muttering had started behind him. The festively dressed spectators were hugging themselves and stamping suddenly against the boards and looking up at the clear sky. And then Karlini felt it, too—the wave of cold, a chill harsh enough that it felt like an abrupt dip in a vat of ice. Not from the heavens, though.

From underfoot.

Karlini pushed aside the final woman ahead, took a quick glance to verify his suspicion, and then, even more quickly, before his better judgment had a chance to kick in, vaulted over the low railing. The seagull cast an incredulous glance at Karlini, seeming to ques-tion whether he'd taken leave of his species identity, and flapped convulsively off his shoulder and away from him into the air. Below Karlini for a second was open slack water, and next to the open area a barge in the shape of a trumpeter swan occupied by a group of spectators in the process of falling over as their vessel was shoved rudely away. The space was immediately filled by the vessel that had done the shoving; undoubtedly the houseboat Haddo was shouting about in his ear, appearing from beneath the pier with the remains of a mudbank draped over its prow and dank mist freezing to its superstructure. As he landed atop the cabin, Karlini noted behind him in the stern gallery a howling human figure writhing in a pool of piercing white and orange flame.

Unexpectedly the boat lifted; another bow wake from whatever creature was passing down the Tongue. The stern quarter of the boat bashed against a piling, scraped with hair-raising intent, and caught up. The lee side of the breaker poured over the gunwales, mounting quickly almost to the top of the cabin. Karlini felt a swirl of trigger-releases from the figure in the stern. A matrix locked into place, and with a blast of arctic wind the water atop the ship froze solid.

The boat staggered under the weight of the ice. Dortonn, now trapped in a bubble inside the ice himself, was continuing to struggle with the fire that enveloped him, although from the cloud of steam that was hiding him from view the ice might be helping him out. Even if Dortonn was merely lashing back out of reflex or was being assisted by previously programmed automatic safeguards, the tactical situation might very well be shifting in his favor. Karlini disliked causing death or severe personal injury through direct magical action, but perhaps this was a case that warranted it. Shaa had taught him how to inflict acute cirrhosis, and sudden heart failure was always a classic. Karlini braced himself on the canted roof and reeled off the proximate parameters. Except—why did his stomach seem to be sinking?

Karlini looked off to the side and immediately grabbed for the nearest handhold. The wharf with its gape-mouthed crowd was retreating, that much wasn't surprising . . . but it was retreating *down* as much as away! The boat rocked again, more violently, and traversed an arc that must have been fifteen feet wide. Karlini had a quick view straight down at the foaming water and the sparkling wall rising up out of it.

The houseboat was embedded in the top of a growing iceberg.

Shaa and Leen were both looking straight toward the blast. In the quick moment before Shaa's outsweeping arm carried them both down to hug the pavement, they could see the closest pillars supporting the observation deck disappear in red fireballs and clouds of black smoke and an expanding hailstorm of hurtling stone and fragmented steel. The bridge was shuddering beneath them—but was it starting to lean? Would the entire structure go down?

Shaa lifted his head for another update. In the midst of the billowing smoke, he could see the grandstand platform collapsing in twisted sections onto the main roadbed. Part of the far edge was still in place up above, the charges on those pylons perhaps having failed to detonate. A vast shrieking clang of metal and the cry of victims made pandemonium around the major part of the wreck, though—and now a chunk of the maindeck and the adjoining southside railing were separating out and tumbling free toward the water.

A banner of flaming letters was rising from the smoke, its message something about liberation and self-determination and free rights that seemed somewhat irrelevant in the present context. Not that too many in the immediate vicinity were spending the time to take it in—the part of the crowd that could stand had begun to surge away from the center toward the banks off the bridge, pressing with increasing force against the equally packed mass on the approaches and the shore. Making their way upstream, though, in a purposeful charge toward the main mess, were a group of armed men, whether police or troops or Imperial guards was impossible to tell. The detachment that had surrounded the observation deck had disintegrated into a rabble of individuals still pulling themselves dazedly out of the wreckage or trapped in its midst. Some of them did seem to be pulling themselves together and reorganizing, though. "We'd better get out of the way!" yelled Leen.

She clearly *was* yelling, yet Shaa's hearing at the moment was also clearly unequal to the task of comprehension since meaning was lost behind a vast ringing. It was like old times. Also like old times was the usual leading question—"Where's Max?" Shaa said, yelling himself. Max hadn't been *under* the platform when it had started to drop, but he had been squarely in the path of one burst of fiery debris.

Then Shaa felt a hand on his collar yanking him to his feet. He swung on the person behind him, his hand going to the sword he was still wearing out of habit in his belt, even though the workout of actually employing it was beyond him at present, but felt another hand grab his arm and yank it behind his back out of the way. The point of someone else's sword hung before his face. Manacles clanged behind him. "Get them off this bridge!" someone else was hollering.

"What is the meaning of this?" Shaa asked reasonably. "The priority at the moment would seem to be disaster relief, not apprehending bystanders."

"Shut up, scum!" the man with the sword in his face said, and then whacked him over the side of the head with the flat of his blade for good measure. Next to Shaa, Leen was similarly being dragged aside. If it was a case of mistaken identity it would all be straightened out in due time, unless this was some sort of quarantine or witchhunt. But what if it is wasn't a mistake?

Where *was* Max?

It wasn't the blast; that much he could have ridden with. No, it was obviously more sheer back luck. Although it could have been worse. If it had been a twenty-pound chunk of flying pylon that had walloped Max in the back, instead of probably only half as much, the thing might very well have overwhelmed his personal protection field and continued straight though his spine to exit through his chest. As it was, the projectile had merely knocked the wind and momentary consciousness out of him while smashing him to the roadbed.

And leaving a good-sized indentation in his back, too, Max thought dazedly. He twisted, letting the piece of bridge roll off his shoulders, and pushed himself to his hands and knees. For some reason none of those trademark flips that would send him in one graceful motion to his toe-tips seemed quite accessible at the moment. Max shook his head. He should be trying to help rescue survivors, he should be—

Wait a minute. That explosion had been no accident. Someone had planned this . . . those terrorists, that must be it. What if they had a followup attack planned? He should be preparing. . . .

No, that wasn't it. Something was nagging at his mind, something remaining perversely just out of his grasp. On the ground in front of him, Max noticed a full head of hair lying free of someone's body, with a hat just beyond—some poor soul obviously scalped by another fragment of flying debris. Where was the victim?—oh. He really was dazed. The hair was the wig from his own disguise, and the hat the same, and now he noted that the putty and greasepaint he'd applied to his face had been scraped clean by his encounter with the cobblestones.

There was certainly a lot of shouting going on around him, even above the shrieks of trapped victims and the roar of the fires and the bashing as the bridge seemed to be pulling apart behind him. Where was Shaa—and Leen! And Phlinn Arol had been atop the grandstand, the Emperor also, and who knew how many others. None of the voices sounded like anyone he knew. Except possibly one, louder than the rest, bellowing, of all things, "There he is!"

Something was waving in front of his face. The point of a sword? Max looked up. He was surrounded by a solid ring of soldiers. They were *all* pointing swords at him. Then the two men in front of him parted and let a new person stride importantly out. *Now* Max recognized him; it was the same person who'd been shouting. "Maximillian V'Dirapal," said Gadol V'Nora, leader of the Hand, "you are under arrest."

"Arrest?" Max said groggily. "On what the hell kind of trumped-up charge is it this time?"

Gadol's thin smile grew somewhat wider. "That should be obvious. You should scarcely have begun consorting with terrorists, much less advanced to be their leader."

Hands were relieving Max of his sword, others were dragging him to his feet, and now his arms were being lashed behind his back. Through the circle enclosing him he could now see down the confused bridge toward the shore, could see Shaa and Leen being hustled toward the open door of a waiting carriage by a similar detachment of forces. He thought Leen might have cast him a direct glance over her shoulder; regardless, though, it was finally time to go into action. Max waggled his fingers to limber up and subvocalized a triggerword—

BLAM! The blow to his head threw him to the side. He would have gone back to the ground if it hadn't been for the hands holding him upright and the swords poking him in the back. Still, someone had obviously had an arm free to bash him with a mace. His own hands were feeling cramped, confined. Gooey? Another figure stepped into view. "None of that, Max," said Chas V'Halila, the sorcerer. "You want me to cast your mouth in plaster, too?"

Max glared at him, feeling the material encasing his fingers harden into stone. Gadol was saying something about getting off the bridge, but a flicker of bright motion from off to the left caught Max's eye. Beyond the bridge, heading down the river toward them at a hefty clip, was—what? What the hell *was* that?

This made no sense, no sense at all. Leen might not have known Max very well, or for very long, and she might indeed have her own solid grievances with him, and he might unquestionably be involved in more than his share of unlikely escapades, but being publicly associated with terrorists—being publicly associated with *anyone*—was clearly the direct opposite of his style. Subterfuge in the shadows was his mode of operation, intrigue behind the scene.

On its face it made no sense, but that only meant the surface was not the appropriate level at which to look. What else had—

Oh! That broadsheet campaign! Suddenly it *did* make sense—Max's enemy had resorted to a program of character assassination to link him in the public mind to the terrorists and their depredations. That implied that this enemy was associated with the terrorists in some way, if they weren't actually the same. Max had served as cover for the terrorists and their goals, and Max was now being taken off the playing board as an active factor.

But that was far too abstract. As the men dragged her toward the end of the bridge, she could see Max back over her shoulder and hear the taunts of the leader of the band surrounding him. Even if Max got away, he'd been branded as the head of the terrorists—and with such an outrageous act to his credit as the one just accomplished he'd be ripped to shreds by the first crowd that caught sight of his face. And if he didn't escape, he'd clearly never leave custody alive.

But what did *she* have to do with it—and Shaa?

On the step up to the carriage she paused, straining against the hands shoving her inside for one last glance backward. Max was still beset by his captors. Off to the side, though, rising out of the river, was a glinting white wall. No, not a wall, a cliff—a *moving* cliff. What could that—

But then the hands thrust harder. Leen lost her balance and went sprawling after Shaa into the carriage. A set of outstretched legs kept her from falling completely to the floor, although she did manage to bang her head on the opposite windowsill.

"Ah," said the owner of the legs, "at last you grace me with your personal attention."

The owner was not Shaa. Leen twisted and looked up.

"Don't worry about old Maximillian," continued the Scapula. "He is in the best of hands. As are you, my dear, and of course my dear brother."

It was trite and lame and stock, she knew that, but it was the only retort she could muster at the moment. "What is the meaning of this?"

"Why, it's all very simple," said the Scapula. "I'm about to get some good news, and I thought the two of you would like to help me celebrate."

In for a penny, Karlini had figured, when Haddo had asked him for his backup against Dortonn, in for a pound. But he hadn't counted on anything like this. Alone on the top of an iceberg in the middle of the Running of Squids; alone, that is, save for a pain-crazed powerhouse of a sorcerer who obviously didn't care who else he took down with him. For all his flailing and trying to stay out of the way, Karlini had still had a leg ensnared by a looping tongue of ice. The stuff he'd been hurling at Dortonn had apparently not had full effect, either, unless Dortonn was being uncharacteristically active for someone whose heart had stopped. With the clinging fire still eating at his skin, too, and entombed as he was underneath the sweep of ice, kidney and liver failure might not be Dortonn's primary worries at the moment anyway.

If Karlini could get his leg free, it might be just as well to cut his losses and get away.

After all, the navigation channel wasn't all that deep. If Dortonn's iceberg kept growing, which it was clearly doing now under its own self-feeding chain reaction, it wouldn't be long before it grounded itself. The grounding wouldn't be the real problem. That would be the brisk flow-tide current pushing against it, the current and its tendency to tip the precarious iceberg over on its side. Abruptly the iceberg quivered violently, a high shrill grating shriek radiating through its mass and into the air. Karlini scrabbled for purchase and held on, feeling as though his bones were trying to pop their way out from under his skin.

Then, in an act of significant mercy, the scraping stopped. The iceberg, however, did not. It had cleared the momentary shoals. The fact that the iceberg had come that close to grounding in the middle of the channel, though, did not augur well for the future. Karlini decided to let Dortonn stew on his own and went to work on his leg. A few shaped-charge blasts should crack the ice sheet without losing him his foot. . . .

A quick shadow passed over him, and in the corner of his eye, a glinting object. ''Favored?'' Karlini said.

The shiny object, a huffing brass sphere, banked around him and headed away, trailing a string of white steamclouds in tight little balls. ''I could use some help here, Favored,'' called Karlini.

The ball kept going.

The plug in Karlini's ear popped and hissed. ''I just got a priority call from the bridge,'' Favored's voice crackled.

Bridge? *What* bridge? ''Favored!''

Then the noises from the plug stopped entirely. Favored had cut him off. The berg itself was busily creaking and groaning, of course, a cacophony Karlini's present efforts against the ice were only serving to increase, but suddenly there was a new additional sound, closer to hand and more regular; an added noise of cracking and chipping. It was—

A hand appeared over the spire of ice encasing the stern, then another matching hand next to it bearing a dagger. The dagger plunged into the ice with the same regular sound—which was, of course, the sound of someone cutting his way up a sheer wall of ice. The associated head rose into view between the hands. ''I should know by now that this kind of thing is always happening around you people,'' said Svin.

"Uh, Svin?" Karlini called. "Would you give me a hand here?"

Svin, who had been looking down through the ice at Dortonn, glanced up at Karlini. His eyes widened. Karlini squinted back at him, then twisted to look back over his shoulder. His own eyes went big, and his jaw dropped for good measure.

Looming ahead of them was obviously Favored's bridge. The center section, shrouded in flames and oily black smoke, was just slightly below the level of Karlini's present perch. As he gaped at it, a section of wreckage tore free and went tumbling away toward the surface of the water.

Actually, come to think of it, Karlini probably didn't need Svin's help after all. He kicked violently, and the ice encasing his leg, chipped and abraded down already by his careful employment of pulse-bursts, flew off in shards. His leg came free. The released force sent him rolling back on his side, temporarily without a good handhold, and as he skidded backward on the slick ice sheet covering the contorted roof of the houseboat, the iceberg began to shudder again beneath him, even more vigorously than the last time. The peak whiplashed forward. "Aah!" Karlini began to yell.

Svin was too far away, though, and Karlini already had too much momentum. He felt the cold of the ice leave his back and felt the rush of air in his face, his stomach began to drop out from under him, and as he continued to twist in the air he caught a glimpse of the surface of the water far too far below, a group of dots that might be sea lions scattering in confusion as the iceberg bore down upon them.

What he needed to do was concentrate on spellcraft. His mind, though, was perversely fixating on the last time he had found himself in midair over a substantial body of water. The reflection was not encouraging. There was no giant bird around this time to pluck him from mid-fall.

Svin, used to working around ice from his youth in terrain whose primary characteristic was frost, hung on to his embedded dagger with one hand and found purchase for the other in a crevasse. The large tremor died. The iceberg lurched forward again. Beneath him and ahead, though, the ice was caving in. Svin eased himself back and turned his head aside. With his face averted, the storm of jagged icicles that suddenly erupted as the depression in the ice stopped collapsing and instead blew out did no more than slice the skin away from his neck and puncture his ear, rather than putting out an eye. The dagger began to shift and his other hand was now clutching nothing but a detached and crumbling ice cube, and even though the pulverized ice in the air had produced a sudden whiteout Svin knew what lay at the bottom of the fresh ice crater anyway, so he flung himself forward into the hole, turned in the air, and did his best to aim.

Tildy Mont had seen her share of preposterous and overblown situations since encountering the Karlinis and their associates for the first time, but the present sequence clearly set some new sort of record. Not that she'd found anyone she knew. She'd just kept making her way through the crowd, and then the proclamations had started and the trumpets and cheers, and so she'd settled for just watching the aquatic procession from the place she'd squeezed herself into on the bridge.

But then the bridge had tried to blow itself to pieces.

Tildy was far off to the side, merely on the abutment, really, so she hadn't been hurt; more just shaken up. In the relative still after the blasts the cries and screams of the people further along had come clearly through, though, and then people started to stampede in every direction and she was caught up and spun around in the press. She couldn't see a thing except the rioting people immediately around her, and then the dust rose and the smoke from the explosions drifted over and she realized that she was in danger of being trampled to paste on the pavement if she happened to trip, so instead of being dragged along she tried to thrust her own way free. Was she still on the bridge? Was she back on land? There was no way to tell. She felt an unfamiliar desire to scream. . . .

She clamped down on it and forged ahead. Then suddenly there was daylight ahead, and a gap in the mob, and a crew of police or troops or somebody official trying to sort things out and channel the flow and generally set things back in order. Tildy burst into the open. She was off the bridge—back on that main street, in fact. The police were forcing open a lane for traffic. A closed carriage swept off the bridge as she watched, swerved to miss an oncoming wagon crowded with more police, and rattled off at high speed down the boulevard.

Suddenly a new shadow loomed over her—a man, in a silver and black outfit with a cape. Her breath froze—

Oh, come on, Tildy told herself. *You're not the fluttery sort.* But there was no denying she was on edge.

"This is not a healthy place to be," the man said to her. "May I escort you home?"

Tildy forced her heart back out of her throat again as she realized that the voice was familiar. He was . . . he was that guy she'd met at the club, the one who was so interested in her, the one who, well—

But whether she'd liked him or not was beside the point at the moment. *It* might be better to have help getting clear of this mess. "Thank you," Tildy told him. "That would be great."

Suddenly he was sweeping her along, a strong hand on her arm. "Unfortunately my vehicle is in use, so we will have to walk," the man said. "Let us first get away from this vicinity and then you will give me directions."

"Thank you," she was babbling again. Tildy forced her mouth shut. *If you can't talk intelligently,* she told herself, *don't.* There was nothing to worry about now, not with this man at her side.

Although, relieved or not, she did have to admit he

was looking even more attractive now than he had the other evening.

Again a wave washed over his head. Again? How was he alive, then, and not drowned? Assuming he *was* alive? But he *must* be alive—death could hardly be this unpleasant.

He was in the middle of a paroxysm of coughing. Not just from the water, either, he realized. He was sick to his stomach. He wasn't by any means the only thing the water had floating in it. Shaa had warned him against the water, and especially the Tongue, and yet here he was floating in *something*, and he had been for—for who knew how long?

Jurtan Mont flailed around with his arms. One hand hit a squishy embankment rising up out of the horrid water. That was it, Jurtan realized. He'd fallen through that pit into an inlet off the Tongue waterfront, but instead of going full into the water he'd hung up on the edge, on that mudbank. A mudbank that people apparently used as a convenient place to dump their sewage. Now the water was being agitated by these waves and the bank had been undermined, precipitating him into the water and finally waking him up. Just then another wave rolled through, shoving Jurtan up against the mud and letting him slide, thoroughly slimed again, back down.

He'd never make it up that incline. The thing was totally unstable—he'd risk bringing down a mudslide that would bury him once and for all. Jurtan's head throbbed horridly, he was on the verge of throwing up, not (he was sure) for the first time, on top of that he felt wretchedly queasy . . . but the waves weren't the only reason he'd woken up. Music was pounding full force in his skull; music telling him to get going, and *fast*.

A glimmer of light showed ahead, illuminating the curve of a semicircle three times as tall as he was. Jurtan launched himself toward it. For a moment he could touch bottom, a bottom even squishier than the slope behind him, and laden with clinging sea-grass and vines, but then the surface dropped mercifully away and he was fully paddling. This was actually a culvert, Jurtan recognized, and up ahead should be—

The largest wave yet came spilling around the corner. Jurtan felt himself lifted, pressed against the top of the culvert, scraped backward as the space filled entirely with water. Then he was dropping again. Jurtan kicked madly and dug in with his arms, trying to ride the ebb tide back out, felt himself bash off the wall as the current dragged him around a corner—but now that was full sunlight was up ahead. Another moment brought him through.

Off to the right a forest of pilings signaled the start of the wharves. The long shadow to the left and the stone island ahead announced the presence of the bridge. Beyond the island and its stout vertical pier some kind of large gray smooth-skinned fish were leaping clear of the water and dancing backward on their tails. Behind them was the much larger bulk of a lumbering whale. From his vantage point low in the water himself he could see the superstructure of a small boat cutting back and forth ahead of the leviathan.

But Jurtan wasn't here for sightseeing. The music was urging him on—on, and up. Behind him the bank of the Tongue Water was faced with a heavy stone wall linked to the shoreward arch of the bridge. Was there a stairway, or a ladder? There was, and a floating landing stage at its base. Both were crowded with people, people hanging on the ladder, people shouting and waving, people—jumping in? They'd spotted him! They were coming after him . . . no, they weren't. They weren't waving and pointing in his direction, either. Jurtan broke his awkward stroke long enough to cast a glance back over his shoulder. Now, looking further up, he saw what his first cursory inspection had missed. The center span of the bridge was in flames. Stones and girders and unrecognizable chunks of wreckage were pouring toward the water in

the path of the leviathan. And people—people, too.
Could he help?

The music roared at him. That wasn't what it had
in mind. There was something more important going
on? The music was weaving multiple themes and melodic lines together in a dark tapestry; Jurtan could
recognize Max's motif, and Shaa's, and his sister's,
and . . . What *was* going on out there?

By the time he reached the landing stage a few moments later, it had emptied enough for him to pull
himself from the water and grab for the ladder without
having to shove anyone out of the way. Not that he'd
have had the strength to push through a crowd, but
then again the music was quite serious about egging
him on. Just behind Jurtan a dory was putting in with
a cargo of people pulled from the water; above him,
though, a line of people hanging onto the ladder were
helping to guide him up, regardless of his slime-caked
clothes and thoroughly subhuman appearance.

More quickly than he would have expected, Jurtan
was collapsing over the top of the seawall onto a short
riverwalk stretching beneath the final arch of the
bridge. He found his feet and shambled ahead. Now
people were falling back from him; now, catching a
whiff of his own scent, Jurtan would have fallen back
from *himself,* if possible. A broad stair beyond the
arch led up to the bridge, though. His shoes were sliding and slurching on the pavement, and the slick stone
of the stairway was even worse; he *did* fall, halfway
up, smashing both knees into the edge of the step and
scraping the fresh scabs off his palms. He wobbled to
his feet and lurched onward.

The top of the broad staircase formed an even
broader plaza which merged on the side with the road
where it flowed off the bridge. As he came off the last
stair and tried to get a fix on whatever the music was
trying to tell him, a carriage tore past heading from
the bridge into the city. A strange sense of disorien-
tation gripped Jurtan—but, no, that had to have been

yesterday that he'd chased after that carriage the first time. He took a step after the coach and then paused.

It *was* the same carriage. The theme he'd heard yesterday that had attracted his attention to the vehicle, though, the one belonging to that guy Tildy had been spending time with, was absent. The man wasn't *in* the carriage.

He *was* hearing that person's motif, however. He was hearing a whole bunch of them. Max's was coming from his right, and Shaa's from the left, and—

What did the music want him to do? It had to—

But no, it didn't. The music didn't know. There was too much happening; Jurtan's internal sense couldn't figure out what was most important. They were leaving it up to him.

Tildy's themes floated in from the left, to, and weaving through it the sinister slidehorn snarl of the man from the carriage. Jurtan swung in that direction and headed after them.

Favored swooped low over the twisted grandstand. Sections were still collapsing onto the lower deck, and through the lower deck toward the river, but here and there small knots of people were extricating themselves from the wreckage, and a detachment of rescuers was working its way in from the west end of the bridge. At least two sorcerers were at work as well trying to damp down the fires and stabilize the structure before the whole center span of the bridge gave way. No one had taken the time to squash the terrorists' message, however, and the flaming letters and sigils were still casting a flickering red wash over the rising clouds and the smoky pall below.

Smoke should not be a major concern to him, though, or more precisely to Flotarobolis. Favored brought the vehicle to a hover at about twice head-height for a tall human and went into a slow tracking spin. Fortunately he'd brought the flyer along in the wagon; it never hurt to be prepared. But prepared for what? Who'd sent out that call? It had to be a god, no one else could have—

"You—Favored-of-the-Gods—" came a shouting voice. There he was, waving at Flotarobolis, standing erect atop what might have started the festivities as a table of refreshments, covered in soot and grime, a dark stain that might be blood dripping down his side. Favored floated toward him. "Hurry up!" the god snapped. "I am requisitioning your vehicle."

"You couldn't fit inside it," Favored yelled back through the speaking-tube, "and you couldn't fly it if you could!"

"Of course," the god said impatiently. "I am requisitioning you, too."

I had no idea how long I'd been swimming in mist. For all I knew it had been days. I didn't know either when—if ever—I'd decide to come back out. It didn't bother me much one way or the other. It felt like a lot of thinking of some sort was going on, but it was happening somewhere in the neighborhood, not right in my own head where I could get at it. It was more like someone across the room was having a conversation that I couldn't quite hear than a discussion I was involved in myself.

All of which sounded to me like a pretty solid picture of somebody going firmly and quite unequivocally out of his mind.

But like I said, I didn't much care. Maybe the sensation of crossing the divide from moderate inebriation to total anesthetization of the brain was—

"It's time to get up," someone was saying.

Someone? Well, yes, I guess so, except the "someone" happened to be me. At least it was my voice, although I didn't remember asking it to speak up just then. "Just a second," I said. "What—"

All of a sudden the mist was gone. Around me was still the wreckage of my room at the Adventurers' Club. From the fact that the dust had largely settled and everything that had been on the verge of falling over or apart had made its decision and was now resting in fragments further littering the floor, it *could* have been hours or days since the last time I'd been conscious. I'd not only gotten cleaned up from the battle and my encounter with the pit, I found myself dressed in a different outfit, too, obviously ready to go out.

This was clearly a new slant on ways to be productive while you were asleep.

Except I hadn't *been* sleeping, had I? Or was it that part of me had been up and active while another part of me—

"There is only so much of this entertainment I have time for," I said, with a decided sneer. "It is too bad to hurry things after this long, but—"

"Who *are* you?" I interrupted.

I chuckled again, that same nasty cackle I'd heard before. *I* chuckled? No, *he* chuckled. But how could there be "me" and "him?" There was only one of us. Wasn't there? "Who are *you?*" he said, and then broke into another cackling roll.

Why don't you *tell* me *that?* I thought at him.

"Who I am or who you are? No matter, you don't want to know either one."

Well, he was right in a way; I didn't but I did.

But in the same way I didn't know who he was, but I did. Or at least I *almost* did. The knowledge was down there, bubbling slowly up toward full comprehension. Then—

"You're Iskendarian," I said. "Right?" Which meant I was Iskendarian, sort of, which meant—which meant I'd have to sort it all out later. "But you invented the Spell of Namelessness, or something like that, didn't you? So how could you let yourself be— unless you—"

"Of course, you dolt. I used it on *myself.*"

Of course. He'd wanted to disappear, totally and completely. What better way than to be dead? He'd spread around the story he was dead, and to keep anyone from finding him by probe he'd cast his own custom spell on himself before going into hibernation; cast his spell and shifted his physical appearance, too, no doubt. Then when he'd woken up, he'd used me as a false front to disguise himself from the world and as a hiding place to put his capabilities back together. He'd been peeking out every so often to check up on events and he'd stepped in when magic had needed to be employed. He'd—

"I made you," he said, in a tone that clearly stated that our conversation was coming to a close. "Now your usefulness is done. And there is at present a window of opportunity I do not choose to miss."

"Wait a—" I said, but he didn't. The headache exploded out through my mind. I hung on to the fragments of my consciousness—I would have shouted, except he had control of our mouth; I would have fallen to the floor, except I'd lost control of our body, hopefully I at least managed to vomit, although I wouldn't have known it if I had; I would have. . . .

26

There was *still* no giant bird, the Great Karlini observed. He had half-expected that the bird, given as it was to melodramatic gestures, would have chosen just this moment to make its entrance, triumphant from its stay at the ancestral breeding grounds. But apparently not. Now Favored had walked out on him as well, and there was no one else in sight between him and the surface of the water coming up at him now quite rapidly, no one except of course for one of the namesake guests of honor of the festival now cruising through his probable point of touchdown. It was probably too much to expect for a flailing tentacle to pluck him from the air . . . wasn't it?

If only he hadn't always been so quick to lump levitation with transmutation of metals and perpetual motion in the "useless" bin reserved for the old wives' tales of sorcery, perhaps he might have been able to come up with something. Unfortunately it seemed a little late at the moment to be—

A shadow passed overhead. Had Favored returned? No—and it wasn't one shadow, either, it was a bunch of little ones. Not a giant bird, but a flock of small ones?

Screeching madly, the birds dove on him. Beaks and claws closed on every available edge of clothing, on feet, hands, hair, on—

Karlini's stomach flipped again as his rush toward the surface abruptly paused. He was rising—no, actually he wasn't, he was still falling, but more slowly and under some semblance of control. Feathers were drifting down past his nose, the sound of frenzied flapping surrounded him, wings beat his back and thrust gusts of winds along his side—but he *was* still falling. They were only small birds, after all; they were . . . seagulls?

Of course, Karlini thought, totally dazed, *what else?* An exhausted bird peeled free and soared off in a long glide, then another nosed over at his feet and dropped headfirst toward the water. The squid was off to the side now and up ahead, waving its tentacles regally at the Imperial grandstand, where from the look of things no one was paying the slightest attention. "Can we make shore?" Karlini asked, but just at that moment a particularly loud squawk blared at him from about six inches overhead, and with a chorus of relieved wails the flock of seagulls let him go.

They had released raggedly. Karlini found himself turning a deranged mid-air cartwheel, legs and arms sprawled in every direction, but he was barely becoming aware of the situation when he hit the surface of the water and went through in a shower of foam.

Something squishy went "ooph" beneath Svin's feet as he landed in the bottom of the ice crater. Svin crouched low, dagger at the ready, and peered through the haze of pulverized ice. "You are Dortonn of the north?" Svin demanded.

The man immobilized beneath him opened a bleary eye and gazed up past his sagging eyelid. "Who are you?" he wheezed. Then he made a hollow rattly sound deep in his throat. "But I don't care. Just end it."

Truly Dortonn was battered. The exploding ring and the clinging fire had done their work, and indeed the fire was still licking at one charred arm and a bare section of chest. It would clearly be the honorable thing to dispatch this creature from his misery.

But would it also be the wisest? If Svin thought he'd

learned anything, it was not to waste the possibility of information about what really might be going on. Then there was the question of the current tactical situation to consider too. "Can you stop this iceberg?" Svin said.

The eye goggled at him as though he was out of his mind. "My powers are drained," Dortonn stated. "*I* am drained."

"That is no excuse," Svin told him. Suddenly he was standing not on Dortonn's belly but at his side, and almost in the same blurred instant Dortonn had been slung over his shoulder with one of Svin's large hands wrapped securely around his neck. As he crouched again and sprang forcefully up the side of the crater, Svin noted that Dortonn had found enough strength for a weak wail . . . then they'd cleared the crater's lip. The frost cloud had settled enough to see the looming structure ahead. "You can still become even less comfortable," Svin suggested.

Dortonn's eye rolled, absorbed the scene, and abruptly widened. The hand that had not worn the ring, which was still significantly more intact than the other contorted claw, began gesturing. A strange word bubbled in his throat.

I gradually became aware that I was gradually becoming aware. Thinking straight was still a highly problematic proposition since my head still felt like someone with a large lead mallet was trying to play it like a bell in pace with each heartbeat, but I wasn't about to complain. With his last nasty move, Iskendarian had made it sound like he was doing away with me for good. The fact that he'd pulled his punch, or maybe that I'd proved a little more tenacious than he'd allowed for, was enough to hang onto for the moment. I wasn't about to ask him about it either, especially since he was showing no sign he realized I was still in the vicinity.

Of course, it wasn't surprising my head felt like it was going to explode; it had to be pretty crowded with two of us in there. On the other hand, I wasn't sure it was our head that *was* hurting, per se. I couldn't actually feel the rest of our body, and sight and hearing were pretty erratic, too. On the whole, it seemed like I'd been wadded up and shoved away in the attic.

Not that I was thinking of just giving up and going to sleep. No, I would have been happy to do something about the situation, except I couldn't think of what. I couldn't hit him over the head; he was controlling our arms. I couldn't knock him over, unless I could pull off some kind of commando attack on our center of balance and rely on him to trip. I didn't even seem to able to give him back the headache he'd given me.

I wasn't overhearing any of his thoughts, either. From the fact that he wasn't trying to eradicate me again I hoped that also meant he couldn't detect mine. Even if I couldn't tell what he was thinking, though, he was obviously up to something. He was striding down a winding street, then turning a corner without hesitation, then charging straight through an intersection with only the barest glance at the road sign. The traffic seemed surprisingly sparse. I was wondering where everyone had gone, until it occurred to me that perhaps I had been unconscious for a day or two before Iskendarian had roused me, and that everyone might already be down at the waterfront for the Running of the Squids.

I decided to concentrate harder; maybe I could pick up his thoughts if I really pushed myself at them. It might have been my imagination, but it occurred to me that he was considering how to go about taking the gods up on their offer to make us their chief if we got rid of Max. Of course, it *could* have been my imagination, but it was also totally consistent with what I'd seen of Iskendarian's personality so far.

As I concentrated, though, I might not have only been receiving emanations from Iskendarian. I had enough of a rapport with Monoch to know he was up to something too. What it was I couldn't tell; that obviously was the story of my day. Monoch was probably transferring his allegiance to the new boss, I wouldn't be surprised. Monoch seemed to be as unaware of me as Iskendarian. If he was throwing in with Iskendarian, that was undoubtedly just as well.

We had entered another cobblestoned street lined with small warehouses and strange thaumaturgical signs, and Iskendarian had started looking at the numbers on the buildings, when I suddenly realized where we were. I hadn't been there myself but I knew the address—and sure enough, that was it. His hand made a few quick gestures, something sparkling lit up the locks, and then they all clicked simultaneously as their bolts withdrew. He pushed open the door and stepped in.

The lamps and wizard lights were dark and gloom hung over the interior. At the end of a short wall was an open two-story room. Iskendarian had his head cocked to the side, clearly listening with more than ears. Then he stepped ahead, apparently satisfied, and we were standing in the Karlini workroom.

Another gesture brought up the hanging wizard lights. "Where would she be keeping them?" Iskendarian muttered, gazing around the room. "Surely not in plain sight? But what is this?" He strode across to a work table strewn with old papers, next to a bookcase overflowing with more. I felt him smile. "Ah!" he said, and started quickly gathering them up.

He stopped for a moment, gazing at the top sheet in his hand. "Good, good, exactly as I'd hoped," he muttered, and as he said this I realized I understood what was happening. Iskendarian hadn't been certain all his memory and skills would survive his hibernation, so he'd written out the story of his life and plans, and he'd left himself instructions.

Max had done him the favor or making sure the stuff was right at hand.

Iskendarian was adding another sheaf from the bookcase to the tall pile he'd assembled on the table when his eyes fell on a nearby blackboard. "What's this?'' he murmured. ''Interesting, very interesting. A worthwhile extension. Perhaps—''

''Who is it?'' said a woman's voice from the top of the staircase at the side of the room. ''Oh, it's you. But what are you doing here?''

I threw everything into it. I had to try to warn her— all it would take would be a peep, half-a-second's control of our vocal cords, that wasn't asking for much, but Iskendarian never flinched. I heard him mouth, ''So much the better,'' and raise his arm.

Roni was going into her strike mode, but she wasn't a field operator, and even if she had been she wasn't Iskendarian. Even penned up in the back of my brain and comatose for however long it had been, he still had the power of legions at his fingertips. A fireball blasted across the room and tore into the staircase and blew it apart. The wall behind it crashed out and the ceiling above fell in. The next story above started to follow it down in a rain of screeching wood, the tall barrels beneath the staircase burst their staves and gushed forth jets and waves of oily iridescent liquid, blast waves rolled past us—and I couldn't see Roni. She'd vanished in the center of the ball of flame.

Goddamn, I thought. *He's killed her.*

''Were you responsible for that disaster back there?'' Zalzyn Shaa asked his brother as the coach continued jouncing along.

''One cannot bear all the world's calamities on one's own shoulder,'' said his brother. ''You of all people should know that.''

''I assume that means you don't intend to answer the question.''

''He's always been like this,'' the Scapula told Leen in a calmly reasonable tone.

''*Were* you behind that massacre?'' said Leen.

''I am behind, as you put it, quite a lot,'' Arznaak acknowledged. ''But I, a terrorist? Surely not—I am a force for order. Your friend Max, on the other hand, was clearly implicated—''

"You may have me chained up," Shaa inserted, "you are most certainly up to something nefarious, but you don't have to make me listen to this."

"What about the Emperor?" Leen asked. "Did anyone see what happened to the Emperor?"

The Scapula gazed idly out the window. "Phlinn went after him, good old Phlinn. That *is* his kind of job, anyway." He shrugged. "Who knows? Perhaps Phlinn even rescued him, and survived himself in the bargain. Regardless, rest assured he behaved in a manner archetypically befitting an archetypal god of heroes. Ah, here we are, home at last."

The carriage had indeed clattered to a halt. An attendant was opening the door, behind him a serious contingent of guards. "Show our guests in," the Scapula instructed. "Has anyone else arrived? Not yet? Well, he should be along momentarily." With an energetic spring he bounded from his seat into the courtyard. As Leen and Shaa were being dragged, less comfortably, from the cab, Arznaak suddenly turned back. "You are awake," he addressed his brother, "so you are certainly contemplating some bold move. Before you act so as to quixotically accelerate your own death you might consider a truth your friend Maximillian has always failed to appreciate."

"And that truth is?" Shaa said.

"Why, that not every problem has a solution, of course."

"Have you noticed that a gigantic iceberg is heading straight toward us?" Max remarked.

"You are reduced to this?" smirked Gadol V'Nora. "Such an old trick? No, Maximillian. You—"

Max shrugged as much as possible, given the number of hands still holding him. "Well, don't say I didn't try to warn you," he said.

"If you—" Gadol began, but he broke off as something swooped toward them from the ruined section of the bridge, something round and shiny and trailing gouts of steam. Clanking madly, it made an erratic leap and gained perhaps five feet of altitude, then equally abruptly reversed course and dropped back toward the roadbed. Atop the reeling prodigy was sprawled a human form clutching frantically for purchase. Just when it seemed the thing would surely crash into their midst, a fresh steam cloud enveloped it. When the cloud shredded, the contraption was bounding again into the sky.

"Read the formal indictment and let's get him out of here," said Chas, the magician, looking after the apparition with a clear expression of disbelief.

Gadol turned back from the retreating vapor trail and favored him with a brief frown. "Very well. In our power as Special Auxiliary to the Municipality of Peridol I arrest you in their name for—"

"What's that?" one of the Hand's troopers interrupted. "That big white—"

Every head in the group swiveled to follow the man's pointing arm. Every head, that is, except one. Max threw himself back and around, ripping free of the restraining hands through the element of forceful surprise, put his head down, and charged the gap between two of the Hand. They spun away under the impact just far enough for Max to plunge on through. The low wall at the margin of the bridge was just beyond. Did he really want to do this, with his hands still frozen in a block of stone behind his back? Did he have a—

A titanic spine-rattling teeth-clenching screeching scraping sound came up from behind, and then with an equally loud crunch and THOMP! the bridge jerked out from under him. Max, still in forward flight, felt his footing vanish. He cartwheeled ahead, barely cleared the railing at the upside-down limit of his somersault, and went over the side. In the brief glimpse he caught behind him before beginning his drop toward the water below, Max saw several things of particular interest. The part of the iceberg he could see had fractured into a collection of boulder-sized ice fragments that were even now cascading onto the roadbed and careening across it, knocking people aside like tenpins. Overhead above the toppling ice cubes, caught in the midst of a prodigious leap from what a moment before had been the top of the iceberg, was a mightily thewed figure with another dangling person slung over his shoulder.

Max tumbled toward the water. Fortunately he had a second quantum level force burst pre-prepared for emergencies, and on voice trigger too. He began to subvocalize the release sequence—

Something slapped him across the back and knocked the wind out of him. No, not merely a slap, whatever-it-was was wrapping itself around his body. A hurling net—the edges weighted with bolo plumbs, the mesh slathered with some clinging adhesive, the—

Max hit the water. His mouth still open, he gulped fluid; his arms and legs securely swaddled and his hands still weighted down by Chas' clay block, he began to sink. He could barely even writhe.

But something was hauling at his feet. One of the Running leviathans, some carnivore of the sea? No—a casting line was attached to the net. He was being drawn in. A gaff caught on the webbing behind his back, then another one near his ankles, they yanked together, and he came free of the water into the air.

Max coughed, retched, hacked—

"Oh, come now, Maximillian," said a man standing over him. "Forget the show."

Max spat up a final gout of water and opened his eyes. He was sprawled on a flatboat. Several men around him were nailing corners of the net to the deck. "You always were the smartest Hand," Max stated, and coughed again.

Romm V'Nisa put his hands on his hips. "It was prudent to anticipate you would attempt to reach the water. *I* would have."

"Thanks, teacher," Max told him. Beyond the flatboat, what remained of the iceberg with its top lopped off had come to a stop partway under the bridge. The sliced-flat upper surface had wedged itself beneath the damaged section of the center span, where it now appeared to be serving as an effective, if temporary, splint.

"Since Gadol surely failed," Romm said, "I should pronounce the indictment. Maximillian V'Dirapal, I arrest you under the authority and in the name of . . ."

The Great Karlini finished crawling from the water onto the ledge at the base of the bridge pier and collapsed on his face. "Thanks," he managed. "I know I couldn't have done this without you."

Behind him, the bottle-nosed sea mammal that had towed him from the channel nuzzled him again and made another comment in its high-pitched squeaky voice. The creature had dragged him out of the way of the iceberg with not too much time left to spare. As far as Karlini was concerned, though, it was time for a vacation. The world could go on with its plots without him for—

A scream split his head from the inside out. Karlini jackknifed convulsively up, his ears ringing as the shriek cut suddenly off, even though he knew his ears hadn't actually been what had done the hearing. The low-level back-of-the-mind link they'd maintained for so long he'd barely thought about it in years had exploded with so much agonal force that—

Karlini looked miserably across the intervening water at the city-side seawall and its crowded staircase, then sighed and jumped back in the water. With a cry like that he knew he'd be too late—he was too late already—but he had to know. Roni—

"Why is this vehicle so slow?" yelled Gashanatantra. "And so unstable," he added, as the brass ball beneath him suddenly quivered, rolled, and lurched again toward the ground. For an instant the top was the side, and he was hanging over a five-story drop with only his precarious grip on a protruding circulation vent saving him from entering free-fall above the pavement.

"It's not designed for this!" honked the speaking-tube. "You could just land and commandeer a wagon."

"Shut up and fly! Time is critical!"

"Then you might have planned ahead for your transportation," muttered Favored. Another block of flats slid past below them in a reasonably straight diagonal line.

"I didn't think he would move so fast," Gash said grudgingly, almost to himself. His head was cocked to the side as though he was listening to something not in the immediate vicinity. "Or with so much force. Faster!" he repeated. They were still too far out of range.

Behind us echoed a despairing wail. Iskendarian turned. He'd been contemplating the scene in front of us for what had felt to me like minutes but had probably been only a second or two. Atop the vista of exploding fire and collapsing woodwork had been added the glittering meshwork of spells going off, scooping up and channeling the broth gushing from the vats through overlapping balls glowing azure and aquamarine. As his vision shifted, though, it became apparent that the destruction was thus far limited to the corner of the building he'd struck. The entry hall was still intact. Backlit by the light from the street and tinted dancing red by the flames was the open-mouthed figure of Tildamire Mont, chest heaving from her run through the front door Iskendarian had left unlocked, the horrified anguish on her face clearly visible.

Beneath Iskendarian's arm was the stack of paperwork he'd gathered up, and in that hand Monoch the walking stick, but that still left the other arm free. He raised it and pointed it at the girl. I could feel the power crackle as he spoke the trigger-word—

Another person dove in through the open door, snatched Tildamire away with one arm, carried her to the floor with him off to the side, and hugged the boards, covering her with his body as the entry hall erupted into flame.

* * *

"Isn't there anything you can do about this?" Leen hissed at Shaa.

"I can see what develops," Shaa told her. "You might choose to do the same. You don't look too uncomfortable."

Indeed, he *was* the one chained to the wall. Leen was merely tied to a chair, and an overstuffed armchair at that. Of course, unlike a straight-back chair, the armchair would be impossible to lift with oneself and move, and the deep cushion gave exactly the wrong leverage to try to manipulate oneself to one's feet. "This is no dungeon, either," he added. "You don't have to worry about rats." Shaa hesitated, then went ahead, addressing his words to the man across the room. "Also, I swore an oath."

Arznaak didn't bother to turn to face him, instead continuing to busy himself clinking glasses at the sideboard. He waved his free hand idly; it was a matter of little significance. "Then I absolve you of it."

"That is one thing you can't do. The oath was to Dad, not you, as you know quite well."

Arznaak leaned back against the sideboard, twirling a snifter in his hand. He raised into position for a toast. "To Dad, who isn't around, t'sk t'sk. Very well, then, it's your choice. If you want to consider this a convenient excuse to prepare for suicide, be my guest."

"How can you two be *acting* this way?" Leen sputtered.

They both opened their mouths to provide each his own dryly barbed rejoinder, but just then a new person appeared in the doorway. "Ah," said the Scapula, "the true guest of honor."

"I have it," Jardin panted. "I have it at last. He went through with our bargain, the fool human."

"What bargain?" said Shaa, his voice much flatter than usual.

"In time," his brother told him. "Bring it here, then, my friend."

Jardin dragged himself across the room. His shoulders were sagging, he was carrying himself stiffly as though he was covered with bruises, his sling-supported arm was clearly weighing him down, even his voice lacked energy; he was clearly thoroughly exhausted. Who had he fallen afoul of? Shaa wondered. Had his reverses, whatever they had been, caused him to make the bargain he'd mentioned? Jardin reached into a pocket and held up a ring.

"Keeping your jaw dropped in such a manner lacks decorum, my brother," chided Arznaak. "Now—"

"Now you will examine this ring," Jardin ordered.

"Very well," said the Scapula. He caressed the air above Jardin's hand, closed his eyes—

"I thought you had very little advanced training," Shaa observed. "If anyone here is examining anything it should be me."

Arznaak sighed and made another pass. "Unfortunately my brother has his own agendas. It would be foolish to trust him. I—"

"Does he know?" said Jardin.

"Also in time; everything in its time. Jardin, this ring is clean. Maximillian's trivial safeguards will fall away before your mighty power."

"If you're lying, I'll eat your heart," Jardin said, took the ring from his palm, and slipped it onto his finger.

What had he wandered into? With Max out of circulation, his plan would have left the way clear to pursue his added goal of insinuating himself into the company of Max's compatriots. There were undoubtedly secrets there ripe for the taking, information that would help him position himself against his own patron. The girl had been an obvious target, and she had been fulfilling her ordained role with remarkable precision. With everyone else in Max's organization out at the Running—who would be anywhere else?—it had seemed a perfect opportunity to raid their facility. Tildamire could get him through the defenses and reveal through her enamored talk any caches of hidden worth—

But then where had Spilkas come from, and where had he developed such destructive power—and why was he *using* it? And why had he looked so nasty, too, in the brief glimpse Fradjikan had had of him as he'd dove through the door?

Fradi knew he should have turned around and left the vicinity as quickly as possible at the first sight of this scene. Instead, he'd acted on impulse. Yes, he'd saved the girl, for the moment, but that only meant that Spilkas would try to finish the job with the next blow. They had to get out—

Except the doorway they'd just used to enter was now a solid cauldron of flame, and the ceiling above was coming down on their heads. There were no side exits. The only way out was ahead, straight toward Spilkas. There was nothing to be gained by waiting. Fradi came to a low crouch and flung himself weaving down the hall.

Was he the cavalry? Whatever his secrets were, whatever he'd thought he was really up to, I was happy to see him. Fradjikan had seemed deadly enough in our earlier meetings that he might actually be able to take Iskendarian on—

Except if he triumphed over Iskendarian, where would that leave me?

This was all far too confusing. The only clear part was that Iskendarian *had* to be stopped, and stopped fast. Iskendarian levered his arm again, shook it, then looked at it with an expression of puzzlement I could feel. "Drained already?" he muttered. He *was* tired; I could feel that, too, but surely he wasn't down to his last dregs. I threw myself against him again, straining as hard as I could to make him realize he was more than tired, he was *exhausted*, he needed to take a nap, anything to distract him from—

Another shockwave hit us from behind. Iskendarian glanced over his shoulder and reflexively spat a word-string. The ethereal containment balls swayed and leaned away as though struck by a sudden high wind, tables covered with beakers and trays blew over and slid toward the wall, and then the wall itself and the whole corner of the building leaned away too, the vertical wood planks rippling and snapping, and both corner walls and their structural posts pulled away from the building and fell over.

I didn't know if I was having as much of an impact as a gnat, but I was still shouting at him and pummeling—or thinking hard about pummeling, anyway. Iskendarian was swinging back, though, and with him I could feel something dangerous approaching rapidly . . . and there it was, Fradjikan, coming straight toward us out of a crouch into a lunge, his sword in his hand outstretched toward Iskendarian's chest. Iskendarian started to step away, started to bring Monoch around, the papers under his arm going flying, but Fradjikan was clear on target. He hit Iskendarian off-center on the left between two ribs in perfect position to slice through and into his heart—

—and the impact threw us back as Iskendarian's protection field went rigid around the sword. I felt ribs crunch up and down his chest as the force of the blow distributed itself, but the triangular point had not gone through, and now the end of the sword was glowing red and drooping and even the hilt was melting around Fradjikan's hand. The sword dropped to the floor and Fradi sunk to his knees after it, clutching his hand to his chest.

Another explosion blasted behind us. Iskendarian ignored it. He levered himself off his back, gritting his teeth, and climbed to his feet. Then he picked Monoch up off the floor, raised him over Fradjikan's neck, and spoke the phrase to activate his shift from stick to blade.

Someone was yelling, "Tildy! Tildy!" and crashing around in the flames. Being hit from behind and crushed into the floor might well have saved her life, but the experience had left her so dazed she could barely move. Still, she managed to get one arm into the air and wave it around. An apparition like an ambulatory creature of mud loomed over her and seized it. Even through the smell of the smoke and the dust and the flaming wood, whoever-it-was stank. *Reeked!*

But it—or he—was trying to drag her, then lift her. "Come *on,* Tildy," he was saying, "you've got to get out of—"

"Jurtan? Where did you come from?"

"Right where we're going back to, through the wall." He shifted his grip to grab her under the arms and staggered toward a splintered shaft of daylight.

Jardin slipped the ring onto his finger. Shaa noted that his brother had taken a step back away from Jardin; he also appeared to be holding his breath. "So, you have not betrayed me after all," Jardin commented to the Scapula. "Perhaps you are as wise as you would have me think. Now—"

Which was when Jardin stiffened and fell to the floor with the heavy clunk of a sudden stone statue.

"Good old Max," said Arznaak. "Always so predictable. But a nice job. Simple, direct, to the point. Ah, yes—here comes the other part."

Indeed, the ring was staring to glow, and the paralyzed form of Jardin seemed to be withering, his skin wrinkling and tightening over shrinking muscles, its color becoming ashen, frigid veins showing prominent blue. "That fellow in the ring is drinking well, isn't he?" Arznaak added. "Surely Max wasn't about to leave him a way out, though." He glanced over at Shaa. "Enjoying the spectacle, dear brother?"

"You obviously have that side of affairs well covered by yourself," Shaa told him.

Arznaak put on a pout. "Oh, but of course, you're not in any mood for entertainment. Been feeling rather directionless, have you, overwhelmed with ennui? Life seem not worth the trouble of living?"

Surely he couldn't mean . . . but he obviously did.

"I thought the curse restricted who I could fall in love with," Shaa said slowly. "I never heard about any of this other stuff."

"Well, you know. Even a god can't do everything. The mysteries of the human heart . . ." His brother shrugged an untroubled shrug. "So sue me." The Scapula raised a finger. "But not right at the moment, if you don't mind."

What was Arznaak doing? He was rummaging in a service drawer beneath his sideboard, and then in a cabinet underneath the drawer, withdrawing from the former several silver instruments and from the latter an ice chest. "Hold still," Arznaak told the paralyzed Jardin, who clearly could do nothing else. Arznaak knelt carefully next to Jardin, gingerly took hold of the end of the finger wearing the ring with an ice tong, avoiding all other contact with his rheumy, aged skin, and brought up his other hand. Shaa had barely enough time to appreciate the honed edge of the knife as Arznaak positioned it over Jardin's hand and brought it forcefully down. The knife embedded itself in the floor with an unambiguous *thunk*.

"One must avoid crosstalk contamination," Arznaak commented, bringing the ice tongs up to eye level so he could inspect the liberated finger, still wearing the ring. "And who knows what other surprises Max might have had hidden?" He flipped open the ice chest, dropped in the finger, and clicked the lid shut.

"But there remains one important step," said Arznaak. Positioning himself out of the way of the pool of blood spreading across the hardwood floor from Jardin's spurting hand, he felt inside Jardin's jacket. "Ah, here we are." He transferred Jardin's slate of reference to his own pocket, then rested both palms flat on Jardin's chest. Jardin shuddered rigidly.

Shaa was unable to tell if Jardin's eyes were tracking at all, or whether his pupils were widening and retreating. A guttural moan escaped his throat, though, his head jerked back and forth, and his heels drummed once against the floor.

"Well," Arznaak said, climbing to his feet. "That should do for that. Clive!"

One of the assistants who had brought Shaa and Leen into the room appeared in the door. "Sir?"

Arznaak indicated the prostrate Jardin with a backward wave of his hand. "Take this out and dump it in an alley somewhere."

Clive jumped forward to grab Jardin under the shoulders. "No," Arznaak said, studying the situation. "By the heels, I think."

"Yes, sir," said Clive. A moment later he and the thumping Jardin had vanished out into the corridor.

"All quite simple, really," Arznaak observed, shaking his head, "especially since the Administrator of Curses is not very smart. Or the former Curse Administrator, I should say, and in the past tense as well. Nor was he careful enough with the secrets of his office. But one god's folly is, shall we say, another god's opportunity." He straightened, stretched, cracked his back. "In fact, I can feel the aura settling into place quite nicely."

He crossed the room, stood gazing down at his brother, then chucked Shaa under the chin. "You've always been the perfect pawn, dear brother. Still, family is family; I could scarcely celebrate such an exciting occasion without at least one of you present, now could I? You've been an adequate audience, I suppose, if scarcely more than that. But now to business. First up, I think is to reinstate your curse. Oh, you don't want to give me the pleasure of a verbal retort, do you? Well, no matter, I can see the question in your eyes. I had wondered if you'd feel anything at all different, but I expect my little diversions here have served their purpose. Do you understand what has transpired here, at last?"

"Max traded the ring to the Curse Administrator behind my back in exchange for his removing the curse on me," Shaa said grimly. "We know Jardin's been after the ring anyway, and whatever got him bashed up like that drained his energy so much it made him desperate to get it immediately; he needed the transfusion of energy. Except you were guiding things behind the scenes. You were advising Jardin, but you never told him Max would booby-trap the ring regardless of whatever bargain he made. So you got Jardin to set the trap off and get consumed, and now you've taken his place." He shrugged. "Perfectly straightforward."

"Well, close enough," said Arznaak. "Now, shall we proceed?"

Monoch flamed on. I braced myself—I didn't know how much of my experience Iskendarian had access to, but I remembered the trouble Monoch had given me the first few times I'd tried to wield him and figured there was a chance Iskendarian would be thrown momentarily off his stride. As Monoch solidified and started to arc down at Fradjikan's bowed neck, though, it looked like Iskendarian had matters well in hand. He must have thought the same thing, because I could almost feel him relax and let Monoch's weight begin to do the work. That was when Monoch suddenly jerked in the air, jarring Iskendarian's arms in their sockets so hard his teeth snapped together with a crunch, and then, having established some sort of pathway, sent a blast of lightning through the hilt into his body and up into his brain.

Iskendarian staggered back, hands trying to loose their grip on Monoch's hilt, body jiggering uncontrollably, his vision going dark. Monoch hit him with another electric jolt. Iskendarian's head whipped back farther than should have been possible given that it was still attached to his neck, his mouth opened for a shriek, but his whole body had now locked up, all muscles so rigid he might have been trying to pull his tendons out at the joints. He fell over toward the floor.

I hit squarely on the back of my head. My throat hurt as much as you'd expect given that a moment before Iskendarian had been trying to force our lungs out past our teeth, but I still managed to croak, "Don't—it's me!" at Monoch before he came around and took my head off with a single chop. Instead, he spun in the air again and tried to drag me back to my feet.

It was either go with him or decide whether to lose my arms at the elbow or the shoulder. Since my joints were still locked, it worked about the same as stepping on the business end of a reclining rake to raise the handle to the vertical. Where Fradjikan had been was now another heap of erupting debris. The entire front of the building was going up, and as Monoch jerked me tottering away it was clear the rear area was totally lost as well. I could barely even make out the tracery of defense spells now, but from the way the flames were shaping themselves across invisible arcs and roiling within unsupported balls something had to still be at work. I might have shut my eyes then; whatever I was doing obviously didn't concern Monoch one way or the other. I thought he might have even cut his way through a wall at some point, and he must have dragged me straight through some significant amount of flame, but it was just as well. I wasn't too excited about having to live with myself right at that particular moment.

But no one asked me. I finally realized I was lying on my back; when I reluctantly dragged open my eyes, I saw overhead continuing billows of smoke, and slightly below the smoke on either side a pair of blank walls, and lower than that a familiar fellow I was not at all surprised to find there.

It was my old pal Gashanatantra.

He had shifted farther away from his tweedy Jardin disguise, of course, but I was coming to think I'd recognize him in any incarnation, even if his wife and other odd friends didn't. At the moment, the air of intrigue and menace and wheels revolving within wheels that usually hovered over him like a habitual warning of dangerous weather ahead was somewhat frayed as a result of the fact that he was covered in soot, his clothes were shredded and had apparently been close enough to a fire to leave them totally singed except for the patches that had entirely burnt through, he was holding one hand against a dark-stained patch on his side, and one temple was covered with matted blood. Next to him on the ground, barely as tall as my chest would have been if I'd been able to stand up, was a brass ball studded with gears and linkages and sighing steam cylinders venting their tired wisps of lackluster vapor.

Monoch was lying across my chest at an awkward angle, his point embedded in the alley muck at my side. Both of my hands were still locked around his hilt. I ignored Monoch and regarded Gash. "Should I be thanking you?" I said to him, ignoring the stabbing pain from the broken ribs in my chest.

"All things considered," Gash said evenly, "I rather think you should."

"Just so I know," I added. But he wasn't exactly giving his full attention to me. He was now gazing down the alley at what was clearly the smoldering mess of the Karlini lab. From the look of him, too, I had a feeling this wasn't the only wreckage he'd been involved in today.

"This is not how events should have turned out," Gash was saying to himself, "not at all." Then he turned back to me, eyeing me with a glance of new appraisal. "Apparently I was mistaken about certain things, but—"

"Such as?" I croaked.

"Nothing material, except possibly on the question of scale." Now he was favoring Monoch with a glare. "You could have given me a little more warning. I might have been standing by closer to hand." He shook his head. "Instead things are clearly worse, significantly worse, worse even than I had expected."

"Great," I told him. "Now you're an optimist."

TO BE CONCLUDED IN
SPELL OF APOCALYPSE

DAW

Mayer Alan Brenner

☐ CATASTROPHE'S SPELL (Book 1)   UE2357—$3.95
Someone was on a power trip—and far too many acquaintances
of Maximillian the Vaguely Disreputable (Max to his friends)—
were being unwillingly caught up in the sorcerous struggle.
Trying to free two people trapped in a wandering castle, Max
runs straight into a war between Death Gods, necromancers,
and a sorcerer/detective who becomes mortally ill whenever he
tries to cast a spell. With inept wizardry running wild, can even
the mighty Max avert the catastrophic doom rushing to meet
him?

☐ SPELL OF INTRIGUE (Book 2)   UE2453—$4.50
Resurrected by one of the gods, Fradjikan the Assassin had
his work cut out for him, spying on Maximillian the Vaguely
Disreputable, the Creeping Sword, the Great Karlini, and all the
rest—as they followed separate pathways which would lead
them into the midst of a god-generated plot to find and gain
control of a missing ring of power.

☐ SPELL OF FATE (Book 3)   UE2508—$4.99
Return again to Brenner's world of hilarious havoc. This time
trouble is brewing for mortals and gods alike, as Maximillian
the Vaguely Disreputable comes closer to solving the laws of
conservation of magic and toppling the gods' power base,
while the Creeping Sword, who still can't remember his own
name, is drawn more and more deeply into the fighting between
warring factions of the gods.

Tanya Huff

☐ **THE FIRE'S STONE** UE2445—$3.95
Thief, swordsman and wizardess—drawn together by a quest not of their own choosing, would they find their true destinies in a fight against spells, swords and betrayal?

☐ **GATE OF DARKNESS, CIRCLE OF LIGHT** UE2386—$3.95

The Wild Magic was loose in Toronto, for an Adept of Darkness had broken through the barrier into the everyday mortal world. And in this age when only fools and innocents still believed in magic, who was there to fight against this invasion by evil?

VICTORY NELSON, INVESTIGATOR:
Otherworldly Crimes A Specialty

☐ **BLOOD PRICE: Book 1** UE2471—$3.99
Can one ex-policewoman and a vampire defeat the magic-spawned evil which is devastating Toronto?

☐ **BLOOD TRAIL: Book 2** UE2502—$4.50
Someone was out to exterminate Canada's most endangered species—the werewolf.

THE NOVELS OF CRYSTAL

Ardhan is a world slowly losing its magic. But one wizard still survives, a master of evil bent on world domination. No mere mortal can withstand him—and so the Elder Races must intervene, giving Ardhan a new champion, Crystal—the last-born wizard who will ever walk their world!

☐ **CHILD OF THE GROVE: Book 1** UE2432—$3.95
☐ **THE LAST WIZARD: Book 2** UE2331—$3.95

Buy them at your local bookstore or use this convenient coupon for ordering.

PENGUIN USA P.O. Box 999, Bergenfield, New Jersey 07621

Please send me the DAW BOOKS I have checked above, for which I am enclosing $_____ (please add $2.00 per order to cover postage and handling. Send check or money order (no cash or C.O.D.'s) or charge by Mastercard or Visa (with a $15.00 minimum.) Prices and numbers are subject to change without notice.

Card #_____ Exp. Date _____
Signature_____
Name_____
Address_____
City _____ State _____ Zip _____

For faster service when ordering by credit card call **1-800-253-6476**

Please allow a minimum of 4 to 6 weeks for delivery.

THE DRAGON TOKEN
Dragon Star: Book Two
by Melanie Rawn

In this exciting sequel to STRONGHOLD, the flames of war continue to blaze across the land. Till now the beleaguered forces of the High Prince have been forced to retreat, leaving abandoned castles and towns to desecration and destruction at enemy hands. But the time for retreat is coming to an end, and Prince Pol and Maarken— his most valued general and fellow Sunrunner—must rally their forces in a desperate attempt to halt the advance of the unknown invaders' army. But ancient rivalries begin to weaken their alliance as several of the princes seize this opportunity to further their own ambitions. Only time will tell whether those loyal to the High Prince's cause can defeat both the foreign invaders and the betrayers within their own ranks.

And as Pol leads his troops forth to fight a new kind of warfare, Andry, the Sunrunner Lord of Goddess Keep, is also determined to take the attack to the enemy, to claim vengeance for loved ones slain, and to protect his Sunrunners from this mysterious foe which has sworn to slay all workers of magic.

Yet the invaders, too, have an agenda of conquest, and they are readying to strike at the very heart of the Desert, stealing treasures which both Andry and Pol would pay any price to reclaim—even if the price should prove to be their own lives. . . .

- Featuring spell-binding Michael Whelan cover art

☐ **Hardcover Edition**   UE2493—$20.00